W9-BYR-501

by Madeleine L'Engle

NOVELS

The Small Rain
Ilsa
Camilla Dickinson
A Winter's Love
The Other Side of the Sun
The Love Letters
A Severed Wasp

NON-FICTION

A Circle of Quiet
The Summer of the Great-grandmother
The Irrational Season
Walking on Water

A
SEVERED
WASP

[A wasp] was sucking jam on my plate and I cut him in half. He paid no attention, merely went on with his meal, while a tiny stream of jam trickled out of his severed esophagus. Only when he tried to fly away did he grasp the dreadful thing that had happened to him.

GEORGE ORWELL, *Collected Essays*

A SEVERED WASP

Madeleine L'Engle

Farrar · Straus · Giroux

NEW YORK

Printed in the United States of America

Published in Canada by
Collins Publishers, Toronto

Designed by Tere LoPrete

Library of Congress Cataloging in Publication Data
L'Engle, Madeleine.   A severed wasp.
I. Title.   PS3523.E55S4   1982   813'.54   82-15694

Contents

A
SEVERED
WASP

The Cathedral

The very size of the Cathedral was a surprise. The old woman looked around at the columns rising up into shadows, at the vast nave sweeping the full length of a city block. Despite a sudden, unseasonable heat wave that had turned April into summer, she relaxed into a strange coolness of space and height, of soft light filtering through the stained glass of the high windows.

She could sense deep love in the retired bishop's voice as he propelled her farther into the nave. "I've never known a cathedral more beautiful than St. John the Divine, and I've preached and visited in many. The fact that the building started out Romanesque and got changed to Gothic in midstream doesn't matter. Somehow, the mishmash of architecture works."

Katherine turned slowly, enjoying the coolness that seemed to breathe from the stones. The soft light shimmered against the columns so that they shone like mother-of-pearl.

The bishop said, "I suppose you're familiar with most of the great cathedrals in Europe."

"Felix, I'm a pianist. I work hard. I've had little time for sightseeing."

He smiled slightly. "There are other reasons for going to a cathedral than sightseeing."

She laughed. "*Touché.* You've obviously changed since our non-churchgoing days. I haven't."

Somewhat stiffly, the old bishop said, "I realize you thought my way of life was—"

"Casual," she supplied.

"Thank you. That is a most generous way of putting it. I'm not certain that one is capable of much basic change. You might say that my priorities have shifted."

She put her hand lightly on his arm. "I'm not sure I was even aware your cathedral existed before you called me last week."

He reached for her hand. His skin was dry and felt crumply, like old leaves. "Remember—we used to come uptown to see the old French and Russian movies at the Thalia. But, as you say, we weren't thinking about church then. How I'd have laughed if anyone had told me I'd end up as Bishop of New York, and that this gorgeous monstrosity of St. John's Cathedral would be my true home."

He moved on down the nave. He wore a long, loose, off-white robe: a what? a caftan? That was not it, but she could not remember the right word. She knew that priests wore this kind of garb on occasion even now; it was, perhaps, coming back into style after all the years of clergy being more secular than the congregation. It was belted with a knotted silk rope from which dangled some kind of wooden beads, a long string of them, with a cross at the end. Not a rosary. All in all, it was a becoming costume.

"What do you call your caftan, or whatever it is?"

"Cassock. Katherine, my dear, you are kind indeed to come all this way up to meet me this evening. I can't tell you how much it means to me."

She would not tell him she had accepted his invitation simply out of curiosity. The idea that Felix Bodeway, that lightweight young man she had known half a century ago when they were both living in the Village, should have ended up a bishop struck her as hilarious. Felix? Had he experienced some kind of conversion, then? She was at loose ends, back in New York, widowed, retired—why not see what had happened to Felix?

Was it just that one is never quite aware of one's own age that made her feel that he looked older than she? He had shrunk, but not inordinately, and he still had most of his hair, although it was yellowish white. His eyes were a faded blue.

And now he was a bishop, frail, more stooped than she, but not doddering, like many of their contemporaries. That was a relief. She glanced at him again, at ease enough now to look to see if she recognized the old Felix and, if so, if he would still awaken the long-ago pain which had been part of the past to which Felix belonged. But so much deeper pain had come in the intervening years that all she felt was a vague nostalgia for her youthful anguish.

Brilliant sound startled her, a vivid calling of trumpets, red and blue and gold like the great stained-glass windows, she thought, and then came the mighty strains of a Bach fugue pouring from the organ.

Felix looked toward the choir loft. "Ah. Llew Owen is practicing. Since his wife's death he sometimes plays till two, three in the morning. I'd hoped he might be here this evening."

Without thinking, she shook off his hand and stood absolutely still, listening. Light and music wove and interwove; stone and sound became one. She stood absorbing, participating, until the last note of the fugue moved slowly along the length of the nave.

"Well?" Felix demanded.

She turned to him, incomprehending.

"What do you think of it—Llew's playing?"

"He's superb. Although I'd guess he's fairly young, isn't he?"

"Around thirty, I suppose. How did you know?"

"I'm a musician. How did his wife die?"

"In childbirth. The baby, too. Doesn't happen often in this day and age, and he almost went mad with grief."

"He'll be all right," she said with authority. "His music will see to that. While I was listening to him play, I realized how futile it is to try to transcribe that fugue for the piano."

"I've heard you play it, and magnificently."

"Don't flatter me, Felix."

"I often flatter, I suppose." His voice was rueful. "But not you, Katya, never you." The old nickname still sounded strange to her, so long was it since it had been used. "On the phone, when you realized who I was, you called me 'window cleaner.' I was deeply moved that you remembered."

"I have a good memory, Felix." —Too good. "Is becoming a bishop a way of becoming a window cleaner?"

"Becoming a priest. That was my hope." He sounded weary, and sad. He turned as they heard footsteps coming toward them, and raised his hand in greeting to an armed guard. "Evening, Steele."

"Evening, Bishop. You all right?"

"Yes, fine."

"Mr. Owen is up there practicing."

"Yes, we heard him. Everything quiet this evening?"

"So far," the guard said, nodded at them, and walked on.

The music started again, Messiaen now, and Katherine sat in one of the folding chairs which were lined in neat rows across the nave, with no fixed pews, as in most European cathedrals, or, at any rate, the only one she knew at all, the cathedral in Munich. She regarded the bishop in his light caftan—no, cassock—and thought that he looked pale and lonely and, despite his thinness, not as lightweight as he had been in his youth. Life had taken him a long way from the feline young man she had known for no more than a year. He had represented for her the cheapest part of *la vie de Bohême*, or hippiedom, or whatever it was called now, and she had tried to forget him as quickly as possible. She had not thought of him in all these years, until he had called her, less than a week after she had left the house in Paris and flown to New York, to her house on Tenth Street.

The stiff cathedral chair was uncomfortable. She rose, pushing herself up with the ivory-handled cane which she carried largely because she felt that it helped her get the service and consideration that she demanded in her old age. She did not want to need the cane. Her back was still straight, and though she likened her fingers to gnarled carrots, they were nearly as strong and nimble on the piano as ever. She practiced daily, and if it was not for as many hours as it used to be, it was a minimum of four. "All right, Felix. You've got me all the way up here for something. What is it?" The organ had stopped now, but almost immediately began again, the gentle sound of one of the more meditative chorale preludes.

He continued down the nave, stepping like a child around large, circular bronze insets. "The Pilgrim's Pavement," he murmured. "We have St. Peter's and St. Paul's towers completed, and are doing well with the transepts thanks to a completely unexpected bequest. However . . ."

She stiffened. When he had urged her to meet him at the Cathedral, he had promised not to ask her for money.

"My job in my retirement is to work with the Cathedral Arts Program. I want you to give a concert, a benefit concert for us."

She shook her head definitely. "I am retired. You know that."

"You gave a concert in Paris less than six months ago. And I'm retired and still working and you're younger than I am."

"Felix, my feet hurt on this stone. I'm hungry. What about that dinner you promised me?"

"In a minute. I want to show you the ambulatory."

Her voice was sharper than she intended. "I'm tired. I'm still on French time, and it's past my dinner hour."

"All right. I never could say no to you. I hope you won't say no to me, though you were always good at that. But this time . . . Come, we'll go out by St. James chapel and you'll at least get a glimpse of the ambulatory."

Still cross, but trying to soften her tone, she asked, "What's an ambulatory?"

"More or less what it sounds like. It's a half circle behind the high altar, and off it are rayed seven chapels. My idea is for a series of distinguished chamber-music concerts in St. Ansgar's chapel. Acoustically it's excellent for the piano, and we've been given a particularly fine Bösendorfer." He offered her the bait with eager anxiety.

Fine pianos were nothing new. "Dinner," she said firmly, "before I faint."

He jingled his bunch of keys. "I thought it would be more pleasant to take you home for a quiet meal than to go to a restaurant. Dinner's all ready, waiting in the fridge. Vitello tonnato and a bottle of Frascati."

"*Allons y, alors.*"

Reluctantly he led her to an elaborately grilled iron gate, to the right of which stood an antique carved chest the size of a small coffin, with a hand-lettered sign reading DONATIONS.

"Does it ever get filled?" She smiled slightly at the size of the chest.

"We have to empty it every day, because of thieves and vandals, but you'd be amazed at how much gets put into it in a day, widow's mites, mostly, but it mounts up." He selected a key from the ring that was attached to his belt, on the other side from the beads—were they prayer beads of some kind?—opened the gate and led her up the shallow steps. "Everything gets locked up at five, but I still have the keys to the kingdom, and now that we're well into spring it's light till late." He pointed. "Look on your left for a glimpse of the ambulatory."

Obediently she turned her head and saw a curve of shadows and paneled wood holding paintings which in the twilight appeared to be early Renaissance. To the right were more grilled gates and a feeling that everything was reaching up, soaring to the vaulted ceiling. Felix opened another door, a wooden one this time, and they were out on a landing, leading to a steep flight of iron steps. The door closed on the notes of the organ. "Careful," Felix warned. "Hold on to the rail. We're still working on the south transept. I'll go first." He started down, leaning heavily on the iron rail. "I've hardly shown you anything." He sounded like a disappointed child. "We haven't gone near the Stone Yard—but of course it's closed for the night. Next time—you will come again? The Close is at its most beautiful right now."

"Close?"

"The grounds," he answered. "All this loveliness."

She looked around at the flowering trees, the young green grass. Everything was spring-fresh, and this first premature wave of heat was bringing all the buds into quick bloom. The thermometer was well into the eighties but the heat was not oppressive; the buildings had not yet absorbed the heat as they would during the long summer. She was grateful that she had come home in the spring rather than into the sweltering humidity of New York in summer.

"Haven't you read any Trollope lately?" Felix was asking.

"No, and I'm not sure I've ever been this far uptown before. I've tended to stay close to Tenth Street and Lincoln Center when I've been in New York."

"People are often amazed at this island of beauty in what is surely not one of the cleanest parts of our fair city." He paused to wave to two young mothers, one pushing a stroller, the other carrying her infant in a bright blue baby sling. They both returned his greeting, smiling. "This is a happy place," Felix said, "in an often unhappy city. People come here to play, to pray, to cry, to sing. All this green space is one of the greatest gifts we have to offer in an overcrowded metropolis. You will come again, won't you?"

"We'll see." And then, because she did not enjoy being unkind, she added, "We both do rather well in our old age, don't we?"

"You do. Better than I. I tend to get tottery if I'm overtired. Come. These are the flying buttresses. I'm enormously fond of them."

She looked at the great curved stone reinforcements, heavy to bear the adjective of flying, and jumped as a raucous scream cut across the air.

Felix laughed at her startled reflex. "One of our peacocks. They've become a tradition. They came with—" He paused, pondering. "When Donegan was Diocesan, or Moore? Anyhow, we've had several generations of them. They have become, as you might say, part of our image."

She glanced back at the great buttressed bulk of the cathedral looking, she thought, like many cathedrals in many cities where she had given concerts. Perhaps this was larger; Americans always wanted to make everything larger than everything else, as though that would make it better. She sighed lightly, thinking, —But I am an American. And I have always been small.

"Come look here." Felix prodded her, and they walked around to the front of the building, which had a façade of Greek columns, strangely in contrast to the prevailing Gothic architecture. "It used to be an orphan asylum, if I remember correctly, and it's now our museum. We have some very fine pieces." He turned again, leading her toward an open area of grass, trees, flowering bushes, azaleas just beginning to bud. To their left and ahead of them were grey stone buildings, their severity softened by spring plantings. The bishop looked around, sniffing appreciatively. "The Close runs from Amsterdam to Morningside, and from 110th to 113th Street. Ah, Katya"—he used the nickname he had picked up from her stepmother, her beloved Aunt Manya, and as he smiled she saw for a moment the young Felix—"you are as lovely as the Close—as strong as the stone of the buildings and as new as the spring—I would have recognized you anywhere. But then I've come to hear you every time you've played in New York."

"Have you, then?"

"Your hair turned white early, as I remember, but then black hair usually does."

"Felix, if you've come to hear me play over the years, why haven't you come backstage? Why wait till now to get in touch?"

He lifted one slender shoulder slightly. "Our paths have diverged radically. I thought I should not remind you of a time that surely was not happy for you. But now I want something."

He paused at the head of a short flight of stone steps. She stopped beside him. "Felix," she reminded him, "I've told you I'm retired."

"Wait. This is Cathedral House on our left, designed after a French château. Diocesan House is ahead of us, just down these steps and along the path. The library is there, and the diocesan offices, and my own little office. Several of the canons have apartments upstairs. Most of the married priests live off the Close."

She turned toward him. "Married priests?"

"Katya, St. John the Divine is an Episcopal church, not Roman Catholic. I thought you realized."

She traced a vague gesture with one hand. "I hardly knew that there were Episcopal cathedrals—or Episcopal bishops."

He took her hand and pressed it. "I told you our paths had diverged."

She looked at the beautifully kept gardens, smiling to see a group of young people, probably college students, dancing morris dances on the spring-green lawn, while one played a mandolin, another a recorder. "Yes. Sorry, Felix, you must know more about my path than I do yours, since you've come to my concerts. I've been rather isolated in the world of music."

"And your family."

"Yes. Of course. My family."

He looked across at the grey stone building he had called Diocesan House. "Since I'm long-retired, I'm more than grateful that I have my tiny office in this building where there's an elevator. Allie has been—is—extraordinarily kind to me."

"Allie?"

"Alwood Undercroft. The sixteenth Bishop of New York; I was fifteenth. I'm still moderately useful in my modest way, and being allowed to remain useful is a great and uncommon privilege. The government ups its retirement age, and the church lowers its, and out you go, arse over amice, whether you're still in your prime or not. I'm long past my prime, but I wasn't at retirement, and I'd die quickly if I was just turned out to pasture."

She shifted the strap of her handbag from one shoulder to the other. She had not got over the habit of carrying music manuscript around with her. "Artists have no mandatory retirement age. I'm not at all sure what I'm going to do with my retirement."

"You'll play the piano, of course. Anyhow, aging isn't done according to strict rules. One of our bishops is in his fifties and looks like Fu Manchu at ninety. He had one of those weird pneumonias a couple of years ago and he's gone down steadily ever since. Anyhow, I'm enormously grateful to the present Bishop of New York, and I try to be as inconspicuous as possible and not get in the way."

All about them was the scent of freshly cut grass, of spring bulbs: hyacinth, daffodil, narcissus. Her ears enjoyed the shifting of leaves in the breeze, the gentle twittering of birds. Across this oasis of peace came the peacock's scream, and a large bird stepped out from the shadows of some rhododendron bushes and crossed in front of them, screaming again, something which sounded extremely rude, then spread its magnificent tail, quivering with iridescent color, and strutted onto the lawn.

Felix applauded. "I'm glad he showed off for you, though they aren't beasts one can get fond of."

The door of Cathedral House opened, a handsome door of glass and ironwork, clanging shut heavily, and a tall, dark-skinned man emerged, dressed in a light grey suit and clerical collar. Perhaps clerical collars were more worn in America than in Europe. Or perhaps it was an Episcopalian affectation.

He waved. Felix waved back, then beckoned. "Dean Davidson—"

The tall man paused, shifting a briefcase from one hand to the other. "Bishop. Good to see you." His voice was warm and deep. A cello.

Felix gestured dramatically toward Katherine. "I want you to meet an old friend of mine from the days of my youth, Katherine

Forrester, as she was then, Madame Katherine Vigneras, as she is known now."

The dean's face lightened with a quick, open smile. He set down his briefcase and took her hand in his. "This is indeed a great pleasure. I'm one of your many admirers, and we have, I think, nearly all your recordings."

"The dean plays the English horn," Felix said. "I'm hoping Madame Vigneras will agree to give at least one benefit concert for us. I'm trying to tempt her with our Bösendorfer."

That was unfair. "It is not a good thing for an artist to go on for too long."

Again the dean gave her his brilliant smile. "Don't let the bishop bully you. For all his quiet ways, he's a great bully."

"How can you say that, Dave?" Felix sounded wounded, although he continued to smile. "I must now feed Katherine— Madame—or she will, she has told me, faint from starvation. Oh—" He put one hand lightly on the dean's. "Here come the Undercrofts! How fortuitous!" He hailed them delightedly. "Bishop! Mrs. Undercroft!"

The couple coming toward them were strikingly handsome, the man fair and fine-featured, the woman tall and dark, with an exotic air. But it was the man who made her reach for Felix's arm as though giddy. His resemblance to someone she had known almost as long ago as Felix, a German officer in Paris during the Occupation, who had been in charge of the makeshift prison in which she had been interned—the resemblance was startling. Lukas von Hilpert had had grey eyes, and the young bishop's were a bright, light blue. Otherwise, he was so like him he could have been his son. In fact, the bishop seemed somewhere near the age that von Hilpert had been when she was in his prison.

The woman beside him was tall, unusually tall even in this day of tall women, and beautifully proportioned. Her features were strong and Latin, and her eyes were so dark a brown that it was difficult to tell the pupil from the iris.

Bishop Undercroft greeted Felix with pleasure. "What are you doing wandering around at this time of evening?"

Felix stretched out his arms in an embracing gesture. "Bishop and Mrs. Undercroft, I want you to meet an old and very dear friend, Madame Katherine Vigneras."

The younger bishop's reaction was as swift and appreciative as the dean's. "Madame Vigneras! What an unexpected and lovely pleasure! I met Felix many years ago at one of your concerts— you were playing in San Francisco—so you were, in a way, the cause of what has been a lifelong friendship." He took her hands in both of his.

"Allie was very young," Felix said tolerantly.

"But I had good taste—in music, and in choosing friends—didn't I?" He dropped Katherine's hand and deferred to his wife, calling her name lovingly. "Yolande?" She smiled at him, nodding, and then turned the smile to Katherine, a warm smile, but behind it, Katherine felt, there was something sad, something unresolved.

"I don't want to pressure Katherine," Felix said, "but I *am* hoping that she will give a benefit concert for us."

"You *are* pressuring me, Felix." She glanced once more at Undercroft; the memories he awoke in her were far more painful than anything Felix could evoke.

"I'm so sorry, my dear." Felix took her arm in a proprietary gesture. "You don't have to give us your answer tonight, of course. And now I really must take you home and give you something to eat, mustn't I?" He slipped into a perfected ritual of farewells, then led her down the steps and turned west, past Diocesan House. As they neared another stone building, he gestured, "This is Synod Hall. The bishops' offices are here, and it's here that we hold Diocesan Convention." She did not know what Synod Hall was, nor Diocesan Convention. She remembered vaguely that Felix was wont to give long answers to simple questions. So she said, "The flowers are beautiful."

"Lovely, aren't they? Especially after some of the odors on Amsterdam Avenue."

They came to a gate in the fence which surrounded the grounds. Felix again shook his key ring until he found the key he wanted, and as he was opening the gate, two little girls in plaid school jumpers came hurrying up, one brightly pretty, with fair, curly hair and heartrending violet eyes, the other a little older, a little too fat, with brown hair strained torturously back from her face in braids which seemed to stretch her skin.

"Oh, good, Uncle Bishop," the fair child called out. "You can let us in. I left my gate key at home. Thanks." She made a slight, graceful curtsy in Katherine's direction, and then caught the other child's hand, saying, "C'mon, Fatty, we'll be late and Mrs. Undercroft doesn't like that."

Felix clanged the gate behind them, explaining, "The pretty one is Tory, the dean's youngest. The other's her odd friend, whose name is actually Fatima."

"Poor thing. The nickname becomes obvious."

"She ought to lose some of that puppy fat soon, or she's in for trouble. She's lucky to have someone like Tory on her side. Come. That's my building across the street, just east of that Con Ed monstrosity." He looked at the light, which was redly flickering DON'T WALK. His voice became petulant. "There's no safe way to cross 110th. Even with the green light saying WALK, cars can swing round at you. Every few years someone is hurt or killed, and they change the lights for a month, and you begin to relax, and then they change them back, with no thought for the pedestrian. Hurry. Even when the cars don't come at you, the light barely stays green long enough for you to cross unless you race." He broke into a bobbling trot, which slowed down, rather than speeded up, his progress.

Katherine remembered that Julie had said, a good many years ago, 'Don't bobble, Maman. You waste your energy going up and down instead of going forward.' She continued to walk calmly beside Felix.

--- 2 ---

When they reached the sidewalk, he was panting, and pulled a linen handkerchief from a capacious pocket and patted his upper lip and brow. "I freeze in winter and melt in summer. It's part of growing old." —It was not that hot, she thought. Felix had overexerted himself simply crossing the street. "It's reasonably cool in the apartment," he reassured. They went in through glass doors to a vestibule filled with a formidable array of names and numbers. Felix followed her glance. "What you do is find the name of the person you're trying to visit, the apartment number, and then press the button and wait for a voice to come out of that round grille, and then you identify yourself, and your host buzzes that

buzzer and the door unlatches, and you can go in." He waved
through the closed doors at a uniformed guard sitting at a desk. The
man rose, patting the gun conspicuous in his holster, and let them in.
  "Evening, Bishop."
  "Evening, Pio. This is my friend, Madame Vigneras."
  "*Buenas noches*," the guard said to Katherine, who returned his
greeting. Then Felix led her down a long hall to a bank of elevators.
  Even in most of the best hotels in Europe, there were now self-
service elevators. She had never learned to be comfortable with
them, and she was glad that Felix was with her. One of the doors
opened and unloaded a motley assortment of people, white, black,
yellow, and in between, speaking Spanish, German, English, and a
few other languages she did not understand. Felix put his arm
about her to keep her from being bumped, then guided her into
the elevator.
  "I'm on the twentieth floor, so it's moderately quiet, and I have
a pleasant view."
  The elevator rose swiftly, and the door opened onto a long
corridor painted institutional green. He led her past several doors
and then opened one with yet another key and took her into an
apartment which was cool and unexpectedly beautiful.
  Felix urged her into a comfortable chair. "I'll be with you in
just a moment. There are only one or two last-minute things to do."
  She felt weary and irritable. She scarcely smiled when Felix put
into her hand a chilled glass of pale, very dry sherry.
  Why had she come? Loneliness makes people do strange things,
she supposed. Loneliness and curiosity. The old Felix had given no
hint that one day he might become a bishop. She had met him in
the Village one night, after the theatre, and their first conversation
had occurred when she was left alone with him in a rather scruffy
apartment on Bank Street, while the young man she had thought to
marry had gone off to buy beer with the young woman who was to
take him from her.
  'Shall I tell you about myself?' Felix had asked. Long and pallid,
he had sat hunched on a yellow wooden cube, holding his nose
between two fingers. A lock of drab, blondish hair fell across his
forehead and over one eye. 'I'm a window cleaner.' He let his nose
go and straightened his bow tie.
  She had been informed by the young woman that Felix was a

superb violinist. 'A window cleaner and a violinist?' she had asked as he paused expectantly.

'No *and*. Music is my window cleaning.' And he had gone on, with unexpected passion for one who seemed so languorously wan, to talk about the human isolation 'in this fragile bag of bones, where all our windows have been so fouled with futility and folly that we can't see out. So there have to be window cleaners.' Artists, he said, would clean the muddied windows with the purity of their art. He was naïve, self-centered, rather pompous. Nevertheless, under the shallow surface of his words there were depths which she, too, believed. Still believed. And so, when she had realized who was behind the voice on the other end of the phone, she had said, "Window cleaner!"

Perhaps in a way he was a window cleaner now, still isolated in his fragile bag of bones. But real.

In the dingy, pseudo-Swedish-modern studio on Bank Street he had gone on talking about himself. Katherine, unused to this kind of immediate self-revelation, did not reply, but sat there looking at this soft young man who belonged to a world so different from hers it might have been another planet. And yet, when he talked about music, it was in a language she could understand.

But then he shifted, waving his long fingers, which were much too tapered and delicate for a piano but might be all right for a violin. 'I'm not in the least in love with Sarah. Nor she with me. But it might be convenient for us to marry. She has enough money to support me in the manner to which I would like to become accustomed, and we get on very well.'

That was Felix, a combination of idealism and pragmatism, the pragmatism, at least back then, winning over the idealism. But perhaps he had become a window cleaner after a fashion.

Now, in his apartment across from the Cathedral Close, he puttered about, bringing things in from the kitchen. An oval rosewood table was placed in readiness in front of a window which looked east across the city to the river. He set out silver dishes of food, opened a bottle of wine. His living room was small but uncluttered and everything in it was beautiful.

When he was satisfied with the table, he sat on a small stool at her feet (reminiscent of the pose on the yellow cube) and raised his glass of sherry. "To the renewal of a friendship I bitterly regretted losing."

—Why, then, has he waited so long before trying to renew it? How much has he changed? How far have I come from the naïve adolescent unprepared for love or pain?

She noticed that his fingers were moving rhythmically over the chain of wooden beads. "Is that a rosary?"

His fingers paused. "Not exactly, though occasionally I use it as one. They're Russian prayer beads, given me by an old Orthodox priest, so they have been well prayed with. I don't suppose you use a rosary?"

He sounded, she thought, hopeful. She shook her head. "I have one. Also given me by someone I admired and loved—or, rather, they were given me after his death."

"Who?" he asked with open curiosity.

"You may have heard of him. He was a great friend of Justin's and mine. Cardinal von Stromberg."

"But of course I've heard of him!" he cried. "I have all his books which have been translated into English. How did you and Justin happen to know him?"

"Wolfi was a lover of music. We were very fond of him."

"Katya, dear Katya." He drained the small crystal glass, rose, and led her to the table. He lit the candles, adjusted a single iris in the bud vase. China and crystal gleamed. He did not pull out her chair for her, but stood at his own place opposite her. She started to sit, then realized that he was in the process of saying grace. "Benedictus, benedicam. Amen." He crossed himself and sat.

The food was superbly prepared and she was hungry.

He watched her eating and smiled, slightly smugly. "I always thought I'd be a good cook, given a chance. Katya, why didn't you keep your maiden name professionally? Why are you Vigneras instead of Forrester?"

She took a sip of wine, which was dry enough for her definite taste; Justin had taught her about wines. "Forrester was my mother's name, and I spent a good bit of my life in her shadow. Forrester meant Julie Forrester, not Katherine."

He demurred. "Surely not now. You saw how both the dean and the bishop reacted."

"No, not now, but definitely when I was starting out. My mother made an indelible name for herself in a very short time. Her records are collector's items, going for enormous prices. They still teach me. And then—my husband wanted me to use his name."

"I thought he was a pianist himself."

Her voice was chill. "He was. His career was cut off abruptly, sooner than my mother's."

The bishop, ignoring her coldness, leaned across the polished surface of the table. "What happened?"

"The Nazis. Among other things, they broke his hands. They mended well enough for all normal purposes. Not for the piano." She tried to lighten her voice. "The Second World War is old-hat now. Not many young people have even heard of Hitler. But for those of us who were caught up in it, it has had lasting aftereffects."

"Yes." He winced slightly, as though in pain. "So your Justin fulfilled himself in you?" He pushed back from the table and padded to the kitchen, which was little more than an alcove off the dining area.

"He was no Svengali." Again, Katherine's voice was brusque. "We worked extraordinarily well together. And then he did a great deal of composing."

"I know." Felix turned, asking gently, "Do you still miss him very much?"

"I do."

There was naïve curiosity but no malice as he asked, "Was it the perfect marriage all the articles and interviews would have led the public to believe?"

She laughed. "The press tend to believe that any couple who stay together as long as we did must have a perfect marriage, but there is no such thing. We had some very bad times. But as marriages go, it was, in its own way, good. Very good." She added simply, "I will always miss him."

Her memory had stored in it a series of film clips (as it were) for her to take out and look at as needed. A treasured one was of a brief vacation in Chamonix, when they had skied in the morning, and in the afternoon had skated, waltzing to a loudspeaker that poured forth nostalgic dance music. Katherine, always clumsy at sports, staying on the beginners' slopes in skiing while Justin went off for magnificent jumps and grand slaloms, was unexpectedly graceful on skates, and the waltzing with Justin was sheer joy, as the early night fell between the Alps and the stars came out. It was a glorious kind of intercourse, the two of them moving as one, skating to the accelerating tempo of the music so that it was almost as though they were flying among the stars.

And then, back to earth, to the simple physical pleasure of hot chocolate heaped with whipped cream, and crunchy pastries, served at long tables at the side of the skating rink.

It was good. It was very good.

"Oh, my dear—" Felix came back to the table bearing a silver coffeepot.

But Katherine had risen. "Felix, I must go."

"No coffee, my dear?"

"No, thanks. I have long been too old for coffee at this time of night—even decaffeinated."

He set the pot on a trivet and came round the table to her, taking her hands in his. "I may keep in touch?"

"If you wish."

"You will consider my request?"

"I will consider it, Felix, but please don't be optimistic. I heard Paderewski's last concert."

"I know," he said quickly. "I was there with you listening to the radio."

"People laughed."

"Oh, Katya, Katya, you still play as well as ever, you know that. Come. I'll see you to a taxi."

"Don't bother. I can manage."

"You don't know this neighborhood. Taxis are almost impossible to come by on Amsterdam. We'll have to go to Broadway."

She put her hand lightly on his. "I'm capable of going to Broadway on my own. As you said, Felix, you tend to get tottery."

"You will be careful?"

"Of course. I am well aware that the streets of New York are not safe, but then there is no longer any place in the world which is safe. One cannot live in perpetual fear. One has to be as prudent as possible, and get on with life. Don't worry about me."

He sighed, "In the old days I'd have called one of the guards to get a cab for you. But now—there's so much vandalism and petty thievery, we can't spare a guard for even a few minutes.

Anyhow, the Church becomes more and more a business and can't spare time for Good Samaritan acts. Let me at least see you across the street."

He kissed her lightly after they had crossed Amsterdam, the bishop still bobbling, she walking calmly. She was certain he had never kissed her before. Auld Lang Syne does strange things.

She felt she ought to wait to see that he got safely back across the dangerous intersection and to his building, but decided that would be discourteous, so she walked west without looking back. Swinging her cane loosely, she walked at a brisk pace. She had long held a theory that if you looked vague, at any age, or old and frail, you stood a good chance of being mugged. But if you moved along as though you knew where you were going and what you were doing, you were apt to be let alone.

Gutters and sidewalks were littered with papers, broken bottles, dog turds (in disregard of signs), general filth. A shadow moved swiftly across a pile of garbage; a rat, she thought. She shuddered. She had a horror of rats. There was a pervasive, unpleasant stench of decay. Just as she was beginning to despair of getting a taxi, she felt a light touch on her arm and looked down to see a young boy.

"Want a taxi, lady?"

His skin was a clear olive, his eyes huge and lashed with a thick, dark fringe. There was something endearing about him, and she would be glad of his help. "Yes, and they all seem to be filled."

"Topaze will get you one. Topaze can do lots of things. You want to know anything?"

She looked at him with amusement. She suspected that he was small for his age, and wise with the ways of children of the street, though he was less grubby than most, and his dark curls were clean. "All I want at this moment is a taxi to take me home."

He was scanning the street. "You don't want to know anything about anybody? Anybody at the Cathedral? I could tell you lots."

She continued to search for a taxi with the roof light lit. "Why would I want to know anything about anybody at the Cathedral?"

"Saw you with Bishop Bodeway. The peacock came and spread out his tail for you. Saw you talk to the dean, and to the other bishop, too. So you want to know anything?"

What was this? "No, thanks, Topaze."

"My sister and I know lots. She knows who goes to St. Martin's chapel to make confession to who."

Katherine turned her eyes from the street to look at the boy, who was gazing up at her with large, innocent eyes, like a Renaissance angel. "That's nobody's business."

"Sez who?"

His cynicism was distressing to her. "Topaze, if you can get me a taxi, I'll be glad to give you a quarter."

"Mrs. Bishop gives my sister a dollar."

She looked at him severely. "I'm looking for a taxi, not information."

"Hey, lady, don't be mad. I was just trying to help."

At that moment an empty taxi came by and she waved at it. Topaze sprang forward to open the door. She took a quarter out of her change purse, gave it to him, and gratefully got in. There was no reason to be disturbed by the child. Small children all over the city picked up money any way they could, standing with soapy sponges at the entrances to bridges, waiting to wipe windshields, selling wilted flowers that had probably been filched, running errands—it was surely better than groups of children, many of them no older than Topaze, who mugged and sometimes killed the old and weak.

She directed the taxi driver to her home downtown.

Tenth Street

 I

Home.

Home was arbitrary, the place she had designated as home, the house on Tenth Street, rather than the farm in Connecticut, or the house in Paris; New York, rather than France, where she and Justin had shared so many years of their married life.

As soon as she had been able to afford it, she had bought the brownstone on tree-lined Tenth Street where she had lived briefly with her mother. It was as close to roots as she could get, this building she had lived in when she was a child, closer to roots than the old farmhouse which she had inherited from her Russian stepmother, and where she had spent far more time than in the city. Odd, how the heart will put down roots in what was, at the time, only a temporary shelter.

Tenth Street had not changed much over the years. The trees were taller, that was about all. It was still a street of well-kept brownstones. Nearer Fifth Avenue, men still sat solemnly at tables in the windows of the Marshall Chess Club. The sameness was comforting to her. Despite all that had happened in the intervening years, Tenth Street between Fifth and Sixth was an affirmation of constancy. She had a home which bridged chronology.

However, the brownstone on Tenth Street was an investment as well as continuity, and rents from the upper stories and from the garden apartment were a welcome supplement to her income. Often she had rented her parlor-floor apartment for years at a time. Now it was hers. She would not rent it again.

She climbed the outside steps slowly, annoyed at not being able to run up lightly. Yes, she was tired, but by no means as tottery as Felix. She took out her keys; her apartment had its own separate entrance in the vestibule, to the left of the main inner door.

She had left on the piano lamp; continuing energy crisis or no, she was not willing to come home to a dark house. She moved immediately to the familiar instrument, pausing only to turn on one or two lights on the way. For a moment she stroked her fingers lovingly over the polished wood. Then she sat, and stretched her fingers over the keyboard. Her hands were broad and strong; the true pianist's sledgehammer hands, they had been called. They still moved to her bidding, but the memory of the old master's last broadcast was, for some reason, in the forefront of her mind, probably because Felix had been one of the group when they turned the radio to the Boston station from which the program was being transmitted. She had been sitting on the floor, next to the young man she had expected to marry, waiting in eager anticipation for the first notes.

And the old man could no longer play. The authority was gone. The fingers fumbled. The insensitive laughter had made her furious, and she had left the group, sick with shame, and retreated to the bathroom. Had Felix laughed? She did not think so. If he had laughed, she would have remembered. But the others had. Even the young man who . . .

She started to play. Bach. Always Bach when she needed reassurance. Her fingers did not fumble. No matter to what she likened them—turnips, carrots—they were still as nimble as ever. The notes came clear and true. Years after Paderewski's last devastating concert, she had also heard Rubinstein play on television, when he was older than she was now, his fingers, too, looking gnarled and knotted, but fleet and swift and potent. There had been no diminishment there.

The notes of the *Fifth French Suite* dropped from her fingers. That would get one through almost anything, memories, strange resemblances, echoes of sounds better forgotten . . .

She came to the gigue, the notes merry and lighthearted and

young. How old was Bach when he wrote that? Not very young. Old enough to be able to write about youth. The promise of youth was in the music and her fingers, the future open and available and changing as it always must be, regardless of age.

Age—Felix had brought it to the forefront of her mind, but most of the time she did not think about it. She was Katherine Forrester Vigneras, not a chronological digit. She did not want to lose any part of herself. In her seventies she was still seven, and seventeen, and thirty-seven, and fifty. She was the music she played. She had been formed as much by Bach and Brahms as by her parents. No doubt the fact that her father had been a composer and her mother a pianist had made her awareness of herself as being part of music come far sooner than it might otherwise have come; but they were too preoccupied with their own careers to give her the kind of day-to-day guidance which is part of the life of most American children. Perhaps it was her lonely childhood which had made her, with Justin's full cooperation, try to give Michou and Julie all the family love possible. And there, she thought, she had failed, as much as, if not more than, her parents had failed her, and for much the same reason. She had often been off on the road giving concerts when her heart longed to be at home; but she had not stayed home; she had gone.

She looked above the mantelpiece. The wall was bare; her pictures were not yet uncrated. The one which would hang above the fireplace was a portrait of herself and Michou, her firstborn, when he was an infant.

She sighed and turned her thoughts to her daughter. Julie, named after Katherine's mother, black of hair and fair of skin like Katherine. Married, mother of four, a tall, vibrant woman. Who was Julie? Does a mother ever know her daughter? Katherine had been fourteen when her mother died, mature physically, but young in every other way, too young to have reached the time when she would have needed to separate herself from her mother. Parents fail their children and children fail their parents, but is it really failure? When people love each other, they hurt each other, parents, children; husbands, wives; friends, lovers.

And was a normal, happy childhood really desirable for an artist? The pain of her parents' separation, her father's remarriage to the volatile actress, Manya Sergeievna, her mother's death—all these griefs had been exorcised and redeemed through music. How does one survive even the normal vicissitudes of life without a driving passion and its concomitant demanding work?

Was she going to be able to keep herself going now, with no more concerts to prepare for? Was her own discipline of daily practicing going to satisfy her? It would have to. She might feel like a young woman in an old body, but there was no denying that the body was old, and she had little patience with people who could not face their own aging. She had had a full, rich life—surely that should be enough.

—◦◦❧{ 2 }❧◦◦—

At first she did not hear the knock at her door, the inside door that led from her small kitchen into the main hall. It was only as the last, joyous notes of the gigue died away that her attention was caught. She moved slowly from the piano, her knees less flexible than her fingers and wrists. "Who is it?"

"Mimi Oppenheimer. I heard you playing, so knew you were still up. My God, you play superbly."

Mimi Oppenheimer rented the third- and fourth-floor duplex. A young couple had the garden apartment, and a man who was abroad most of the time rented the second floor. Dr. Oppenheimer was an orthopedic surgeon, fifteen or so years younger than Katherine, a tall, distinguished woman, big-boned; not overweight, just amply proportioned. Her rather wild blond hair was barely touched with grey.

"Don't hesitate to send me upstairs if you want to get rid of me. But something about your playing—not the gigue, but the more pensive movements . . . Perhaps you might enjoy relaxing for a few minutes over a cup of tea?"

Katherine glanced at Dr. Oppenheimer's astute surgeon's eyes. "Relaxing for a few minutes would be pleasant; but no tea, this late in the evening."

"Herb tea," the doctor stated. "I have an excellent tisane which is far better than a synthetic tranquilizer. Will you come up? Or shall I bring it down? Yes, I'll bring it down. Go back to your piano. I'll keep the kitchen door ajar." She left in her wake a faint scent of perfume—chypre?—and of freshness.

Katherine returned to the piano. Dr. Oppenheimer had rented the duplex apartment ever since Katherine had owned the building, and they were comfortable, if casual, acquaintances. She had often thought that, when there was time, they might be friends.

A spring breeze stirred the light curtains at the long front windows. She began to play her husband's best-known concerto, written at the time of the Vietnam war, in memory of the village which had had to be totally destroyed in order to be saved. The hideous irony ran through the piece, which had spoken to a generation dismayed and confused by the series of incomprehensible wars and violences spreading like plague across the planet, but its genesis had been Justin's own experiences during the occupation of France and, later, in Auschwitz.

Sometimes the music, which touched deeply on her own experience, was more than Katherine could bear, and she was not sure why she had turned to it now. It might be because it had been a day for recalling the past; first, the meeting with Felix; and then seeing the bishop who was so reminiscent of Lukas von Hilpert, who, like the war, had exploded into her life not more than a short time after she had left New York and the young man she did not marry; and had said what she thought was a final goodbye to Felix.

She heard Dr. Oppenheimer come in and close the door gently. "Don't stop playing. I'll make the tea."

But Katherine took her hands from the keys. "It's time for those few minutes of relaxing you promised me. I don't think I'm over jet lag yet."

Dr. Oppenheimer splashed water into the kettle. "It takes me two weeks coming to New York. It's supposed to be the other way around, what with the direction the planet turns and the prevailing winds, but I find it easier to go to Europe than coming home."

Katherine sat in a silver-grey wing chair, leaning back wearily, watching the doctor deftly preparing the tisane.

"That was your husband's music?"

"Yes. It's thin without the orchestra."

The doctor opened cupboards until she found cups. "Music is one of my best ways of unwinding. But for the past year or so I've been too tired to go out to concerts in the evening as I used to. So I depend on records and tapes. Now that I'm doing more teaching and spend less time operating, I must start getting out again." She set a steaming cup of something nostalgically fragrant on the small table by Katherine's chair. "I like your apartment. All soft greys and silvers. Peaceful."

"Thanks. I'm not nearly settled in yet. The pictures aren't up, except for a few snapshots. Half the silver and china is still in crates. I have some rather lovely sea-green damask curtains for winter, but for the summer I think the shutters and glass curtains are all I need. I'm glad you like it." She took a sip from her cup. "Ah, that's lovely. Justin was fond of tisanes."

"How long since his death?" The question was concerned, rather than abrasive.

Katherine looked into the cup, pondering. "Nearly twenty years, I suppose. Chronology has less and less meaning as I grow older. Things that happened only a short while ago—like closing the house in Paris—can seem longer ago than events in the dim past. Actually, I met someone this evening I hadn't seen since the days of my extreme youth. He was a bohemian type who thought he played the violin better than he did. And now he's a bishop."

Mimi smiled. "Bishop Bodeway. Funny and appealing old gent."

Katherine turned in surprise. "How—"

"How would Mimi Oppenheimer, with her name and profession, be conversant with Episcopal bishops? Well might you ask. One of my late interns and roommates is married to the present dean, Dave Davidson, and I sometimes go up to the Close for a meal or a concert with them, and Bishop Bodeway is often there. I'm very fond of the dean. Those of my girls who marry make interesting choices of mates, and do not neglect their own careers. Suzy is an excellent cardiologist. She's on the staff at St. Luke's, and they're lucky to have her. It's convenient for her, too, 113th Street, just above the Cathedral. Even so, Dave doesn't like her coming home alone at night."

Katherine remembered vaguely that, throughout the years, Dr. Oppenheimer had had a series of roommates—or women tenants—living in the back bedroom of the duplex.

The doctor rose and refilled Katherine's cup. "You've moved back for good, now?"

"I think so. My house in Connecticut is still rented. If I find I can afford it, I may keep it open for myself for the summers. I find this spring heat bothersome, so how am I going to feel in July and August?"

"You're home for good?"

"Yes. No more concert tours."

"But you loved them."

"Yes, I loved them. But I don't want to go on beyond my prime."

It was apparent that Katherine considered herself still within her prime. Dr. Oppenheimer smiled. "You'll never stop playing."

"Not until I stop breathing."

The younger woman took the teapot back to the kitchen, returned to the living room, and held out her hands. Like Katherine's, they were broad and strong, though her fingers were more tapered. "Good hands for a surgeon. As yours are for the piano." Katherine looked at Dr. Oppenheimer's outstretched hands, then at her own, and the surgeon said quickly, "My dear, have I touched a sore spot? What's wrong?"

Katherine shook her head. "Nothing. Nothing at all. It is just that I always marvel at my hands because there was a time when it looked as though arthritis was going to cripple them."

The doctor took Katherine's hands in her own and studied them. "There's no sign of it, no untoward thickening in the joints—"

Katherine withdrew her hands. "They are my miracle. I have some small arthritis in my knees and one hip, but not enough to bother me."

"Thank God, then," Dr. Oppenheimer said briskly. "Your hands have given solace as well as pleasure to a great many people." She smiled. "Would you call me Mimi, please?"

"Thank you. I'd like to. And I'm Katherine."

"I'm grateful for the gift of your name. I used to go to all your New York concerts. I thought of you as belonging to the older generation, but as the years increase, the distance between generations decreases. I, too, am pushing toward retirement." She moved to the kitchen with her cup, pausing at a bookcase where several framed photographs were propped on the shelves. "Your husband was older than you, wasn't he?"

"Fifteen years. But, as you say, chronologies make less and less difference."

Mimi picked up the photograph to study it. "Handsome, your Justin. Christ, he's attractive, the kind of pensive eyes and fine-bridged nose with those lines of tension moving to the mouth which make me a pushover. But a bit moody, I'd say, and not easy to live with on a day-to-day basis."

Katherine's laugh pealed out. "He was impossible! Moody is hardly the word for it. But then, I am impossible, too. How we managed to have so much fun together I'm not sure, but we did. We loved having people in for small dinners, and talking long into the night—music, of course, but politics, books, philosophy—and we two could talk about anything."

"That's it, isn't it?" Mimi asked. "Someone to talk with. Someone who can talk about the things in our own concerns. We need that." A bleak expression flitted across her face. "I did a hip replacement a few weeks ago on a delightful woman who's been widowed for a few years, and she talked about how much she missed someone to talk with about the silly little things, the small diminishments and wearings out of the body, someone to look at in the morning and say, 'Did you have a good B.M.?' And then to argue with— Did you and your Justin ever fight?"

"Of course. Enormous, shouting battles. When we were working up a program for me we would quarrel violently—about interpretation, about presentation—but the important thing was that in the end I always understood the music better and so, I think, did he. Music in a sense started the battles and, in the end, resolved them. A good argument is a splendid thing."

Mimi looked pensively at the photograph of Justin. "A good clean one. I can see that you did not indulge in bitterness or recriminations."

"What for? Neither Justin nor I was capable of going to bed mad. We couldn't stand it. Everything was all right at the end of the day." Not quite true. Or at least more true about herself than about Justin. If he started to 'go to bed mad,' it was she who could not stand it and who managed to resolve whatever had been the cause of the anger.

Mimi put the picture back in its place. "And these are your children?" She indicated a photograph of a boy and a girl, the blond little boy perhaps seven, the dark-haired little girl younger, standing one on each side of Justin, holding his hands.

"Yes. I love that picture. Justin adored the children, and he was a wonderful father, romping with them, listening to them, while I, too often, was away on tour. That's Julie a few years ago." Katherine nodded toward a snapshot of a handsome woman standing with a tall Viking of a man, both carrying skis.

"Her husband?"

"Yes. Eric Olaffsen. They live in Norway. Eric's a stepnephew of Erlend Nikulaussen—the conductor. Eric himself has a shipping business, and they have a house on one of the fjords. I don't see them nearly enough, though we're appallingly extravagant with the phone. I'm nowhere near finished nesting. I'll get the more current pictures out eventually. Julie's middle-aged now, and her hair's as white as mine, and my eldest grandchild is well in the twenties. I have four grandchildren, charming young people. They, too, add to my phone bill, especially Kristen, who's a flautist with the symphony in Oslo. We talk music too often—no, not too often. It's a great joy to me."

Mimi turned to the picture of the small boy and girl. "Your son—who on earth does he remind me of?"

"His father." Katherine's voice was sharp.

Mimi looked at the snapshot of Justin Vigneras, dark and hawk-like, and at the fair boy, and shook her head. "Where is he now?"

"He is dead," Katherine said, and Dr. Oppenheimer did not pursue the question.

She said, "You have a gracious apartment, very much reflecting your personality. But all those bookshelves! Do you realize that a plethora of bookshelves lowers the real-estate value of your house?"

"Not true, surely?"

"Very true, alas."

"Fortunately, I have no intention of selling." Katherine put her hand to her mouth to stifle a yawn.

"I've stayed too long," Mimi said. "Thank you for letting me come. Sleep well."

"You, too. Good night." Katherine saw her out by the kitchen door. The tisane, or the hour, had made her sleepy and she yawned again, fully. Then she turned out the lights and went to her bedroom. The long windows looked down on the garden in the back,

charmingly kept by the young couple. There was a small fountain
playing, and the sound was cool and springlike.

She turned down her bed, not the big bed she had shared with
Justin, which had been sold with most of the furniture from the
house in Paris, but a smaller mahogany bedstead which had been
her mother's. The head and footboards were beautifully carved,
with swans curving in graceful intertwining. The furniture for the
bedroom had come from Connecticut, where it had been stored in
one of Manya's barns. It, too, gave her a feeling of continuity.
Both her mother and her stepmother had used the graceful high-
boy, had sat at the low dressing table and looked in the mirror,
perhaps had even lighted the candles in silver holders which
branched from the oval frame. The rug, Chinese, soft blues and
silvers, had come from Manya's apartment on the East River. It
was a quiet room, a restful room.

She removed the light summer spread and pulled down the
cotton blanket. Likely she would need to pull it up during the
night. This weather was absurd for April. Nevertheless, she took
a hot bath. When she was on tour she was always drained and
chilly after a concert, and a hot bath was needed to warm and
relax her enough for sleep. It had become part of her evening
ritual, of shedding the tensions which had built during the day.
Michou and Julie had had their evening rituals, too, as small children. Perhaps we never lose the need to put a frame of quiet and
comfort around the events of the day.

It was too warm for bath oil, so she sprinkled in a handful of
lightly scented lavender salts, and climbed into the tub, dropping
with a small splash into the water. Her creaky knees and aching
hip made getting in and out of the tub no easy matter. Here, as in
Paris, she had installed a handgrip, without which she did not think
she could have managed. When she was on tour she had often
had to ask her maid to help her out of difficult and unfamiliar tubs.
She would miss Nanette, for that and many reasons, Nanette who
had come to her as a fresh-cheeked, still-adolescent Breton girl, to

be a nurse for the children, and then had stayed on to take care of Katherine. It was nothing for Nanette to pick Katherine up in her arms, as she had earlier picked up Michou and Julie, and carry her across a filthy stage-door alley. So, too, she had lifted her from the tub, as she had lifted the children.

The water, she noted with irritation, was slightly muddy, but she had been informed that this was now taken for granted in the city. The bath salts, however, smelled clean and fresh, and she lay back and closed her eyes and let the warm water soothe her.

But her mind would not relax. She tried to quieten it with trivia: she would wash her hair in the morning under the shower. After Justin's death she had had it cut short, and felt that it was more becoming than the heavy masses of long hair he had loved, and which took forever to dry and dress. The short, well-styled hair toweled dry in a few minutes, and fell in becoming waves over her high forehead, her small delicate ears, showing the graceful curve of her neck.

She could not keep her mind on anything as simple as a shampoo. Whether it was seeing Felix after all these years, she did not know.

The bath water suddenly felt cold and she turned on the hot-water tap. Going to Paris after the bitter breakup with her young man had been the first step into what she considered reality, the world of the serious artist. How gently Justin had guided her then, when she was barely more than an overgrown adolescent, working with her through the music, relaxing the rigidity which had been her instinctive defense against rejection. After a few months he had started taking her out to dinner, to this favorite bistro or that, and then they would go back to his attic rooms and she would play—or, rather, he would seat her at the piano and demand that she repeat something he had not been satisfied with at her last lesson. Ultimately, when she had corrected the phrase which she had not, during the cold light of day, been able to master, he would walk her home to her small studio.

It was difficult for people now to realize that she had ever been so shy that she spoke in a mumble, looking down at her feet, so insecure that she came to life only at the keyboard. Justin had grown her up, she thought, and that is no small thing.

She wondered what had grown Felix up. And what—or who— had turned him from the self-indulgent young man to the far more interesting person he was now. She was vaguely relieved that he had not talked about religion, and yet she found herself wondering what he believed.

With the help of the handrail she pulled herself out of the tub and put on a white terry robe. She moved slowly about the apartment, making sure the doors were locked: the door from the kitchen into the front hall; her private door into the vestibule. She could leave the windows open because of the iron grillwork which protected them. Although she had had the beautifully wrought grilles sent over from Spain, she still resented the necessity for barring herself in.

She paused in the kitchen to pour a glass of water from the large bottle which was replaced weekly. It was tepid, but she had been away from New York long enough so that she had become indifferent to iced drinks, just as they were becoming *de rigueur* in Europe. Back in the bedroom, she put on her reading glasses and stretched out on the chaise longue by the windows to read until she was dry. In the garden below, two couples were lingering over coffee. Candles burned in glass globes, and voices and laughter came up to her. It was still not eleven o'clock and they were not being noisy.

She was hot in the terry robe, so she moved back into the bathroom, finished drying with dusting powder, and put on a light cotton-batiste nightgown. Getting her book from the chaise longue, she lay on the bed, throwing off the sheet. She felt too tired to read, and after a few pages put the book on her nightstand and turned off the light.

---··❧{ 4 }❧··---

The sound of the phone, raucous as the peacocks, broke across her.

Automatically she reached for it, first on the wrong side of the bed, the side it had been on in Paris. She rolled over, groping for the light, then the phone. A phone call after she had gone to sleep could well be her daughter, Julie, or one of the grandchildren, knowing that this was the one time she could surely be reached. Or it could mean something wrong, an accident to one of the children, to . . .

During Justin's last years, when he was not well enough to travel, it could be her husband calling to chat. Or it could be, as it had been several times before the final call, a summons to his bedside.

As she said "Hello," chronologies swirled. She did not know when she was, or where.

"Katherine, did I wake you?"

"Yes. Who is it?"

"Katya—"

Chronology still had not settled. She almost called out, "Aunt Manya!"

"It's Felix."

The past, like a weary bird, dropped into place. She was in the bedroom of her house on Tenth Street, in New York. "Felix, what on earth—"

"I'm sorry I woke you. I don't sleep much nowadays."

"I do. Eight hours—when the phone doesn't interrupt." She looked at the traveling clock. Nearly one in the morning. He was presuming on friendship, on old times. She was not feeling apologetic for sounding angry.

"Katya, please don't be cross, I need you."

"Felix, I told you not to badger me about that benefit."

"Not the benefit. I need you. I need to hear your voice. I need to know there's someone at the other end of the phone." His voice rose in anxiety.

"Surely I'm not the only person you know in the City of New York."

"Katherine. I'm afraid."

She sat up in bed. "Felix, what on earth is this? Why are you calling *me*?"

"You're not involved."

"In what?"

"The Church. The Cathedral. And you could call Dr. Oppenheimer if—"

"If what?" Felix had always tended to theatricality. She could not tell if the terror in his voice was feigned or real.

"I had a nightmare . . ."

"Why tell me?" She did not know why she did not hang up.

"I don't want to bother Dave—the dean. He has enough on his

hands. I'd wake Suzy and the kids. And Llew is too involved in himself. And the others—I don't want to be laughed at—"

Had he been drinking? He had never had much of a head for alcohol. Even if he'd only finished the Frascati— "What is all this about? Why are you calling me at this hour?"

"I'm afraid," he repeated, and there was no doubting that his fear was real.

Her voice softened. "Are you ill?"

"No, I'm not ill."

"You're not in pain? Your heart's all right?"

"My heart is fine. It's thumping only because I'm frightened."

"Of what?"

"There are noises . . . I thought if they heard me talking on the phone . . ."

"Who?"

There was a small, choking sound.

She tried to be gentle with what sounded close to hysterical panic. She had known terror in the night, although she could not imagine what was frightening the bishop. "Isn't there somebody closer you could call? Someone who could come over?"

"No, no, I don't want any of them. It's helping just to hear your voice. You've always been so strong—people have always been able to talk to you. You've done me a world of good. You've saved my life."

That sounded more like the old Felix, prone to hyperbole. "All right for me to go back to sleep now?" —If I can.

"You've made all the difference. Just hearing your voice has reassured me."

"Why don't you turn on your radio? There are some good all-night stations."

"Yes, yes, I'll do that. Forgive me. I've been drinking."

Had he? She was not sure. "Good night, Felix."

"Oh, bless you, Katherine, bless you."

It was an appropriate way for a bishop to end a conversation. She replaced the receiver in its cradle. What had all that been about? She felt baffled and vaguely concerned. There was only one thing of which she was sure: Felix was afraid.

But why had he called her?

There was no answer to that, this night at any rate. And he had thoroughly wakened her. Fear is contagious, and she had caught some of his.

--◦◖{ 5 }◗◦--

Slowly she stretched out her hands to make sure they were all right. Her memory would never lose that time during the war when she had been beaten; she had clenched her fists so tightly against the pain that she could not open her fingers without agony until the next day, and she had been afraid they would never open easily again. The unremitting damp of the Nazi prison and then the beating had been the beginning of the arthritis which had for so many years been a sword of Damocles hanging over her head. Once again, in the infectious terror she had caught from Felix, she was afraid that the thread might break, so that, after all these crowded years, she needed tangible reassurance that her hands were all right.

She opened her bed-table drawer and pulled out a small, tooled-leather box. Inside was a rosary of small, carved myrtle-wood beads, the patterning almost worn down by Cardinal von Stromberg's fingers. Although her own praying was little more than an anguished cry of "Help!" or a "Thank you!" in the startlement of joy, the rosary held the strength of von Stromberg's prayers, and her heart slowed its rapid beating.

She eased herself out of bed, moved to the living room, and sat down at the piano. Bach. The last prelude in the second volume of *The Well-Tempered Clavier*. Her hands were all right. As Justin's had not been. Nor her mother's, whose right arm had been so injured in an automobile accident that it cut off her career, broke her marriage, nearly drove her to drink—

Ravel's Piano Concerto for the Left Hand had been composed for a friend whose right hand had been blown off in the trenches during World War I. Surely Felix could not believe in a God who made a world where people were given great gifts, only to have those gifts smashed, irrevocably, while the life which was no more than a vessel for that gift went on and on, meaninglessly. Are there other gifts to replace the broken one? For her mother, there had not been.

Justin had turned to composing as well as nurturing Katherine's talent, maturing her, expanding her, never forcing or manipulating, but helping her serve the gift for which she had been born. She played the Prelude and Fugue through to the end, then dutifully returned to bed, returning the rosary to its box and the bed-table drawer. To her surprise, she slid almost immediately into sleep. And dream. Her dreams, of late, had been reliving the past, as though her subconscious mind was helping her to recover all the things she had not had time to think about. It was not so much that she had deliberately repressed the memories as that she had been too busy for them. The present had been too full, even in these years after Justin's death. Now the past was returning to her in her dreams, not to shock and frighten her, but to help her complete herself. Even when the dreams were nightmares or, rather, reviewing what had been living nightmares, she welcomed them. But this dream was as much of a chronological muddle as she had been in when Felix's call had roused her. She was in his Cathedral, listening to the organ, and in the dream she could see the organist, Llew whatever his name was, and he wept, wept for his wife and child, wept for Bishop Undercroft. Why was he grieving for the bishop, who was very much alive? But he wept, and his tears became part of the music, bathing the columns of the nave with a gentle, cleansing flow. She ran the length of the dark building to hold him, to give him a light, because he was afraid of the dark.

She woke up, her face wet with tears, Llew's tears, she thought vaguely, and then was astonished to find herself in an old body, a body which could not run as fleetly as she had just run in the dream.

There had been many nights when she had held Justin, as she had been running to hold Llew, when they had wept together. Perhaps what she missed most was someone with whom to shed tears.

It was three o'clock in the morning, and the light curtains at the windows hung limply in the humidity. Her various routines for inducing sleep took no account of the warm weather. She went to the kitchen to heat up some consommé, and took it to bed to sip. Sometimes that would quieten her when she had an attack of the past. But this was past and present all kaleidoscoped. She did not like it. In her mind's ear she played through thesis and antithesis of Busoni's *Fantasia Contrappuntistica*, letting the rich fusion of counterpoint and fantasy clarify her mind. She felt Justin's presence behind her, as he had so often stood behind her while she worked, and in the comfort of his presence she drifted into sleep.

⸙{ 6 }⸙

Toward morning, the air lightened and her sleep became restful. She did not stir till nearly nine.

She was waiting for her coffee to drip through the filter when the phone rang. It was not surprising to have it be Felix.

"I hope I didn't disturb you?"

"No, I'm up."

"Did I call you last night?"

"You know you did."

"No, I don't know. I got drunk, and when that happens, I forget."

"You didn't sound drunk."

"I was. It doesn't happen very often. But last night—"

"What about last night?"

"What did I talk to you about?"

"You were afraid of something."

"You mustn't take it seriously. I sometimes get the screaming meemies. I can't apologize enough for bothering you."

Frascati or no, she had believed his fear the night before. She did not believe his excuses this morning.

"Fears—" he murmured. "They don't end when one is consecrated bishop. Do you remember the horrible ads they used to have in the subway when we were young? Pictures of coffins looking, oh, so cozy, as though if we made the corpse comfy that would take away the sting of death."

"Felix, will you hang on a minute? Let me pour myself a cup of coffee."

"Of course, my dear. Take your time. It's a gorgeous spring day, in the seventies, with the sun lovely and warm."

She fixed her coffee and sat down comfortably. She wanted to know what had put him in a state of near-panic the night before. "Here I am. What were you saying?"

"I'm not sure. I have no memory. I think I was talking about fears, all the human fears. I don't think I'm really afraid of dying now, at least not the way I used to be when I was so appalled at pictures of satin-padded coffins."

She was silent. Whatever was making him talk this way had to do with whatever had frightened him the night before.

"All I meant to do was call and apologize for drinking too much and bothering you, you of all people. Did I wake you?"

"I told you, I'm drinking coffee."

"I mean last night."

"It doesn't matter. Don't fret."

"Bless you, my dear. I'll be in touch, but I won't bother you. I promise."

She hoped he would keep the promise. She hung up, vaguely disturbed, and warmed a croissant to go with her second cup of coffee. She would spend the morning at the piano.

The Hunter Portrait

 1

During her busy professional life, she'd appreciated her rare hours alone. In hotel rooms all over the world she had made herself at home by putting an herb-scented pillow on the bed, pictures of Justin and the children on tables and chests of drawers, scattering books and music about, carrying with her two small vases for flowers, given her by thoughtful admirers. Her times of solitude were treasured, a few hours snatched here and there between television appearances, newspaper interviews, recording sessions.

Crowds backstage after a concert. Small supper parties afterwards, carefully organized by Jean Paul Yvert, her manager. Formal dinners with heads of state. Gifts from music lovers, not just the great bouquets of hothouse flowers, but more thoughtful things, like the vases, the first herbal pillow, a book someone thought she might enjoy.

Sometimes she would take two weeks off, in the mountains, or by the sea, sleeping great drenches of sleep, swimming, reading, walking. In the periods between tours, when she stayed in Paris, there were daily visits from Jean Paul as the next concert was planned, the guest appearances with various orchestras. She was always on the move, to airports, hotels . . .

After the last long tour, when the house had been sold, the farewell concert given, the champagne flat, the flowers wilted, the plane ticket to New York in her bag, she had said a final farewell to Jean Paul, who had so competently managed her career since Justin's death. He had tried to hold her back, begging her to marry him, to stay in France.

She was not sure why she felt she had to leave Jean Paul, to leave the house where she had lived with Justin, to return to the city of her birth, where she had spent only the smallest fraction of her life. But if she was to retire, and she was convinced that the right time had come, then all connections had to be cut.

'It's absurd to think of marriage at my age,' she had told Jean Paul. 'You are young enough to be my son.'

'So was Colette's third husband. And he took care of her till she died.'

'I have had only one husband, and I have no intention of dying in the near future,' she had replied with asperity. 'I intend to enjoy the peace and quiet of my retirement. I own a brownstone in New York and a farmhouse in Connecticut.'

'But the farmhouse is rented and you need the income, and New York is not safe.'

'It's no less safe than Paris. All big cities are dangerous. They have always been.'

'But New York—its reputation . . .'

'Jean Paul, I want to go home.'

'But Paris has been your home—why go so far? What about Norway? Your daughter is there, and your grandchildren. I know Erlend Nikulaussen is dead, but—'

'Norway is out,' she said flatly. 'I have no intention of dumping myself on a daughter who, in any case, would not welcome me. And, as you say, Erlend is dead. He was my great good friend, and a fine conductor, and I was probably happier playing with him than with anyone else, but the past is past and I do not need to go to Norway, where I do not speak the language.'

'But your daughter—after all, Julie is married to Erlend's nephew, and you love to talk on the phone with your grandchildren—'

'Jean Paul, stop trying. I am going home. I do not speak Norwegian and I am tired of talking French.'

'But, my love, you think in French.'

'It is now time for me to return to thinking in English.'

At first she had felt that she was translating; her idioms came out with a Gallic twist. But after a few weeks she would have to stop herself and check to see in which language she was thinking, or in which language she had been dreaming. One morning in early May when she was setting out to do the day's marketing, and passed Mimi Oppenheimer in the vestibule, she inadvertently greeted her in French, and to her surprise Mimi replied in French, explaining, "I was born in Paris. My mother was American, so we spoke French and English interchangeably at home. It's delightful to have someone to speak French with."

"I'm trying to remember to think in English," Katherine said ruefully. "This was a slipup."

"You don't really think in any language," Mimi told her. "You think in music. By the way, Suzy Davidson called me this morning to say that Llewellyn Owen is giving a concert this afternoon after Evensong. He's an unusually fine organist. Could I persuade you to join me?"

"I think you could. I heard him practicing last month when Felix was showing me around the Cathedral."

"Good. I'll pick you up at three-thirty. I'm off to give a lecture now and I'm running late." With a quick wave, Mimi loped down the street, swinging a black briefcase, moving more like an overgrown adolescent than a professional woman on the verge of retirement.

Katherine did her marketing and let herself into the apartment. It was beginning to feel like home. All the pictures were now unpacked, the photographs hung. The music was arranged in a tall cherry cabinet which had been Justin's present to her on her fiftieth birthday, and was one of the pieces she had brought over from France. The barrels containing silver, china, linens, had been taken away; the sawdust, real and plastic, had been swept up by Raissa, the cleaning woman Mimi had found for her, who came for a few hours twice a week. She had called a piano tuner who understood the piano. She had discovered a good butcher, a stand with really fresh fruits and vegetables. José, the superintendent she shared with half the block, was full of excellent if nearly incomprehensible advice. The exterminator Mimi had recommended would come on the first Monday of each month. An old house in New York, Mimi had warned her, is a favorite habitation of cockroaches and rodents.

'I can stand the mice,' Mimi said, 'but not the rats. And not the cockroaches. Do you know that they can survive almost anything: heat, pressure, even the aftereffects of an atom bomb? If human beings eliminate themselves in atomic warfare, the cockroaches will inherit the world.'

Katherine had shuddered and promptly called the exterminator. 'And be sure to have plenty of candles on hand,' Mimi had added. 'I note you have candlesticks on your table, but you should be warned that the power system of this great city is getting more and more unreliable. The power tends to go out in one borough or other far too frequently, and Manhattan, of course, is likely to suffer most.' Katherine heeded Mimi's advice—the doctor, she thought, was not a doom-monger—and put several boxes of candles in her big closet under the stairs in the main hall. It had a strong padlock and was as close as she could come to having an attic. There she stored some silver she did not use regularly, and a few pictures she could not find room for in her limited space. Too many bookcases? No, she could not do without her books—though half a dozen cartons were also stored in the back of the hall closet, waiting until she could figure out a new place for shelves.

She was, she was confident, settling in, becoming once again at home in her native city and her native tongue.

But she was not falling asleep easily at night. After all these years of widowhood she kept reaching out for Justin's warm and sleeping body, as she had so often in the night reached out to give or receive comfort. Even in the hottest weather they had always slept in the same bed, in order that touch be available, the loveliness of a beloved body.

When she was not at the piano, she had an uneasy sense of being displaced. There was no busy time during the day when she was planning a new tour. When she checked her music, it was not to prepare a program for a new concert. One morning after two hours of aimless practicing she went to the record player and put on one of her mother's records. It was a new pressing, taken from one of the old 78 rpm discs, and even with all of modern technology there was a faint roaring as of distant vacuum cleaners in the background. But the music rose above it, brilliant and alive. Scriabin.

Julie Forrester had been one of the great interpreters of that complex Russian composer. The dense Slavic music twined itself into Katherine's attentive listening. Why was she playing it? Her mother had been known for her Scriabin, Liszt, Chopin. Not Katherine's music. So why was she playing it now? What was she looking for?

Love, perhaps? Reassurance? Even now, was she looking for figurative lap-sitting, the petting, the coddling she had not received as a child? But surely she had received more than enough affirmation from Manya, once she had been able to turn to her stepmother. But, like all human beings, she still had unfulfilled longings. She could still be as lonely and frightened as a child, and with as little reason.

The music still playing, she returned to her desk. Her correspondence was large, and likely to remain so. She had received many fan letters over the years, and some of them had resulted in lifelong friendships and continuing correspondence. Many of the letters were from fellow musicians, others from people who appreciated music and understood it. Only the day before, she had received a letter from a man who had heard her last concert in Vienna—how long ago? a year?—and had remarked that when an audience listened to Vigneras, there was no curtain of protection between player and audience, that there was a sensation of music not so much being played as creating itself, of its own volition. He surely deserved a reasonable thank-you letter. During the height of her career she had needed a secretary to take care of the bulk of the mail. For the past few years she had been weaning herself of this assistance, and had devoted at least an hour a day to answering letters, and this now gave her some needed structure. But she did not want to be an old woman dependent on fans for a sense of self. Absurd. Letters were fine, and she treasured the friendships, and was helped, as all artists need to be helped, by reassurance; however, she spent only a small part of each day at her desk. Time stretched ahead of her with no structure she herself did not impose. Perhaps she had been overhasty in retiring.

Nonsense.

But she was restless. She was lonely. She was grateful for Mimi's invitation.

--◦◦⊰ 2 ⊱◦◦--

When the doctor arrived, a little ahead of time, Katherine offered her a cup of tea. The spring weather had been unwontedly variable. The day before, after a warm beginning to May, she had needed a coat. Now, with one of New York's unpredictable switches, it was summer-hot.

Mimi accepted a cup with alacrity. "I'm glad I came early. The students were particularly dull today, and I did not think I was being that obscure. I have a reputation for being an attention-holding if slightly flamboyant lecturer, and one young creature yawned." She settled herself comfortably on the sofa, one leg tucked under her. "You're looking more rested. Everything going along all right?"

"Fine. I'm not accustomed to total lack of schedule."

"You practice regularly."

"Oh—that. Yes, of course. But it's for no particular purpose."

"Have you heard from Bishop Bodeway since your dinner together?"

Katherine shook her head. Felix had honored his promise not to bother her. She did not want to betray him, and as the weeks had passed, she had put the two strange phone calls from her mind, but she heard herself asking, "Has he ever had a drinking problem?"

Mimi smiled. "Did he go rather heavily on the wine that night at dinner?"

"No. We had only one glass apiece. And one small glass of dry sherry beforehand."

"Then—forgive me—but why do you ask?"

Katherine prevaricated: "He used to drink more than I thought was good for him back in the days of our extreme youth."

Mimi's eyes were shrewd. "But that's not why you ask. Never mind. No, I don't think he has a drinking problem. I gather that a long time ago he drank heavily, but he was not an alcoholic, and he's had no problem with drinking ever since I've known him. From all I can see, he has none of the telltale signs of the secret drinker. I think he is, in fact, a temperate old boy."

Mimi rose, and stood by the bookshelves, pulling out a volume. "You have eclectic taste in reading."

"I've tried to keep my horizons a little wider than music."

"Where's the picture of your son and daughter?"

A small hesitation. Then, "Oh—I have so many pictures I rotate them. There he is, Michou, standing by Julie in her cradle." She pointed to a snapshot which was focused on the baby; the small boy was in shadow, only his fair hair visible as he bent over the cradle. "And"—Katherine pointed toward the fireplace—"there he is again with me."

The doctor turned to regard a portrait of a young woman, half-veiled by loose dark hair, nursing a baby, a beautiful subtle painting. "Gorgeous! Whose?"

"Philippa Hunter's."

"I should have known. Her use of light and shadow always awes me. Did you know her?"

"Slightly. She was a protégée of Aunt Manya's—my stepmother—who was an actress—"

Mimi said, "I recognized her photograph on your wall, there. I'm old enough to remember Manya Sergeievna."

"Lots of people your age don't. Anyhow, Philippa asked to do the portrait. Aunt Manya bought it for Justin and me and we always loved it—it's probably my most treasured possession."

"Small wonder. It's one of the best Hunters I've ever seen."

Katherine, too, gazed at the portrait. "Everything's uncrated and unpacked and put in its place—at last. I'm feeling very much at home."

"Yes, this is a home. And I'm very glad you're in it."

--⋅⊰{ 3 }⊱⋅--

In the taxi, Katherine said, "Felix wants me to give him a benefit concert."

"Why not do it? It won't be like preparing for a tour, but it will at least give you a small sense of purpose."

"I'm thinking about it."

"The completion of much of the Cathedral—though it's still not finished—was largely because of Felix. You know, despite my friendship with Suzy and Dave, the workings of the Church are completely beyond my ken, but I have a hunch Felix Bodeway was a good bishop. It would make him very happy if the Cathedral could be a little nearer completion before he dies."

Katherine held on to the cracked leather strap as the taxi swerved to avoid a truck. She did not reply.

Mimi continued, "The designs for the towers and the transepts came about long before Felix's time. Dean Morton brought in a master builder from England and started a project of training local kids to cut stone. But the world was in its usual state of chaos, inflation was rampant, and things were slower than they should have been. The dean's vision was brilliant, and despite all the problems the towers of Sts. Peter and Paul got built amazingly quickly. But after Morton left when he was called to be a bishop, things came almost to a halt for lack of imagination and money. Time passed. Then along came Bodeway."

"And gets the money?"

"Wait," Mimi said. "It's not as easy as that. Felix is, I believe, a man of prayer, but he never hesitated to ask for money, whenever and wherever he could. But the amount of money he needed isn't raised by importunate bishops, or even professional money-raisers. Not any more. Things cost far more than anyone could have anticipated when Dean Morton started rebuilding." She tapped on the glass separating them from the driver. "Go up Amsterdam, please." Back to Katherine. "When your friend Bodeway was elected bishop, he did all kinds of things that were thought odd. Unless his duties took him elsewhere, he was apt to turn up at the Cathedral for the early communion service, and for Evensong. And he made hospital calls, not just on staff and employees and old friends who were ill, but to the wards of St. Luke's. He didn't make any public business about it—I got all this from Dave Davidson, by the way, not Felix. He would go visit someone in the private pavilion, and then he would wander around the hospital, looking more like a monk than a bishop, and if anyone wanted him, there he was. Not that he stepped on the toes of the chaplains, but they were woefully understaffed, and he was so gentle and deferential with them that they were only grateful for his help. When they were exhausted, which was frequently, he took around the early communions. But I digress."

Again she tapped on the dividing glass. "It's on the right, just below 112th." She leaned back again. "I don't know why I put all this in the past tense. For all I know, he still does it. But—and this is definitely in the past—before the north transept got built, there was one old indigent woman he visited daily, week after week. One of those thousands of pathetic cases. No family. No friends. Old and alone and ill in an unfriendly city. And she took a long time dying. One foot came off, then the other. Weeks before her death, she smelled of putrefaction, so that she had to be put in a tiny cubicle because none of the other patients in the ward could stand the stench. There are a lot of unpleasant smells in a big city hospital, but hers really got to the doctors and nurses. Bishop Bodeway never let on it wasn't a rose garden. And he was with the old girl, holding her hand, when she died." Mimi opened her billfold. "Here we are." She glanced at Katherine reaching for her bag. "You pay on the way home." She unfolded herself out of the taxi and held out a hand. "Are you going to be all right on these steps?"

"As long as you don't expect me to gallop."

They started the climb, and halfway up Mimi stopped. "Let me finish my story. The old girl had left a will and she wasn't indigent after all. She was loaded. She wasn't a unique case. I've never understood why there have always been millionaires who choose to live in penury, but I'm an orthopod, not a shrink. The money all went to Felix. Naturally, some distant cousins turned up to contest the will, but under the circs they didn't have a chance. They didn't admit her existence when she appeared to need financial help in the worst possible way. They weren't sitting by her bed, holding her hand, when the stench was enough to make the most hardened nurse retch. And it was obvious that the bishop was as surprised as anyone at the will, and he had an entire hospital staff to back him up, from the head medic to the lowest cleaning woman. So the money went to Bishop Bodeway. Some he gave to the hospital. But there was enough for the Cathedral, so that St. Paul's tower got finished and the transepts started. Not entirely on the old woman's money, but such bequests, with their publicity, and articles all slanted in Bodeway's favor, tend to beget more bequests, and money came in, in amazing amounts, I gather, despite hard times." She saw that Katherine had regained her breath. "Let's go on up the rest of these ghastly steps and get in early enough so that we can get my pet seats."

Katherine continued the climb, grateful for the respite. "That's a nice story, about Felix. Thanks for telling me. I'm glad to know he turned out to be that kind of person."

"Suzy and Dave think the world of him. I do hope you'll give him his benefit concert."

"You've convinced me," Katherine said.

--⊰{ 4 }⊱--

Once again she felt the coolness of the stones, of the great vault of the Cathedral, light and space as much part of the architecture as the soaring columns. Mimi took her the length of the nave, treading briskly on the bronze medallions around which Felix had carefully walked, past the carved oak chest which received widow's mites, up the wide marble steps to the ambulatory and into the choir stalls.

"We'll be more comfortable here than in those folding chairs. And the acoustics of this place are such that we'll hear as well here if not better than in the crossing."

There was already a clustering of people in the choir stalls, in the nave. Half concealed in a carved and hooded seat at the front of the choir sat the dark man she had met with Felix—the dean. Mimi caught his eye and waved discreetly, and he smiled at them, leaning his chin on one hand, looking, Katherine thought, worn and tired.

"Evensong's just over," Mimi whispered in her ear. "I didn't think you'd care to be here for that. It makes a long time to sit on uncushioned seats. A lot of music lovers come in after the service. Llew waits to begin till people have found seats and quieted down."

Assorted groups were milling about the nave, greeting each other, chatting, looking for seats, acting more as though they were in the lobby of a concert hall than in a cathedral, Katherine thought; but then, she was not at all certain how people were supposed to behave in a cathedral. What she looked for was a rich silence, like the pause between the movements of a sonata.

Years ago, so long it was like another lifetime, Cardinal von Stromberg had sent her into the cathedral in Munich, not to pray, just to be quiet. There was no service going on. The silence seemed as ancient as the wooden carving of a Madonna and Child before which she stood, drawing strength from the other young woman's stillness. She looked about Felix's cathedral but saw no statue of the Virgin. Instead, she noted four nuns walking in, dressed in light-blue summer habits. They headed for the choir, and one, taller than the others, paused for a moment as she passed the dean, to speak to him, and he reached out his hand for hers.

"Mother Catherine of Siena," Mimi said. "She runs St. Andrew's, the school the Davidson kids go to. She's quite a gal, Mother Cat, a priest, and a canon of the Cathedral."

"I didn't know nuns were priests."

"Episcopal nuns," Mimi said. "And most aren't. Some are. Mother Cat's qualified, all right. She has a Ph.D. in Byzantine theology, and she also has—though this is rumor—an M.D. I wouldn't put it past her."

Katherine shook her head. "The Episcopal Church is an enigma to me. Just when I think it's like the Catholic Church, I discover there are nuns who are priests."

"Not just nuns. Other women, too. Why not? People used to think that only men could be doctors, that women had to be nurses. The Catholic Church is on the verge, I gather. But you'd know more about that than I. You *are* Catholic, aren't you?"

"Nominally, I suppose, since Justin was, also nominally."

"You must meet Mother Cat. You'll like her. She knows music— I wonder if there's anything she doesn't know?"

The four nuns seated themselves in the choir stalls opposite Katherine and Mimi, and a small boy, with dark, curly hair, was crowded into the stall with Mother Catherine of Siena, leaning against her confidingly. Katherine started as she recognized the child who had tried to get her a taxi and offered to sell her secrets. "Who is the little boy?"

Mimi followed her glance. "Topaze Gomez. His mother is Yolande Undercroft's cook, and he has a funny, fat older sister. The nuns do tend to pick up waifs and strays. Kids who don't get enough love at home—which the Gomez kids certainly don't. No wonder Topaze hangs around the Sisters. He's a beautiful child, too beautiful to be true, I suspect." And then she turned the subject, asking Katherine, "Where were you during the war?"

"Which war?"

"Ours. World War II."

"Paris."

"The whole time?"

"No. I was in prison for a while, and then my father and step-mother managed my release, and I came back to America."

"And your husband?"

"I was an American citizen, so it was easier to get me out. He was in Auschwitz for about a year."

"I didn't realize he was Jewish."

"He wasn't. A good many people went to concentration camps for refusing to collaborate."

Mimi beat one fist lightly against her breast. "*Mea culpa.* We sometimes forget that other people besides the Jews suffered during the Holocaust."

"My—Erlend Nikulaussen—the conductor—"

"Of course."

"He took his boat between Norway and England countless times, carrying men to safety—flyers who had escaped, anybody wanted by the Germans. Many Norwegians lost their lives, either in the bombings or the Resistance."

"Yes. Sorry. We have services remembering the Jews in the Holocaust and forget the Dutch—or the towns in Greece where all the able-bodied men and boys were shot down in front of their women—and the English, and—well. The dean, too, has had occasion to remind me of this. So, you refused to collaborate. Was that why you were in prison?"

"Yes."

"Quite a few well-known musicians did collaborate."

"Yes," Katherine said flatly. "I was stubborn to the point of pig-headedness."

"As for me," Mimi continued, "I had no choices to make. I was a small child and whipped off early to my American grandmother in South Carolina, where I stayed for the duration. Odd, isn't it: if you're half English and half Dutch, say, you have a choice at twenty-one which to be. If you're half Jewish, you're a Jew—or even an eighth. Which is fine with me, even though that was Hitler's idea."

"Oh, come," Katherine said. "I don't suppose most people feel that way."

"Oh, don't they?" Mimi demanded. "What about blacks? The

head of ophthalmology in my hospital is fair-haired and blue-eyed and lives on Washington Square, but he calls himself a black. Dave Davidson is a mixture of Puerto Rican and Indian and—I think—Welsh, but his skin is dark enough so that most people call him 'the black dean' in private, if not to his face. So I'm a Jew, and happy to be one, because Jake, my father, was a Jew. As my mama pointed out, before the war broke out we were in the midst of things and couldn't see the forest for the trees, and if it hadn't been for Grandmother Renier's urgent transatlantic calls in a day when such were not usual, we'd never have got out in time. We had to leave France because Jake was a Jew; though I never felt any anti-Semitism in Paris, there was plenty in South Carolina. Some of my Huguenot Renier cousins could be pretty insular."

"And yet—it's a good thing you left Paris, or you'd have felt anti-Semitism soon enough, and drastically."

"I know. We might all have been marched into the gas chambers. So here I am, a Jew, an atheist, and devoted to an Episcopal dean. Life is full of surprises. Grandmother Renier, who was a devout Episcopalian, would be delighted."

A small stir of anticipation moved like a breeze through the audience, and the concert began. At first the notes of the great organ were muted, no more than a whisper. Then, slowly, a series of rich chords rose, swelled, burst into brilliant life. Katherine leaned her head back against the carved wood of the stall. Mimi's chatter was gone now, Mimi was gone, there was nothing but music.

The Cathedral was gone. Memory, memories were gone. The power of the music caught her up into pure being. Into is-ness. Reality. It was this transcendence into which music drew her which had been her salvation during the most intolerable periods of her life.

The concert may have lasted an hour, but music, which is inextricably intertwined with time, is also paradoxically a release from time, and when enthusiastic applause greeted the final notes, Katherine was scarcely aware of time having passed.

"He *is* superb, isn't he?" Mimi was still beating her hands together.

"Glorious. Of course, he played some of my favorite things."

Katherine reached for her cane and the lacy shawl she had brought in case the weather should once again change suddenly.

Mimi put a restraining hand on her arm. "Let's wait until the place clears out. It's hell, isn't it, but Llew's playing has deepened enormously since he lost his wife and baby."

"Hell," Katherine agreed. "But that's the way it works. Look at Beethoven. The worse his deafness, the greater his music. And the best was composed when he was totally walled into a silent world. Did you notice that your Llew played one of Justin's pieces? Justin might never have started composing had his hands not been broken in Auschwitz."

"Christ, I didn't know about that," Mimi said. "Yes, it's hell. Oh, shit." She heaved a sigh. "Suzy's invited us to the deanery for a drink. I told her just to leave it open, we'd come or not according to your inclination."

"Would you like to go?"

"It's really up to you, but it would mean a lot to Llew to meet you."

"As long as we don't stay too long—"

"Just give me the high sign whenever you feel like it and we'll cut out. I think you'll enjoy the Davidsons. They help me retain a faint shred of hope for the institutional church. Grandmother Renier diligently took me to church with her every Sunday, but it did nothing for my soul, to her sorrow—and mine, because she was a great lady. No anti-Semitism in her. She and Jake adored each other, and there were many tears when we returned to France. When"—she turned the subject with typical abruptness—"when were you and your Justin married?"

"The week before the Nazis knocked on our door and arrested us."

"Did you expect the knock?"

"No. We were unpardonably naïve."

"Was it a good week, before the arrest?"

—Americans have no hesitation in asking personal questions. Felix. Mimi. The butcher, the baker, the candlestick maker. They all want to know everything. Too much psychiatry. "Yes. A good week. One can get through almost everything on the strength of one good week."

"I sometimes wonder"—Mimi reached for her handbag, which she had stashed under the stall—"if I have ever had that kind of good week? It involves a commitment I'm not sure I've ever been able to make. I'm closer to Suzy and some of my other tenants than I've ever been to my lovers. The trouble has been that the men I've enjoyed most in bed would have been inadequate as marriage partners and companions. And those whose friendship I've enjoyed haven't been exciting at sex, or have been gay."

—And Americans tell all as well as ask all. And I *must* remember that I am American.

They took the same exit Felix had used, Mimi running down the steps and waiting for Katherine. The four nuns were getting into a car, and Katherine saw that one was old and gnarled with arthritis, and the curly-haired boy was helping her in. Mimi waved to them, and the tall nun, who was waiting to get in the driver's seat, came over to shake hands.

"Dr. Oppenheimer, I might have expected to find you here for Llew's concert. He was magnificent, wasn't he?"

"Better every day. Mother Cat, I'd like you to meet my landlord and friend, Madame Katherine Vigneras."

The nun's thin, intelligent face lit up. "Madame Vigneras—truly? I'd heard you'd come back to New York."

"Katherine," Mimi said, "this is Mother Catherine of Siena—two Katherines I admire, though you spell it differently."

"Madame Vigneras, I'm delighted." Mother Catherine of Siena shook hands warmly. "We often play your records during Recreation, especially when we are overtired and need to be together without talking. May I drive you anywhere?"

"Oh, thanks, but no," Mimi replied. "We're just on our way to the Davidsons'."

"Do give them our love," the nun said.

"And my love to everybody," Mimi said, "especially Sister Isobel."

"She has a nasty cold, otherwise she'd have been here this afternoon." Mother Catherine of Siena looked down at the child who was pulling at her skirts. "What is it, Topaze?"

"C'n I come back with you for Vespers?"

"All right. Hop in the back." She waved, and got into the car.

"She's beautiful as well as bright," Katherine remarked.

"That she is. Come along, it's just across here, past Ogilvie House, which is sometimes lived in by bishops, sometimes by deans. The bishop has it now, which seems a pity, since he and his wife have no children, while Suzy and Dave have their four still living at home. But Mrs. Undercroft, the present Mrs. Undercroft, that is, isn't about to give up any of her perks. What matter that she doesn't need all those rooms? Topaze's mother is her cook, and she could perfectly well let Mrs. Gomez and the two kids live somewhere up on the third floor but no, they have to live in a filthy tenement up on Washington Heights."

"The present Mrs. Undercroft? Is he widowed?"

"Divorced," Mimi said flatly and with disapproval.

"I'm staggered enough at married bishops, much less divorced ones."

Mimi shrugged. "All is permissiveness nowadays. Express yourself, fulfill yourself, no matter at what cost to others. I liked his first wife, and he threw her aside like a used tissue."

"I gather," Katherine remarked dryly, "that you don't care for him?"

Mimi sighed. "I have unreasonable likes and dislikes. I'm aware that he's brilliant and charming, but he's too young for my tastes, or I'm too old for his charm. Anyhow, Dave—and your Felix— are the only clerical types I can abide."

"I'm still surprised at a divorced bishop."

Mimi put out her hand to help Katherine down the stone steps. "There are plenty. Like most non-churchgoers, you have high expectations of bishops."

"Not really," Katherine demurred. "I'm pretty realistic about clergy now. When I was young, it was a shock to my childish idolatry to discover flesh and blood and human frailty instead of marble perfection. But I discovered it." Carefully, she did not over-emphasize her words.

"Dave and Suzy chide me for what they call my false expectations of the clergy. I do get the message. People tend to have false expectations of physicians, as I know only too well." They had reached the French château which Felix called Cathedral House. Mimi pulled open a large glass and ironwork door with considerable effort. "These doors put on weight every year." She rang a bell and, at the sound of the buzzer, pulled open another heavy glass door. "I'm afraid there are quite a few stairs." She looked at the cane.

"No problem if I can take it slowly. I won't complain about rheumaticky knees as long as my fingers aren't affected."

"There really ought to be an elevator—" Mimi led the way.

A flight of stone steps. Then a steeper flight of carpeted stairs. Mimi climbed them slowly, looking back to see if Katherine needed help. Halfway up she paused to give Katherine a chance to rest, and said, sounding slightly guilty, "I didn't mean to prejudice you against Allie Undercroft. Dave says he's a fine bishop."

Katherine breathed slowly and deeply, grateful for the respite. "I find him rather fascinating, particularly because he reminds me of someone I knew—oh, thousands of years ago."

"Who?" Mimi was quickly curious.

"A German—a Bavarian—who was in charge of the prison outside Paris where I was interned at the beginning of the war."

"A bad memory?"

"Yes." Her tone precluded further questioning, and they continued up the stairs.

--◦◦{ 5 }◦◦--

The dean and his wife were standing in the doorway to greet them, Dr. Davidson in as much contrast to her husband as Mrs. Undercroft to the bishop. Against the dean's darkness, Dr. Davidson was brightly blonde, and looked far younger than she must, in actuality, be.

Within the apartment there was a hubbub of conversation which dropped as Katherine entered, and she found herself surrounded by people eager to meet her. Somehow she had expected lionization to vanish with her retirement; another misconception.

A bevy of little girls was going about the room, offering drinks and sandwiches. One was the pretty child Katherine and Felix had met at the gate; there was no question that she was Dr. Davidson's daughter, the same buttery hair, the fringed gentian eyes. Standing near her, as though she were about to drop her tray of sandwiches, was the plump child who had been with her: Fatima.

Katherine was introduced to two men who were called Canon

Ulgrade and Canon Dorsey; Felix explained that "canon" was a title used in cathedrals. More introductions. She had not expected this many people. She caught a glimpse of Bishop and Mrs. Undercroft across the crowded room, talking to two tall young men. Dr. Davidson followed her gaze and said, "Those two monsters with the Undercrofts are my sons. Internships, residencies, and so forth, play havoc with family planning. Women still have a lot more juggling to do than men, no matter how supportive their husbands."

Katherine was relieved that the doctor had not noticed her involuntary start as once again the resemblance between Bishop Undercroft and Lukas von Hilpert struck her. Everyone was supposed to have a Doppelgänger, but Doppelgängers were identical, if she remembered correctly, and Bishop Undercroft's bright blue eyes were very different from von Hilpert's sober grey ones. The past does not leave one alone, she thought. It is always there, erupting into the present when one least expects it.

Dr. Davidson continued to chatter, pointing out her daughters among the children. Emily, the older of the two girls, was thin, with straight, flaxen hair, paler than her mother's and sister's, against a coppery skin, and eyes nearly as blue as the bishop's. She was an odd-looking pre-adolescent, but the very oddness would likely turn into beauty in a few years.

"My infants," Dr. Davidson said fondly, and moved Katherine toward the fireplace, where there were two comfortable chairs, one of which was occupied by a young man with black hair and fair skin and brown shadows under his dark eyes. He looked very Welsh, so he was likely the young organist.

Before Dr. Davidson could get Katherine to the empty chair, she had to introduce her to several more people. But at last she was seated, thinking that if Mimi had warned her that there was going to be this kind of mob she would never have agreed to come.

A welcome breeze blew in the long French windows. In the fireplace was a great bunch of mountain laurel. The furniture had white summer covers, and despite all the people, the room had an air of comfortable coolness.

Dr. Davidson said, "What can we get you to drink? We have iced tea, and the children have made lemonade, and there's sherry."

"Lemonade would be perfect," Katherine said.

"Tory!" Dr. Davidson called across the room to her youngest. "A glass of lemonade for Madame Vigneras."

The child called back, "Coming up," picked up an empty tray, and left the room.

"Now," Dr. Davidson said firmly, "Llew, we've run the gamut but we're here at last. Madame Vigneras, our organist, Llewellyn Owen."

Llewellyn Owen leapt to his feet to take her hand.

"That was a splendid performance, Mr. Owen," Katherine said. "I especially enjoyed my husband's Toccata and Fugue. Far too many people play it at a gallop, and you hit exactly the right controlled and serious tempo."

A quick flush suffused his pale skin. "Thank you. That means more to me than I can say, coming from you. I'm particularly fond of that piece—there's so much—so much acceptance in it."

She nodded. "Justin was not a very accepting person, but he worked through a good deal while he was composing that."

The young organist's eyes were bleak. "Is it worth it?"

"Oh, yes, Mr. Owen. It is worth it. I promise you that."

"In spite of—death and war and terror—"

"In spite of everything." He looked at her with so much pain that she repeated, "I promise."

A swarthy middle-aged man, in clericals, came up and introduced himself to Katherine as Bishop Juxon, one of Bishop Undercroft's suffragans. When she looked politely vague, Bishop Juxon smiled and explained that it meant only that he was an assistant bishop and what he really wanted to talk to her about was music.

Llew rose, and Bishop Juxon said, "Don't get up, Llew. I can stay only a few minutes."

But the young organist offered the older man his chair. "I want to get back to the organ. There's a phrase in the Hovhaness I'm not satisfied with, and I want to go over it while it's still fresh in my mind. You understand?" He looked at Katherine imploringly.

"Of course, Mr. Owen. Go right ahead." She wished she could go with him. As he left, he nodded goodbye to the Davidsons, and to Mrs. Undercroft, who was sitting on a sofa, surrounded by a twitter of little girls. She looked up from speaking with one of them, waved goodbye to the organist, caught Katherine's eyes, and smiled at her.

Bishop Juxon perched on the edge of the chair. "You've heard about Llew's tragedy?"

"Yes." And then, because it seemed that something more was expected, she added, "One survives."

"Some are better survivors than others." Despite his name, Bishop Juxon with his oily black hair and olive skin looked Levantine and spoke with a trace of accent. "You have survived considerable, haven't you?" His dark eyes were warm and friendly.

"Considerable," she agreed, and accepted a glass of lemonade from the younger Davidson daughter.

"You have many fans on the Cathedral Close," Bishop Juxon continued. "We're great lovers of music around here. And Llew is, as you have heard, a musician par excellence. What he can do with a choir is remarkable. His children's choir, particularly, draws crowds; he takes a pack of little wild creatures and turns them—at least while they're singing—into angels. If you enjoy choral music—"

"I do."

"Then I'm sorry you weren't here for Holy Week. Llew does a superb *St. Matthew Passion*, which I consider probably the greatest piece of music in the world."

"Merv! Listen to this!" Bishop Juxon and Katherine both turned to see Bishop Undercroft standing near the dean, holding up a book. "It's Orwell, and I've just discovered it, though Dave says it was old-hat when he was in seminary. He—George Orwell, not Dave—talks about 'a rather cruel trick I once played on a wasp.'" He looked down at the page. " 'He was sucking jam on my plate and I cut him in half. He paid no attention, merely went on with his meal, while a tiny stream of jam trickled out of his severed esophagus. Only when he tried to fly away did he grasp the dreadful thing that had happened to him. It is the same with modern man, and there was a period—twenty years, perhaps—during which he did not notice it. It was absolutely necessary that the soul be cut away. Religious belief, in the form that we had known it, had to be abandoned.' I suppose you've read it, Merv?"

Bishop Juxon nodded. "But I'd forgotten it till this moment. It's a powerful image."

"What do you make of it, Allie?" the dean asked Bishop Undercroft.

The fair young bishop shook his head. "It is all too easy to see the Church in that image, the greedy wasp unaware of its brokenness. And I don't mean just the Episcopal Church which still hasn't rid itself of its image—"

"God's frozen people," Bishop Juxon murmured.

Undercroft nodded. "It's also the Romans, the Evangelicals, the Pentecostals, all of us who believe we profess Christ."

"Don't we?" a small Chinese priest asked.

Bishop Undercroft looked sober; some of the brightness seemed to dim in his blue eyes. "Some of us do, thank God. You do, Chan. But when Christian bodies war together as bitterly as we are doing, then it would seem that some of us must be professing Antichrist, perhaps honestly believing him to be the Christ."

Bishop Juxon unobtrusively indicated the Chinese priest to Katherine. "That's Ming Chan, our other suffragan. A fine priest."

Felix moved from the Davidson young men to enter the conversation. "Once we recognize that we're broken, we have a chance to mend. You're a healer, Allie, that's what you're called to be."

Bishop Chan said, "Felix is right, Allie, and your parish priests need your healing gifts. So do Merv and I."

Katherine turned away as Mimi headed toward her. The men discussing the Orwell passage seemed genuinely fond of each other, she thought. There was no pomposity, no—so far as she could see—jostling for power, only a shared and deep concern.

"It's easier in this troubled world," she said to Mimi, "to be a pianist than a priest."

"Christ, yes," Mimi agreed, and looked toward the men, who were still deep in conversation. "Katherine, I do apologize. Suzy and Dave had no intention of collecting a mob. I didn't have any idea of getting you into anything like this. But word must have got round that you were going to be here, and you've given a lot of people a thrill. And you really helped Llew. It's just around the anniversary of his wife's death, and he's having a rough time."

"It's all right," Katherine said moderately graciously, as Fatima Gomez came up to them, almost bumping into Katherine with her plate of sandwiches.

"Ubiquitous creature," Mimi murmured, "she's always underfoot. Have you gathered that she and Topaze are siblings?"

Katherine nodded. "Did you know that Topaze and Fatima sell information?"

Mimi splashed tea on her dress and began mopping at it with a paper napkin. "Where on earth did you hear that?"

"Topaze wanted to know if I wanted to know anything about anybody—for a dollar, I think."

Mimi whistled. "I'm not surprised. Yolande and Allie pay for their tuition—they go to St. Andrew's, with the Davidson kids—but their mother is supposed to take care of their pocket money, and Mrs. Gomez is convinced that if they have one penny to rub against the other they'd buy drugs."

"Would they?"

"I doubt it. They've seen what drugs can do, and they aren't like their father."

"What do you mean?"

"Gomez was—is—a smalltime pusher. Right now he's in jail. The children think he was framed, and maybe he was. He was only on the fringes of a large drug ring—the big wheels don't get caught; they keep the Gomezes of this world for that. He was found with a large quantity of heroin."

"I thought the drug traffic was supposed to be slowing down."

"It can be slowing down and still be big business. In an unhappy world there's always someone who wants to buy oblivion. I use various morphine derivatives for my patients who are in extreme pain, and I've learned to assess those I have to be particularly careful with. Pain is better than addiction, even if they'd argue with me. Some I don't have to worry about. They're grateful to have their pain alleviated, but as soon as it drops to a bearable level they're happy to cut out their shots. Odd. It doesn't run to a predictable pattern."

Katherine returned to the original subject. "Who would want to buy the kind of information a child could pick up?"

"You'd be surprised what a child can pick up, just because the adults don't pay them any attention. As to who'd want to know—oh, all kinds of people. That's why gossip and scandal sheets are so popular."

"So—that's a kind of addiction, too?"

"And probably as dangerous as drugs. Oy veh, I understand it only too well. I have a strong streak of nasty curiosity myself."

Katherine looked at Fatima, who was handing her plate of sandwiches to a group of priests. Selling information was nothing new, she supposed, even for children.

--◦◦◦⊰{ 6 }⊱◦◦◦--

Mimi turned toward another group as the two Davidson young men approached, the elder with a pitcher of fresh lemonade.

"I'm Jos," he said, refilling Katherine's glass. "The number-one Davidson offspring."

"Chronologically," the younger boy said. "I'm John, and I'm number two. Jos—his real name is Josiah, but he prefers Jos—is in his first year at N.Y.U., pre-med, and I'm a junior in high school."

"John's a musician." Jos set the pitcher of lemonade on a long table behind a sofa. He was a big brown bear of a young man, not handsome, but good-looking in a reassuring kind of way. "He plays the violin."

"Like Bishop Bodeway," John said.

Felix had left his conversation and come over to them. "Much better than Bishop Bodeway. John's a real musician."

"But you did—" Katherine started.

"I had delusions of grandeur," Felix said wryly. "Actually, I played fairly well, and still do. But John's the real thing."

A soft, adolescent blush suffused John's cheeks. "Uncle Bishop is my great encourager. Dad plays the English horn, and we sometimes get together and play."

Josiah said, "Lots of it sounds horrendous, but we have fun. Sometimes Bishop Bodeway comes, too."

"It doesn't really sound that bad," Felix protested. "I've taped some of our Sunday evenings."

Josiah said earnestly, "We play your records a lot, Madame Vigneras. It's a real privilege to meet you."

And John, shining, added, "It really is."

"Thank you. You're very kind." Her answer was less automatic than with most of the people she had met at the Davidsons'. John's admiration was the kind that comes only from an artist; she suspected that Felix was right and the child was going to be good.

The priest who had been introduced as Canon Ulgrade came up to shake her hand and say goodbye; she had the feeling that he had no idea who she was, but had been told she should be treated with respect. Mrs. Undercroft rose, shaking small girls away as though they were flower petals.

"We really ought to be going," Katherine murmured. She was tired.

Felix reached for her hand. "Katya, it is so *good* to see you. Allie and I've been reminiscing about our first meeting at that concert hall in San Francisco. Allie doesn't play an instrument, but he loves music. Dave, by the way, could have made a career of the English horn if the priesthood hadn't called him."

Katherine looked around for Mimi, but did not see her. This gathering of bishops, deans, priests, was an alien world and she wondered that Mimi was so comfortable in it.

"Madame Vigneras." Bishop Undercroft had come up to them. "I realize it's time for you to go home, but may I take you into the library for just a moment?" He held out his arm and she took it. He slowed his pace to match hers, and led her into a room filled with books and comfortable chairs. There was a fireplace with a bouquet of shasta daisies in a white vase, giving a spring-like feeling to the room, which would be cozy in winter with the fire lit, but was, on this May afternoon, stuffy, smelling of crumbling leather.

"Parties sometimes creep up on Suzy," the bishop said. "The Davidsons more or less keep open house, but this afternoon they asked only Yolande and me, Felix, Llew, and you and Mimi. Or so they thought. Wind of your presence drifted across the Close, and people are so used to the Davidson hospitality that they tend to come crowding up, uninvited, despite all those stairs, and of course Suzy and Dave would never turn anyone away. Did you enjoy the concert?"

"Yes, very much indeed. Mr. Owen is a fine musician."

Bishop Undercroft nodded. "Felix found him for Dave. He has a nose for discovering the right people at the right time, and Dave is enough of a musician himself to recognize quality when he hears it. Perhaps Felix has found you again at exactly the right time."

"I'm very fond of Felix," Katherine said quickly, not knowing what was coming. Bishop Undercroft's resemblance to Lukas von Hilpert still took her off-guard. Their voices at least were totally different. Lukas had been a bass, and while his English was fluent, far better than Katherine's German, it had been heavily accented. Bishop Undercroft's voice was lighter, the inflections crisply English.

"Felix needs you," he said now. "You and he come from the same worlds—or at least the same generation. I worry about Felix being lonely. He has no family—though the Davidsons come close. If Yolande and I had been able to have children—but we couldn't, and while we do a considerable amount of entertaining, largely in the line of business, Yolande is not very strong and needs a great deal of privacy. But I didn't bring you here to discuss our problems or even to thank you for being Felix's friend. I know he's spoken to you about the possibility of a concert in St. Ansgar's, and I just wanted to add my voice to his."

"I will think about it." Katherine had definitely decided that she would give Felix his benefit, so why couldn't she say so to Bishop Undercroft? Was it because she had refused to give a concert for Lukas von Hilpert? Was the past getting in the way of and distorting the present? There was no reason she could not say yes to this pleasant man who—

"I need a glass of water," she heard herself saying in an echoing voice, and she moved blindly to the nearest chair.

She had never fainted and she did not faint now. Color faded from the room, as though she were seeing an old black-and-white movie. She bent over in the chair, putting her head down on her knees until blood returned to her brain and color to her eyes. Then she leaned back, eyes closed, trying to calm her breathing. This weakness of her body frightened her.

"Madame Vigneras." The voice was dusky, gentle.

She felt a cool cloth being touched to her forehead, her cheeks. She opened her eyes to see Yolande Undercroft, a wet cloth in one hand, a glass of iced tea in the other. Bishop Undercroft stood beside his wife, looking distressed.

"Shouldn't we call Suzy or Mimi?" he suggested.

Katherine took the tea. "Please, no. I do not need a doctor. I'm all right. I don't want any fuss." She took several sips of tea. Her pulse was steady now, her head clear. "It was just the heat—I'm not used to New York yet—"

"May can be hellishly hot," Mrs. Undercroft said, "and there's no air in this room. Almost all of the guests—half of them, you know, uninvited—have left now. As soon as you feel able, we'll go back to the living room. There's a good breeze there."

Katherine nodded, sipping more of the refreshing tea. Mrs. Undercroft was not prying, and she was grateful.

The younger woman moved a strand of silky black hair from her brow. "Go on, Allie. Madame Vigneras doesn't want people poking their noses in. Go and be charming to the lingerers and send them on their merry way." She chattered on, softly, one eye on Katherine. When the bishop left the library, she sat on a hassock by Katherine's chair. "Better?"

"Much better. Thank you."

Mrs. Undercroft continued to sit at Katherine's feet, her dark eyes full of pain. "I'm sorry my husband upset you."

"No—no—" Katherine sat up straight in her chair.

"It's all right." Mrs. Undercroft's voice was soft. "I'm not going to ask you why. Allie sometimes does, you know, upset people, but it's different with you . . . Are you up to going back to the living room?"

"I'm fine, yes, thanks." Katherine finished the tea and Mrs. Undercroft took the glass and set it down.

As Katherine pushed herself up out of the chair, Mrs. Undercroft again gestured wearily, brushing her hand across her forehead; Katherine noticed with surprise that her fingers were nicotine-stained. "How I admire you—not because of your music—unlike Allie, I don't know much about your kind of music. But your expression—even when you were feeling faint—there was such, you know, repose in your face, no trace of bitterness. There is still so much anger left in me, so many regrets, so much guilt, oh, so much guilt— Do you suppose I'll have come to terms with it all when I'm your age?"

"Very likely," Katherine assured her. "It took me a long time."

"Truly?" The dark brown eyes were supplicating.

"Truly."

They moved back to the living room as a group of little girls left, thudding down the stairs like a herd of young elephant calves. Tory Davidson and her friend Fatima stayed, both carrying plates with the remains of hors d'oeuvres. Tory held her plate out to Katherine. "There's not much left, but you might try the egg salad. It's special. Fatty's mother taught us some of her secret recipes."

Katherine accepted one of the bite-sized sandwiches and then, as Fatima rather forlornly proffered her plate, took one from the lumpy child, too.

Felix came over to her. "Did you have a nice chat with Allie?"

So the bishop had said nothing about her faintness; that was both perceptive and kind. "Very pleasant."

John Davidson charged up, carrying a pitcher in each hand. "Lemonade or iced tea?"

"Neither, thank you, John, I'm already floating." She looked with appreciation at the boy's still-untried good looks. He was likely in his mid- to late teens, with a fair complexion and light brown hair, and his father's dark eyes and brows, an arresting contrast. Josiah and Tory were attractive young creatures, but John and Emily had received the most interesting combination of genes and chromosomes.

Felix urged Katherine to one of the fireplace chairs. Mimi, carrying an empty decanter, paused apologetically. "Katherine—I truly didn't mean—just let me help Suzy tidy up a little of this mess and we'll leave." She moved on to the kitchen.

Emily came into the living room, passing Mimi; Katherine noticed for the first time that she walked with a slight limp. "May I get you anything, Madame Vigneras?"

"Not a thing, thank you." Emily was going to be the spectacular-looking one of the family when she put a little weight on her bones and her childish angles softened. The bronze skin, though not quite as dark as her father's, was startling with her fair hair. She and John exchanged looks, then John spoke.

"Madame Vigneras, Em and I were wondering—we—that is the Cathedral—there's a Bösendorfer in St. Ansgar's chapel, and we were wondering if you'd like to try it?" Silence followed and he broke it by asking, "Is that a terrible imposition or something?"

Felix said, "John, I'm trying not to pressure Madame Vigneras about the benefit."

John looked baffled. "I don't know anything about a benefit. I just thought she might like it—sort of as if someone offered me a Strad to play."

Emily added, "It's cooler in the Cathedral than it is here. Mom and Dad don't have air-conditioning, because of conserving energy, you know—" She stopped, as though she might have said something rude.

"I don't have air-conditioning, either," Katherine reassured her. "My doctor in Paris was convinced that air-conditioning in summer and overheating in winter are responsible for sinusitis, bronchitis, arthritis, and most of the physical ills we suffer from nowadays."

Josiah said, "I bet your doctor's right. At any rate, my biology prof would agree."

John said, "But about the Bösendorfer—"

Katherine looked at John and something about his eyes reminded her of Michou, and she wondered briefly if Michou might have turned out to be anything like John if he had lived. Michou, too, had played the violin, extraordinarily well for one so young . . . She said, "Yes, John, I'll go try your Bösendorfer. And, yes, Felix, I'll give you a benefit concert."

Before Felix could reply, John cried, "Bishop! Now we can get the tower of light!"

Josiah explained, "The Cathedral is cruciform, you see, and from the air it looks like a great cross—it's beautiful—lots of planes fly over it coming into New York."

Felix's voice was high and excited. "Katya, you're an angel! What we want is not a stone tower, but something quite different."

John broke in, "It was Dean Morton's dream—Dad's a great admirer of his. St. Paul and St. Peter are tall towers, so the central tower would have to be even taller, and if it were made of stone, then it would destroy the cruciformness and look sort of top-heavy—"

"So what we are hoping for," Felix continued, "is a tower of light, laser beams of incredibly condensed light rising up in the shape of an almost infinitely high tower."

"That sounds fascinating," Katherine said, "and highly innovative."

"More than innovative," Felix said. "Dean Morton had great vision, and the idea that it might really and truly be realized—I'm overwhelmed."

Katherine smiled at the general enthusiasm. "It sounds like a worthy cause for a benefit."

"It would be absolutely gorgeous," John said.

"If you know anything about architecture—" Felix started.

"I don't."

"Well, then—all I can say is that to see it come about would fulfill my wildest dreams."

"Wait, Felix, I doubt if one benefit concert will do all that."

"It will be a start, a good start."

"I'll be glad to provide a start. Let's go to the Bösendorfer; I'll have to go down the stairs slowly. Can someone tell Mimi to meet me in half an hour? I can't manage to climb these formidable stairs twice in one day."

"I'll tell her," Jos said, "and I'll drive you home. I'm sure Dad will let me have the car."

"Just tell Dr. Oppenheimer," John urged. "We don't want the world coming with us to St. Ansgar's. Just Bishop Bodeway and Em and"—an afterthought—"you, of course."

"I'll slip in when I've checked everything out," Josiah said. "You go ahead."

Emily turned her blue eyes on Katherine. Although she had not spoken, she had been listening intensely. "I'll show you the way."

There was something about Emily's quiet focus which reminded Katherine of herself at the same age. Emily, therefore, must be a difficult child.

⋯❖{ 7 }❖⋯

It was indeed cooler in the Cathedral. As they entered, Llew was leaving the organ loft, carefully locking the door behind him.

"Madame Vigneras is going to play the Bösendorfer." John's

enthusiasm raised his changing voice to a high pitch and then abruptly lowered it. "Come listen."

"Children!" Katherine remonstrated. "I'm not giving a concert. I am simply trying out an instrument I have been promised is excellent."

They heard the thud of heavy footsteps and a guard came toward them from the direction of the nave, raised a hand in recognition, and turned away.

"Have you got the keys?" Llew asked.

John nodded, and took Katherine's arm, very gently, as though she were made of porcelain, and led her around the ambulatory, pointing out the various chapels.

"We've named the girls' johns at school after the chapels." Emily's eyes twinkled. "St. James, St. Ambrose, St. Martin, St. Saviour, St. Columba, St. Boniface, and St. Ansgar." She was limping along beside them. "All the chapels here have to be kept locked. The gold candles and crucifixes have been removed, but people are still looking for something to rip off."

"Or vandalize," John said. "This is St. Martin of Tours, the French chapel."

"St. Martin gave half his cloak to a beggar," Emily explained.

They continued around the half-moon until John said, "St. Ansgar's," and pulled out a ring of keys as formidable as Felix's. He opened the ornate grilled gates and led the way in, turning on lights.

Felix was pointing out a small red cross inserted in the stained glass of one of the windows, explaining that it was the mark of the maker and that these particular windows were very old and had come from England, but turned as John let out an expletive. "What's up?"

John pointed at some pennies placed in a pattern in front of the altar. With an outraged gesture he bent and swept them up. "They're at it again!"

"At what?" Katherine asked.

"Black magic," Emily said, scowling. "Witchcraft. It's supposed to be more potent in a church. One time Dad even found a dead chicken at the foot of the high altar."

"A chicken?"

"A sacrifice to the devil." Felix's voice was heavy. "Cathedrals attract a lot of darkness."

John sounded a little uncertain. "I suppose darkness doesn't go where things are already dark."

Felix nodded in agreement. "Black magic has been on the increase in New York since—oh, way back in the forties when the Haitians first began to move into the city; and of course it's not only the Haitians; there are plenty of other groups involved in the worship of alien gods."

Llew held out his hand. "Give me the pennies, John. I'll put them in the garbage."

John dropped them into the organist's hand. "On All Souls' Day the guards have to watch to make sure the blessed candles aren't stolen."

Felix agreed, somberly. "And we have to be careful that only experienced priests celebrate communion on that day, to make sure the Hosts are swallowed. Otherwise, one will be used for a black mass."

Katherine shuddered. "How ghastly. I'm afraid I've been completely out of the world of anti-religion as well as religion."

"Anti-Christianity," Felix corrected. "Devil worship is a religion, and a powerful one."

John, too, gave a convulsive shiver as he led Katherine to the piano. "Music, please. That will clean all the ugliness away."

She started off, as always, with Bach, then played her father's merry *First Kermesse Suite* (never the *Second*).

John was kneeling on the stone floor by the piano, and when she turned from the keyboard she saw his face, rapt, ravished by the music. She would like to hear him play the violin.

Emily's face was solemn, almost expressionless, with a hidden intensity which again reminded Katherine of herself as a child; even the slight limp was reminiscent, as she, too, had had a troublesome hip which caused a mild limp that she outgrew with adolescence. John was able to show his delight openly, vulnerably. Katherine, like Emily, had found it excruciatingly difficult to reveal her innermost feelings.

"Katya—" It was the bishop. "I hate to mention time, but it's well over half an hour, and Mimi will be waiting at the garage."

She rose, stiffly, reaching for her cane, which John handed her.

"Yes, you're right, John, this piano does become an extension of the fingers."

They started out of the ambulatory and down the marble steps, and saw Mimi Oppenheimer and Suzy Davidson coming toward them. Emily whispered, "Don't say anything about the pennies. Mom hates it, and it scares Tory."

"It scares me, too," Llew said grimly. "I'm going back to the organ for a while." And he left them.

--••{ 8 }••--

As the rest of them drew together, Suzy said, "Dave has been called out—there's been another stabbing a few blocks down Amsterdam."

Josiah said, "People seem to think Dad can work miracles."

Felix said softly, "No, he reassures them, and that's why they want him."

Suzy added, "And he speaks Spanish and makes them comfortable because he's one of them. I wish I could do the same with my Spanish-speaking patients."

John turned to his mother, saying, incomprehensibly to Katherine, "V & T?"

"Just what I was going to suggest." Suzy turned, pausing to explain. "My offspring love pizza and the best pizza in New York is made just across the street at the V & T—one of our local restaurants. Just up the street there's excellent Hungarian food at the Green Tree—"

They started down the steps, John at Katherine's elbow. "And French at—"

"And Israeli—"

"And Greek—"

Felix cut into the young Davidsons' recitation. "How about it, Katya? When did you last eat pizza?" They stood in the shadow of one of the great buttresses.

"At least a thousand years ago."

"Why not, then?" Mimi strode ahead.

Katherine turned to Felix, "Not since—" She broke into laugh-

ter. "Not since I had pizza after the theatre with you and Pete
and—what was her name?"

"Sarah."

"Yes. Did they marry?"

"No. I married Sarah." He rode over her surprise. "Forget it."
He looked around as though to be sure no one had heard. "Will
you come with us? It really is good pizza, and there are plenty of
other things on the menu if you like good, solid south Italian
food."

Felix married to Sarah? Curiouser and curiouser.

Once in the restaurant they were welcomed like old friends,
which no doubt the Davidsons were, and shown a table by the
window, looking across Amsterdam Avenue to the Close. The
place was crowded with what Katherine took to be graduate students from Columbia; a few uniformed policemen; white-coated
doctors and technicians from St. Luke's Hospital. Occasionally a
pocket beeper would sound, and someone would hurry out. There
were several people in clerical collars, to whom the Davidsons
nodded or called out greetings. Katherine recognized the Levantine-
looking Bishop Juxon sitting at a side table with a young woman
who was trying to conceal the fact that she was weeping.

Felix murmured, "Our local restaurants often take the place of
confessionals," and helped Katherine into a chair.

"Pizza with everything," Tory announced with enthusiasm.
"Peppers and anchovies and mushrooms and sausage and onions
and pepperoni—"

"I'm glad there's a doctor in the house," Katherine said.

"Halt!" Suzy cautioned. "I deal with hearts and I doubt if pizza
will give you a coronary."

And Mimi put up a restraining hand. "And I try to mend bones.
I haven't pumped out a stomach since I was an intern. However,
I don't think one piece of pizza will do your innards any harm,
and I'll give you a settling tisane when we get home."

"For an orthopod," Suzy said, "you do hold great stock in your
home brews."

"It's my French blood, and they haven't failed me yet. I prescribe them for my patients; they help bones to knit."

Suzy began to involve Mimi in a discussion of some especially
intricate heart surgery, and the young men were talking with

Felix, so Katherine turned her ear toward the girls. Emily and Tory were evidently at the age of constant bickering.

Tory's voice was irritatingly smug as she said, "Mrs. Undercroft happens to prefer me to you."

Emily rose to the bait. "Mrs. Undercroft is a frivolous fart."

"You're just jealous."

"You're welcome to her."

"My theory about *you*," Tory continued the attack, "is that you were an accident. Then they had to have me, to go along with you. So I was planned, and you weren't."

Suzy turned from her conversation with Mimi. "Girls, if you're going to fight, you can leave."

"We weren't fighting," Tory defended. "We were talking."

"It sounded unpleasant. Therefore, desist."

The pizza arrived and was, as promised, excellent. "I would have asked you up for dinner," Suzy said, "but I know our stairs are too much for someone who is not used to them, and cooking is not one of my many talents. You'll get a much better meal here than if I'd prepared it."

"You're not that bad, Mom," John defended. "And you always cook lots."

"Quantity, if not quality," Suzy agreed.

"A voracious vulva." Emily's voice rang out during a lull in the conversation."

"Emily!" Suzy snapped.

Emily scowled. "It's a perfect description of her."

"I don't know who you're describing and I don't want to know. Do you know the meaning of your words?"

"They're alliterative."

"The next time you want to be alliterative, look your words up in the dictionary."

"Okay." Emily's odd, fair brows drew together. Somehow she looked frightened, rather than angry.

Felix reached across the table for her hand. "You can use my dictionary." A glance of the intimate love which occasionally exists between the very young and the very old passed between them.

"Thank you," Emily said softly, and then smiled at Katherine. "As you can guess, Madame, we're all mad fans of yours."

"That's very kind of you," Katherine said. "And I'm pleased. I don't think you're 'mad fans' indiscriminately."

"No, we aren't. We're frightfully discriminating."

"And you play the piano?"

Emily spoke in a calm voice. "I had been preparing to be a ballet dancer, but that's out, so I have to acquire a new passion. I've been thinking for the past year that it's going to be the piano. If I could be like you, I'd be sure it was."

"It's a lot of work," Katherine said.

"I'm not afraid of work. But my piano teacher—well, I don't know whether or not I have the gift, the way John has."

To her own surprise, Katherine heard herself asking, "Would you like to play for me?"

"Oh, yes, please! But not yet—I need a while to prepare some pieces for you."

"Just let me know when you're ready, then."

"I will, and, oh, thanks."

The conversation continued generally, and amicably now.

Once Katherine heard Emily asking softly, "Uncle Bishop, are you ever afraid in the night?"

Felix replied, equally softly, "Yes, Em. I am."

Mimi, too, had heard, because her brusque voice joined in. "Good heavens, everybody is afraid sometimes. It's part of the human condition."

"Even you?" Felix asked.

"Christ, yes. Even I."

Suzy said, "I do hope Dave won't be long. I worry when he gets involved in these internecine shootings."

Katherine turned her mind away, and then realized, when Felix asked her a question and had to repeat it, that the below-the-surface part of her mind was busy planning the recital she would give on the Bösendorfer for Felix, who held the hands of old women who were dying badly. And who had married the young woman who had replaced Katherine in Pete's arms.

Bishop Bodeway's Past

When Katherine and Mimi were alone on Tenth Street, sipping a tisane, Mimi asked, "Would you like me to take mine upstairs? Have you had enough of me for one day?"

Katherine knew that if she said, "Yes, go," Mimi would go, and there would be no hard feelings. But she said, "I'm tired, and when I've unwound a bit, I'd like a bath and bed. Meanwhile, I enjoy relaxing over this delicious concoction of herbs you've put together to settle that pizza."

Mimi sat in her typical position, one foot tucked under her, posture and movements still clumsily adolescent in contrast to her incisive look and manner. "This will not only settle the stomach, it will help you do your unwinding. You liked the Davidsons?"

"Enormously."

"Especially John." So Mimi had noticed.

Katherine nodded. "Emily reminds me of myself at that age, prickly and rather difficult. But John—John reminds me of my son."

Mimi glanced at the portrait of Katherine and the infant. "John is an artist, and like all artists he has fluctuating moods."

"Felix says he has the makings of a fine musician, and from the way he listened to my playing, I suspect that's true."

"Dave is a superb horn player, so John inherits it legitimately."

"I'd like to hear him play."

"I'll arrange it. He'll melt your heart. Incredible technique for an adolescent, but there's a quality of—love is the only word I can think of—that has depths far beyond his age."

"Does Felix still play?"

"Occasionally on Sunday evenings when the Davidsons get together to make music. He's not bad, by the way, but he's probably a better bishop than musician. He plays adequately, but he doesn't have that quality that all the technique in the world can't buy."

Mimi, Katherine suspected, had it as a doctor. She sipped her tisane, which was indeed soothing.

"Felix is full of surprises. I didn't know till tonight that he'd been married."

"Married? Felix!" Mimi's voice rose in astonishment.

"Yes. We were on our way to the restaurant—I think you'd gone on ahead with Suzy—and I said I hadn't had a pizza since I used to go out after the theatre with Pete, the actor I was briefly engaged to, and with Felix, and his friend Sarah. My engagement to Pete was broken off because of Sarah, and I thought they'd probably married, and Felix could have knocked me over with a feather when he said that it was he who had married Sarah."

"You could knock me over with a feather, too." Mimi said. "My word! Felix married! Will wonders never—I wonder what happened?"

Katherine regretted bringing up the subject. "I shouldn't have said anything. I suspect it's something he doesn't want talked about."

"Don't worry, love. A doctor learns to keep secrets as well as a priest. I won't say anything. It's just—I thought I knew old Bishop Bodeway pretty well."

"I'm glad you told me that story about him."

"Which?"

"Visiting hospitals, and not being afraid of old women who stank. It's a side of Felix I've never known."

Mimi picked up the teapot and refilled their cups. "Christ, you'd think I'd be used to the complexities of human nature by now. From what Felix tells of his youth, I think he was early used to odd smells."

As vividly as in a dream Katherine saw in her mind's eye a

'favorite' bar Felix and Sarah had taken her to. The stench still assailed her nostrils, spilled sour wine, sweat, vomit. It had been, she realized now, an early and surely one of the worst 'gay' bars, and there had been nothing gay about it. There had been nothing of love there, either. It was Sarah's idea of slumming. Why Felix went along with Sarah in being amused by it, she could not guess.

Mimi continued, "I don't think Felix would mind your knowing, if you don't already, but his father was a pig farmer somewhere in the Midwest."

"I didn't know. I was preoccupied with the piano and Pete. Felix was—peripheral."

"His job as a child was to clean out the pens and feed the pigs their swill. His parents fought continuously, and his home conditions were so appalling that ultimately he got sent to a foster home. He got away as soon as he could and came to New York and lived in the Village—but that you know."

"Yes. No wonder the seamier side of life didn't bother him."

"He's been fastidious as long as I've known him," Mimi said. "My shrink friends say that his background makes it all the more remarkable that he can stand bad odors now. Well, evidently I know more about him than you do, and maybe that's because I have no family, no brothers or sisters, no husband or children, no deep commitment to anyone, and so I've become insatiably curious. I don't think I like that about myself."

Katherine looked over her cup at Mimi, thinking how quickly they had become friends. Setting the cup down, she asked, "Why does Emily Davidson limp?"

"She has an artificial left leg. She was hit by a car two years ago on her way home from school. The car went out of control and up onto the sidewalk, and crushed Emily's leg so that it had to be amputated just below the knee."

Katherine shuddered. "In likening myself to Emily, I remembered my own limping as a child, because of my bad hip. Isn't there an Eastern proverb that talks about a man being sorry for himself because he had no shoes until he met a man with no feet?"

"Don't be sorry for Emily," Mimi warned. "She'd hate that."

"Yes. I know. But how matter-of-factly she talked about not being a ballet dancer."

"Em's not one to go in for self-pity. She was one of the child dancers at the City Ballet, but after the accident she never looked back."

"When she gets rid of all those childish angles she's going to be extraordinarily beautiful."

"And she'll be somewhere," Mimi agreed. "She's fiercely proud and determined to compete. She doesn't have John's sweetness, but she has intense vocational drive. Tory is like Suzy, pretty and sharp, and everything comes easy for her, though she has shown no particular aptitudes, and I think she's jealous of Emily. Jos is going to end up a solid good citizen, a good if not brilliant doctor, but caring. John and Emily are the special ones. I'm glad Em is so close to Felix."

"Yes, I noticed that. It's good for them both, I'm sure."

Mimi nodded. "I think Felix is Emily's confessor. As a doctor, I think that confession, psychologically speaking, is probably a very good thing. And I know that one of the things Felix still does is hear confessions."

That, too, was a side of Felix Katherine had never encountered. The old Felix had been a talker, not a listener.

"Despite the fact that he does tend to run off at the mouth," Mimi went on, "Felix is also a good listener. And that's probably the most important work of the confessor, to listen intently, so that whoever it is can see the problem spread out, and then see it objectively instead of subjectively. Do you ever go to confession or anything like that?"

Katherine, smiling, shook her head. "Not anything like that. I've never been what you might call a real Catholic. It must be a heavy burden, to hear all the darker aspects of the human heart."

"Doctors get their share of it. I wouldn't want to be a shrink."

"I suppose in a way I *have* been to confession, or an equivalent thereof," Katherine mused. "Justin and I were very fond of a cardinal we met in Munich shortly after the war, Wolfgang von Stromberg, a great music lover. We certainly told Wolfi things we'd never have told anyone else. Have you heard of him? He wrote quite a few books which were translated into English. Felix knows them."

"Sure, he's very well known," Mimi said. "I recommend one called *Curing and Healing* to some of my patients. Was he as interesting as his writing?"

"As interesting, and as complex. A great man. He was Vatican Secretary of State when he died." But she was not ready to talk about Wolfi.

"More tea?" Mimi asked.

"No, thanks, I still have a bit, and it's doing its work; I'm relaxing. But I can't get Emily out of my mind. How horrible the person who hit her must have felt."

Mimi looked into her cup for a long time, as though trying to read the leaves. "The driver of the car got out and ran, and was never identified. The car turned out to have been stolen. So I doubt if whoever it was lost much sleep. Don't worry too much about Emily; she'll turn her talents in another direction; she's still young enough. You were a dear to ask her to play for you. Finished?" She saw that Katherine's cup was empty, and went to the kitchen and began washing up. "How did you and Justin happen to know Cardinal von Stromberg?"

"He came backstage after one of my early concerts and invited us to supper. It was our first trip to Germany after the war, and we—or at least I was horribly shocked at the devastation done by American bombers. Wolfi was warm and open and accepting. I've learned a lot about acceptance from him, and there's a vast amount of difference between accepting and being resigned. I've never been one for resignation."

Mimi grimaced, "Nor have I. So your friendship with von Stromberg was something like mine with Dave Davidson—proportion-making."

"Some of the time. As I said, he was complex." She turned the subject. "Bishop Undercroft added his voice to Felix's in asking me to do a benefit. He and Felix seem very fond of each other."

"I think they are. They're old friends."

"What kind of bishop is he—Undercroft?" She tried to keep the question casual. She did not want the perspicacious doctor to guess that she was fascinated by the attractive young bishop.

"I'm the wrong person to ask. Probably the best thing he's done was to make Dave dean."

"Who made him bishop?"

"That's an elected office. There's a huge Diocesan Convention in Synod Hall, and it's sort of like electing a pope—without the white smoke. They just keep on balloting till someone wins by some kind of margin. Allie evidently got in by a landslide, and he's still very popular. He knows how to gather good people about him. He's not jealous of other people's talent, I'll have to say that. And he's done a lot to continue the work Felix was doing in cleaning up the slums around the Cathedral, and in training and employing local kids." Mimi paused. "He's a nice guy, your Felix."

"More yours than mine, it seems."

"Ours, then. And I'm glad you like Dave. The work he did in the slums of Atlanta is largely why Allie called him here. It's sort of full circle for Dave; he sang in the choir here when he was a kid, and was the foster son of the then dean."

— ·•{ 2 }•· —

In the morning Felix called Katherine to discuss a date for the concert.

"Sometime in August, I should think," she said. "That will give me time to work up a program."

"I'm eternally grateful to you," Felix said. "We get a lot of visitors to the city in August, and you'll be a real draw. But most of our regulars are away and I'd hate them to miss you. Would you consider another concert, say, to begin Advent? You could use the same program."

"Don't push me, Felix. One thing at a time."

"But you'll think on it?"

"I'll think on it. Felix—did I hear you correctly last night when you said you married Sarah?"

"You heard me correctly." His voice was gritty. "It isn't something I talk about, by the way. I don't think anybody knows about it except you and Allie. I don't know why I—" His voice trailed off.

Mimi, Katherine knew, would say nothing. "Felix, dear—I shouldn't have brought it up. I'm sorry."

"No, no, I suppose I must have wanted you to know, or I wouldn't have mentioned it. And you are, in a way, involved. You were engaged to Pete, and Sarah deliberately set out to seduce him. And, after they broke up, she turned her wiles on me. It must seem very strange to you. You have a right to know what happened."

"I have no right at all, unless you want to tell me. If you don't, we'll forget it."

"No. If we're going to be friends now, as we weren't able to be back in those days when most of us were just playing at being artists—if we're to be real friends, which is my deepest desire, I want you to know about it. I want you to know me, Katya, because I know that you will accept me." There was a long pause. Katherine sat on the side of her bed, sipping coffee and waiting. Why not? With professional pressures gone, there was no need to rush.

At last Felix spoke again. "You've always been an accepting person, Katya. That's why so many people confided in you, even when we were very young. I suppose people still do—bare their hearts to you."

"Some."

"So please don't mind if I do it, too. I took getting married seriously. Granted, Sarah's money was attractive to me. I don't discount that. I wanted everything her money could buy for me, and I don't suppose I've ever had a completely pure motive in my life. But the money wasn't all. I wanted the rest of it, children, and the whole family picture. But it wasn't long before I realized that Sarah didn't, and that she didn't want me to change. She just wanted me as a—a pet poodle, someone to come home to if and when she felt like it, someone to see that dinner was on the table. We had servants, so it wasn't a great demand. And mostly she wanted me as an excuse—'Oh, I couldn't, my husband, you know.' Anyhow, the marriage was annulled."

"Felix. I'm sorry."

"That makes two of us she's hurt, doesn't it?"

"Does it? Yes—but I'd almost forgotten. I'm sorry, Felix, it must have hurt you abominably."

"Don't be sorry. I learned a lot. And I've told it from my point of view. I'm sure Sarah's version would be different. 'Poor Felix, he just wasn't cut out for the marriage bed. I tried to help him, but it was a losing battle—' "

She winced at the pain in his voice. "Oh, Felix—"

"It's all right. I do believe that all things work together for good to them that love God. I wouldn't have discovered that I had a vocation to the priesthood if I hadn't had to learn to accept myself just as I am, without one plea, and to know that I do not have to earn God's love. Sarah once said that people became priests only if they couldn't do anything else. But you can give that two readings. I discovered that because I was called to be a priest I couldn't, in fact, do or be anything else—although that wasn't till long after the debacle with Sarah. And although I may not have been cut out to be a husband, I am a good friend."

"I'm glad. And Mimi says you were a good bishop, too."

"Does she! How amazing! But I *am* still useful."

"Of course you are."

"I found Llew for Dave. I went off to do some preaching in the boondocks and heard Llew and then brought him East for Dave to hear. Dave is as much musician as priest, and he recognizes quality when he hears it. But I sometimes wonder—would Llew's wife still be alive if they'd stayed in Idaho?"

"You can't hindsight, Felix. I learned that the hard way."

"You're right. And I do bring good musicians to the Cathedral—such as you."

When she had hung up, she turned from this new and deeper Felix to the cherry music cabinet, to planning what she would play for his concert, surprised at her eagerness as she leafed through piles of music. —I'm like a race horse, she thought. —They'll have to shoot me to stop me.

And then, —But I can still run the race. I'm still good.

Fleetingly she wondered if the benefit would be covered by the papers, and then assumed that of course it would. She was far from forgotten. None of the notices in the past few years had even hinted at any diminishment of her powers. She knew that she did not look her age. Her hair had been white since she was thirty. Justin, and then Nanette and Jean Paul, had seen to it that she used enough face lotions and creams so that her skin was scarcely wrinkled. They had not allowed her to sit overlong in the sun, ski overlong in the cold. She missed Nanette and wished momentarily that she had been able to afford to bring her to New York. But while Justin and Jean Paul had invested her money wisely, and she lacked for nothing essential, regularly increasing inflation meant that when she stopped giving concerts she stopped affording Nanette.

She had asked Mimi about a massage parlor and had been non-plussed at the doctor's spontaneous shout of laughter as she informed Katherine of the current meaning of the words. "Most of the people I know who give massages are specially trained physio-therapists, and you don't need that. I'll ask around. Sooner or later I'll know somebody who knows somebody."

Tant pis. Never mind. Massages were a luxury, and she did not want to be a spoiled old woman.

⚜ 3 ⚜

It was mid-June before Katherine brought herself to invite Felix down for tea to discuss the benefit. As she set off for the patisserie, she met the young woman from the garden apartment and they exchanged greetings.

"I live downstairs," the young woman said shyly, looking down at her sandaled feet.

"I know, and isn't it amazing that this is the first time we've bumped into each other?"

"That's New York," the young woman said, "and our hours just haven't happened to coincide. I've seen you a couple of times, but I haven't wanted to bother you."

"As your landlord, I should know your name," Katherine said, "but I've forgotten." A competent man at the bank took care of the rents and all the other business of owning a house in the city.

"Dorcas. Dorcas Gibson." She looked up, and Katherine noticed that her eyes were shadowed, as though she had not slept well. When she smiled, however, the shadows diminished. "I love to hear you practice. There's one place in our living room where I can hear you quite well, and I often sit there—I hope you don't mind."

"Not at all. But practicing is often one phrase repeated and re-peated. I should think it would be intolerable to listen to."

"Oh, no, I'm used to repeating and repeating. I'm a dancer, or was, till—"

Katherine saw that the floating dress concealed a swollen abdo-men.

"And will be again, after the baby's born."

"Oh, yes. Did it stop you? I mean, you did have children, didn't you?"

"Yes. It didn't stop me for very long. But one can play the piano for quite a while after one has to stop dancing. Enjoy your baby. I enjoyed mine, but I didn't take as much time for that enjoyment as I should have."

"Oh—thank you, Madame!"

Katherine waved at her and walked off. The child was adoring her and she did not like to be adored. Appreciated, yes. But adoration turns one into an idol, and when the one who idolizes discovers flesh and blood instead of marble perfection, there is apt to be trouble, if not disaster.

A young girl recently married and large with her first child should have no need to idolize. Were the shadows under the eyes entirely the result of pregnancy?

At Dorcas's age Katherine herself had not outgrown hero-worship—the kindest way of putting it. After adolescence, hero-worship becomes blindness; idols offer nothing but disillusionment, as she had found out to her cost. Idolatry and love are incompatible.

Felix had offered to come to Katherine in order to spare her the trip uptown. Nevertheless, he was cutting into piano time. Her one brief experience with the Bösendorfer and the Cathedral acoustics had suggested nothing romantic or lush, no Scriabin or Fauré. She was going to risk ending with the *Hammerklavier Sonata*, but before Beethoven she would play Couperin, Scarlatti, Bach. The organ was an instrument that could afford to send wave after wave of sound lapping the length of the nave. From her short time in St. Ansgar's chapel, she had decided that the Bösendorfer and her own style would collaborate best with music of clarity and precision.

Felix arrived promptly at four. He had continued to keep his promise not to bother her. There had been no further unexpected ringing of the phone at one o'clock in the morning. But the night before, she had dreamed of him, dreamed that Emily had been in his apartment and had asked him tenderly, *"Hast du Angst?"*

He was dressed, this afternoon, in a lightweight grey suit and clerical collar. He wore a panama hat, which he doffed as she opened the door, and he carried his cane.

Katherine had the tea cart in readiness, and water on the boil. She, who had not cooked for herself in years, found pleasure in puttering about her small but well-planned kitchen. She had kept the tea simple; cucumber sandwiches and pastries. She vaguely remembered that Felix had a sweet tooth.

He ate hungrily. "I skipped lunch so that I could enjoy tea. I adore cucumber sandwiches. Um—Rigo cakes?"

"Yes." She passed the plate to him.

"Now, my dear, you know this concert is going to involve a certain amount of publicity."

"Oh, Felix, I had hoped—"

"Katya, you'll do no good raising money for us if you keep your light under a bushel."

She should, of course, have recognized that. But publicity had always been Justin's and Jean Paul's business, and so she had been free to concentrate on music. She sighed. "You do whatever is necessary."

"Doing publicity is not my thing. I get the artists. Yolande Undercroft has been working on the rest. There's a bright young thing from the *Times* who's coming to interview you. She'll call to set up a date." He fumbled for his glasses and consulted a piece of paper. "Her name's Jarwater, if I read Yolande's handwriting correctly. I think she may be West Indian. Anyhow, I've read her stuff and she knows music and she has a sense for people. When she calls, you're not likely to forget the name Jarwater—or is it Farwater? All right? I told Yolande no late TV or radio talk shows. The young tend to forget that we need our rest. And our minds are not at their brightest at the end of the day. Do you remember, during the war, the Germans used to send for Pétain in the late afternoon when they knew his old brain would be fuddled? Dirty pool. Anyhow, I reminded Yolande that we are not her age."

Katherine thought that Yolande was at least pushing half a century and was probably several years older than her husband. Still, young enough to be able occasionally to burn the candle at both ends.

Impulsively she asked Felix, "You're very fond of Bishop Undercroft, aren't you?"

"I love him," Felix said simply. "One advantage of celibacy is that one does tend to acquire children one way and another, and

I've known Allie since he was little more than a child. And then, of course, one tends to worry about one's children."

"What worries you about Bishop Undercroft?" she asked gently.

"Allie's not had an easy life. Orphaned early—I'm as close to a father as he's had. And right now—well, he's worried about Yolande. I am, too. Sometimes she looks at me with eyes so full of—oh, I'm not sure—pain, fear, anxiety—that I want to put my arms around her and say, 'There, there.' "

"What do you think is wrong?" Mrs. Undercroft's eyes had seemed to Katherine, too, to be those of someone in pain.

The old bishop shook his head. "Yolande has never been a simple personality." He knew more than he was saying, Katherine felt. "She loves Allie, that's the main thing. They have a deep and happy marriage. And she's generous with other people. Every afternoon a gaggle of little girls comes over to Ogilvie House to tea, and she gives some of them singing lessons. Not Tory. Tory gets tea, but she has a voice like the frog in the fairy tales." He sighed.

Katherine handed Felix the plate of sandwiches. She said, "If Allie's like your son, he may be trying to spare you."

"Do yours?"

"Of course."

He laughed, then. "How stupid we all are. I wonder if there's ever been a civilization where people weren't caught up in these conventional games? At least, circumstances have seen to it that you and I have never needed to spare each other. So let's not begin now. Here I am, worrying in front of you like a dog with a bone." He reached for the cake plate. "Katya, I am so grateful to you, for being my wise counselor, as well as for giving me the concert. One of the most difficult things about reaching our advanced age is that we have so few contemporaries. I feel out of context with the rest of the world. Memories which formed and shaped me have no relevance for people even twenty years younger."

"Such as?" She probed him gently, feeling an unexpected tenderness toward him. She guessed that Mimi was right and that he had indeed been a good bishop.

"The war. Ours. The Second World War."

"Yes." She refilled their cups. "It changed our lives irrevocably. What did you do, Felix?"

"I was in graves registration. When I was called before the

draft board I was sure they'd reject me. After my marriage broke up, I fell apart. I decided there was no such thing as faithful love, and I picked up partners in the shabbiest sorts of gay bars, in a kind of frantic and stupid rebellion. There is no love, no friendship, nothing beyond jerking off with someone in the john at the back of the bar." He stopped abruptly. "I've offended you. My language—oh, God, Katya, I'm sorry, I've shocked you."

"It's all right, Felix." She knew that her expression had betrayed her. "Really."

He said, "I'm telling too much, as usual. But—oh, God, I can't accept myself unless I know that you know the absolute worst of me, and still don't—don't—"

"I don't," she replied firmly. "Go on, Felix, dear."

"I hated myself. I hated the world. I didn't give a damn about the war. Forgive me, please, Katya—but the medieval scholastics believed that you could not love someone you didn't know—really know, all the bad as well as the good. And I want you to love me."

She reached across the tea cart and touched his hand, but said nothing. There was much about herself that she would never tell Felix, or anybody else, but she would not stop him from revealing himself, if that was his need. She asked, "What about the war?"

"I got called up, like everybody else, and I found that I could not do what a lot of people were doing—getting turned down by deliberately announcing their unacceptable sex preferences. We've changed a lot in that area, haven't we? Anyhow, I didn't want to get out of the war that way, I'm not sure why. I felt so inadequate as a human being, I was sure they'd give me a 4-F card. But they didn't. I went overseas with graves registration. I still, after all these years, wake up screaming, rushing through the apartment crashing into furniture. I don't think the nightmares will ever leave me completely."

"When you called at one in the morning, the first night we'd had dinner, was that what was wrong?" She was concerned with his almost physical distress.

"Of course." He jumped at her suggestion so quickly that she knew it was not true. He continued, "When I've been asked to talk about my war experiences to groups—Rotary, and so forth—I've managed to give them things they could listen to. They couldn't have stood what really happened. Katherine—we had to go out and find bodies, so they could be registered and identified and families notified. We—we came across aviators who'd fallen with their parachutes into trees and hung all stretched out and elongated over a branch like pieces of spaghetti. You can't forget something like that. It's printed indelibly on the retina."

"Felix, dear—"

"I sometimes wonder if they did it deliberately, put someone like me in a job like that, spending the war identifying and piecing together the remains of bodies that had once been human beings. One time, three of us sat in front of a heap of bones that was all that was left of six aviators, and we had to try to sort out the bones so that each man could be buried. The bones didn't sort out evenly, and the only way we could cope was to get drunk, good and drunk, and just play games, chanting 'Eeny, meeny, miney, mo,' to the bones. We had a chaplain who used to give us his liquor ration so that we could get drunk on decent whiskey instead of rotgut. I'd always thought of religion as being irrelevant, having nothing to do with real life. I don't even remember his name, but perhaps he was the beginning of my conversion." He laughed. "Funny, I never made the connection till this minute."

Silently Katherine refilled his cup, adding a small lump of sugar and a thin wheel of lemon.

"Once I took a helmet off a corpse, and the man's whole scalp and face came off with it, just slipped off the bones. Another time I was going over a dead soldier looking for identification. I took off one jacket, then another. Then I took my knife and tried to cut off what looked like another jacket. It was the man's skin." He covered his eyes with his thin hands, dropped them to his lap. "So I dream. And I scream. And—" He straightened up abruptly, as though waking. "And then I do unpardonable things like calling you in the middle of the night." The tone of his voice had changed completely. Again she did not believe him—not the horrors he had just been recounting; they were real enough—but that they had been the reason for his call. He smiled at her, a forced smile of courtesy. Then, "Why didn't I wipe God out once and for all? There's nothing abominable I didn't see and hear. But war was so horrible that it was—oh, what the jargon would call a 'conversion experience.' Maybe it was because God *had* to be there, he *had* to come to us because we'd have gone raving mad otherwise. When things go well we don't cry out for God as we did then, in anguish, in rage. I was closer to my God in my abysmal nakedness of soul than I was when I was consecrated bishop. We get complacent and self-satisfied. Alas. But when you're in the middle of hell you don't have that choice." He gulped down his tea. "Do we have to know hell before we're fit for a vision of God?" He stood up, then sat down, looking around as though he did not know where he was. "Katya, I can talk to you because you've gone through hell, too. I can—I can tell you the worst about myself and you will not reject me." His voice trembled. "Will you?"

"No." She would not reject him, but what did she have to offer him, to ease the pain that was still there after all these years?

He told her. "Play for me."

--᠁{ 4 }᠁--

When she had finished, he sighed in a relaxed way. "Ah. St. Johann."

"Saint?"

"Oh, I have my own saints. St. Johann Sebastian. St. Albert."

"Which Albert?"

"Einstein. Sts. Ralph and Henry."

She raised her eyebrows in question. He was out of the pain of the past now.

"Emerson and Thoreau. How surprised they would be to be canonized, even by me. I might add St. Ludwig—you know him—and St. Will."

"Shakespeare?"

He nodded, back to himself again, old, frail, but no longer anguished. "*Re* those interviews—I'll try to keep them to a minimum, my dear. And I will be eternally grateful to you for this. The Cathedral is—well, one cannot canonize a building, but it represents for me all that makes life something to be rejoiced in, despite all the desperation, which isn't as quiet as it used to be. I don't think you can know quite how much your willingness to play a benefit means to me. Katherine, if there's ever anything I can do for you . . ."

She replied briskly, "I'd like to come up to the Cathedral once or twice to practice on the Bösendorfer."

He hit the palm of his hand against his forehead. "How stupid of me! I should have thought of it. Of course, just let me know when. Almost any time, as long as it's not during a service." He fished in his pocket and handed her a card. "This has my office number on it, as well as my home number. Thanks for the lovely tea and the yummies." He broke off as the phone rang, startling them both. She reached for it. "It's for you."

"Why on earth would anyone want to track me down here?" His voice was irritable, but he took the receiver. "Yes, Bishop Bodeway . . . What? Oh, my God, no . . . Of course, I'm just leaving, I'll be right there, Dave." He put the receiver down and turned to Katherine. "The present is very much with us. Mervin Juxon has just been shot."

"Felix—how ghastly—" She remembered the Levantine-looking man she had met at the Davidsons', with his deep, kind eyes. "Killed?"

"Yes. It was down Amsterdam—some kids mugging an old woman and Merv intervened and they pulled out a gun. Dear God . . . I've got to get back to the Cathedral as quickly as—I'll be in touch . . ."

⸻⸱❈{ 5 }❈⸱⸻

After Felix had gone, she turned to the piano, still shocked by the distressing news. In a world where even children had guns, no one was safe.

But music took her into its affirmative structure, and she rested there.

She had given Mimi a key to the apartment, at the doctor's request. 'Not that I expect you to fall getting out of the tub, but it's just a good idea for someone to be able to get in to you, if necessary.'

So she had no idea how long Mimi had been curled up on the sofa, listening, although it was no surprise to see her, since they had planned to get together that evening. Katherine suspected that

Mimi had suggested dinner, thinking that Katherine was apt to neglect fixing herself a meal after the tea with Felix, which, of course, was likely.

"My God," Mimi said when Katherine turned from the piano, "and to think that Beethoven was deaf when he wrote that."

Katherine flexed her fingers. "Maybe that's why it's so extraordinarily difficult to perform. An interior sound is not easy to externalize."

"You externalized it, all right. How was your tea with Bodeway?"

Katherine looked at the tea cart with the remnants of their tea, two cucumber sandwiches now withered, a melting blob of chocolate on Felix's plate. "Just as he was leaving, he got a phone call from the dean telling him that Bishop Juxon had tried to help a woman who was being mugged, and got shot. Killed."

"Merv? Killed?"

"Yes."

"Oh, Christ." Mimi's face darkened with outrage. "What a hell of a world we live in. What a hell of a way for Merv to die."

Katherine looked at the messy tea table. "Somehow it's never who or when we expect. And even when we expect death, it comes as a shock anyhow." She started to push away from the piano. "I forgot to clean up. I've been spoiled. I thought I was used to doing for myself, but I see I'm not."

"Stay where you are and play for me, and I'll wash up," Mimi ordered. "Something for Merv—not a dirge, he'd hate that. Something light. How about that merry-go-round thing of your father's?"

Thomas Forrester had been moody, preoccupied, could never understand the point of a joke, and yet his music bubbled with merriment, and it was this quality that kept it alive. Mimi wheeled the tea cart to the kitchen and Katherine turned to the *First Kermesse Suite*. When the last notes trembled into silence as though through gentle laughter, Mimi called from the kitchen, "I'm putting together a Greek salad. I hope that's all right with you."

"Fine. I enjoy Greek food. I even like retsina if it's thoroughly chilled."

"That's a good thing, *ma mie*, because I brought retsina, and it's out of a very cold fridge." She placed a platter on the dining table, glancing at the portrait over the mantelpiece. "I'm glad Sergeievna gave you that. I see something new in it each time I look at it."

"You'd have liked my Aunt Manya, I think," Katherine said. "You remind me of her."

"Was she Jewish?"

"I don't know . . . I never thought about it. She was Russian, very Russian. And she was warm and outgoing and generously understanding with me when I was a prickly, frigid little adolescent. She taught me a lot about generosity of spirit—like you."

"Many thanks. I hope I won't let you down." Mimi flushed. Then, "I'd better give Dave a ring later on. Merv's death has to be a terrible blow to him."

"Yes, we were deep in the past, and the telephone jolted us roughly into the present."

"Was that a bad time for you? The past you and Felix share?" Kindly but piercingly, Mimi's surgeon's eyes probed Katherine.

Their shared past was before the war, many years ago. "Some of it was gloriously happy. And some of it was bad. Music and love clashed, and I was young enough not to know I couldn't have both, with Pete. I'm grateful, whenever I see Felix, to know that I can look back on it now and not relive any of the pain."

"Are all your memories that cleanly healed?"

Katherine, shaking the stiffness out of her knees, walked to the table where Mimi had the meal in readiness. "By no means."

"And did you have both—music and love—with your Justin?" Mimi seated herself on the kitchen side of the table, and helped their plates.

Katherine sat, unfolded her napkin, and laid it across her lap. "Yes, though possibly not as the world would see it."

Mimi poured the wine, and the faint, resinous odor filled the room. Then, suddenly, her expression changed, and she looked around, her ears almost visibly pricking. Katherine heard nothing, but Mimi rose, crossed the room to the front door, and peered through the peephole. Then she flung open the door. "Iona! What on earth!"

--◦◦{ 6 }◦◦--

"Come in, come in, don't just stand there." Mimi drew the other woman into the room and shut the door. "Katherine, this is Dr. Iona Grady, the very first of my tenants, who came to share my apartment when she was interning at St. Vincent's. Iona, this is my landlord, otherwise known as Madame Katherine Vigneras."

Dr. Grady shook hands, smiling politely. She had a firm, cool grip.

Mimi laughed. "Iona's ear is even tinnier than Suzy's. Love of music was one thing we did not share in common. So—to what do we owe the pleasure, Iona?"

Dr. Grady slid the bag off her shoulder. "At least you're home. I was beginning to think I'd have to call Isobel and spend the night at the convent."

"I was lecturing all afternoon."

"Is the back bedroom available?" Iona pushed her short-cropped hair from her forehead with a weary gesture.

"For you, yes. But what brings you to New York?"

"One of my colleagues was to give a lecture tomorrow morning at Memorial, and he slipped and sprained his shoulder, so I was asked to pinch-hit. I agreed, because I was beginning to realize I needed a break, and even twenty-four hours is a help."

Katherine asked, "Have you eaten? There's lots of salad."

"Thank you, Madame—uh—"

"Vigneras."

"Vigneras. You and Mimi go on with your meal. I'm not hungry, but I'd love a glass of wine."

"It's retsina," Mimi warned.

"It could be rhinoceros pee—it could be anything, as far as I'm concerned. I'm tired, I need to go over the lecture notes I put together on the plane, but I'd love a glass of wine. Am I interrupting something?" She seemed entirely impervious to her abrasiveness.

"We've both had a hard day. One of the suffragan bishops was killed this afternoon, and we were trying to relax." Mimi handed the other doctor a glass of wine.

The younger woman sipped, made a face, and sat down. "Do I know him?"

"I don't think so. Merv Juxon."

"A good guy?"

"Very."

"It always seems to be the good who die young, doesn't it? Or was he young?"

"Not fifty. Young."

"That's lousy. I'm sorry. How's Suzy?"

"Busy."

Dr. Grady sighed. "Aren't we all? I could really do with a two-week vacation, but I can't get away until August." She reached to Mimi's plate and picked up a black olive. Katherine noted that there were stains of fatigue under the hazel eyes. "I'll just drink this and go on up and take a shower, if you'll let me have the key. Have you been in touch with Isobel?"

"Last I heard, she had a bad cold."

"Just as well I didn't go to the convent, then. I'll give her a ring tomorrow."

Mimi explained to Katherine, "Iona's sister is a nun, up at the Convent of the Epiphany—one of Mother Cat's Sisters."

"At least one of us is saved." Iona's mouth was suddenly bitter. "The Church has made a heathen of me. Are you churchy, Madame—uh?"

"Vigneras. No."

Dr. Grady's fatigue was expressed in a barely controlled irritation. She made Katherine feel slightly uncomfortable. Mimi said, "But Katherine is an old friend of Bishop Bodeway's."

"I hadn't seen him for ages until a couple of months ago. I lived mostly in Europe. But I'm retired now, and Felix called me shortly after I got home."

"Were you a doctor?" Iona asked.

"I'm a pianist."

"Oh." Dr. Grady's eyes strayed to the piano. "Mimi's right. I'm tone-deaf. I know I've missed a great deal, Madame—uh—Vinegar."

"Vigneras."

"Sorry. I'm bad about last names. My patients are kids, and we're on a first-name basis." Dr. Grady drained her glass and pushed back her chair.

"What's your rush?" Mimi asked.

"Those lecture notes. I've got to gather my thoughts together."

Mimi tossed Iona a key ring." "Make yourself at home." She let Dr. Grady out the kitchen door, then returned to the table but did not sit. She took a sip of wine and made a face. "Ugh. You're right about tepid retsina." She picked up the bottle and put it in the refrigerator; came back to the table.

"What's the matter?" Katherine asked.

Mimi pulled out her chair, and dropped into it so that it creaked alarmingly. "Sorry."

"What is it?" Katherine pursued.

"You're bound to hear about this sooner or later—"

"About what?"

Mimi picked up her fork and poked at her salad. "Felix hasn't said anything?"

"About *what*, Mimi?"

The doctor sighed, gustily. "Iona's sister is, as I said, one of Mother Cat's nuns."

"Yes." Dr. Grady hadn't sounded particularly enthusiastic about the convent, but that did not strike Katherine as enough explanation for Mimi's reluctance.

"She was also," Mimi plunged, "Allie Undercroft's first wife."

"Who?" Katherine asked in surprise.

"Isobel. She was Allie's first wife. They were both very young and untried. Isobel as much as Allie."

"What happened?"

"They had a child, a beautiful little girl. She was Iona's goddaughter as well as her niece, and named after her. She was called Ona, and Iona adored her. She adored her brother-in-law, too. A nice setting for disaster, eh?"

Katherine was not deceived by the facetious tone. "Go on."

Mimi sighed again, then continued. "When Ona was a little over two she developed cancer, one of the devouring kinds we still can't do anything about. Iona knew enough about medicine to know how negative the prognosis was. She told Allie and Isobel—false hope would only have made things worse in the long run." Mimi shoved back her chair, got the retsina, refilled their glasses, and put the bottle back into the refrigerator. "Iona didn't expect medical miracles, and she didn't expect Allie to pull some kind of religious miracle out of a hat, but she wasn't prepared for him not to be able to cope. As I said, she adored him. He had a reputation for being regular about hospital visits, giving courage and strength, almost as good as Felix, but not when it was his own child. He simply couldn't cope, not with the baby, not with his wife, not with his sister-in-law. He withdrew into work. He was cardinal rector of a big East Side parish, and he was available with compassion and understanding for everybody except his family. A backhanded compliment, in a way. He hurt so much he couldn't bear it. Iona took a leave of absence from St. Vincent's, and went up to Boston to be with Isobel and the baby. Allie called, daily, I grant you, but he stayed in New York, and Ona died in Iona's arms."

Mimi put her palms down on the table in a flat gesture, as though she was finished. Then she looked up and added briefly, "And Iona changed from orthopedics to pediatric oncology."

"What?"

"Kids with cancer," Mimi explained. "I'm not sure I could handle it, tough cookie that I am. Iona's one of the best in the field, and she goes through considerable hell."

—And well she might, Katherine thought. —One seven-year-old's death is all I've been able to handle, and that not well. Without work, without the piano, it would have killed me. Of course, for Dr. Grady it *was* work; they were not her own children, bone of her bone, flesh of her flesh. Still . . . "What about Allie's wife—Isobel?"

"Isobel. She understood Allie's pain far better than Iona did. Even though he let her down abysmally when the baby got sick."

"It must have been hard on him, too," Katherine remarked.

"I quite agree. But he let Isobel and Iona bear the burden."

"And now Isobel is a nun. Isn't that unusual?"

"Unusual, but not unheard of. Quite a few nuns have been married before circumstances, or what have you, turned them to religion. Isobel's faith carried her through the long months of Ona's dying. Allie and Iona cursed God. Isobel's a very special human being. My shrink friends tell me that it takes seven years to get over a child's death. It was ten years after Ona's death that Isobel entered the Community of the Epiphany."

"What happened to her marriage?"

"My shrink friends also tell me that something like Ona's death either makes or breaks a marriage. It broke Isobel and Allie's. As I said, they were both young and untried. Allie blamed Isobel for the whole thing—his way of avoiding his inability to cope. And he did a good bit of sleeping around. Very discreet. No gossip. But it's not the kind of thing you can keep from your wife for too long, especially if your first mistress is—anyhow, I learned to dislike Allie Undercroft long before I met him. Sorry to have bored you with all this ancient history."

"I'm not bored. So you've known Allie a long time?"

Mimi shook her head. "Only by hearsay, through Iona, until Suzy and Dave moved to the Cathedral and at last I met him in person. So undoubtedly I came to him with many prejudices, probably unfair. I think I'm just as glad this came out tonight. So Allie reminds you of your old jailer, eh?"

—All men have their weaknesses, she had been thinking wearily. —We ask too much of each other.

She replied, "So there's no possibility of my seeing him objectively either."

"Was your jailer a complete baddie?"

Katherine shook her head. "No. Oh, no. He, too, was complex. Can you be truly bad if you don't also have the capacity to be truly good?"

Mimi twirled her wineglass between her fingers. "I might put it the other way around. Don't judge Allie Undercroft by Iona or me. I'm anti-clerical on principle."

"What about Dave?"

"I'd never have gone near him if Suzy hadn't up and married him. But—yes—I'm very fond of Dave."

"Just what does a dean *do?*"

Mimi laughed. "You're asking me? He's administrator of the Cathedral, I suppose. But where the administrator of a hospital doesn't have to be a doctor, a dean has to be both administrator and priest, and the two are constantly in conflict. Dave somehow manages to maintain a creative balance." She went to the kettle, which was simmering, and prepared two cups of herb tea, which she brought to the table. "Your jailer who reminds you of Undercroft —or vice versa—what was he like?"

"Like Bishop Undercroft, and utterly unlike. His eyes, for in-

stance, were grey, like the sea in winter. Bishop Undercroft looks
—well, rather sunny. Lukas was more somber—like his eyes."

"This von H—"

"Hilpert."

"You called him Lukas. Does one ordinarily call one's jailer by
his first name?"

"No. I learned to call him Lukas many years later."

"After the war?"

"Yes. After." Katherine found that she was trembling. She
pushed up from the table and went across the room to the piano.

"*Ma mie*." Mimi crossed swiftly to her. "I didn't mean to do this
to you. There's too much emotion floating around here tonight,
with Merv—and Iona coming in."

"It's all right." Katherine lowered herself onto the piano bench.
"I have to learn to remember it without reliving it. Have you come
to terms with all your memories?"

"Christ, no. And my life has been—emptier than yours."

"Lukas—or Kommandant von Hilpert, as I first knew him—was
an extraordinary jailer. He knew music—he had even known my
mother when she played in Germany when he was little more than
a child. He allowed Justin and me three hours a day to practice on
the school piano—the Nazis took over a school—" She struck a
diminished seventh, resolved it. "Not together. I practiced in the
early morning, Justin in the afternoon."

Mimi sat where she could watch Katherine, who was moving her
fingers soundlessly over the keys. "That cannot have been usual."

"No." Softly she struck a minor chord. "He was a man of strong
convictions, and he believed in the Nazi dream. Later he likened
it to the Grand Inquisitor in Dostoevsky's *The Brothers Karama-
zov*—" She paused. "During the war—at least in the beginning,
when I knew him, he believed it all. But later—it was a terrible
disillusionment for him—"

"Don't," Mimi urged. "I can see that this is being extremely
painful for you."

"It's all right. It shakes me to find that the old wounds still bleed
when probed."

"Enough probing for tonight. I've asked around, and most people who give massages want you to come to them. So my suggestion
is that you go take your bath and get ready for bed, and I'll do the

same, give Dave a quick call about Merv, and come down and give you a back rub. I think you'll find I'm not half bad."

"But Iona—you should have gone up to her long ago."

"She meant exactly what she said; she came to me because she knew she could go right to bed and not have to talk. She'll be asleep by now. Don't worry."

"Oh, Mimi—" Katherine protested halfheartedly; she felt achy and a back rub would help her to sleep. "That's way above and beyond the call of duty."

--→{ 7 }*--

Katherine bathed and then lay on her bed, waiting for Mimi, who knocked lightly and came in, carrying bottles of alcohol and lotion, and wearing blue striped pajamas.

"Iona was sound asleep with the light on and half a dozen pages of notes scattered about the bed. I picked them up and turned out the light and she didn't even move."

"Did you call Dave?"

Mimi nodded. "They caught the kids who did it. They're all underage, so they'll be back on the streets again in no time. And they'll find another gun and kill someone else. It's easier the second time. I've seldom known Dave to be so upset or so angry. Now, enough of all that for tonight. How do you like your rub? Rough or gentle?"

Katherine leaned up on one elbow. "Not rough. Firm enough to knead the muscles a bit, and then gentle enough to relax me."

"Take off your nightgown and roll over onto your stomach."

Katherine obeyed, and jerked slightly as the slosh of cold alcohol took her by surprise.

"Relax. I'll follow the alcohol with lotion." Mimi's fingers worked over the tense muscles in neck and shoulders, in the lower back. "Christ, Katherine how did you get these scars on your back?"

"Do they still show?" Katherine asked in surprise.

"Not to the naked eye. But I can feel them. What happened?"

"I was beaten when I was in the Nazi prison, for refusing to give a concert."

"Your von Hilpert did this? No wonder you don't like to talk about him."

"No, no, he was away. There was another officer in charge, a Von Stroheim character. Lukas would never have countenanced corporal punishment. It was only the one time—since it didn't accomplish its purpose. And it wasn't long after that that my father and stepmother managed my release and got me back to America."

Mimi's fingers were gentle on Katherine's back. "I knew about the vile stuff that went on in the concentration camps, but not—"

"Hush." Katherine turned her head to a more comfortable position on the pillow. "It's been over for a long time, and the scars healed quickly. I'd forgotten all about them."

Manya Sergeievna, closer in time to what happened, had been even more shocked and angered by the beating than Mimi. Katherine had been too weak to hide the scars from her stepmother. She had had pneumonia on the ship to New York, and was taken to the farm in Connecticut and put immediately to bed. She was still coughing; she still had nightmares about the French prison, about what might be happening to Justin.

When Manya had helped her undress and had seen the still-unhealed slashes on the fair skin, she had burst into a stream of Russian invective. But it was her nursing which helped to heal the scars so that in a few months Katherine was able to wear a low-backed evening dress to play a concert for GIs. As soon as the welts were healed enough, Manya rubbed them with lanolin, with cocoa butter, with infinite love. Surely Katherine had always had the best of Manya, while her stepmother had had to put up with all her adolescent rebellion. But Manya's patience had eventually won her over, and the love between them grew and deepened.

Mimi rubbed a delicately scented lotion into Katherine's skin. "You've taken good care of your body," she said. "Smooth skin, despite the scars. God, I hate the loss of elasticity that comes with aging. Your skin's at least forty years younger than you are." Slowly the tensions eased from Katherine's body, and memories slid away.

The Kommandant

A sudden electrical storm awakened Katherine. She turned onto her back and watched lightning illuminate the night outside her windows. Almost immediately a crash of thunder followed, and then the rain. After a moment, realizing that it was driving in the windows, she got out of bed and shut them, getting wet enough in a few moments to make her nightgown cling to her body. She pulled it off and went to her chest of drawers for a dry one. This storm would certainly break the heat. June was hotter and more humid than she remembered. She thought with longing of the house in Connecticut, where there was always a breeze.

The storm had also broken her sleep. She glanced at her clock: 2 a.m. A miserable time to be wakened, out of the best and deepest sleep of the night. Resolutely she turned out the light, determined to sleep, yet knowing that the determination itself would keep her awake. She rolled on her side, taking the herb-scented pillow with her.

In her mind's ear she played through the program she had chosen for Felix. An hour's program. She played some encores. Sleep was still far away.

A Vivaldi horn concerto. During her nocturnal concerts she could play any instrument she chose. Tonight it did not help. She got up and went to the kitchen for the ritual cup of consommé, adding a good dollop of lemon juice. Back to her chaise longue. The garden below was empty, the fountain playing, mingled with the rain, which was still coming down, although the electrical storm had passed.

Lukas. She had in no way explained to Mimi (nor did she intend to) why she thought of the man who had been her jailer as Lukas. She had already said too much. No more.

Kommandant von Hilpert.

She had not been prepared for his courtesy, as she had not been prepared for the occupation of Paris. The other Germans in charge of the makeshift prison had been different and he could not always control them, although she learned later that she and others in the school had been treated far more humanely than those in similar detention sites.

Nor had she been prepared for the first meeting with him. The knock on the apartment door, the uniformed Germans, the sudden departure from her home, Justin taken in one car, she in another, had been a nightmare, but somehow less unexpected than the summons to the office of the Kommandant, which had been the office of the headmistress of the school. The gracious room had been untouched. There was a fire burning in the fireplace. Lamps were lit against the dull skies of a rainy day. Spring in Paris could be cool. The Kommandant had sat at the headmistress's desk, so that for a moment the nightmare reminded her of boarding school.

'You do not look like your mother,' he said.

This nightmare of reality had less coherence than a dream. Such a statement was not part of any reasonable script. 'How did you know my mother?' she demanded.

'Sit.' He pointed to the straight chair in which no doubt students had sat after being summoned to the office for some misdemeanor.

'How did you know my mother?' she repeated, still standing.

'Sit.' When she had obeyed he said, 'I loved her.'

'You knew her?'

'I was an adolescent when she played in Berlin. I was studying music, seriously, and I had free tickets to many concerts. I heard her play, and I fell in love with her, with her playing, with the vibrancy of her self. She was charming to me, charming as one is to a puppy. I do not complain. How else could she behave with a callow, adoring youth? But you do not resemble her.'

'No. I look like my father's mother.'

He regarded her across the desk. 'You are quite beautiful, with that splendid black hair and marble skin. But you do not have the—the feral quality of your mother.'

Katherine replied stiffly, 'I did not think of my mother as wild.'

And he had laughed, a warm, relaxed laugh. She had not realized then what an unusual interview this was, because she had not yet realized what had happened, to herself and Justin, to France. Had they been taken to any other prison than von Hilpert's, things would undoubtedly have been different.

He had escorted her that first day to the grand piano in the school salon, a Pleyel. She had obeyed his command to play because this was not a public performance; it had, in her mind, to do with her mother, because this man had admired her. He sat, in his immaculate uniform, on a stiff, yellow satin-covered chair while she played, and when she was playing she was out of nightmare, the waking nightmare in which she did not yet believe.

He had said then, 'You do not look like her, but the quality is in the music. Less mature, perhaps, but there. Every man who hears you is going to want to make love to you.' There was no lust in his voice; nevertheless, prickles went up her spine. He continued, 'It would be a pity to let such talent go to seed. I will see to it that both you and your husband have time to practice.'

She did not ask if they would be expected to play in payment for the hours of practice. She did not need to ask. They would have to deal with that when the time came. (A beating for her. Auschwitz for Justin. It might have been different if von Hilpert had still been there.) She asked, 'Where is my husband?'

'The men are in the servants' quarters. He is not being mistreated, I assure you. You are not, after all, criminals.'

'May I see him?'

'That would not be wise.'

'But we've just—'

'I realize. You have just been married. I am sorry to interrupt the honeymoon. If you would like to be together again it is very easy. A concert or so, for audiences who will be, I assure you, appreciative.'

She shook her head.

The phone rang.

It was not the phone in the headmistress's office in Paris all those years ago. She was in New York. Preparing for a benefit concert. And who would be ringing her at four in the morning? She pulled herself up from the chaise longue, and sat on the bed, reaching for the phone.

"Mormor, it's Kristen. Did I wake you?" Mormor, Norwegian for the maternal grandmother, literally Mother mother. The paternal grandmother was Farmor, Father mother. She was delighted. "Kristen, how lovely. You didn't wake me, but I was having a waking nightmare, and I'm grateful to you for freeing me. What's up?"

"You're going to be a great-grandmother. I thought you might like to know."

"My dear, I'm delighted."

"Do you want a great-granddaughter or son?"

"Either will do. Or both. Don't twins run in Martin's family?"

"Mormor, don't wish that on me! By the way, I've just been promoted to first flute in the orchestra, so I'm not spreading the news of my incipient motherhood—seven months off. It's between us."

"I'm silent as the grave."

"I haven't even told your esteemed daughter yet. You're the first to know, except Martin, of course." As Katherine was silent, Kristen added, "Don't worry, Mormor, I'm learning to be the soul of tact. Only you and I will know of this call. I'll give Mor a ring this evening when she gets home from work. How's life in the great U.S. of A.?"

"Interesting."

"Life's always interesting for you, Mormor. I'm glad you haven't changed."

"I'm preparing for a concert."

A chuckle from Kristen. "I thought you were retired."

"It's only a benefit for an old friend. Gives me something to do. How's Martin?"

"Ecstatic. You'd think he was the one to be pregnant; he felt queasy this morning at breakfast."

"And my other grands?"

Her grandchildren were as dear to her heart as her children, and had been spared the inevitable publicity Michou and Julie had endured. Who could blame her for more than skimming the surface with the journalists? If there were the normal family tensions, there was no need for them to be revealed. She did not tell of their anxiety about baby Juliana, slow to speak, not quite up to the other three grandchildren, Juliana who was loving and happy, not severely retarded, but not able to get along with schoolwork, happy with animals and hurt things, ultimately marrying an inarticulate but gentle man who treasured her fey childlikeness and took her to his farm to live away from tensions and competitiveness.

"Last I heard, darling Juliana"—a tenderness touched Kristen's brisk voice—"is contented as a kitten on the farm and has created some new breed of chicken which lays vast quantities of enormous eggs. I wish people wouldn't underestimate Juliana. Nils is on something like page 972 of his novel. Ole and Dagmar are talking about having children, so you're apt to be inundated with greats. When are you coming to see us?"

"Who knows? If I had a fortune I'd bring you all to New York for Christmas."

"Wish you could. Mormor, I'm glad you're giving a concert. I never approved of your retiring. I'd better hang up, or Martin will have a fit over the phone bill—though he did suggest that I call you about our babe."

"Call collect next time."

"*Tusan tak*. I will. Have a fine morning, Mormor."

"It may be morning in Oslo. It's still night here."

"Yes, I know. You're still a gallivanting old lady, and I love you for it. Lots of love, Mormor."

"To you, too."

--◦⊰ 2 ⊱◦--

Kristen's call had achieved what the consommé had not. There had always been a special bond between Katherine and her grandchildren, perhaps particularly with Kristen. With Julie, her own child, she never felt completely secure; it is not a kindness, she thought, for people with demanding careers to have children. In her own case, she had never felt left out or displaced because of her mother's career. She had lived so much more with her father and stepmother that Julie had been able to remain a special icon to her; there was no competition. And during the brief time she had lived with her mother, before Julie's premature death, Julie had, like Justin, turned her energies to Katherine's talent. —It's a wonder, Katherine thought, —that I was able to retain a sense of my own identity. I am, thank God, me, Katherine, not a creation of my mother's or husband's.

Julie, her second-born, had not been an artist, despite her parentage. From somewhere she had been given a shrewd sense of business, so shrewd that as soon as her children were old enough she took over the books for her husband's shipping business. Katherine admired her daughter, but she was never sure of the love between them. She felt an unspoken resentment of her career which time had only diminished, not taken away. But with her grands, the biological remove made it easy for them to have a deep, delighted love. And was Julie resentful of that, too? In any event, she did not tell her daughter how often she talked with Kristen, with the other three. With the grands, she felt relaxed and secure. Secure in their love, and does the need to love and be loved ever lessen? Is anyone completely secure? She doubted it.

Kristen was, in a way, her link with Julie. It was Kristen who had told her, maybe ten years earlier (she was both vague and indifferent about chronology), that Eric was having what the jargon then called a mid-life crisis. 'It's very trying for Mor,' Kristen said. 'But Far's basically a homebody and I'm sure it won't last long. He's just trying to see how far he can go. What he needs is for Farfar to put him over his knee and wallop him. But his parents think he's God, and they have their eyes tightly closed.' It was Kristen who had told her, 'Far's over his philandering phase. Things are pretty good with him and Mor right now, sort of a new honeymoon stage.' Had it not been for Kristen, she would have known none of this. She hoped the younger children were not as aware of their father's foibles as Kristen, and thought they were not.

She fell asleep, slipping into a pleasant dream, set in a falling-down hotel in Jamaica where she had once spent some time with Erlend Nikulaussen, whose stepnephew Eric was.

A smell of flowers and the wind blowing in the palms pervaded the dream, and the sound of surf and the warmth of sun. She moved from the solace of the dream to a quiet and deep sleep.

--◦◄{ 3 }►◦--

A little before nine she roused, and made herself get up. If she stayed awake half the night and then slept half the day, she would set a pattern, one which she had been used to on her concert tours, but which she did not want to fall back into now, when the structure of her days was logically different. When her children were little, and she was home between tours, she had always carefully made the transition from being a night person to being a morning person, so that she could have breakfast with the children, be with them as much as possible.

Coffee was dripping through the filter when she heard a knock on the kitchen door. Mimi would have knocked and come in. "Who is it?"

"Iona Grady."

Katherine opened the door. "Good morning."

Iona looked rested; the shadows under her eyes were less apparent. "Good morning to you, too. May I come in for just a moment?"

"Of course. I'm about to have coffee. Will you join me?"

The doctor shook her head. "Mimi and I have been drinking coffee for an hour, and I've had my quota. Go ahead with yours, please."

Katherine filled her cup, added milk, and then sat down at the small dining-room table.

Iona said, "I want to apologize for my unexpected arrival last night, Madame—uh—"

"Vigneras. And it's quite all right. I hope you slept well."

"I went out like a light. Mimi said she told you about Allie and Isobel."

"Yes. And the baby."

"I've seen a lot of worse things since, but we were very young and it was hell while we were going through it. Don't judge Allie by Mimi or me. I gave her a very prejudiced picture before she ever met the guy, and Mimi's the most loyal of friends and, where her friends are concerned, not very objective. Nor, I suppose, am I. Allie and Isobel made their peace years ago. He calls her for advice and, I may say, listens to her when he won't listen to anyone else. Anyhow, my apologies, Madame—uh—Vigneras."

"Katherine."

"Thanks. That's what Mimi calls you, so that's how I think of you. I just wanted to—well—put in a good word for Allie. It was all too long ago for any of us to hold on to bitterness. It's been nice to meet you. I'm glad you're here for Mimi. She's terribly generous, but she can be very lonely. Okay—I'm off to give that paper."

After she had gone, Katherine boiled herself an egg and went to the piano. She was running scales when the phone rang, jarring her almost as much as it had at four in the morning.

It was Bishop Undercroft. "Madame Vigneras, I hope I haven't disturbed you." His accent was English, his tenor voice not like Lukas's at all. "Felix tells me you'd like some time with our Bösendorfer. If you'd care to practice this afternoon, he'll pick you up."

"Thanks, I'll be most grateful."

"Will around two-thirty be convenient?"

"Fine, thank you. The acoustics will be very different from a concert hall."

"Of course. You'll have a number of adjustments to make. Then perhaps you'll join Yolande and me for an early dinner?"

She was, she had to admit, more curious than ever about the young bishop and his present wife. "Thank you. I'd be delighted."

"We've invited Felix, too, and the Davidsons *mère* and *père*. Of course, Merv is lying in state right now, and it's possible that Felix or Dave or I may have to leave to take our turn at the coffin."

"I'm so terribly sorry about his death—it seems so reasonless—"

"Reasonless indeed, and Merv was a man of reason. Asking you to come to the Cathedral today when normally we wouldn't have anything going on is by way of being a tribute to Merv. Dave and I talked it over and agreed that it was what he would have wanted."

—Yes, for life to continue. An affirmation of value. "I liked him very much at our one brief meeting."

"And he, you. It was a great shock to us all. Violence grows worse daily, but we tend to get blunted unless it hits home. Now.

We'll get you back early tonight. Felix reminded me to promise you that."

"Thank you. I'll appreciate it." She hung up and returned to the piano. She moved into the music for Felix's benefit, so that she was within harmony, outside time and space. Mimi had to pound on the kitchen door before Katherine heard.

The doctor stood in the open doorway. "Sorry to disturb you."

Katherine turned on the piano bench. "I was deep in music."

Mimi came into the living room, carrying her briefcase and a small overnight bag. "I wanted to tell you that I'm taking the shuttle up to Boston with Iona. I'm just going to spend the night, and I'll be home tomorrow."

"Have a good time. You look very nice today."

Mimi looked down at her khaki traveling suit. "It's always chilly on the plane." She looked at Katherine's half-empty cup of coffee. "I'll hot up some milk for the coffee. I'll even wash the pot. I have a while before time to leave, and I'd like a fresh cup myself."

"I'd like some more, too. Thanks for sending Iona down."

Mimi turned from the refrigerator, holding a carton of milk. "It was her idea, not mine."

"Well, thanks, anyhow."

"Iona is very fair-minded, and she knows that sometimes I'm not. I know I'm interrupting your piano time. Sorry. I'm feeling depressed."

"You're never an interruption. Why are you depressed?"

Instead of answering, Mimi said, "You fit my description of a contented person."

"What's that?"

"Being happy to snuggle down in bed at night and go to sleep. And being eager to wake up and get going with the new day in the morning."

Katherine watched Mimi pouring coffee and hot milk. "It's a good description, and very apt for *you*."

"Not always." Mimi handed her the steaming cup. "Sometimes I look at my life and think that on the surface I've accomplished a lot, but I'll be alone at the end."

"Most of us are."

"It's different. You've had Justin. I've only had lovers. And friends. A life-line of friends. But sometimes—" She set her cup on the table in front of the long sofa. "What kind of wedding did you have?"

Katherine moved from the piano to sit beside her. "Tiny. And yet enormous. Justin and Anne—his sister—had no family, and Aunt Manya was on tour with a play, and it was long before the days of jet planes and weekends in Europe, so my father cabled us some money for a honeymoon, which of course we never had a chance to take. Marcel—Anne's husband—was an organist, and we were married in his church, and he played for us as though for a court wedding. All that music alone made me feel very married."

"A nice memory," Mimi said.

"Very nice."

"What happened to them, Anne and Marcel?"

"Marcel went to Africa with de Gaulle. Both his arms were blown off, so we were grateful that he took only a few days to die. Anne was active with the maquis—she got away right after Justin and I were taken. Ultimately she got TB from overexposure and died a few years after the war."

"Christ," Mimi said, "I understand why you sounded so sharp when I thought your Justin was a Jew."

"It's all water under the bridge now. It doesn't do to dwell on it."

"You've hardly cheered me up." Mimi smiled ruefully. "What I am glad about—and I am truly glad—is that you will be here when I get home tomorrow."

"And I'm glad you're coming home," Katherine said.

"Anything I can get you before I go? Food? My fridge is full of salads and cold meats."

"Thanks, but I've plenty in mine for lunch and I'm going up to the Cathedral to practice this afternoon, and have an early meal with the Undercrofts."

"Good, good. As Iona warned you, I wasn't very fair about Allie. I'm more shook about Merv than I realized, and I had to dump somewhere. Damn. Why Merv? Allie's going to miss him terribly. Just remember, Katherine, that most people love Allie, and Iona and I are in the minority. Oh, damn. I thought I was trying not to give you unfair preconceptions of a man who is extraordinarily complicated. Felix has had occasion to remind me that Allie was going through his own hell when Ona was dying, even if he showed it in odd ways. His faith fell to ashes and he couldn't get any kind of phoenix to rise from them. Not, at any rate, until it was too late for him and Isobel. Dave says he has a very deep faith now. And, according to Felix, he saved Yolande."

"How did he meet her?"

"I suppose he saw her first when she was performing. Allie's always loved the theatre."

"Was she an actress?"

Mimi looked at Katherine in astonishment. "Katherine Vigneras, you don't know who Yolande Xabo is?"

"Yolande Xabo? Yes, it does have a familiar ring," Katherine said vaguely. "Was that her name before she was married?"

"Oy veh." Mimi wiped her eyes. "I forget you've lived mostly in Europe. But even there, in the evening, on television—"

"We never had a television set."

"And on tour, when you were staying in hotels, you never turned it on?"

"It never occurred to me."

"Ah, me. You have been rather one-sided, haven't you?"

"I read," Katherine said, smiling. "Lots of things."

"Yes, I know you read. And if you'd inadvertently switched on TV and tuned in on Yolande, you'd probably have changed channels or turned her off. She was a singer—*the* singer for a good number of years."

"Opera?" Katherine asked, still vague.

Again Mimi laughed. "Dear Katherine—not opera. Pop stuff. Post-rock. Not my cup of tea, either, but she was as much of an idol in her own day as—to turn back the clock—the Beatles were in mine. She married Allie when she was at the peak of her popularity, but she had the sense to know that her star was beginning to descend."

"What did she sing?"

"Stuff written especially for her. Some of it good. And, to do her justice, she always transcended her material."

"You heard her?"

"Yes, Quillon Yonge, your tenant below me who's abroad most of the time, was a big fan of hers, and he took me to hear her several times. In a world daily more fearful of atomic destruction,

Yolande Xabo sang of hope—hope that the planet would not be blown apart, that people could go on coupling and birthing."

Katherine nodded. "And so we have, more and more precariously, somehow managing to hold the balance."

"Yup. And what Yolande did was to keep hope alive, and terror at bay."

"No small thing," Katherine said.

"No small thing indeed. She was almost like a mother soothing an entire audience of frightened children."

"Did she make any recordings?"

"Oh, millions, I suppose, selling wildly, but you had to have seen her to understand her power. She fostered the illusion that she could see into the future, and there was a carefully publicized rumor that she was a daughter of the Incas. She's still a beautiful woman, I have to concede that, but her life has taken its toll. She was staggeringly beautiful when she was young. It was all over the papers, of course, when she married an Episcopal bishop."

"Felix says it's a very happy marriage."

Mimi shrugged. "As marriages go, it seems to be lasting."

"So she was a singer," Katherine mused. "That does explain her. I was rather baffled by her."

Mimi made an apologetic gesture. "I don't suppose it occurred to anybody that you didn't know who she was. Their marriage was widely publicized—abroad, too."

"When I was on tour, especially behind the Iron Curtain, I missed weeks of news at a time. Now I understand why she moves like a performer."

"Katherine, I'm sorry. I didn't mean to give you the impression that life at the Cathedral is like *Barchester Towers* as written by Dostoevsky and heavily edited by John Updike. It's basically a happy place, a loving, caring place. I'm sorry I took it all out on Allie last night. It was Iona, appearing out of the blue—"

"Why don't you have anyone sharing your apartment now?" Carefully, Katherine changed the subject.

"I sometimes go years alone." Mimi stood and stretched. "It's only when I find someone who needs a place to live, someone interning at St. Vincent's, which was how I met Suzy, someone I think unusually gifted, someone I think I'd enjoy, that I'm willing to give up my privacy. Especially now as I grow older. I like my own bathroom. Okay, I'm off. Have fun up at the Cathedral. See you tomorrow."

-··❖{ 4 }❖··-

A little after two, Felix rang her doorbell. He bent over her hand in a courteous obeisance. "Your chariot awaits."

As he held the taxi door open for her, she asked, "Please get in first. It's no courtesy to the lady for the gentleman to stand back and let her crawl across these drop-bottom taxis," and then wondered, as she watched him struggle, if she weren't, despite creaky knees, considerably more limber than the bishop.

He caught his breath and directed the driver to the Cathedral. "Allie thinks I'm selfish to insist on coming down for you instead of letting Jos bring you. But I *have* been good about not bothering you, and I thought this would give us time to talk. I hope you won't mind a dead bishop at the high altar while you practice. You'll be in the ambulatory, and you can't see the high altar from there."

"Felix," she demurred, "I'm going to be practicing, not performing."

"That's all right. I just want to make sure the vigil won't be disturbing to you."

"I don't see how it could be, unless he leaps out of the coffin."

Felix sighed. "How I wish he could. I still find it so difficult to realize that he's gone. It was so sudden—I do want to apologize for dashing off that way without even saying goodbye. I'm still in a state of shock. Merv was so young—and I keep going. I used to talk a lot to him. He was like you, that way—people talked to him. His death is another link with reality gone. But even Merv was too close to it all, and so is Chan."

"To close to what?"

"Oh—the mishmash of human nature on the Close, the hates and loves and jealousies that all seem exaggerated when they're contained within a few blocks."

But then he was silent. It was not an easy silence, so she broke it. "Mimi tells me that Bishop Undercroft was married to Sister Isobel when they were very young."

He made a sharp exclamation, looked at the taxi driver, then back to Katherine. "That's true, but I'm sure Mimi gave you a biased version."

"I think she tried to be fair."

"What on earth possessed her to tell you, then?" he exploded.

"Iona Grady spent last night in Mimi's apartment. She's giving a lecture here today."

"Oh." He did not sound happy. "Iona tries to be fair, I grant you that. The way Mimi carries the flag, you'd think Iona had been married to Allie, not Isobel. I suppose it was inevitable that someone would say something, sooner or later. People won't leave the past alone, and the longer ago it is, the more likely the facts are to be distorted. It was tragic. Tragic for them all. But it's over, long over."

"All right," she said mildly.

"Allie's finally forgiven himself. That was hardest of all. He accepted Isobel's forgiveness, and God's, long before he could forgive himself. Why are we so hard on ourselves, Katya?"

"Part of the human predicament, I suppose."

"Lack of forgiveness—it's one of the worst of all sins. I know this, and yet there are things for which I haven't completely forgiven myself. It's odd, Katya—at tea, yesterday, before Merv—I needed to tell you about myself, warts and all. I suppose I think of you as a sort of confessor extraordinary." She made a murmur of negation, but he went on. "I'm not sure the human being has the capacity for self-acceptance without first being accepted. Perhaps it's because we're of an age, we've lived through a lot—not much shocks us." They were crawling up Sixth Avenue, with cars behind and ahead of them honking impatiently.

Felix leaned back, saying, "You really do accept me, after all that I told you about myself and Sarah—and after?"

"Felix, dear, don't brood over it. The past is past."

"Is it? Never completely, I think. It intrudes on the present."

"Then you have to look at it, just as it is, and accept it as part of you. If we were made up only of the parts of ourselves of which we approve, we'd be mighty dull."

"You're right." He looked out the window at the traffic. "For once I'm grateful that we're crawling. It gives us a little more time. Katherine, there's something else I didn't tell you about when I was in the army."

Now their driver leaned on the horn.

"You don't have to tell me anything," Katherine said.

"I know I don't. I *need* to tell you. I'm an old man, and in the nature of things I don't have long to live."

"Felix, I'm an old woman."

"Yes, but you're younger than I am, and you're—you're better about your memories than I am."

She dropped her eyes to his hands, which were tightly clasped over the head of his cane, the raised veins blue.

"Katya, when I left the army I didn't leave with an honorable discharge."

She waited until she knew that it was she who would have to break the silence. "What happened?"

The taxi inched its way up to Twenty-third Street. "It was, I suppose, the height of irony. We were all totally exhausted, and a couple of men had already fallen apart, gone totally bonkers and been taken away, screaming. God knows what happened to them. So we were sent to London—desk jobs, nice and safe. But during the first week I had the beginning of the nightmares. A corporal heard me screaming—one of our own graves registration men— one of our own group—so he had an inkling of what I was going through. He had his arms around me, trying to wake me enough to calm me down, when in walked a sergeant. Not one of us. A man who'd spent his entire war behind a desk."

Again Katherine had to break the silence. "Felix, I'm sorry, but I don't understand."

"We were given dishonorable discharges for sodomy."

"Oh, Felix, no, how stupid—"

"Keith, the corporal, was as straight as they come, wife, kids— he fought it, and eventually got an honorable discharge."

"Why didn't you fight it, too?"

"Because at that point I didn't, as they say, give a damn. I testified for Keith. That was more important for me than clearing myself. And I didn't have a wife and kids. Also, unlike Keith, I hadn't led a blameless life. This was just one more proof that we live in a lousy world, and I wanted no part of it. Once Keith was cleared he urged me to clear myself, too, and said he'd get the chaplain to testify for me. But I had a fit of stubbornness and I wouldn't. Let the world think whatever it wanted. Later, after I was priested, I was terrified that Sarah might open the whole thing up, just to get a good laugh. But she was too busy being a society wife on Long Island to want to bother. She did call one night and hold it over my head when she was drunk."

"Why did you tell her about it?"

"Because, when I came back to New York after the war, we got together again for a few weeks. I was fool enough to think she was serious in wanting to put our marriage back together. We both got very amorous and very drunk one evening, and I was still young and foolish enough to think that there should be no secrets in a marriage. But she was already involved with this Long Island banker, and she was just using me as bait, to make him jealous, to make him come to heel. I never should have told anybody, much less Sarah. I was very young. I know better now. I've never told anybody else, except Allie, and now you. That makes a trinity. I'm still, on occasion, fearful. When I was Diocesan I had the feeling that someone might look up the records. But now—who would want to?"

"No one, I should think." But she wondered: was his fear connected with this sad and ancient history?

"All I know"—he made a convulsive sound loud enough so that the driver turned around briefly—"is that some people hold on to hate. I need to know that you don't hate me."

"Why on earth would I hate you, Felix. Of course I don't."

"Are we friends?"

"Yes, we are friends."

They were silent then, a quiet silence. She looked out the window as they passed Lincoln Center and then turned on to Amsterdam. Restaurants. A gas station. A funeral parlor. Barney Greengrass, the Sturgeon King. Someday she'd like to stop in and see what was sold there besides sturgeon. Antique stores. Churches. Buildings with boarded-up windows. Clean new housing developments. Bodegas. Broken windows. Indeed, a little of everything.

Potholes. "Don't they ever fix these streets?" she asked in exasperation.

"New York isn't in the best fiscal shape."

Finally they were nearing the Cathedral. "If I bring you in by the entrance across from St. Luke's Hospital we won't have steps to climb, and I can give you a quickie glimpse of the Stone Yard." As the taxi turned, he said, "That's St. Luke's, there on our left. Suzy's office is across on Amsterdam. Here we are." As she climbed out of the cab she saw a large woman in a grey uniform purposefully pushing a shopping cart. The woman waved at Felix, with a rather sour smile, and headed toward Broadway. Felix waved back. "That's Mrs. Gomez. I have an irrational dislike of her. She looks like the Beast of Belsen, but she's one of the best cooks in the city."

"Topaze's and Fatima's mother . . ." Katherine murmured.

"The same, though it's difficult to imagine her doing anything as intimate as giving birth. We go in here. I've got the keys." After he had clanged the gate shut behind them, he put his hand on her elbow to help her along the rough flagstones of the path, then turned right across what seemed to be a playing field to a large, open shed. Between the shed and the Cathedral, stacked on the grass, were piles of stone, each one carefully marked by letter and number. As they neared the shed, she could hear the sound of machinery on wet stone. "I can imagine Mrs. Gomez being the matron of a concentration camp. I'm sure she hits Fatty for being clumsy, and she lets Topaze roam the streets and do anything he wants. And she cooks like an angel. No matter what, we'll have a superb meal tonight."

They approached the pile of stones and he nodded toward them. "These will finish the north transept. Most of the work is done by hand, just as it was in the Middle Ages. When Dean Morton started all this, stonecutting was a lost art in this country. We have only a few modern machines, a big gantry crane, and two stone saws, which work like gigantic dentist's drills, with water constantly flowing." He held her arm more firmly as the terrain roughened, and led her into the shed, where he was immediately greeted by an assorted group of young men and women, some at wooden worktables, chipping away at the stone with great wooden mallets and chisels, others working the machines. The only thing they had in common was an expression of love in their faces for the work they were doing.

Felix waved at them, and told them to get on with what they were doing. He led her across the ground again, and they entered the Cathedral. As they neared the ambulatory, she saw someone slip out of the shadows and skitter away into the dimness.

"Fatty Gomez," Felix said in annoyance. "When she's not with Tory, she's afraid of her own shadow. Mrs. Gomez makes the kids wait for her to go home on the subway, and once summer school is over for the day, they don't have any place to go."

One hand lightly on her elbow to guide her, he walked her up the nave. She glanced toward the high altar, and saw Bishop Undercroft kneeling at one side of a coffin draped with a great pall. A shaft of light touched his fair hair. His body was erect and although she could not see his face there was a feeling of peace about him, and an air of authority; he was very much a bishop. He did not move or sway as he knelt.

At the other side of the coffin was a much younger man, looking like a refugee from the sixties, with long hair and blue jeans, and an enormous cross dangling on his chest. He shifted position and swatted at what appeared to be an imaginary fly and scratched at the back of his neck. There was none of the repose which emanated from the bishop.

As they climbed the steps to the ambulatory and the altar was lost to view, Felix reached for his keys to open the chapel. He looked up and sniffed, then looked toward the long-haired priest. Katherine smelled a ropy, rather unpleasant odor.

"Pot," Felix said.

"In the Cathedral?"

Felix wiped his forehead with his handkerchief. "Pot in cathedrals is nothing new, unfortunately. Whenever there's a big concert here, people tend to think they're back in Woodstock in the sixties, particularly if it's something to do with ecology or saving the whales. The Davidson kids, I'm glad to say, take a dim view of priests having to get stoned in order to grieve."

Katherine glanced again at the altar. "Maybe I'm being European, but it doesn't seem very appropriate for a vigil."

"It isn't. And it would have made Merv furious. When there's a huge concert of non-churchgoing people it's a little understandable, though it's strictly forbidden, and we monitor it as much as possible. Don't judge us by this; it truly doesn't happen that often. Did you ever smoke?"

"No."

"I did, for a while. But I didn't like the people around me. Bless Allie. He's doing his grieving the appropriate way. Maybe it will have some influence on the others."

She walked over to the piano and opened the keyboard.

"Sorry," Felix said. "I'll try to see that nothing else eats into your practice time. I'll leave you. Canon Dorsey and I are due to take over the vigil in a few minutes."

She ran a few scales. The superb instrument was not far from needing a tuning. She would mention it to Felix. Then, in deference to Bishop Juxon, she played through her program. She looked up, briefly, and saw that Fatima and Topaze were sitting in one of the carved pews. She had not noticed them come in. Ignoring them, she turned to some phrases which she felt needed honing, then played over, and then over again, and then over again, a Scarlatti toccata, listening to hear if the rapidly repeated notes would remain clear or blur in these acoustics.

Clumsily bumping into the pews, so that Katherine's attention was momentarily distracted, Fatima left the chapel. Topaze, hardly seeming to notice, sat quietly, and it was only then that she noticed Emily sitting beside him. The child's face was somber, severe. Perhaps it was her accident which caused her to look far older than her years, but once again Katherine recognized herself in that young, carefully expressionless face. Justin had thawed her so that she was able to drop her mask of self-protection and reveal her vulnerability, and likely Emily would thaw, too. Thawing hurts, and Katherine ached for the child.

--※{ 5 }※--

She turned from Emily to the piano, and her memory shifted gears (was it because Justin had taught her the toccata?) to her return to Paris to study with Justin when she was perhaps less than half a dozen years older than Emily now—enough to change her from near-adolescence to near-womanhood.

After the breakup with Pete, her father and stepmother had decided, with blind oblivion to her youth and the state of the world, to send her to Paris to study with her beloved Monsieur Vigneras, who had been her piano teacher during her time in boarding school in Switzerland. Concerned only with healing her unhappiness, and with their own careers, it never seemed to have occurred to them that they were sending her into danger, nor that she was extraordinarily young for her seventeen years. Through friends a small studio apartment was found for her, and a passable piano, and she started weekly lessons with Justin, knitting up her raveled spirit with music. She lived an almost entirely solitary life. The young doctor friend they had expected to look out for her had gone with his wife to Zurich, to a post in the big university hospital there. It did not occur to her any more than to Tom and Manya that she should have been finishing school. She lived from one lesson to the next, hardly aware that she was lonely. In the early winter, walking home in the rain from her lesson, she caught cold, and in a day or so her sore throat and headache turned into a mild case of flu, and she lay huddled on the sofa, with aching bones and fever, trying to pull herself over to the piano. By the day of her next lesson she was on her feet again, belting her raincoat about her, pulling on her beret, and heading for Justin's studio.

He seemed abstracted, standing by the window, looking down into the street as she played. She finished the Scarlatti, and then he directed her to play the Franck Prelude, Chorale and Fugue, on which she had just started to work. When she had finished, he turned toward her. 'Katherine, there is something about your playing which puzzles me.'

'What?' she asked, and, as he didn't answer immediately, 'Is it bad?'

'It is, but I don't think it's irremediable. Your technique is remarkable for someone your age, clear and brilliant and sure. And I believe in technique—don't mistake me. But you appear afraid to let anything come through yours, and this puzzles me. There's deep emotion in you; I sense that, though you certainly don't show it. Not even in your playing.'

She sat at the keyboard, nodding slowly. 'You're right. Of course you're right. Maybe I haven't got over that boarding school.'

'It's more than the school. You were badly hurt at that abominable place, but that was a child's hurt. This is more. I think that you have been hurt now as a woman, and that you're afraid to allow yourself to be vulnerable, for fear of being hurt again.'

How did he know? But, tangled with self-consciousness, she

said, 'That's an awful impression to give. Everybody gets hurt. I'm no exception. Anyhow, being hurt isn't bad if you use it the right way.'

'If you know that, why have you pulled such a tight little shell around you?'

'I didn't know that I had. I didn't know it seemed that way. And I don't know why it should, right now, because I'm terribly happy.' Happy in adoration of Justin (adoration still far from being transformed into love), of learning from him, being with him once a week.

His stern eyes became gentle. 'Are you happy, little one?'

'Can't you tell?'

'You make it difficult for people to tell anything about you.'

'I don't mean to.'

'You shy away from people so. You seem afraid. For instance, I know that you haven't been well this week. That's a bad cough you have, and I think you still have some fever. But if I were to come over to you and put my arms around you and tell you I was sorry you feel poorly, you would stiffen up like a little ramrod. It would be like putting my arms around a poker.'

'How do you know that?'

'Experience. Whenever I come near you, you freeze into a little icicle. Why is it?'

She looked down at the piano keys and felt the blood mounting to her face. 'I don't know. I don't feel that way.'

There was a sudden silence between them. He took a step toward her, then stopped. She waited, but he didn't approach her. Instead, he said, 'Play the Franck and put something of yourself in it.'

She started to play, trying to forget everything except what she wanted to tell him and could only tell him through music. She blundered a couple of times but it seemed unimportant and she continued.

Justin said softly, 'That's all I wanted to know.'

Her heart began to beat violently. Her hands were cold.

He continued. 'You can do it, Katherine. You're an artist. I knew there was something in you to be said, but I was beginning to wonder if you were going to be able to express it, if possibly music wasn't the means. But it is, and you're all right.'

'I'm glad,' Katherine whispered, but she was filled with shame.

She had given him her naked heart and now she felt that she had betrayed herself because he didn't want what she had offered (and how right he had been not to take it then, to wait).

'Little one,' he said, 'you feel ill. Go home and go to bed. But don't wait till next Friday to come. Have a lesson on Tuesday. I have a cancellation that afternoon.'

'All right.' She got up from the piano and stood shivering inwardly as he helped her into her raincoat.

'That coat isn't warm enough.'

'I have a sweater on,' she answered, buckling the belt. 'I'll come back Tuesday. Goodbye, Monsieur Vigneras.'

'Now, isn't it time you started calling me Justin?'

'I'd rather not.' —Idiot, why did she say that when in her daydreams she had called him Justin forever?

'Then must I start calling you Mademoiselle Forrester?'

'Of course not.'

'Then it must be Justin. You are no longer a schoolgirl. Your music tells me that.' How gently he had prodded her out of frightened adolescence into vulnerability.

'I'll try. But I'm in the habit of calling you Monsieur Vigneras.'

'Habits can be broken.'

'All right. Goodbye.'

'Justin.'

'Justin.'

She did not cry until she reached the street, and then she couldn't stop herself. She hurried through the grey winter rain, her head ducked against the wind so no one would see her tears.

Justin was a man, and she was behaving like the adolescent she still was, offering him adulation, not daring to believe that it could be transformed into love.

—We do change, she thought, looking briefly from the piano to Emily's face, which was no longer closed but open, vulnerable, as she listened. She was not aware of Katherine's glance.

And Katherine realized that she had been playing, not what she had prepared for Felix, but the Franck.

Justin had understood even then that the frozen child, locked into idolatry, had the capacity to become a woman. It had taken a long time for the tight bud of love to open fully, but Justin had opened it and she was still reveling in the glorious process when they had so roughly been interrupted by the occupation of Paris.

Lukas von Hilpert, gentle and courteous and yet exigent, had said, 'Why do you freeze every time I touch you?'

'I've just been married. I'm a bride.'

'But not a woman?'

She flushed. 'Yes. I am a woman. And as a woman I made marriage vows and I intend to keep them.'

'That needn't and doesn't mean that you aren't as attracted to me as I am to you. War is unnatural. During times of war the old rules do not hold.'

'They do, for me.'

He, in turn, had become angry. 'Your virginal integrity is insufferable. I can take you if I want to. You have no choice.'

But he had not taken her. And the opening bud had remained unbruised, free to grow naturally.

--◦◦◦{ 6 }◦◦◦--

When she had finished the last notes of the Beethoven she realized that she was tired, and reached her arms over her head, rotating her neck slowly, doing the relaxing exercises Justin had taught her. As she turned her head she became aware of movement in one of the pews, and she saw that whoever was there was not Emily. She squinted against the light over the piano: Topaze was still there.

"Sorry, lady. Sorry to bother you."

She looked at him severely. "I am trying to practice for a concert."

His dark eyes filled with tears. "I just wanted to sit . . ."

"Very well, child, sit. But please be quiet." She did not mean to be unkind, but he disturbed her.

"My father's in jail."

"I'm sorry."

"Ma says he's no good. He did bad things. But he makes his confession to Bishop Bodeway. He made his confession before he went to jail."

"Topaze"—she tried to keep her voice kind; it must be dreadful for the Gomez children to have their father in jail—"I'm very sorry. But it's getting late and I don't have much more time . . ."

"Fatty told Mrs. Undercroft."

"Told Mrs. Undercroft what?" The child was making no sense.

"Who goes to confession. When. I wouldn't have told. Not that kind of thing. That's private. Sacred. Especially Pa. I wouldn't tell anybody anything about *you*. No matter for how much."

She did not know what he was driving at, but it was apparent that he was distressed, and that the distress went beyond his father's jail term. "Shouldn't you go home?" she suggested.

He shook his head. "Can't go till Ma's through at Ogilvie House. Fatty and me has to wait for her at night."

"Sit down, then."

"Topaze will be quiet. Will listen."

Determinedly she turned away from the child, to Beethoven, trying to find ways to make the intricacies of the music collaborate with the acoustics of the chapel, working and reworking phrases until sound and space united. She forgot Topaze.

A sharp noise startled her, probably a truck backfiring out on the street, she looked up. She did not see the child. Llew Owen was sitting in one of the pews, next to the Oriental bishop.

Llew rose. "Madame Vigneras, we didn't mean to disturb—"

Her back was tired. She needed to stand and stretch. "It's time for me to have a break. Where's Topaze?"

"I sent him off," Bishop Chan said.

Llew nodded. "He's very upset about Bishop Juxon. Ah, Madame, Merv would have loved the way you interpreted that sonata. Beethoven was his favorite."

The Chinese bishop rose. It was impossible to tell his age, but his skin was like parchment; he did not look well. "You have helped us all, Madame. Merv's murder was a great shock, and your presence and your playing have helped us to put it in perspective."

"Perspective," Llew said, "is something we don't have much of around here. At least I don't."

"Llew," the bishop warned softly.

There was a whiteness about the young organist's mouth and

nose. "Madame Vigneras, have you ever been somewhere you should not have been at a time when you should have been somewhere else, and against your will?"

"Often. I was in Poland when my husband died. I knew the end was near, though the doctors didn't, and neither Justin nor Jean Paul would let me cancel my tour. They were insistent that a concert tour behind the Iron Curtain was important. Maybe it was. I don't know."

Llew sighed. "I was hoping—"

The bishop, too, sighed, and sat down, almost hidden by the high wood of the pew.

Llew said, "Listening to you play—there was something so certain, as though you had no regrets."

Katherine looked at the young, pained face. "I'm not sure I do."

"But you just said—"

"Nobody can live as long as I have, or even as long as you have, without being somewhere when you want to be somewhere else. Or doing things you would never in the world have planned to do or wished to do. But when they're done, they're done. Regrets are useless."

Bishop Chan peered over the pew. "Are you listening?" he asked the organist.

Llew, neither turning nor acknowledging, asked Katherine, "And the people, then, who made you be places you didn't want to be—how do you feel about them?"

"Mostly they were seeing to it that I did my duty—unfashionable word, but I've learned not to take it lightly. Sometimes, if I thought they were wrong, I was angry. But there's no point in staying in anger. It becomes a festering sore."

"You didn't hate them?"

She asked, "Who do you hate, Llew?"

His voice was brittle. "There was a big diocesan service, one of our major events, all tied in with the UN and peace, and I know it was important—but I'm not the only organist in the world."

"What are you trying to tell me?"

"Dee—my wife—went into labor—two weeks early—the morning of the service. Bishop Undercroft said my place was at the Cathedral, that everything would be all right. And it wasn't. The baby—the baby wasn't right, and Dee—started to bleed—and they couldn't control it—and I wasn't with her, I was here, at the Cathedral—" He was choking on dry sobs.

Katherine did not move to touch him, but sat quietly at the piano, waiting.

"It was his fault." The words were muffled. "I could at least have been with her. I'll never forgive him."

"Or yourself?"

"Both of us. I wasn't there, and she died."

"I wasn't with Justin when he died. I knew he was ill, and I still went on with my work. I was in Poland. I know something of what you've been going through. As for Bishop Undercroft, I gather he was brought up in the British tradition, where the chief purpose of education is to train you to do what you have to do, when you have to do it, whether you want to or not. It isn't a bad tradition, you know." —Without it, how could I have gone on playing, giving that first concert after Michou's death? "It wasn't Bishop Undercroft's fault that things went wrong."

Llew was half kneeling, half sitting on the stone floor, and he put his head in her lap. She touched his fine, thick hair. "The doctors said it was something that no one could have predicted."

"Then let it go. Stop blaming. You have to get on with things. You *are* getting on. I have heard you play."

"I'm alive only when I'm at the organ. Everywhere else I'm lost. I want to kill someone, to—"

"That's all right at first," Katherine said, "but you can't let it go on too long. If you do, it will destroy your music, and you are not permitted to do that."

"Who won't permit me?"

"I, for one."

He laughed then, a strangled sound. "At least you didn't say God."

She continued to stroke the lustrous black hair. His head was heavy on her lap, and suddenly she realized that he had fallen asleep, there on the hard stone floor of St. Ansgar's chapel.

Bishop Chan emerged slowly from the pew. "Thank you, Madame. You've done more for Llew than the rest of us together."

"But I haven't—"

"You're Katherine Vigneras. He can hear a musician where he cannot hear a priest."

"He's asleep—"

"I'll wake him in a moment. He was holding vigil for Merv most of last night. You've been a catalytic agent among us, Madame. We get very lost in our own world, here on the Close, very ingrown." The bishop leaned down and touched Llew on the shoulder. "Son." Llew shuddered and opened his eyes. "We must leave Madame Vigneras to the piano."

The young organist sprang to his feet, looked around wildly. "What did I do? I dumped it all on you—"

Katherine spread out both her hands and made a gesture as though throwing. "There. I've dumped it on these stones where it can't hurt anyone. Let it go. Serve your music."

He nodded. "I'm tired of being told to serve God. Serving my music is something I understand."

"Isn't it the same thing?" Bishop Chan crossed to him. "Come."

- ·⊷❈{ 7 }❈⊶· -

As they were leaving, in trooped the Davidsons, all four, and Fatima Gomez. Jos approached her. "We're here to escort you to the Undercrofts'. We haven't been invited, as we're still considered children."

"Perhaps it's because there are so many of you?" Katherine suggested.

John said, "The Undercrofts have a maid as well as Mrs. Gomez. I think they could have coped. Mom can manage any number."

Tory shrugged. "Mom's used to it. And she doesn't much care what the food tastes like as long as there's plenty of it. People who don't have kids can't cope with numbers. Anyhow, Mrs. Undercroft said if it was only me, she'd invite me."

"Teacher's pet, as usual," Emily said.

Fatima sounded smug. "I'm going to be there. I always help out when there's company. I help serve at dinner, and then I help with the dishes."

"What about Topaze?" Emily asked.

"Ma says it's not man's work. Anyhow, I'm older than he is, and I need the money."

"Mrs. Gomez likes me," Tory said, "and she doesn't like most people."

"She can have you, as far as I'm concerned," Emily snapped.

John said, peaceably, "I don't want to go to the old dinner party anyhow. They'll do nothing but talk about a new suffragan and when to call Diocesan Convention."

Fatima ventured, "Perhaps Mrs. Undercroft will sing."

"Yuk," Emily said.

"Okay, kids," Jos reprimanded. "That's enough. Ready, Madame?"

As they left the ambulatory she glanced again at the high altar. Felix and Canon Dorsey were at either side of the coffin. The tall candle flames moved softly as though some interior breeze touched them. The two men were motionless, intent on prayer. Felix knelt with an air of quiet expectancy. Canon Dorsey was as still as a black marble statue. In the front row in the nave, Topaze was kneeling, his eyes dwelling on the great gold cross which hung over the high altar.

Tory said, "He's so pi it makes me want to puke."

Jos said, "His mother encourages it. She prays every day that he'll be a bishop."

Emily looked at Topaze dourly. "To Mrs. Gomez, being a bishop means having money."

John stood quietly looking at the altar and the coffin.

Katherine asked, "Is this—the vigil—held for everybody?"

"No," Emily said, "but it ought to be. When I die I don't want to be off in some funeral parlor. Quite a lot of churches in the diocese are doing it—candles and vigils and all. Uncle Bishop encouraged it when he was Diocesan, and Bishop Undercroft agrees. Of course, the undertakers' union is against it."

John said, "I still haven't quite taken it in. Bishop Juxon was alive, and then he was dead, without any warning, just because he was trying to help an old woman."

Emily's voice was suddenly brittle. "Things can be going along, and then all of a sudden everything is changed." Then, her voice quieter, "The old woman—we don't even know her name, and Bishop Juxon died for her."

A Concert in Munich

The Davidson contingent left Katherine at the door to Ogilvie House, which was opened by a maid in a grey uniform and white apron. Ogilvie House, like most of the buildings on the Close, was of stone, and impressive. Katherine was taken down a few steps into the living room. A beautiful Chinese fan was spread open in the fireplace. The great mullioned windows had window seats covered with unbleached linen cushions. The room was furnished in a felicitous combination of eighteenth-century English and Oriental.

Bishop Undercroft came hurrying to meet her. "Welcome, Madame! I think you will find it moderately cool here. Yolande has a weak chest, so we do use a modicum of air-conditioning."

Dean Davidson rose and held up a hand in greeting. Suzy was sitting on one of the cushioned window seats, one foot tucked under her, and Katherine wondered if she had picked up the position from Mimi. She, too, rose, and smiled in greeting. Mrs. Undercroft, dressed in white satin pants and a white embroidered Chinese top, came quickly across the room. Now that Katherine knew of her background, she was considerably more comprehensible. In any room her beauty would have been exotic, and it complemented the decor of the living room.

The maid offered Katherine an assortment of drinks from a

silver tray. She chose a dry sherry, and accepted a small plate of hors d'oeuvres from Fatima, who wore a frilly white apron and radiated self-importance. "I'd like a glass of water, too, please," Katherine said to the child. "Piano playing is thirsty work."

Fatima bobbed her clumsy curtsy, as though she had been paid a great compliment.

The bishop seated Katherine in a wing chair which had similar lines to her own favorite chair on Tenth Street, and she leaned back in it wearily. The bishop himself brought her a tall glass of water, with one cube of ice. "I remember that you don't like it too cold."

"That's very thoughtful of you. Thank you."

"I've gone to hear you several times with Felix, not only that first concert in San Francisco where we met. But there's something very different about being so close to you, in St. Ansgar's, from hearing you in a concert hall. I sat and listened for a while. It was magnificent."

"He was nearly in tears when he came home." Mrs. Undercroft put her hand protectively on her husband's arm. "I'm not sure I want you to make him unhappy."

"If the music made me sad, Madame, it was a joyous sadness."

She nodded. "I'm still experimenting with the acoustics—and with the Bösendorfer."

"Please feel free to come as often as you want. There will always be someone delighted to drive you. As I believe you know, Josiah is taking summer courses at N.Y.U.—he's a bright lad—and the organist at the Church of the Ascension, just up the street from you on Fifth, is a friend of Llew's, so he's in your neighborhood fairly often."

"Thank you. Once more will probably be sufficient. I haven't always had this much time before a concert with a new piano and a new room. When I was young, there was sometimes no more than half an hour before the performance."

"You've earned the right to as much time as you like. You are a great artist, and a remarkable woman."

Katherine smiled. "I do fairly well for an old woman."

"You are ageless. You see, Madame Vigneras, you have lived and suffered and rejoiced, and it's all there, in your face as well as your playing, and it is this quality of abundant life which is what draws me to people. Yolande, before she was twenty, had lived more terribly and more richly than most people in a lifetime. Merv had this quality, though very differently. But when he talked to anyone he was there completely, so whoever it was felt more alive. That's a rare gift. It would be my greatest joy if someone could say the same of me."

"There's a theory, which I take seriously," Katherine said, "that we live until we do whatever we're meant to do. Mozart started composing at an incredibly early age, and when he died young he had accomplished the purpose for which he was born."

Undercroft nodded. "And Conrad didn't start writing novels till he was nearly forty and died in his sixties. But what about you, Madame Vigneras? Surely you started your career as a young woman—"

"And here I am, an old one? I'm not sure I like what that implies."

"Bach, too, had a long career and a long life." The blue eyes smiled at her. "It may also mean that God has uses for you beyond your music."

Mrs. Undercroft summoned her husband, and the maid and Fatima brought around a tray of fresh hors d'oeuvres. More drinks were poured. Katherine leaned back in her chair and looked around the room. She looked at the pictures, and was sure that she saw a Seurat, a Mary Cassatt.

Felix, in a white cassock, entered and crossed to her chair. "Katya! I'm sorry I'm late. How was the practicing?"

She flexed her wrists and fingers. "Tiring. But it is a superb instrument."

He accepted a glass of sherry from the maid and followed her gaze. "That's a Philippa Hunter." It was a painting of an Alpine pasture with a spring sun slanting across drifts of snow in the shadows, and small flowers in the full light.

"Yes, I know." Katherine continued to look at it, enjoying the contrasts of light and shadow, spring, and the last snow of winter. "The portrait of Michou and me, over my mantel, is hers."

"Is it!" Felix exclaimed. "I thought it might be. How did—"

"She was a friend of Aunt Manya's."

"She knew everybody, didn't she? I count myself fortunate to have known your stepmother even slightly."

Katherine said, "She was wonderful. We had a closeness that

was possibly richer than if we had been biologically bound. But I gave her a lot of trouble in the beginning. I was an extraordinarily prickly adolescent."

"You always seemed to me to get along very well with each other."

"We did, by the time you and I met. She was one of the most generous human beings I have ever known."

"Doesn't Yolande remind you of her?"

Katherine considered. "I hadn't thought of it. I don't think so."

"They're both tall."

"Aunt Manya wasn't unusually tall."

"She seemed to be. And they both have black hair and what the romantic novelists call generous features."

Katherine glanced over at Mrs. Undercroft, who was talking with the dean. Manya Sergeievna could have been nothing but Russian; Yolande Undercroft—Yolande Xabo—was definitely Spanish-looking.

Felix said, "I don't mean to press the point. Manya Sergeievna had a great energy, a kind of cosmic energy; so did Yolande when she was working. How do you like Ogilvie House?"

"It's beautiful. And the pictures—isn't that a Georgia O'Keeffe?"

"It is. Allie has superb taste, and the pictures are an investment for him, as well as an example of his love of beauty." He glanced across the room. "I'm still sorry you had to hear about Allie and Isobel from Mimi. She and Iona have turned Isobel into some kind of saint."

"Not really," Katherine protested.

"Divorce is always ugly, but Allie and Isobel's was far less ugly than most."

She nodded. "I know what a strain the death of a child can put on a marriage."

"You do, don't you? And you and Justin had been married considerably longer than Allie and Isobel. It must have been hell, anyhow. Allie said people avoided them, after Ona's death; as though he and Isobel carried some kind of contagion. He would come to me, and I would try to comfort him, careful not to touch him. We should be allowed to touch each other without innuendo."

"Yes."

"We change, and the Church changes, too, and perhaps it has

swung too far. When I first was priested, you could be a murderer, confess, be absolved, and be welcome at the altar rail. But if you were divorced, you were forbidden. If my marriage had not been dissolved, I couldn't have become a priest, much less a bishop." He looked across the room again at Allie. "Iona Grady is a fine doctor, but—well, I just want you to know that tragedy changed and deepened Allie."

She tried to reassure him. "I really do understand that people change, as Wolfi said, not so much *from* who we are as *to* who we are."

Felix sighed. "Forgive me. We're all feeling fragile and vulnerable because of Merv's death, and the manner of it."

"Did he have a family?"

"No. But he'll be missed by many people. He was a superb confessor. It will be like the loss of a father to more people than I can count. We all carry a full load of counseling. That's another way I can help out—hearing confessions. It takes some of the burdens off the others. There's more and more demand for spiritual directors as the world keeps on getting more and more confused. Being able to make my own confession isn't always easy, and I firmly believe that no one should hear confessions who doesn't make confession. I have a superb spiritual director, Father Fieldstone, one of the Community of the Resurrection. But they're in England, and I don't travel much overseas any more, and he comes here only a couple of times a year, if that. If I'm in a bind I go to Mother Cat, and she is magnificent. But she, too, is overburdened. So now I am talking to you as my spiritual director, Katya. I never dreamed such a blessing would come to me." As she demurred he said, "I can tell you anything—anything about myself, that is. It's the burdens of others that weigh heavily on me. I try to do as John of Kronstadt advised, and hang them on the cross. If I have to carry everything around with me, it means I don't trust God. Sometimes I think that single-handedly I put more weight on the cross than . . ." His words drifted off. He seemed smaller and frailer than ever. He added hastily, "I've never heard those things that come up in plays or movies: should the priest tell that Jack the Ripper has confessed his crimes and so break the seal, or let him go on murdering . . ." He looked around as Fatima was passing more hors d'oeuvres and lowered his voice.

"That child always seems to be wandering around." His tone was irritable. Did he know that Fatima was some kind of spy, that Topaze made pocket money dispensing information? If the children had to wait for their mother before going home, no wonder they got into mischief. Nasty mischief.

—◦◦⟨ 2 ⟩◦◦—

At dinner Katherine was seated to the right of the bishop. At the other end of the table, Yolande ladled jellied madrilene from a silver tureen which sparkled with bright drops of condensation, handed the filled cups to Fatima, and watched her carefully as she served them. It took a certain amount of faith, Katherine thought, to permit the clumsy child to handle the delicate china.

Bishop Undercroft turned to Katherine. "It's generous of you to give us your time this evening. I know you must be tired."

"But now she needs time to relax," Felix said, "and to enjoy a good meal."

"I have to be careful," the younger bishop said, "or I could easily put on weight. Yolande has never had to worry; her tremendous energy burns up calories."

"Do you have to watch your weight, Katya?" Felix asked. "You don't seem to me to have changed any in all these years."

"I haven't much, though I do have to watch it," she admitted. "I've lost the slender waistline I was once so proud of. We tend to become pear-shaped as we grow older."

"Nonsense." Bishop Undercroft took a last swallow of soup. "You still have a splendid figure. Do you remember the old opera singers, male and female, who were mountains of flesh? I'll never forget my disappointment when, as a small child, I was taken to see *Siegfried*. Fafner was a puny and obviously *papier-mâché* dragon, but I still held my breath waiting for Brünnhilde to rise up out of the pyre at the end. And then, instead of a beautiful maiden emerging from the flames, there rose up a great fat cow. It finished opera for me for years."

Felix accepted a second bowl of madrilene. "Like Yolande, I've never had to worry. Although I don't think I could cope with the vast quantity of food those singers must have tucked away."

"In a sense I can understand it," Katherine said, refusing more soup, "at least the after-theatre suppers. One is always hungry after a performance, and it is a time to unwind, let go stress and strain. It's the most delightful and unhurried time of day when one is on tour."

Mrs. Gomez, both tall and muscular, carried in a silver platter which she set down in front of the bishop, and then gazed with small, olive-black eyes at the assembled company with a look of smug satisfaction. At close quarters Katherine saw that Fatima and her mother resembled each other. As far as beauty was concerned, Fatima did not have much to look forward to, though Mrs. Gomez's tight white uniform and short-cropped grizzled hair did nothing to soften her features.

Bishop Undercroft looked across the table at his wife, who was talking with Suzy Davidson. "I am often awed by the artistic temperament. It sometimes seems to me to be a battleground, a dark angel of destruction and a bright angel of creativity wrestling, and when the bright angel dominates, out comes a great work of art, a Michelangelo *David* or a Beethoven symphony."

"It's an interesting image," Katherine said, "but both my husband and my father produced their best work when their dark angel, as it were, was dominant. That is, when their moods were most black, the purest melody seemed to be released."

"And you?" the young bishop asked.

"I'm an interpreter. I, too, have my dark angels, but I can always balance them by someone else's joy, even though that joy, like some of Mozart's happiest work, may have been born out of darkness."

"You are so right," Bishop Undercroft admitted, "and perhaps my image was an oversimplification." Again he looked across the table at his wife, and it seemed to Katherine that he was seeing her dark angel in her dark Spanish eyes.

Yolande was saying to Suzy, "Fatima's voice has really come into its own this year. It's almost as amazing that she should be gifted with a beautiful voice as that her mother should be a gourmet cook."

"Another piece of evidence," the dean said, "that God is no respecter of persons." He stopped, as Fatima came in, passing around a tray of vegetables.

Katherine helped herself from the child's slightly wobbly tray. "You have a magnificent collection of paintings," she said to the young bishop, "all work by artists I especially admire."

"Collecting art is my weakness." He glanced at a Chinese scroll on the wall behind Yolande's head. "But no—the paintings are more than that for me; they are a form of prayer. When I am out of proportion—which, believe me, is a frequent state of mind for an overworked bishop—the pictures will usually restore me, particularly the O'Keeffe, and, perhaps even more deeply, the Hunter."

"Katherine has a Hunter," Felix said, "a superb one."

"Do you collect, too?" Bishop Undercroft asked her.

She shook her head. "My stepmother was one of the first to discover Philippa Hunter, and the picture I have is an early one, of me and my baby, where she was just discovering her amazing perception of shadow and brilliance."

"Shadow and brilliance," the young bishop repeated. "To continue my analogy, then, I wonder how much control we have over the battle of our angels? Van Gogh, for instance. Do you know, I still worry about Van Gogh because he never had the satisfaction, during his lifetime, of knowing that his work would mean what it does now, to countless people. What a terrible deprivation."

"And most artists," Felix added, "never know, consciously at any rate, whether it's the dark angel or the bright angel in ascendance."

Both bishops were thinking, Katherine was certain, not of Van Gogh or Michelangelo or Mozart, but of Yolande. "Perhaps it's really one angel?" she suggested. "I'd think it's most likely the same angel in different guises. At least, that's how it seemed to be with me, and with the artists I've been surrounded with all my life. My stepmother, Manya Sergeievna, had a most volatile temper. If anything went wrong backstage she would pour out her anger on the nearest stagehand, like an erupting volcano, and the next moment she would sweep on stage, radiating serenity, and holding the audience in the palm of her hand."

Felix turned his gaze from Yolande to Fatima going into the kitchen, nearly dropping her tray as she pushed through the swinging door. "Thus far," he mused, "I don't see in Fatima any signs of the artistic temperament, but perhaps it's hidden away somewhere, if Yolande is right about her voice." He sounded definitely dubious.

After dessert, a light-as-air soufflé, they returned to the living room for coffee. Yolande perched on the sofa beside Katherine.

"Dr. Oppenheimer has converted Allie and me to herb tea. So much better than all that caffeine. Dave likes his coffee, so I have it for him. I used to drink enormous quantities of coffee when I was singing. But of course one doesn't need chemical sources for adrenaline. Just let me get near a stage door and my adrenaline starts to pump. Was it that way for you?"

"Very much so."

"We're so pleased that you're doing the benefit. That will be a real boost to the building fund. Have you been through the Stone Yard?"

"Yes. Felix gave me a quick tour this afternoon."

"Oh, good. I know Allie's looking forward to giving you the grand tour himself. As an artist, you'll really appreciate it, you know. Did Felix tell you that one of the early apprentices, back when Dean Morton started it all, you know, is now a well-known sculptor? That bust of Allie in the front hall is hers. Did you notice it when you came in?"

"No. Sorry. But your pictures—they're incredible—"

Yolande rose, holding out her hand. "Do come see the bust. It's quite special."

Katherine let the younger woman help her up. The bust was, in fact, very fine. It was a strong face, done of the bishop at about the same age as Lukas had been when she first knew him. The mouth was sensitive and compassionate, and the eyes showed a quick intelligence, and a humor she had not yet seen in the bishop. "Yes, it is a splendid piece of work. I can understand how much it means to you."

"And here"—Mrs. Undercroft opened a door to the left of the entrance—"is our chapel. Sometimes Allie celebrates the—you know—the Holy Mysteries for me here."

Katherine looked into a small white chapel, with a simple altar, candles, a small crucifix. There was a prie-dieu, and chairs for half a dozen people. The simplicity of the room should have given a sense of quiet, but it did not, and she was not sure why. There was no peace in Yolande Undercroft as she looked fixedly toward the crucifix; instead, Katherine felt distress from the younger woman, feelings still acutely unresolved.

Mrs. Undercroft broke the silence. "I often come here to pray, alone, you know. I was here when I knew that Merv was going to die. Sometimes I can see past the veil, and it is a gift which brings more pain than joy. Merv's death has really shaken Allie. And it is a terrible loss to me, you know. I could talk to Merv. Like me, he had a terrible background, a background alien to all that those born and brought up in this country can ever understand. He understood me, all my anxieties and uncertainties. And guilt—oh, I was so close, you know, so close to being able to unburden myself to him. I'm not sure how long I can go on carrying it alone—I'm not strong enough—why couldn't Chan have died instead? He's half dead with emphysema anyhow—not that I wish him, you know, ill, but Merv—Jesus, what a loss."

"I'm sorry," Katherine murmured lamely.

Yolande seemed wound up like a steel spring. "And Allie—he works so hard. When I complain about my awful childhood I have to remember that his wasn't easy, either—though he always had enough to eat. But his mother was frequently ill, or thought she was, and his father traveled a lot. And then they died and he had that hellish boarding-school experience. English schoolboys are unmerciful bullies. The privileged are cruel. And he spent the holidays with some distant relative of his mother's who, ultimately, left him her money and her name. Undercroft. It's a good name for a bishop."

"It isn't his real name?"

"It's real enough legally. She didn't have any children, and the name would have died out with her. Poor Allie, there's always a line of stress between his eyes. I, too, know what it's like to, you know, work under stress. Strange—the pressures put on a bishop and those put on an artist are not dissimilar."

"I'm sorry," Katherine said. "I've spent so much of my life abroad that I've never heard you sing."

Yolande shrugged slightly. "I didn't have much of a voice, but I did have a presence. Singing—God gave me the ability to put over a song. But there are other things, oh, things more difficult. Knowing things which must be done. And I see things I would rather not see. I saw Merv—and the old woman—and the gun. I told Allie, because I didn't want it to be too much of a shock for him. I thought it would be better if I—you know—warned him . . ."

Katherine continued to regard the younger woman. There was no harshness in her face now, and Katherine felt a tremendous pity for her.

Yolande turned her gaze from the crucifix. Her voice was tired, as though something in her, some spring, had wound down. "We'd better get back to the others. They'll be wondering. I don't know what I'd do if I couldn't come in here to the chapel. Jesus had heavy burdens, too. He knew things that other people didn't know. That helps. And he was kind to women who had been overlavish in love. That was, you know, unusual. Still is." She made a deep genuflection, crossed herself dramatically, and led Katherine back to the living room.

She sat on a low sofa and indicated that Katherine was to sit with her. "Allie rescued me. I was in bondage to my work, to my public. It is one thing to be given a gift, another to be a slave. Do you miss all the travel?"

Katherine replied, "Not the airports. Certainly not, in this country, O'Hare or Atlanta."

Mrs. Undercroft gave a small screech of appreciation. "God, I hated them! Every year travel gets more complicated and uncomfortable. Added to that, my manager, my producers—they all thought of me as theirs, their, you know, chattel. They used me, my talent, to serve their own greeds and their own lusts. I never even knew that love existed until Allie. Your Justin loved you?"

"Yes."

"I envy you. A long, faithful marriage. I hope that Allie and I will have that, though we began later than most."

"War interrupted us," Katherine said. "So, though I was very young when we actually married, we were apart for the entire war."

"The Second World War? Yes. That seems so long ago. It must seem strange to you that it didn't touch my life at all. But I was born in—South America, far away from all your wars. Then, when I was hardly more than a child it was discovered that I had a gift with music and my own—you know—presence. I'm not sure exactly what happens, but when I get in front of an audience, it is as though lightning enters my body, and the electricity is visible—" She paused to light a cigarette and Katherine's sensitive nostrils quivered. Surely if Yolande had a weak chest she should not smoke. "You say you never heard me sing. I've never heard you play. But from what Allie says—does that happen with you?"

"Something like that, when it's at its best."

"That's why I always had an audience when I did TV. But even then, you know, when millions were screaming to hear me when I was at Madison Square Garden, I was still not myself. I was still someone being used for other people's purposes. I'm often asked if I miss the excitement and adulation. Sure—being adored is a kind of addiction, I'm the first to admit it. But what I have with Allie is far more than all the worship the crowds gave me. Allie loves me. I had never been loved before. I didn't even know I was someone who could be loved until Allie gave me myself. Do you mind my telling you all this—I know I've monopolized you tonight, and I've hardly let you get a word in edgewise—but I had a feeling that you knew—you know—only what you might have heard about me from other people. And somehow I wanted to tell you myself. I'm sorry—I hope you don't mind—"

"Of course not. I appreciate it."

"You've been a wonderful listener. And Allie and I are grateful to you for being here to help take care of Felix."

"I'm afraid I'm not much help."

"Oh, yes, he can talk to you. You're a link with the past, you know, someone who has the same memories. Old Felix has a lot to come to terms with in his not-so-saintly past. He has not always been a good influence on Allie. You help keep him occupied, and I thank you for that."

"I'm glad to be of some small help." Katherine did not like the way the bishop's wife talked about Felix. "He's most appreciative of all your husband does for him."

"He does do a great deal," Yolande agreed. "Far more than is expected or warranted. But then, Allie is willing to take on burdens other people would not support. Allie gets so tired, and then I'm the one who has to try to put him back, you know, together again. Forgive me, hon, for bending your ear this way. And now I'd better pay attention to the rest of the guests."

─··◄{ 3 }►··─

The dean came over to Katherine, carrying a steaming cup of coffee, and asked her about the Bösendorfer, and then suggested that he and Suzy drive her home. "It's a beautiful evening, and Suzy and I enjoy a chance to drive through the park. It will be a respite for me, as I'll be holding vigil for Merv most of the night. And then the funeral is tomorrow."

The bishop rose then and clapped his hands for attention. "Would you like to have Yolande sing before you leave?"

There were polite murmurs of assent.

Yolande uncoiled herself from the sofa and stood at the top of the steps that led down from the large hall to the living room. The bishop went to a hi-fi set and put on a record. Music poured out at them—assailed them—from several loudspeakers, so that they were encased in blaring sound. Drums. Marimbas. Amplified guitars. South American music with pulsing rhythms.

At the top of the steps Yolande began to sway to the beat. Then she started to sing. Her voice was hoarse, but it still had power. She started singing beneath the music, the soft Spanish words nevertheless completely audible. Then, as she slowly increased the volume, she increased her body movements. The drums began to beat wildly, and Yolande's voice rose above the beat. She still had an extraordinary range, from deep contralto to the highest coloratura, and if it was more than slightly strained it was still an amazing instrument. Now she was singing about death, a poignant mourning song. And yet, as Mimi had said, there was something comforting about it. Through the grief came a promise of comfort.

The dean and his wife were sitting side by side, staring down. Felix was standing, gazing into the fireplace. Bishop Undercroft, looking at his wife, was adjusting the volume of the record. In the hall behind Yolande, Fatima hovered, in rapt adoration. Behind the child stood Mrs. Gomez and the maid.

Yolande's voice rose in a controlled scream. She slumped, and turned the slump into a deep bow. The bishop raised the needle from the record and everybody applauded. Mrs. Gomez clapped her hands together stolidly. Then she nodded at Fatima and the maid and led them back to the kitchen.

Yolande bowed again and came down the steps to the living room. The bishop took her hands. "Thank you, my dear. Thank you for singing that song for Merv." He looked at Katherine, expectantly.

She sat straight in the chair. "I can understand why Mrs. Undercroft had such a following."

"Yolande Xabo," the bishop corrected. "She drew thousands to her concerts, with people standing out on the streets."

Yolande looked down deprecatingly. "I don't have much voice left. A voice goes long before the music does. A singer's career is, you know, necessarily short."

Katherine looked pointedly at the nicotine-stained fingers, and saw that Yolande, too, was waiting for her to say something, that it mattered. She tried, "You still understand the music, and you make the audience understand it. Piaf sang, and moved audiences, long after her voice was beyond its chronological prime. It is the capacity to touch people that matters."

"P—" Yolande asked.

"Edith Piaf. A French singer, a child of the streets who was wonderfully poignant."

"I'm afraid I didn't—" She came close to Katherine, asking in a low voice, "You really liked it?"

Liked was not exactly the word. It was not Katherine's kind of music, any more than rock had been. "It was kind of you to sing especially for Bishop Juxon. I think everybody appreciated it very much indeed—it was a comfort."

Yolande accepted that. "When I first met Allie—long before we were married—I was young. You know, an adolescent. I started singing professionally when I was thirteen. You pretty well missed the sixties, didn't you?"

What did the sixties have to do with it? Was Yolande already singing then? If she started at thirteen, it was possible. "Not entirely. I was here one year playing with the Philharmonic, and a group of actors and musicians held a peace vigil around the fountain in front of the Plaza. We all carried candles, and it was very quiet and what you might call undemonstrative. Erlend and I were barely middle-aged, then, but we were by far the oldest people there, and I think the young ones appreciated our presence."

"Erl—"

"Erlend Nikulaussen, who was guest conductor at the Philharmonic for a series of Beethoven concerti." As Yolande looked blank, she explained, "He was a well-known conductor, half Norwegian, half Finnish, and a descendant of Sibelius."

"And you were close friends?"

"I became good friends with many conductors, most of them now dead. The music world is small, and we make some deep friendships through music. Erlend and I were both certainly anti-war—particularly one as ambiguous as the Vietnam one seemed to be—our own was bad enough, but it wasn't ambiguous. However, it made us more than willing to add our silent protest. Then some troublemaker shouted out that foreigners had no business there, and I in my naïve idiocy waved my American passport and might well have lost it if some hefty tympanists hadn't surrounded Erlend and me and wafted us away, and before we knew it we were in the Palm Court of the Plaza drinking hot buttered rum."

"How casually you say that—the Palm Court and all the taken-for-granted perks of the privileged."

"I don't think we took them for granted," Katherine murmured, —and surely you can have all the perks *you* want? Why do you still sound so wistful?

"I hated my conductors," Yolande said. "All they wanted was my—you know—body, and they were jealous of my music. How different the world of your kind of music must be."

"There's plenty of jealousy in the world of classical music, too," Katherine said.

--⋅⊰{ 4 }⊱⋅--

Driving home with the Davidsons was certainly pleasanter than a taxi, and the springs of the Saab were in fairly good condition.

Suzy leaned forward. "What did you think of Yolande's singing?"

Katherine replied carefully. "It is not a kind of music with which

I am familiar, and surely she should not smoke if she has a weak chest?"

Suzy said, "I gather that she had asthma as a child. The early medication for asthma was made up into a kind of cigarette, and while that has not been used in the United States for years, it was standard treatment wherever it was in South America that Yolande grew up. Allie has tried to get her to stop smoking, and I think she would like to, but she got hooked early. Having once been an avid smoker myself in the days of my rebellious youth, I have a certain sympathy. I still miss it. But she's been smoking more the past couple of years than she used to."

The dean said, "Hearing her did give you an idea of how she must have mesmerized crowds."

"Indeed it did."

Suzy said, "If I were her doctor, I'd prescribe that she see Bishop Chan at least twice a day—although he was never a smoker, ironically. It meant a lot to Yolande to sing for us the way she did tonight. And she's generous in many ways—with the Gomez children, for instance; she's paying for Fatima's remedial work this summer as well as for their regular tuition. And she didn't stash up the millions she should have. Most of the money went to the crooks who managed her, and when she got out of their clutches they kept everything that should have gone to her. Allie got a lawyer, but they had even cleverer and more ruthless lawyers. Allie inherited a little money, and a bishop's salary is not small pickings, but they aren't rolling in gold the way people assume they are."

"Bravo," the dean said.

"Well, I try to be fair. Most of the time. I'm not happy about Yolande's hold over Tory."

"Do you exaggerate it?"

"I don't think so. Tory absolutely idolizes her. And I suppose Yolande makes me feel guilty for not being home when our kids get out of school. I do *not* like to think of her as a substitute mother for my baby."

"I doubt if Yolande thinks of it like that," the dean said. "At least half a dozen of Tory's classmates are there nearly every day for tea, and I think she enjoys being a kind of goddess to the kids, now that she no longer has her adoring public. It's harmless enough. And just as Emily has seen through the glitter and stopped being part of the group, so, too, will Tory, when she's a little older."

"You're probably right. It's my own guilt feelings . . ."

"Nonsense," the dean said. "By the way, Madame Vigneras, you do know that Emily took you seriously when you offered to hear her play?"

"I offered seriously," Katherine said.

"We do thank you." Again Suzy leaned over the seat. "She's working hard on a little program. I've persuaded her to keep it short."

"She's talented, isn't she?" The kind of drive Katherine felt in Emily occasionally accompanied a second-rate talent, and when that happened, it usually brought disaster.

"We hope so," Suzy said, "but piano got short shrift in her life until after her accident—Mimi told you?"

"Yes. She has a lot of courage, your child."

Suzy nodded. "She's stubborn as a mule. That can sometimes be an asset."

"All inherited from her mother," the dean assured Katherine. "Tory may look like Suzy, but Em's the one who can be pig-headed."

"And thank you very much, kind sir. I always knew you appreciated me."

"You have to have all the faults as well as all the virtues of stubbornness to stay married to me. Anybody else would have abandoned me long ago."

Katherine liked them. There was warm affection between them as well as love. They were good companions. As she and Justin had been. Liking the same books, the same plays, the same people. Even the note of criticism in Suzy's voice as she talked about Yolande Undercroft was a revealing that she was totally human.

"By the way," Suzy said. "We have a family tradition that on the first Sunday evening of the month everybody stays home, we have dinner together, and then we—or at least some of us—make music. Felix is usually with us. You've just missed the first Sunday in June—possibly lucky for you—but we'd love to have you come for our July music-making. Mimi sometimes manages to survive our noise, and we'll ask her to bring you, if you'd like."

"I'd like very much," Katherine said.

At that the dean bellowed with laughter. "I hope you'll be able to stand it. We are always loud and sometimes we don't play together. You can imagine what it sounds like when I finish three measures ahead of everyone else?"

"I can see that it takes talent." Katherine smiled. "I have a feeling that it will sound familiar to me. We used to have musical evenings, too. My son had a lovely voice, and a talent for the violin. He died before we knew whether or not he would have been as gifted a musician as your John." —*And John tears my heart, because I cannot look at him without thinking of Michou.*

She and Justin had been determined not to push Michou; they had dissuaded his teacher from putting him on the concert platform as a child prodigy, insisting that it was better to wait for his talent to mature. She still thought that they were right in having given him a far more normal childhood than he could have had if he had started playing in public. "Justin and I used to sing opera —you should have heard us do Aïda and Radames. Mimi and Rodolfo were in our repertoire, too. Occasionally, when I was on tour, we used to drive instead of taking trains or planes, and we sang the miles away—I might add that neither of us had any singing voice whatsoever. A kind of alto is the best you could call me. I'm not saying what kind."

Suzy and the dean joined in her laughter. Dave said, "We're not quite that elevated."

"I'd hardly call it elevated. We were just in the habit of memorizing music and it came easily to us. I do look forward to Sunday. I love the English horn. I'm not a Wagner buff, but the horn solo in the prelude to the third act of *Tristan* always gives me chills with its haunting loveliness."

"It's one of Dave's best pieces," Suzy agreed.

"And John—I do look forward to hearing John."

"John's good." There was assurance and pride in the dean's voice. "He's also fallen head over heels in love with you. You're an excellent example for him."

"I think I've fallen head over heels in love with John, too," Katherine said. "He's going to be spectacularly handsome, which will do him no harm on the concert platform."

"Thank God he doesn't realize it," Suzy said. "That he's handsome, I mean. He keeps thinking his dark eyebrows and lashes are weird, as he calls them. I don't disabuse him. He knows he's talented, and that's enough for a young adolescent to know about himself."

At Tenth Street, the dean helped her up the steps and made sure that she was in the apartment, and that the lights were on, before he bade her good night.

--◦❧{ 5 }❧◦--

It had been an interesting evening, but she was tired, and moved gratefully into her bedtime routine. The bath water was less muddy than usual, and she lay back, relaxing in the scented warmth, letting her mind drift into free fall.

Yolande Undercroft. Yolande Xabo, singer. Manya Sergeievna. Manya had had an enormous following, too, though probably nothing like Yolande's. Why is it that a serious artist never gets the . . . *Tant pis*. Never mind. Manya had flowers after every performance, so that the apartment always smelled like a hothouse. And Manya had been a star, in every way. She moved with the assurance of a star. The plaudits never surprised her. A rare bad notice brought out a stream of Russian oaths. But her angers never lasted. She was generous of heart. Generous to Katherine when the child, still grieving for her mother, did not know how to return Manya's love. Generous to her as an adult. A warm and loving grandmother to the children, and especially to Julie, after Michou's death, when Katherine's own shock and grief were so great that it was a barrier between her and Julie, even when she rocked the little girl, tried to dry the child's tears, her own eyes tearless, dry as sand.

Manya had always been there to help, to pull the strings necessary to get Katherine out of that prison in Paris, out of France; to fly—once that became the usual mode of travel—to Katherine and Justin whenever she was needed. Only once, and that was the last time, had Manya asked, instead of given.

The overseas call had come early one morning when Katherine was at home in Paris for a few weeks. Nanette had called her to the phone, looking anxious. "Madame, for you."

The voice on the phone was faint, not the wind-filled, echoing faintness which sometimes accompanies overseas calls, but faint in itself. At first, Katherine had no idea who it was; then, 'Aunt Manya! What's wrong?'

'I'm not well, Katya. I'm not well.'

Manya Sergeievna was always well. Katherine could not imagine her except bursting with vitality. Even after Thomas Forrester's death, the actress's passionate grieving had been suffused with life.

But the thin, frightened voice repeated. 'I'm not well.'

'Do you want me to come?' Katherine asked automatically, then realized that Manya, always ready to come to Katherine in any emergency, to change plans, postpone openings, would never herself ask for help; so she said, 'I'm coming Aunt Manya,' understanding with a sense of shock that Manya must be desperate to call at all, to admit weakness. 'Jean Paul will get me on a plane tomorrow,'

'But Julie—' There was little protest in the trembling voice.

'Nanette is here. And Justin.'

She wanted Justin to come with her. She knew that Manya was dying and she was afraid. But Justin was in the midst of some recordings, and Julie, who adored her "Mamushka," would need one of her parents at home. So she caught an early flight the next day. Justin had called ahead, and the farmer who took care of the few animals Manya still had on the farm met her at the airport. 'She's very bad,' he said, his face lined with grief as well as work and age. 'But she's waiting for you. She won't go till you come.'

There was a nurse in a white uniform and cap. She, too, said that Manya was waiting. 'They often do, you know.'

'I didn't even know she was ill,' Katherine said helplessly.

'She didn't want you to worry. And it's gone more quickly than any of us thought . . .'

The great bed in which Manya had continued to sleep after her husband's death was made up, empty. A hospital bed was by the long windows which looked into the woods. A hanging candle gave a soft light on the icon in the corner.

Katherine scarcely recognized the shrunken body lying propped up against the pillows. Manya had lost weight, radically, so that she was as thin as Justin after Auschwitz. Her skin was yellowed and wrinkled. But a smile of absolute delight irradiated her face as she saw Katherine, and she stretched out her arms, so thin that they were only bones with dry flesh hanging from them. But the smile was so brilliant that all else faded and Katherine ran to her stepmother. Was she holding Manya, or was Manya holding her?

'Child of my heart,' Manya said.

Katherine could only murmur, 'Manya, Aunt Manya . . .'

The old woman had talked, then, brokenly, often difficult to hear, about Thomas Forrester, about her life in the theatre. 'Jealousy—it is the ugliest of all human emotions. God has kept me from it. And Tom. And then, I have been practical. I never had on the stage with me any young woman who could replace me, overshadow me. I have seen what that can do to a star. Once a young actress tried to . . . and I fired her. To try to get to the top by leaving bloody bodies under your feet is not . . . and I never . . .'

'Of course you never,' Katherine reassured.

'You will be hated—' Manya's thin fingers clutched at her. 'You will be hated for what you are and who you are and I cannot protect you.'

'But you have, over and over again.' Katherine stroked the thin hand.

'You are not jealous, thank God you are not, but you will suffer from the jealousy of other . . .'

Katherine began to smooth the thin, white hair, softly stroking it back from the old woman's feverish brow.

'I do not want you to suffer from the green bile of jealousy . . .' Manya's voice was so low that Katherine had to bend over to hear. 'I would protect you. But we cannot protect those we love. All I can do is warn you. You have been hurt from sick jealousy; and you will be hurt again, and the worst will be when you are old . . .'

Katherine turned from her stepmother to the present, to the tub which was relaxing her tired muscles. She drew some more hot water, and leaned back again. Manya had frequently talked of her paranormal gifts (another reminder of Yolande?), but there had been no evidence of them until that night of her death. As for jealousy—yes, there had been plenty. And it had been bad. And Manya had still been alive for the worst of it; what more could come, now?

There was the rainy night when a younger artist had followed her out the stage door after a performance and pushed her, so that she fell (accidentally) on the slippery iron steps, hit her head on the cement, and lost consciousness. When she awoke, two days later, in the high white bed of a hospital in a strange city, Justin was sitting by her, had been sitting by her until she came out of the shock of severe concussion, his face haggard, his unshaven jowls bristly. How tender he had been, how gentle—until she was out of danger, at which point he became furious with her for having been hurt, for having put him through so much anxiety.

'It is typical of men,' Manya had said, after flying to Paris to meet them. 'They are always furious with us if we sneeze. Pay no attention to him.'

Far worse had been something which happened less than a year after Michou's death. Manya had been with them, on a brief visit after the close of a play, and before starting rehearsals for a new one. It had been in December, a few weeks before Christmas. Presents from family and close friends were saved, to put under the tree; they were trying to keep Christmas happy for Julie's sake; Wolfi would come for Epiphany and the gifts of the Magi, but there had always been a tree for the children, and surely Julie deserved presents and music and laughter.

Gifts from anonymous admirers Katherine had learned to open ahead of time, after receiving an emerald necklace which she had had a hard time returning to the donor. Nanette brought the mail into the bedroom each morning while Katherine and Justin were having breakfast; Manya ate in her room, in bed, not joining them till lunch. Before Christmas, the mail was always heavy. There were several packages which were obviously books, and she opened them, keeping the cards and addresses aside for thank-you notes. There was another parcel, the size of a shoebox, and this she opened. It was, in fact, under the outer wrappings, a shoebox. She took off the lid, pulled aside the tissue paper. And there was a white rat. Dead.

Utter horror.

Nanette had snatched away the box and its contents. Manya, hearing the noise, had come running, had held Katherine as though she were a baby, while Justin took Julie to the park so that she would not know what had happened, so that the ugliness would leave no mark on the child.

'You are very much loved,' Manya had said, pressing Katherine close, 'and where there is much love, there is, always, hate. But the love is greater, Katya, much greater. Never forget that.'

Somehow Manya brought back sanity, and the horror receded. 'There are sick people in the world, but they are to be pitied. And those of us who are able to love must return the sickness with healing; that is the gift of the artist.'

Manya could not have forgotten those episodes, even in the weakness of her illness. But her urgent warning was about something else, something to come. Thus far, Katherine thought, her old age was being peaceful and pleasant. Her friendship with Mimi, with Felix, her growing friendship with the Davidsons and the Undercrofts, these were keeping things interesting. Heretofore her friends—with the exception of Wolfi—had been professional artists. It was amusing now to meet completely different people, to enlarge her horizons. She could not remember a time when life had not been interesting. Even in the midst of grief it had been interesting.

Her mind drifted back to the house in Connecticut and to the dying old woman.

The late afternoon sun slanted through the trees and across the hospital bed, touching Manya's face, which was still beautiful; the wrinkles seemed to have been smoothed away, and only the purity of the bone structure showed. 'I have been able to come to you, and to love you, but I cannot protect you from jealousy,' the old woman had murmured, and then she shifted position, trying to sit up, and Katherine held her, supporting the thin frame. *'My soul is getting stronger every day.'* Now Manya's voice was clear. *'Now I know, now I understand, Kostya, that in our work—in acting or writing—what matters is not fame, not glory, not what I dreamed of, but knowing how to be patient* . . . Do you remember? Nina. Nina in *The Sea Gull,* my first major role . . . *knowing how to be patient. To bear one's cross and have faith. I have faith, and it all doesn't hurt so much. And when I think of my vocation, I am not afraid of life.'* The voice faded out, but the old woman's arms tightened about Katherine, and they continued to embrace, and love flowed between and through them, stronger than electricity.

It did not cease abruptly, like a light switch turned off; it faded slowly, gently. And then Manya was heavy in Katherine's arms.

6

For Katherine, the memory of Manya's death was a memory of love, love tangible as the sunlight that had fallen across the bed. As she pulled herself out of the tub and slipped into her terry robe, all she felt was love, and the echo of Nina's words. She was in her nightgown and brushing her hair when the phone rang. She reached for it. "Hello?"

"Madame Vigneras."

"Yes, speaking." And then the doorbell rang. Mimi was in Boston with Iona. Who on earth, at this time of night—

"Excuse me," she said to the caller, "while I answer the door. I'll be right back." She slipped on a light robe and started toward the living room. "Who is it?" she called through the door.

"It's Dorcas—Dorcas Gibson from downstairs. Please let me in."

Katherine opened the door and was startled by Dorcas's ravaged, tearstained face. "I'm sorry, I'm sorry," Dorcas started to say, and began to weep.

"Sit down, child," Katherine ordered. "There's someone on the phone. I'll be right back to you." She returned to the bedroom and picked up the phone again. "I'm sorry to keep you waiting, but the doorbell—"

An unfamiliar, grating voice said, "Don't think you can get away from us like that, Madame Vigneras. We know all about you and your—shall we call it unusual—sex life."

She was frozen on the side of the bed, still holding the phone to her ear.

"Oh, yes, we know all about you and Dr. Oppenheimer. And we know that you were Bishop Bodeway's mistress . . ."

Released from paralysis, she slammed down the phone. For a moment she sat on the edge of the bed, trembling with shock and disbelief. The call could not have caught her at a more sensitive moment. Half of her mind was still with remembered jealousies, with Manya's warning—

She remembered Dorcas.

Walking slowly, because her limbs were trembling, although this phone call was no more than an idiocy, a mere nothing, she returned to the living room. Dorcas was curled up on the sofa. She had stopped her uncontrollable weeping, and held a wet ball of a handkerchief.

"Sorry to keep you waiting." Katherine's voice was automatically courteous, but she was not yet completely aware of the child. "What's the matter?"

Dorcas hiccuped. "I'm sorry to bother you like this, but your lights were on, and I knew you weren't asleep, and I had to get away. I walked and walked, and I might have tried just to go to sleep on a bench in the Square, but I was afraid it might not be good for the baby, and I couldn't go home, and I didn't know where to go, my parents are dead and my sister lives in California—" She ran out of breath.

"But what's the matter?" Katherine reiterated.

"Terry—my husband—"

"Yes?"

"He's been having an affair."

Still caught in the cloud of memories, followed by the unidentified phone caller, Katherine simply looked at the girl.

"With a man," Dorcas finished, and began again to cry.

—Oh, God, I've had enough emotion for one evening. "Do you want to tell me about it?" Not wanting to hear, and yet unable to reject the child, whose belly was swollen with the fruit of what had certainly seemed to be the love of two people.

"Everybody in the company thought we were the ideal couple—and I thought so, too—"

—Here we go again, Katherine thought, —with that nonexistent ideal couple.

"He's a dancer in the company—not Terry, but Ric. He's one of the tallest men in the company, and he's beautiful, but I didn't know—he has a wife, and June's nice. We all like her. And they have two kids. So it never occurred to me that he—it's all such a stupid, dirty mess." She wiped at her face with her tear-drenched handkerchief. Katherine went into the bathroom and returned with a box of tissues.

"Dorcas, if I sound unsympathetic, or strained, that phone call which came just when you rang the doorbell was what I suppose you might call a poison-pen call, accusing me of abnormal sexual relationships. People seem to want to define others only in terms of their sexual activity, and I find that highly distasteful. I do not wish to be defined by gender or genitals. I am a pianist. You are a dancer. What does your husband do?"

"He's a lawyer."

"Obviously a successful one. I charge you the limit for that garden apartment."

Dorcas gave a strangled sound that was half sob, half laugh. "He specializes in marital counseling."

"How long have you been married?"

"Two years."

"Have they been good?"

"Marvelous—mostly. I thought he loved me."

Katherine asked, "What makes you think that he doesn't love you now?"

"Well—sometimes he's been terribly late coming home—too often, lately—and now, he and Ric—"

Katherine closed her eyes. She felt weary in every bone of her body. She had enough to do to come to terms with her own experiences, without being drawn into the grief and shock of this strange child. Perhaps Jean Paul was right and she should not have come to New York; she should have stayed with her own kind of people. "Is this habitual?"

"Sorry?"

"Is this the first time?"

"I don't know." The young woman reached for the box of Kleenex and dabbed at a fresh flow of tears.

"Dorcas, no two people are ever totally faithful to each other, and physical infidelity is not necessarily the worst kind." Dear Lord, I sound like a ruddy psychiatrist.

"What's worse?" Dorcas looked up.

"How about alcoholism?"

"Well, maybe. But with Ric!"

"Would you have preferred it to be with a woman?"

"I think maybe it would have been less humiliating."

"What about you, right now?" Katherine asked.

"What about me, what?"

"You're pregnant. Is your sex life going on as usual?" —I hate this. It's waking memories I'm not ready for yet. I want to go to bed.

"Well, not quite. I had a little show of blood, and my obstetrician told me not to, for a few weeks."

"Could that at least partly explain it?"

"I want to make love, too! The doctor said not to. I miss it as much as Terry does, and it's his baby as much as mine."

"Not right now, it isn't. The baby's in your body, not his. It's an intimacy no man is privileged to know."

"Woman's lib wouldn't like that."

"Do I strike you as being unliberated?"

"No."

"I had two children. I'm not talking out of thin air. After the baby is born, or maybe during the birth, if your husband is with you, as Justin was with me when Julie was born, then it will become his baby as much as yours. But for these months of pregnancy, that's not so."

"Ric's wife isn't pregnant."

"How does she feel about it?"

"I don't suppose she knows."

"And you?"

"I went up to watch the rehearsal of a new ballet this afternoon. I'll be dancing in it after—but somehow I couldn't stay. Terry thought I'd be gone all afternoon, but I came home after only an hour, and there they were . . ."

"And?"

"I could have killed them."

"That's a good, healthy reaction."

"It's a lousy way to end a marriage. I never thought I'd say—so soon, and carrying our baby—that the marriage is over." The girl looked at Katherine, expectantly, waiting.

At last Katherine sighed and said, "What do you mean, 'the marriage is over'? There are at least half a dozen times in any good long-term marriage when 'the marriage is over.' Marriage, like the rest of life, has stages. At the end of one stage, that part of the marriage is over, and you move on to the next."

"Or," Dorcas said flatly, "you quit. If you think it's really all over."

Katherine spoke impatiently. "Of course it's all over. It has to be all over before you're free to move on to the next stage. If you want to."

"Why would I want to? What possible kind of next stage can there be for Terry and me?"

"That you'll have to find out for yourself. I don't know Terry. But maybe you can both do some real growing over this. Maybe you can begin to learn what love is all about."

Dorcas pushed back her long chestnut hair and looked at Katherine. "How?"

Katherine dropped her hands in her lap. "Child, a marriage is something that has to be worked at, and too many people give up just at the point where their love could begin to grow."

"Your marriage—"

"It had to be worked at. Hard. Nothing good ever comes free. When you're dancing you have to go to classes, you have to work every day, don't you?"

"Yes, of course."

"Do you think a marriage should be any easier than dancing?"

"I hadn't thought of it that way."

"The greater the thing we want, the higher the price."

Dorcas rubbed one hand absently over her swollen belly. "What I told you about Terry and Ric—you're not shocked."

"Child, I've seen enough of human nature so that I'm not easily shocked."

"But—you had a perfect marriage, didn't you?"

Katherine stirred wearily. "There is no such thing. I don't know where all these extraordinary expectations of marriage have come from. I think we were more realistic in my day. People always hurt and betray each other. It's inevitable. It's what you do with that pain which makes a marriage good or bad. Ours was good."

"How—how did you betray each other?"

—I was whole, and I had the piano career Justin could not have. And he betrayed me by being castrated in one of the 'medical experiments' in Auschwitz.

Aloud, she said, "That is something which should be private between two people."

"I'm sorry. And I've just dumped all my private junk right in your lap. But now—oh, please—what should I do?"

Katherine rose stiffly. "Dorcas, you're a grown woman. You should not expect me, or anyone else, to make decisions for you."

"But you have so much experience—"

"You're getting experience right now, aren't you?"

"I don't know what to do with it."

"When I was a child my nanny used to tell me to make haste slowly. It was good advice."

"Perhaps Terry and I should talk—"

"Perhaps."

"I was thinking of going to see June—Ric's wife. Now I don't think it's such a good idea." Katherine did not reply, and Dorcas rose, too. "Yes, it would be a shitty, bitchy idea. At least talking it out with you has made me see that much. That would just be dragging June into my hurt and trying to slap back at Terry and Ric."

Katherine nodded. "Sorry if I've seemed unsympathetic, but that revolting phone call shook me. There are a few ways in which I'm not unshockable after all."

"I'm so sorry!" Dorcas cried. "I've been thinking only of myself—but oh, Madame, you have helped. I don't know what I'm going to do about it all, except that I'm not going to do anything tonight. I'm going downstairs now, and if Terry wants to talk, I'll listen."

—I'm not going to be *in loco parentis*, Katherine thought firmly. —Renting an apartment in my house gives you no special privileges.

"I do apologize." Dorcas sounded like a prim little girl. With her long hair, she looked hardly old enough to be a wife, much less a mother. "I had no right to bother you. But you're an artist, and you were married for a long time, and I thought you'd understand, and I—I couldn't carry it alone—I apologize—"

"Never mind, child. There were quite a few times, when I was around your age, when I needed to do some spilling of my own." And how often Manya had been there to listen, cosset, comfort. But not about Justin, not about— "The only thing I can tell you is that it does help you to grow, and what you do now should be part of that growing."

"You're not condoning—"

Katherine moved to the piano and leaned against its strong, sustaining curve. "Of course not. But have you—even in your short life—never done anything uncondonable?"

Dorcas was silent. She went without speaking to the door, then said, "I suppose one shouldn't make comparisons: if something's uncondonable it isn't more or less so than anything else. But that still doesn't mean—"

"Of course it doesn't. But I can't work it out for you, child. You'll have to work it out for yourself."

"Okay. Yes. I see. And I do thank you—"

"No," Katherine said. "Please don't. Just make haste slowly."

---◈ 7 ◈---

When the girl had left, she sat at the piano. Her body was trembling with that fatigue which is beyond sleep; fatigue, and still a certain amount of shock from the phone call. Why, after all these years of enduring far worse shocks, was she still so vulnerable? After a more than full life, how could she retain the naïveté which had always caused her so much grief? Unshockable? Hardly.

Was it jealousy again, as Manya had warned? But who?

She closed her eyes. Her mind moved from Manya to Dorcas, to marriage, to betrayal. She had never been able to erase completely from her memory the sight of Justin when she had first seen him after his release from Auschwitz, grey of skin and hair, cadaverous, only his caverned eyes showing his fierce pride. He babbled about divorce, annulment, he was not going to allow her to be tied to a cripple, a eunuch . . .

Manya and Tom knew only that he looked, and possibly was, close to death. They sent him for a month to a sanatorium, to be brought back to some kind of health.

'He was a mature man when this happened,' the doctor told Katherine in the privacy of his office. 'He will be able to be aroused, to have an erection, but there will be no ejaculation, he can have no children . . .'

When he returned from the sanatorium to Manya's farm in Connecticut, he had filled out so that the bones no longer seemed ready to tear through the ivory flesh. His hair, though still grey, was lustrous. His eyes were no longer deep-sunken into the sockets. He still talked about divorce, about annulment, but at least now he listened to her, argued with her rather than throwing statements at her.

'You are young, you need children . . .'

'That's nonsense. I'm a musician. I have my music. I have you. That's all I want. And I need you. You're my teacher.' And, 'I love you. You're everything I need. We had a week together which was more beautiful than anything I could ever have imagined. I couldn't be married to anybody else. It's you I love, because of all of you. We make music together, in every possible way.'

They had gone, at the doctor's suggestion, to a psychiatrist, a kindly old man with a beard, laughably like the father figure psychiatrists were supposed to be. And at last Justin had said, 'I love you, my Katherine. I can't imagine life without you. If you are willing to be married to me, a—'

'My husband,' she had said across the words. 'The man I love.'

It had not been easy, nor had they expected it to be, though it was harder than their most realistic expectations. There were times when Justin's pride was wounded, when he would lash out at her, sometimes in public, humiliate her so that she could not control her tears.

She shook her head, as though to clear memory, struck a major chord, and the pictures in her mind shifted and she saw the strong and compassionate face of Cardinal von Stromberg, known in Munich—and Rome—as Gotte's Wolf. The Great Grey Wolf, as Katherine and Justin had called him.

The cardinal had said to her, holding her face between his strong hands as they stood in his gracious and spacious library, one of the few undamaged rooms in his bombed palace, 'Katherine, my child, I could give you a series of exercises which would control your extreme sensitivity, so that never again would you be afraid of crying when you did not want to.'

And the tears were streaming down her face as she begged, 'Oh, could you, please?'

'I could. But I think I won't, because it might kill your talent, and I will not risk that.'

Wolfi, taller than Justin, with a beak of a nose and steel-grey eyes under powerful brows. Tall, strong, with lustrous hair and clear, unmarred skin, a sign of hope in a devastated city.

She had not been prepared for the destruction of Munich, for the aftermath of the bombings, bombings by American planes, flown by American flyers. She had not wanted to go to Munich, so soon after the war, so soon after their return to Europe, so early in her professional career. There had been concerts during the war, many of them benefits; her name was beginning to be mentioned in musical circles; but she did not feel ready to give a major concert in Munich, for an audience of people many of whom may well have been Nazis, may possibly have been involved in concentration camps . . . But she had been asked to go by the State Department. It was not quite emotional blackmail, but something was murmured about her early release from prison, about Justin's ultimate release from Auschwitz.

Someone had said, with a show of reason, 'After all, you will not be playing for Nazis. The war is over. The Nazi Party is dead. You cannot go on blaming the people of Germany forever.'

It was still playing for the enemy. The war might technically be over, but Justin was an ever-present reminder of the wounds of war which never heal. She protested hotly. She had refused to play for the Nazis during the Occupation. Why should she play for the Germans now?

It was Justin who finally said, wearily, 'Stop talking and go. These people who are planning all this helped get you out of prison. You owe them that much. I'll go with you.'

They were flown over on a Military Air Transport plane, her first flight, met by an army car. She looked out the window at the rubble of a town where the scars of war were not yet beginning to heal. Beside her, Justin sat, quiet, too quiet, his hands clamped, his face stern and unmoving. This might be the city of the enemy, but it was an enemy beaten. She thought that he was as horrified by the city as she.

Their hotel was on the one side of a square which had not been demolished by bombs. They were registered and taken to their room, a clean white room, with white bedspreads, white curtains at the windows, and left to rest. Katherine went to one of the long windows which opened out onto a small stone balcony. The square was filled with rubble, with barbed wire, with gaping holes. She saw children on crutches, a leg or a foot gone, children without hands, without arms. Children still playing in that devastated square, still laughing. She was cold with horror.

She turned to Justin, who was sitting in an upholstered chair that faced an empty fireplace. 'I didn't realize—' she said.

'What?' His voice was harsh.

'What we'd done—Americans. Oh, God, Justin, I wanted to kill, personally and with my bare hands, the people at Auschwitz. I'd have done it gladly—but not this—this random maiming of children and old people and—'

His voice was low and cold. 'Why not? It is only justice.'

'There's a little boy out in the square; he's bouncing a ball with his foot because he doesn't have any arms. He didn't have anything to do with Auschwitz.'

Justin continued to stare into the empty fireplace. 'Children suffer for the sins of their parents.'

'But this—we did this, my people did this—'

Justin's voice continued, low, emotionless. 'Don't be naïve. You should have learned something about war by now. The innocent always suffer. What did you want your country to do? Sit back and let the Nazis take over the world so that we'd all be in a series of concentration camps from Alaska to Africa? That's the alternative. Is that what you want?'

If he had shouted at her, it would have been more bearable. She could not turn from the window.

'Stupid,' Justin said, still not looking at her. 'Lie down and rest. You have a concert to give tonight. That is all the sanity there is in an insane world, filled with people who like to maim and kill. You don't understand anything. You weren't at Auschwitz. You didn't see what I saw.'

Now she turned to him. 'I was beaten—'

A small harsh sound came from his throat, more a snarl than a laugh. 'Did you smell a little blood then? That is nothing. You never knew the smell of roasting flesh. You never heard the screams. You never saw the piles of bodies, useful for nothing but the gold which had been taken from their teeth. I am glad for every bomb the Americans or the British or anybody else dropped on the Germans. There was no other way to stop them. You cannot call them animals, because animals do not behave in such a way.'

She moved slowly to the bed and lay down on the clean, white spread.

Finally Justin turned toward her. 'You are a child. I am not sure that I want you to grow up, because in the adult the human heart is evil.'

'Not everyone—'

'Evil, or stupid. There is nothing else.'

'Father, and Aunt Manya—'

'Stupid, you know they were stupid. They sent you to France into the war.'

'But they didn't know—'

'As I said, stupid. Well-meaning and stupid. To send a teenager alone to France with Hitler already—' He rose slowly, and closed the white shutters. 'You have a concert to give this evening. Rest.'

She closed her eyes. She wanted him to lie beside her, but he did not. She moved her fingers as though over a keyboard, her fingers which moved to her bidding as Justin's broken ones did not.

They took a taxi to the concert hall, the great Herkulessaal, and the assistant manager, waiting to greet them, pointed out the old tapestries which depicted the labors of Hercules, but she scarcely saw them.

Then, when she went into her dressing room, the first thing to meet her eye was a crystal bowl of yellow roses waiting for her, the bowl exquisitely etched with ferns, the roses tiny and fragrant. It was, against the background of the nearly destroyed city, a tangible icon of love. The card tucked in among the roses read, 'With the compliments of the manager.' When she asked for him, she was told that he was away, at a theatre in another city, and that the assistant manager would care for her needs.

She played that evening feeling that her hands had been broken and miraculously healed, that she was playing with Justin's hands as well as her own. She played, she realized after the fact, better than she knew how to play. The silence at the end of the concert was profound, and then followed great ocean waves of applause, and demands for encores and yet one more encore . . .

When she was finally permitted to leave the stage and go to her dressing room, Cardinal von Stromberg was waiting. And although she knew that it was not he who had sent the roses and the vase he, too, was a gift of healing. She had played one of Justin's early compositions, and it was to Justin the cardinal spoke first, understanding more in the music than Justin himself had heard. It was knowledgeable appreciation, not facile praise, and Justin could not help responding to it. The cardinal was not a German, an enemy, while he was speaking, but someone who understood music and saw in Justin a potential he hardly dared perceive in himself.

Then the cardinal turned to Katherine and took her hands in his enveloping strong ones.

--◆{ 8 }◆--

Justin accepted the cardinal's invitation to supper, murmuring to Katherine, 'We can hardly blame him for the entire war.' The stone house by the cathedral was half destroyed, but the great library had been untouched and they sat there, with wine and cheese and bread and pickles and whatever the cardinal could find in the larder, talking, talking as though they had known each other forever, as they talked first about music, and then about the war and its horrors, its scars which would never disappear. And then the cardinal turned to Justin, knelt on the marble floor and confessed, for confession was what it was, all the sins of omission of the Church during the years just past, during twenty centuries of sins of omission and commission. He wept over Justin's hands, and there was a strange power of healing in the tears. The broken hands would never be able to express the intricacies of a fugue, but they would be hands which, in their turn, held healing.

Justin, too, had wept, all politeness gone, tears of rage, of hatred, hatred for the Nazis, hatred for the cardinal whose food he had just eaten.

Von Stromberg, head bowed, murmured, 'So slow I am to learn some of the meaning which infuses the psalms. You show me, for the first time, what it meant to cry out:

> *Du Tochter Babels, du Verwüsterin,*
> *Heil dem, der dir vergilt,*
> *Was du uns angetan hast!*
> *Heil dem, der deine kleinen Kinder nimmt,*
> *und sie zerschmettert an dem Felsen!*

But although your music makes that cry of hate, what ultimately it gives is healing and joy.'

Katherine had looked at the two men, von Stromberg still on his knees, being helped up by Justin, so that the two of them stood together. She knew just enough German to understand that the cardinal had been quoting something about a daughter of Babylon, in misery, and something terrible about blessing those who took her children and threw them against the stones. What was there in those angry and anguished words to turn Justin's vengefulness into forgiveness? For, as the cardinal had confessed to Justin, so, then, Justin in turn confessed, telling Cardinal von Stromberg what they had vowed never to tell anybody, Justin's mutilation. Somehow Wolfi—and it was as though they had been calling him Wolfi forever—by dawn was able to bring healing to Justin, to— somehow—man him again.

He was a healer, the Grey Wolf.

They were in Munich for nearly a week and they saw the cardinal daily, for counseling, for pleasure. Their friendship was his greatest privilege, he told them, and it blossomed swiftly, a beautiful, spontaneous flowering. 'We have nothing to give each other except friendship,' he assured them. 'You can't ask any favors of me, nor I of you.' But he had already given them more than friendship, his warm lovingness thawing the splinter of ice still lodged in Justin's heart.

How hilarious, they thought, that they, of all people, who had not darkened the doorway of a church since their wedding day, should be friends with a cardinal!

(So why was she surprised by her friendship with Felix all these years later?)

He knew music, the Grey Wolf. As he was driven by God, so he understood the music which drove them. Mozart, he said, was of course his favorite, since he was in a way a namesake of the great composer. But he loved Bach, too, and he encouraged Justin to move more deeply into his own composing, to continue to work with Katherine, but to redirect his own talent as well. Would Justin have gone as far as he did without the Grey Wolf?

They left Munich, to continue the tour, with promises of return visits. Never had Katherine felt so swiftly secure in a friendship, so certain that this time there would be no rejection; and he seemed to love them equally, so that they were like an equilateral triangle. There was never any sense of imbalance; never did his love for one in any way exclude the other. He was, of course, older, older even than Justin. What no one else, what none of the doctors had been able to do, he had accomplished in one intense week. Katherine perhaps fell into the trap of feeling that he was a father to her, as her own father had not been. When they were back in Paris, when she was on the road, with or without Justin, she would often call him for the reassurance of his voice, and no matter when she called, it was as though he had been waiting for her, as though she was the one person in the world he wanted to hear from.

And she adored him. Did she feel, back then, about the cardinal the way Dorcas appeared to feel about Katherine?

The thought of Dorcas brought her back to the present. She was not sure whether or not anything she had said to Dorcas was right. Once again she had been plunged into a situation where she did not know what was right and what was wrong, and this had happened so often during her lifetime that surely she should be used to it. 'You do not have to be right,' Wolfi had said. 'Only to care.' And, she added to herself, now, —never to play God.

With an effort of will she started the *Goldberg Variations*. Perhaps they would calm her enough so that she could sleep.

---※{ 9 }※---

Calm, but not calm enough. She repeated her bedtime routine, warm bath, slow drying, a book—not the mystery she was currently enjoying, but philosophy; Kant; she never got very far with Kant; the long Germanic sentences bored her, so that her lids began to droop. It was Wolfi who had first suggested using Kant as a soporific, 'or almost any German theologian. It is said that we German theologians are the deepest-down-divingest, longest-staying-underest, most-with-mud-coming-uppest, thinkers who ever lived.'

More mud was the last thing she needed. Theology was not helping her now. Once again she was caught in old pain, long resolved, but nevertheless occasionally surfacing when she least expected it. Perhaps now it was Dorcas and her problems which had triggered the memory.

It had taken a long time, for Katherine and Justin, before their night companionship had become bearable. For both of them desire that could not be fulfilled rose like an incomplete crescendo. If her peak was reached, then it seemed to emphasize for Justin his own never-to-be-completed passion. Sometimes in longing for all the ecstasy he had given her, all that she in return had given him, nevermore to be attained, she would expel her anguish in streams of silent tears. Or a deliberate act of will. Quiet, Katherine. Hush.

She understood that it was mostly more frustration for Justin than he could bear, to respond to her and then go so far and no further. It was a long time, even after Wolfi came into their lives with his healing hands and heart, before Justin could put his arms around her, without anger or tears. When his compositions began to be played, to receive both critical and popular acclaim, he began to regain his *amour propre*, a sense of his own validity aside from her talent. Then things were better. But still painful, precarious.

At their best they would lie together, arms about each other, quietly, and that was a way of knowing each other. Her childish adulation was long gone (transferred, perhaps, to the cardinal?). They held each other as man and woman on the good nights; despite Auschwitz, they knew each other.

Occasionally the moments of beauty would dissolve into Justin's slow-burning and then suddenly flaming rage, into accusations. 'You stay with me only out of duty, out of pity—'

When he was like that, there was no calming him. Sometimes she would leave their bed and spend the rest of the night on the couch in the living room. Usually, then, she woke early, before Justin, and would go to the telephone to call the cardinal, knowing that he, too, would be awake. She envisioned him sitting at the long table in the library, tall, grey-haired, grey-eyed, strong and stern and wise. His love for them seemed to move tangibly along the telephone wire and, sustained by his swift response, by his understanding and compassion even more than by his words, she would go back to the bedroom, slipping into bed without waking Justin. She thought of separate beds, separate bedrooms, and understood that this would be a rejection which would wound him beyond healing.

When she and Justin were working together, there was no separation, no pain. It was, as the cardinal pointed out, a total intercourse for them, something closer to perfection than most people could even dream of. And, he assured her during one early-morning phone conversation, the pain was infusing her playing, deepening and strengthening both the music and Katherine.

'You talk of Justin's fierce pride,' he said. 'You have a good bit of your own, you know.'

She had hardly realized how dependent on the cardinal she was becoming. As a child she had barely known her father; she had never had the experience of a loving 'daddy.' All the lacks of her childhood were gathered together and fulfilled in the tender wisdom of the Grey Wolf. And he encouraged her, as perhaps he should not have done.

But without Wolfi she might not have been able to love Justin as much as she did, to move into a joyous companionship which gave them both delight. If she still sometimes wept at night, the days were often filled with laughter. And with work. He was a hard taskmaster, and she throve. Professionally they were both flourishing, and this was joy; joy was work and work was joy.

She and Justin even went occasionally to Mass as a courtesy to the cardinal for being there when they needed him. In the amazement of their friendship, they were startled to discover how well known he was, not so much for being a cardinal as for his writings, books which were read not only in theological circles. He had the ability to translate deep theological thinking into language which the interested layman could understand, and his own interests were wide and varied. As soon as they had learned of von Stromberg's writings, they had gone to the Librairie Hachard to buy everything available, devoured the books in great gulps, then gone back and sipped at them slowly, and his words had nurtured them, their love.

'Where have we been all this time?' Katherine demanded when they first learned of von Stromberg's writings.

'Lost in our own insular lives,' Justin had replied. 'It's time we widened our horizons.'

At a party one night, after the premiere of one of Justin's concerti, the cellist, who had been the soloist and who had never struck them as being well-read, startled them by referring to von Stromberg's book on Mozart. 'It's fabulous. But of course he's as vain as the rest of us, and it's natural he'd be interested in a Wolfgang.'

'Oh, come on, Willie,' a flautist said. 'He really understands music.'

'Did I say he didn't?' Willie demanded. 'He surely got inside

Wolfgang Amadeus. And I've just read his latest book, brand-new, all about love in the post-war world. It's a good book, of course. But he should know.' There was something insinuating about his voice.

'Know what?' Justin asked.

'What he's talking about,' the cellist had replied.

Katherine felt her hackles rise. 'What do you mean?'

'Great man or no, he's not above enjoying tail.'

Outraged, Katherine had cried, 'He's a cardinal!'

'Come, little one,' the cellist had condescended from his ten-years and five-inches advantage over Katherine. 'Surely you know that priests are human beings with human needs which sometimes have to be fulfilled.'

'I don't believe it.' Katherine knocked her glass of Mâcon into a plate of brie.

Justin began calmly mopping up the red liquid. 'Cardinal von Stromberg is a friend of ours and a very great man, and people always have to cut the great down to size.'

The cellist added his not-very-clean handkerchief to the plate of cheese and wine, sopping it up absently. 'I, unlike you, go to Mass regularly, so I'm less easily upset. Celibacy didn't come into the Church at all for the first several centuries. You should read his new book. Ginette gave it to me to read, thinking it might nudge me toward marriage. We'll see.'

'Oh, come on, Willie, you'll never marry,' a trombonist said, and the conversation shifted.

When Katherine and Justin were getting ready for bed that night she said, 'Your concerto came off superbly. Even Willie couldn't ruin it.'

'Oh, Willie's not that bad a cellist. Not tops, but all right. Anyhow, I think the concerto came off pretty well, too. But tell me again. Flattery will get you everywhere.'

They talked about the concerto for a while, and Justin sighed contentedly, 'I think the Wolf would have been pleased,' and went into the bathroom.

She asked, 'It's not true, is it?'

Justin called through the open door, 'What's not true?'

'What Willie said about Wolfi.'

For a moment she heard the sound of Justin brushing his teeth.

Then, 'It's the price of fame, Minou.' He came in, tying the belt to his robe. 'The moment anyone is famous, then people have to cut them down. All Willie was trying to do was boost his own lecherous ego by bringing Wolfi down to his level.'

'He can't.'

'Of course he can't. The Grey Wolf stands head and shoulders above the rest of us.'

'He's a cardinal. Why would Willie say such a thing?'

'Precisely because Wolfi *is* a cardinal. Willie's mind is totally phallic.'

Katherine sat on the edge of the bed. 'So you don't think it could be true, do you?'

Justin sat beside her, smelling of toothpaste and cologne, and put his arm around her. 'You are still an innocent child. No. I don't think it's true, though I think it *could* be true. Wolfi is a human being, and all human beings have flaws and faults, even the greatest; especially the greatest.'

'But—'

'Little one—'

Perhaps because the mingled odors of toothpaste, of the cologne she had given him for Christmas, of Justin himself, were strongly aphrodisiac, she answered sharply, 'I'm not a child!'

'Katherine. Minou. Wife. Every human being has a special temptation. For some men it's women, whether they're priests or not. If they go in for womanizing as a fixed policy, then'—he held his nose— '*ça dégueulasse*. But if they occasionally yield to temptation, pick themselves up out of the dirt, say I'm sorry to God or whomever they ought to say it to, then *ça va assez bien*.'

'It's dirty. I mean, Willie's mouth is dirty.'

'*Sale*, yes. But you must allow Wolfi to be human. He is not a marble statue.'

'I don't want him to be. But I don't want him to be what Willie said, either.'

'Wolfi is not what Willie said. That I can promise you. Willie has lived too long in America, where all friendship is assumed to have a genital basis.' A look of bitter anguish moved across his face. 'Who knows what Auschwitz may have spared you? Before I married you, I wasn't much better than Willie. Believe me, Minou, I wasn't. I'm not at all sure I would have been strong enough for complete fidelity.' She put her hands over her face, pressing her fingers against her eyes, and Justin reached and took one of her hands, pressing it against his chest, moving her fingers through the dense, dark hair. 'And, had I been able to go on playing, I might have been jealous of your talent. It is not good for husband and wife to be in competition.' As she shook her head in negation, he added, 'Wolfi is a great friend and confessor to many people, far more than we realize because we think of him as being especially ours. But he is not. He has many people who need him, women as well as men. Don't you realize that if you and I become famous, people are going to say things about us, too?'

'Us? What kind of things?'

'Don't sound so horrified. They'll think of something. That I'm homosexual. That you sleep with half a dozen conductors.'

'You're laughing at me.'

'Not really.' Again he rubbed her fingers against his chest, but his voice was serious. 'Minou, if we do what I expect us to do in the world of music, there will be people out to smear us, and malicious gossip is one of the easiest weapons.'

(He was right; there had been gossip; all far from the truth: Justin and a ballerina; Justin and an Iranian oil princess; Katherine and a violinist with whom she played frequently; anyone, everyone—it did not bother them overmuch.)

She sighed. '*Merde*. You'd think I'd realize it's a vile world. I do, in the big things. How could I not? It's the little things that surprise me.'

He drew her to him. 'I know, *ma chérie*. But there are good surprises, too. Wolfi. His books. How like him to let us discover them for ourselves! And you, Minou, you are my great, good surprise.'

'I'm not a surprise,' she murmured. 'I'm Katherine.'

'That is a surprise. I thought, when you first came back to Paris to work with me, that you would remain a frozen little girl all your life, that you would never become the warm, wise, mature, wonderful—' He broke off and kissed her forehead, her eyebrows, the tip of her nose, her chin. 'That you are my Katherine is the greatest surprise of all.'

There are many ways of love, of intercourse, which the world, including all the Willies, cannot understand.

---⊷❧ 10 ❧⊷---

There were, of course, temptations. In the sexually permissive atmosphere of the world after the war, she was often approached. Perhaps her unmet need was felt; in any event, she had many offers. 'We're in Antwerp just this one night; my room is just down the corridor from yours; I'll be waiting . . .'

The Willies of the world were easy to turn down. With others it was not so easy, especially if they had just been making music together. There were times when it was all she could do not to give in to her need. And why shouldn't she? Wouldn't it have been completely normal and natural? But something, and she was never sure what, kept her from it, and when Justin lay in her arms, and then, in his turn, held her, murmuring endearments, she was grateful that she was wholly his. She did not fully understand why she could not reach out for fulfillment to some of the men who came to her with love as well as desire. It had nothing to do with morals or virtue. Perhaps it was an inchoate knowledge (which she understood more fully later) that she could not give her body to someone for a brief time of pleasure and release, and let it go at that. Perhaps others could hold some of themselves back; she could not.

After Justin's death there were offers of marriage. But no one came up to the standards of companionship set by Justin. She was not interested in compromise or second-best. There were musicians with whom she had enjoyed playing, and perhaps lingering over supper after the concert. But that was enough. For some reason Julie was concerned that her mother might remarry. In this one area Katherine was able to give her complete reassurance. 'No, darling, don't worry. Your father was all the husband I need.'

---⊷❧ 11 ❧⊷---

The volume of Kant slipped from the old woman's fingers and slid to the floor. Not bothering to pick it up, she turned off the light and slid into sleep, not the deep sleep of the early hours of the night, but the shallows in which conscious and the subconscious slide in and out of each other.

She dreamed, not of Justin, or of the cardinal, but of Llew; that he was playing the organ in the Cathedral, with the moonlight pouring muted colors through the windows, and that Dorcas, holding a baby, was standing beside him, turning the pages.

Katherine slipped slowly back into consciousness and reached out with foot and hand for Justin's body. Are such habits never broken? She was alone. Alone in bed as she had been for twenty years. Was it twenty? No matter. Long enough.

The past was always part of the present and some events never lose their power to evoke pain.

One night, as she and Justin were getting ready for bed, he turned to her. 'Katherine, I want children.'

She paused, hairbrush in hand, her hair thrown back. Then, 'All right. We can look into the various adoption agencies. The war has left plenty of homeless children.'

'No.' The lines between Justin's nose and mouth were white with tension. 'Not adoption.'

She did not know what to say, what he had in mind, so she continued brushing her hair, long and black and silky and heavy, so heavy that she felt pulled down by it. Or by Justin.

The brush moved more and more slowly over her hair.

'What happened to me is between you and me. We have told Wolfi, and we will tell no one else. We have come to terms with it, and that is that. But I have heard that there have been rumors—from someone from Auschwitz—I can't have that. I want them stopped.'

Silence lay between them like a chasm.

His voice was angry. 'I warned you that something like this would happen, that when we began to make names for ourselves people would have to find some way to diminish us, the way they do with Wolfi—'

'But that's not true—'

'Katherine, I want this stopped. It is essential to me that it be stopped.' He was almost shouting. 'You can have children. You're still young, you're still in your twenties.'

She felt as though she would never be able to speak again; the column of her throat was frozen.

'My God!' Justin cried. 'Don't act dumb! Don't play the naïve child. You are a desirable woman. There are plenty of men who— stop whimpering! Don't you see what has to be done to stop people? If you get pregnant it will be assumed that I am the father. I will *be* the father. I don't ever want to know who—'

Now she said, sounding to herself old-fashioned, a stupid schoolgirl, 'But when I married you I promised to—'

'Damn it! I don't want you to become a prostitute! Just to get pregnant, to give me a baby. I will love the child, I will . . .'

She had fumbled into clothes, not looking at him, and fled the house, running to a public phone. Wolfi. She had to speak to the cardinal.

He told her to come. 'Take the next train. It's absolutely impossible for me to leave now, or I'd come to you. But we cannot talk about this on the phone. Go home to Justin and tell him that you have to think, and that you need to be away for a few days.'

'Shall I tell him I'm coming to you?'

To her surprise he said, 'No. I don't want anything to come between Justin's and my friendship, and this might. But come quickly.'

Why did it hurt so much? Why wasn't it a reasonable suggestion? Why did it still hurt?

She turned over in bed. The heat had returned to New York, and she took a corner of the sheet and wiped her face. It was being a bad night. Memories were not healing.

When she told people that Justin had been a wonderful father, it was true. Often, when she had been on tour, he had been father and mother to the children. He had adored them. She thought that he sometimes forgot that he had not been part of their conception.

Was it the fact that it was pride which had brought about the original demand (for it was not a request) that still hurt? And why, when love had overcome pride, and so soon . . .

But the past still hurt. And the present hurt.

Who had made that repellent phone call?

Elective Affinities

For the next several days, she was restless. Whenever the phone rang, it was a jolt. But it was always something innocuous, a rug-cleaning service, a wrong number, and, finally, Felix asking her for dinner.

She felt restless enough to accept unhesitatingly, and for a moment he overwhelmed her with gratitude. Then he made plans calmly and considerately. He would come down to the Village and take her to a small northern Italian restaurant which had been there when they first knew each other.

She did not remember it, although as they walked up MacDougal Street he assured her that they had been there several times. The restaurant was down several steps and felt pleasantly cool as they entered. On the wall above the bar was a life-sized photographic portrait of an exquisitely beautiful young woman.

"It was her restaurant," Felix said after they were seated in a quiet corner and given menus. "She wasn't that young when we first started coming here, and she was an old woman when I was elected Diocesan and returned to New York. One of her sons and one of her grandsons are carrying on. They've kept up the quality of the cooking; everything is made on the premises."

As a waiter came by, Felix asked for the wine list. "Wine, I think, all through the meal, rather than cocktails. All right?"

"Fine." She unfolded her napkin and relaxed into the comfortable chair; the chair itself spoke well for the restaurant.

"I'm so grateful you could come, Katya. I've had the screaming meemies all week. I'm grateful not to have to be alone tonight when I'm so out of proportion."

He, too? "Why are you disproportionate, Felix?"

"Oh, Katya, I wish I could tell you. I have too many secrets, and I wish there could be no secrets between us—"

She tried to calm him. "We've both lived such long lives that if we tried to tell each other everything we'd die of even older age before we finished our tale."

"You're right, of course you're right. Do you have secrets, too?"

"A Bluebeard's closet full." A small tremor moved through her.

He peered over the large menu at her. "Has something happened to disturb you?"

Why was she telling him? "Nothing really important. I had a poison-pen kind of phone call the other night, accusing me of sex with both you and Mimi."

"How *dare* they!" His reaction was so violent it surprised her. "Who?"

He studied the menu, then put it down, his voice calm. "Nobody in particular. Anyone who makes obscene phone calls."

"You don't have *any* idea who?" She peered at him in the dimness of the restaurant light.

"No."

"Felix, you're not telling me the truth. Who is it?"

He looked again at the menu. Then, "I don't know. That's the truth."

"Have you had similar calls?"

"Heavens, yes. I can't count how many through the years. This isn't your first, ever, is it?"

She shook her head. "But the first in several years. And the first since I've come home to Tenth Street."

"I'm so sorry . . ." He stetched his hand across the table toward her. "I've had them increasingly in the past couple of years. For someone who's knocked around, I find them amazingly distressing." He was not telling her everything he knew.

"Have you had one recently?"

"No, no . . ."

"Felix." She drew her hand back, away from his.

The menu trembled in his hands. "I had a call this evening, just before I left to come downtown. Someone threatening to tell about Allie and me."

"To tell who, what, about Allie and you?"

He put the menu down on the table and placed his hands on it to stop their trembling. "Katya—after Sarah, after the war, I was, to put it mildly, a mess. As I've told you."

"Don't be so hard on yourself, Felix. What about window cleaning?"

"Thank you. Sometimes I tend to forget that there was ever anything good about me, back then. I don't know why I didn't end up the victim of one of those sordid murders one reads about in the scandal sheets. God knows I didn't deserve to live."

"Felix, don't," she said softly.

The waiter returned with wine in an ice bucket, and waited while they ordered. When he left them, Felix said, "Katherine, I need your friendship, your counsel."

She sighed. "I am a pianist. I can*not* be your confessor."

A thin laugh. "Don't worry. I'm through the nasty part. Sarah gave me some money, but not enough. I got a job as a waiter, since I didn't appear to be making much of a living with the violin, first in a crummy hash house. I was good at it—people liked me, because I listened to them, even when they swore at me. That's how I discovered I had a gift for the ministry. I moved on to a better restaurant and ended up, although I find it hard to believe, at the Pierre. I used to bring breakfast to a Dutch couple who were there for the winter; they were textile people, traveling to various mills, but they made the hotel home base. They read a lot—all the tables and chests were piled with books and magazines—theology mostly —and they'd give me articles to read, I used to come talk with them on my off-hours. The amazing thing is that I fell in love with both of them, Pieter and Wendele. And they with me. Did you know that kind of thing could happen?"

"Felix, I am very naïve."

"All I can tell you is that there was nothing sordid about it, nothing nasty. And I was grateful beyond words that I could feel for—toward—a woman all that I felt for Wendele. After Sarah, I thought I could never love a woman. But I loved Wendele. And then, on one of their trips, they were killed in a car crash. For a long time I asked myself if it was a just punishment—not for them, but for me. I could never bring myself to answer yes to the question, though I went on asking it for a long time. Then, when the will—they were wealthy, but they had no children, no close family. They left most of their money to various charities, but they left a trust fund for me—almost as though they'd known they were going to die. The only string was that the fund was to be used for theological education. It could be any denomination; it didn't even have to be Christian. They wanted me, simply, to give my life to God, and I found that I wanted that, too. I'm not even sure why I chose the Episcopal Church; it was almost coincidence, happenstance, though I don't believe in coincidence. I was living in Chelsea and there was a seminary right around the corner. There. That's enough revelation. And here comes our antipasto. It's really excellent here."

When they were served, she prodded him. "Felix. Your phone call. About you and Allie."

"Oh. Yes. I felt I needed to tell you how I got into this line of work. And I've been good at it."

"Yes. I'm sure you have. Now. You and Allie."

"All right. I'll have to take the long way around."

"I'm in no hurry. And the restaurant's not crowded. We aren't keeping anyone from a table." She was not in a hurry. For the first time in longer than she could remember, she was not. And she wanted to know, not so much out of curiosity as out of growing affection for Felix.

"When I was in my mid-fifties"—Felix took a small bite of prosciutto and melon—"I was dean of the cathedral in San Francisco. On the surface, things were going well for me. I was well thought of, I really was, well thought of enough so that I was shortly elected Bishop of New York, though nothing could have been further from my mind at the time." He let his fork rest on his plate. "What was in my mind was dust, dry dust. I preached brilliantly—you should have heard me, Katya—and I heard confessions and did a lot of counseling and helped people—I really did—and rather casually took part in diocesan politics, because I was good at that, too. But I was lonely. Trying to give one's life to God can be a very lonely business, especially when God often seems to be absent. I knew his presence when I was in the pulpit; I was on fire with his presence. And then: emptiness."

Katherine watched Felix absently pick up his fork.

"I lived in the deanery all by myself, and I had someone to do the heavy cleaning, and a couple who came in to help when I entertained—which I did a lot of, both in the line of business and because I was lonely. At intimate dinner parties I reconciled quarrels which had been going on for years; I raised money; I did all the right things. I had friends, some of them close, most of them dead now because most of them were older than I. Am I boring you?"

"No, Felix. Go on."

"I'm not trying to avoid the subject, but I have to set the stage." He glanced past a table of young Japanese students to the large photograph over the bar, then back to Katherine. "As I said, I was lonely. Admired and surrounded by people, I was lonely. I know—everybody is lonely. But I didn't understand that, not then. I didn't understand that it was all right to believe only part of the time all that I base my life on. Sometimes when I was counseling someone I heard myself saying the right things, but the better the things I said, the less I believed afterwards, the emptier I felt, the lonelier. I took my faith and I gave it away, gave it to people who needed it, and then it seemed that there wasn't any left for me.

"I was due a sabbatical. I knew part of my problem was being overextended and overtired. But that didn't make the emptiness, the unfilled God-hole within me, any easier. I knew I came across to others as a man of great faith, and when I was alone it was ashes, nothing but ashes. I wonder—did that kind of accidie ever attack your friend Cardinal von Stromberg?"

She picked up a forkful of lentils and regarded them. "I don't know, Felix. It wasn't the kind of thing we talked about. He was old enough to be my father, I suppose—but go on." She had talked to Wolfi, endlessly, it seemed. How often had Wolfi talked to her?

"I used to walk a lot in the evenings. It wasn't terribly safe, even with a clerical collar, but it was all that kept me sane. I went occasionally to plays or concerts with parishioners. I heard you play.

Odd, how complex and intertwined life is. Every time I think I'm settling for chance and randomness, then pattern enmeshes me in its strands. Is your antipasto good?"

"Excellent."

"So. I'd gone to hear you play. Odd that it should have happened when I was going to hear you, Katya, in an all-Bach program. I'd been going to go with one of the older women who worshipped at the Cathedral and who'd been recently widowed. But she came down with a virus, so I went alone. We had fine seats, first ring, front row. And during intermission a young man slipped in and sat in my friend's empty seat. Do you remember how we used to do that—buy the cheapest seats in the house, and 'case the joint,' as we used to say, and then at intermission move to better seats?"

"I remember."

"So I wasn't surprised to have a young man take advantage of an empty seat. He was so young! He looked about fifteen, though I discovered later that he was a good ten years older. He settled himself in, and then pulled a paperback out of his pocket and began to read. I'm always impelled to see what people are reading. It was *King Lear*. He saw me looking and explained that he was with one of the small acting groups that tend to crop up in San Francisco, and he was studying the role of the fool. Then he went back to his book, and I could see that it was all marked up. His lips were moving slightly as he studied, and he was deep in concentration. He had very fair hair, and pale skin, too pale. There were lavender smudges under his eyes—he had that transparent skin which shows the blue of veins. His features were clear and clean, like the stone-chiseled features of a statue. He did, in fact, look like a very young Greek god."

The waiter took away their plates, returned with the main course, uncorked and poured the wine, and waited for Felix to taste it. The old man swirled the wine absentmindedly, tasted it, and nodded at the waiter. He continued, appearing hardly to have noticed the interruption.

"The lights went down, and he was focused as intently on you and the music as he had been on his script. Young John Davidson has that same intensity, the total self-emptying. You have it; you've always had it. I love music, but I'm not drawn into it in that utterly concentrated way. I was listening to you, yes, and listening well enough to know that you were playing superbly, but I was also watching him listening.

"And that, I thought, is how one should listen to God, and I wondered if I had ever let myself go that completely, if I had ever fallen into God the way that child was falling into your music.

"You know, Katya, I'd thought of going backstage that night and making myself known to you again. I thought maybe enough time had passed so that you wouldn't mind seeing me."

Where was she in her own life, all those years ago? Michou was dead. Wolfi was dead. She, too, had times when there seemed to be nothing but ashes.

"I wonder what would have happened if I'd gone backstage?" Felix continued. He had not touched his meal. "The concert ended, and they kept bringing you back for encores, and he kept applauding, beating his hands together with that rapt look on his face, and finally people began straggling out, and the curtain came down for the last time, and we stood up, too, and made our way out, not speaking, going our separate ways, although we were close enough to touch, and still were when we got to the sidewalk. He turned right, and I was about to turn left, still thinking I might look for the stage door, when I saw him stagger. He would have fallen if I hadn't caught him. He was very light; it was like holding a child, and that's how I thought of him. He was deathly pale, but conscious enough to bend over, so that the blood came back to his head, and he managed to tell me that he hadn't eaten for three days."

"Signor," the waiter appeared by them, asking anxiously, "is the dinner not all right?"

Felix looked in surprise at his untouched plate, picked up his knife and fork. "Yes, it's fine, fine, thanks," and waved the waiter away, looking at Katherine. "Are you still with me?"

"I'm still with you."

Shaking his head, the waiter moved on to another table. Felix continued, "There was a small, after-theatre sort of restaurant nearby, and I managed to get him there, half carrying him. I was probably as strong then as I've ever been, taking good care of myself, going regularly to a gym, playing a lot of tennis, though you wouldn't know it to look at me now. So I got him into a booth and ordered coffee, because I knew we'd get that immediately, and then soup and a sandwich.

"When he'd eaten—and I had to keep slowing him down so he wouldn't wolf the food and then throw up—I asked him why he'd gone so long without eating, and he said he'd spent his last money on standing room for your concert. His English accent was so strong that I asked him how he happened to be in San Francisco." Felix paused, looked at his plate, cut off several pieces of meat, and put a very small one in his mouth. "He explained that his aunt, who had raised him, had died shortly after he went down from Oxford. He'd read Greats, and taken a First, but he'd always been interested in the theatre. His aunt, of course, was dead against it, and he felt, he said, very beholden to her, as she'd taken him in after his parents' death and been kind to him in a distant, English sort of way, and seen to his education. But after her death he was determined to try the theatre—his father had had something to do with the theatre, though I don't remember what. Someone had encouraged him to come to the States, to Hollywood, so he did. His aunt had left him a sizable amount of money, but until he was thirty he received only a monthly allowance, a reasonable enough sum, but he'd found Hollywood dreadfully expensive, and he didn't find work. At least, he didn't find work which he would or could accept. He received a couple of offers for porno films, for instance. You do know by now that I'm talking about Allie?"

"Yes, Felix. And do take another bite or the waiter will come hover again."

Dutifully, he obeyed. Then, "Somehow he made his way to San Francisco and got in with an acting group—serious kids—but he'd borrowed ahead on his allowance and he was broke and about to be evicted, and when I heard where he lived I thought that eviction was probably the best thing that could happen to him. But then, what?

"Anyhow, I believed his story, and he wasn't lying, it was all true. So I took him home with me to the deanery. It was raining and very chilly—San Francisco in the forties can freeze your marrow. I ran him a good hot bath, and told him he could stay in the guest wing for a few days. He began to whimper like a baby, and didn't want me to go, and for a moment I was afraid—but all he wanted was for me to bring him hot milk, and then sit by the bed and rub his head as though he were six years old. So I did, and left him sleeping like a baby.

"And so at last I had my son, the child I had expected to have by Sarah. And he—he had been deprived of a father when he was a small boy, and I know from experience that if one does not have a father's love as a child, that need simply goes on growing, rather than decreasing. I had an intensely happy month with this cherished son. I have not always been innocent, but this was innocent. My faith came flooding back; I shone with it.

"And then I realized that he was not, in fact, a child, He was older than I thought him that first night. And he was very dependent on me, and I did not want that dependency to become neurotic. His check had come from England, and I knew it was time for him to start looking for a place for himself. He could not go on being a small boy dependent on Daddy for everything. So I made up my mind that I would have to speak to him—and believe me, Katya, it was not an easy decision, because I was joyfully happy with things as they were. Yet I knew that things could not stay that way. Something would happen to—to smirch them.

"How ironic life is: the night I had planned to speak to him he came home from rehearsal and said that he had something to tell me. He babbled about a book by Goethe called—believe me, I can never forget the name of that book—*Die Wahlverwandtschaften*. Do you know it?"

"Sorry." She had long finished her meal.

"It means elective affinities. What a snobbish little group of sods those kids were, working on their ghastly production of *Lear* and dabbling in philosophy and love. But who was I to talk? After all, they were what I was like when I was their age. Only I didn't want Allie to be like that. But he went on about elective affinities, explaining pompously that in chemistry it means a force by which atoms which are of dissimilar natures nevertheless unite. It's like that with human beings, he said. And stars. Stars, two of them billions of light-years away from each other, are drawn together slowly by some unknown force of gravity. He was serious, and all I wanted to do as I listened to him was shake him. I finally asked him what he was trying to tell me. He kept beating around the bush, asking me if I believed that it is written in the stars that certain souls are drawn together by a strange magnetism more powerful than any force on earth. And then he looked at me and waited for me to say something, so I said that I had heard the theory but thought it was romantic nonsense and it had never happened to me. So he looked at me with those guileless blue eyes and said that it had happened with him and the girl who was playing Goneril—*Wahlverwandtschaften*. They were destined to be together; it was written in the stars.

"I had met Goneril. A good role for her. But if the stars wrote anything about her and Allie, it was a dirty joke. Allie was going to move in with her and I did nothing to stop him. I could have, but if he had stayed with me it would have been for all the wrong reasons. He needed to be with a woman, even the wrong woman— and she was.

"For a few weeks he called me ecstatically, spouting more Goethe, or whatever the little twerps were reading. Sorry, that's not fair of me. They weren't bad kids. Their production of *Lear* was no more disastrous than most, and Goneril was a good actress. But then the kids began working on another play, and he began seeing someone else, and I was called to New York, and I got only an occasional card from him. But that, Katya—that's all there's to be known about Allie and me. I loved him. I love him. But nothing ever—maybe I could have made it happen, but I didn't. I wouldn't. If Allie has sins of the flesh they're not in that direction. He's still hung up on this *Wahlverwandtschaften* stuff, but now it's with Yolande, and certainly Yolande has been the only woman in his life for a long time. So why should I be afraid about that phone call, threatening to 'expose' Allie and me?"

"Why indeed—except that I was also distinctly shaken by the disembodied voice accusing me of ambidextrous sexual activities. But there's no point in being afraid, Felix, especially when there's nothing to expose."

"People distort and destroy. If they should bring up that dishonorable discharge from the army . . . Allie's friendship is more dear to me than I can say. I don't want it smutched and smeared."

To herself, as much as to him, she said, "There is still no reason to be frightened."

"Untrue gossip has done all kinds of damage, unmendable damage."

"Isn't it a bit late for that?"

"Gossip knows no time limits. I don't want it. I don't know what started it, who made that phone call, but I don't want it."

The waiter took their plates away, and they ordered cheese and crackers. No espresso.

"Do I—does my return to New York have anything to do with your anonymous phone calls?"

"No, no! It's not you," Felix said swiftly. "You're involved only because of me, I'm sure of that. *I'm* the one who caused your horrid call, not the other way around, and I don't want you touched any more than I want Allie hurt. Why do people always put the ugliest possible interpretation on things?"

"Human nature has always tended to look for scandal whether there's cause or not," she agreed, and heard the echo of Justin's voice after Willie's suggestiveness about Wolfi. "Do you really have no idea who it could be?"

"None."

"But it's likely the same person who accused me of goings-on with both Mimi and you," she suggested.

"Lord, I wish it was true—I mean with me." Felix sighed.

Katherine asked, "How did Allie get from San Francisco and the theatre to the Church?"

"A few months after my installation in New York, Allie arrived. He told me that he was not cut out for the theatre, that he was a good actor but not good enough, because he didn't care enough. But he thought he might have a vocation to the priesthood and he wanted to find out. Of course, I helped him as much as I could. He got a scholarship to seminary, and with his aunt's money he got by. And he did have a vocation, and he's always thanked me for that. He might have discovered it anyhow, but perhaps I had at least a small part in it. We saw a good bit of each other, but not too much. He was popular at seminary, and he always had a string of girlfriends. I was, for him, the father he had lost, and he was the son I'd never been able to have."

"So why should anyone threaten you?"

"God knows."

"Are your calls always about you and Allie?"

"No, no, this was the first time, that's why it upset me."

"What are they, usually, then?"

"They don't sound like much. 'We'll get you.' Or, 'Frightened, aren't you?' Sometimes my doorbell will ring at eleven or twelve at night—I go to the peephole and nobody's there. Once it was the buzzer downstairs, and I called through the intercom and nobody answered. I called the guard, and he said nobody was there. I think he thought I was drunk."

"But you weren't, were you?"

"No."

"You weren't drunk that first night you called me, either."

"No. I was just frightened—such a frightened fool to call you, which I'd never have done in my right mind."

"Why did you call me? We'd only had that one evening together, after all those years, so why did you call *me*?"

He crumbled a cracker onto his plate. "Because you'd just come back to New York and you had nothing to do with the Cathedral or with my life there. I didn't think it could hurt you and I knew I had to reach out to sanity. Katya, I've done many wrong things in my life, but I don't believe in a punishing God. I did work that through after Pieter and Wendele—actions have consequences, and we suffer from them, but I can't think of anything I've done to cause this kind of persecution. It's not paranoia. I've tried to convince myself that it was, but it isn't. Somebody's deliberately out to terrorize me."

"It couldn't be Allie?"

He looked up, shocked. "Oh, God, Katya, no! Why would you think that? Allie would never want me to be frightened."

"Have you told him about it—all the calls?"

"No. Nobody but you. I suppose it was because you received a horrid call yourself—anyhow, I'm glad I told you. It sounds less fearful now that it's out in the open. But I'd prefer you not to say anything to anybody. And, Katya—if you get another nasty call, get your number changed. Change it anyway, to an unlisted number. And—forgive me—but you've no idea how it cheers me to have anybody think that you and I had or are having an affair."

She touched his hand lightly.

"Oh, Katya, bless you, bless you. I'm so glad you've come home. I'm so glad we're friends."

"I am, too. And I think it's time we went home, now."

"Of course. I've talked your ear off." He called for the check. "Thank you for bearing the burden of my past." He handed the waiter a credit card.

She put her napkin on the table. "You made me realize that I have lived a very protected life. I've really been woefully spoiled."

"And loved every minute of it?"

"I never even thought about it. I took it for granted. What I thought about was music."

"And Justin?"

"Thinking about music *is* to think about Justin. I've lived in a narrow world."

"Most of us do," Felix agreed. "Mine has been the Church." He helped her out of her chair. "You wouldn't have believed, would you, that I could be a bishop, and a good one?"

They walked up the stone steps into the warm, late June evening. "Mimi has told me some of the things you've done. She admires you very much."

"Does she? Truly?" He headed into the park, past a group of not-so-young men playing a transistor radio, volume up high.

"Truly," Katherine called above the noise, and Felix hurried them along.

"I'm amazed. You know, Katya, I thought she saw in me only my weaknesses."

"Your strengths are what she's told me about."

"I'm amazed!" he repeated. "I think she sees only Allie's weaknesses. She won't let him change from the young man who was unfaithful to Isobel."

"You don't have to whitewash Bishop Undercroft for me. I find him very attractive." They crossed Eighth Street and walked up Fifth Avenue, where it was quieter than it had been in the Square.

"Oh, my dear, we have so much to share—"

"And now," Katherine said firmly, "it's time for this pleasant evening to end. I'm not going to ask you in—it's bedtime for us both, and you have to get uptown."

"You're right, of course. Thank you, dear, dear Katya."

--*∗{ 3 }∗*--

In the morning she sat at her desk, coffee beside her, to pay bills. She had indeed been spoiled. Jean Paul had taken care of all her bills. One of his parting presents to her had been a small, battery-powered calculator. 'You know your arithmetic is terrible. You'll never get your checkbook balanced without this.' Carefully, patiently, he had taught her to use the machine, and she was grateful for it, although even with its help she found herself counting on her fingers. But the bills were fairly straightforward. The bank had taken care of her rent money for years, and she was happy to have this service continued.

She fought down a feeling that she was wasting time, sitting at a desk punching buttons to add up her bills. She would give one morning a month to it, no more, and she had nothing more urgent to attend to than preparing for Felix's benefit. Although she took a benefit performance no less seriously than a major concert, she was already well prepared. She had chosen works she had played all over the world throughout the years.

Meanwhile, it was about time she learned to pay her own bills, manage her own affairs. She grimaced as she acknowledged that she found it abysmally boring. She kept at it dutifully, however, until the last check was written, the last envelope addressed. She looked up, stretching, and out the window she saw Mimi loping down the street, looking in a hurry as always. Katherine smiled at the retreating figure.

Her back ached much more than when she had been at the piano for the same length of time. She rose, longing for someone to massage her neck and shoulder muscles. She eased herself onto the piano bench and started the Two-Part Inventions and was deep in them when the phone rang. Nanette had usually answered the phone; Nanette had seen to it that she did not have to speak to the hangers-on, the lion-hunters. She reached for the instrument, still half afraid that it might be another anonymous call.

"Madame Vigneras, this is Mother Catherine of Siena—we met briefly after one of Llew Owen's concerts."

"Yes, of course. Hello."

"I was wondering if you would consider coming to speak to the Sisters some Sunday evening? We would, of course, come for you and bring you back home. We have Vespers at five-thirty, then a light supper, and then it would be a great privilege for us if you'd speak to us for a while about your work. We'd have you home by eight or eight-thirty."

It was a perfectly reasonable request. How could she say no? "If you think you'd really be interested—I've lived a very limited life—"

"We'd be deeply interested. After all, you have a sense of vocation probably greater than that of many religious."

"Yes, then, I'd be glad to come."

"How about two weeks from this Sunday?"

"Yes. That would be fine."

"Thank you, Madame. I can't tell you how grateful I am. We look forward to it enormously."

Would Nanette have put Mother Cat through? Probably. Nanette was a devout Catholic. Would she have considered an Episcopal nun a real nun? How ironic, Katherine thought, as she returned to the piano, that it should be through her Jewish tenant, even more than Felix, that she should be accepting an invitation to speak at a convent, that she should become friends with the family of the dean of an Episcopal cathedral, and even the Gomez waifs and strays. Her retirement was not proceeding at all as she had expected. And what had she expected? Did she really think she could sit in her apartment and play the piano all alone and withdraw from the world? And it was Felix, after all, who had introduced her to the great and beautiful cathedral. How strange to live on Tenth Street and have one's unexpected social life largely involved with people whose life not only was the Church but was also geographically at the other end of the island.

Restlessness was undoubtedly a large part of retirement. Without the benefit to work for, she would have been climbing the walls.

June, which had been remarkably cool and pleasant, slipped warmly into July.

"We often have the worst heat of the summer around the Fourth," Mimi said on Saturday evening as they sat in Katherine's apartment drinking a tisane.

Katherine wore a light, loose robe of her favorite silvery sea green. Nevertheless, she felt hot and sticky. "I suppose when winter comes and the north wind funnels through the street I'll wish it was hot. But I do find this weather distressing, partly because of all the weird people who seem to appear out of the cracks. One extraordinary old crone approached me this afternoon and I think she was about to try to rob me, but I was out for my afternoon walk and had only my keys in my pocket, and I turned on her in my most abusive French and she fled."

Mimi laughed. "You're a formidable opponent indeed, but I wish you wouldn't wander about alone so much."

"I have to have the exercise," Katherine explained. "It's the only thing that keeps the arthritis in my knees and hip manageable, and I'm careful which streets I walk on. I tend not to stray far from the West Village."

"I suppose if you carried a small gun," Mimi suggested, "you wouldn't use it?"

"I've lived in a century of total violence"—Katherine leaned back and closed her eyes wearily—"and if I've learned nothing else I've learned that violence is not the answer."

"You live in a city of violence, too," Mimi reminded her.

"I am aware of that. I haven't forgotten what happened to that nice Merv Juxon. Or to Emily. But one cannot live in fear, retreating from life. I have to try to go on living as normally as possible. Otherwise, I'm giving in to, almost condoning violence, and I won't do that."

"Yah," Mimi said. "I suppose I'm asking you to be more careful than I'm willing to be myself, and that's not fair. Emily was certainly not being careless when she walked home from school that afternoon. Speaking of Emily, you *are* coming to the Davidsons', aren't you?"

"Of course. I look forward to it. I gather Llew's going to give another concert after Evensong?"

"In your honor." Mimi took their empty cups out to the kitchen, calling back, "The program's going to be entirely your husband's and your father's works, and he's transcribed several of their orchestral pieces to the organ himself. He's devoted to you."

"He's very Welsh, isn't he? I like him."

"Indubitably Welsh. He's beginning to be a little less bitter. Suzy reports that he actually laughed the other day. After his concert—which will be glorious—we'll go have a quick drink at the Undercrofts'. Or we can back out of that if you like." She stood in the kitchen doorway drying the teacups.

Katherine shook her head. "I'm not anxious to go, because I don't want it to be a late evening. But if we don't go, it will hurt Yolande's feelings and I don't want to do that."

"I wouldn't worry too much about Yolande's feelings." Mimi clattered the cups and saucers back into the cupboard.

Katherine said, "She's feeling raw about something. She's at the point where it wouldn't take much—even a small rebuff—to send her over the edge."

Mimi came back to the living room. "You should have been a shrink. I suppose you're right. Felix says she reminds him of your Manya Sergeievna. Is that why you're so nice about her?"

Katherine shook her head. "Yolande and Aunt Manya both had a foreign and glamorous beauty, and they were both stars in their own fields. Otherwise, they don't resemble each other—at least I don't see it."

"Well"—Mimi crossed the room and looked out on Tenth Street—"we can go for fifteen or twenty minutes, and a glass of wine, for courtesy's sake. Dave and Suzy will be there, and Llew, so it won't be too bad."

Actually, Katherine thought, it sounded quite pleasant. And she looked forward to the concert.

∗{ 4 }∗

Sunday turned out to be one of New York's most beautiful summer days. The air was clear and dry, and a brisk breeze blew from the northwest. The sky was brilliantly blue, with a few fair-weather clouds. Mimi therefore suggested that they take the bus up to the Cathedral.

"It takes forever, but it's such a nice day that I'd rather bounce along in a bus than rattle over the potholes in a springless taxi."

They walked to Washington Square. "How many times I've made this long trek uptown myself," Mimi said. "It's much more pleasant with you."

"Thanks. You've made my retirement a great deal less lonely than it would have been otherwise, you and Felix."

"Lonely. Somehow I don't visualize you as ever being lonely."

"I expect it's part of the human predicament."

Mimi sighed gustily. "And perhaps it's worse for those of us who seem self-sufficient than for the poor little twitterers who always find someone to hover over them in time of need. Everybody except me seems to think I'm omni-competent. Oy veh. Do you know your second-floor tenant, Quillon Yonge?"

"I think I've met him," Katherine said, "but he always seems to be in Europe or South America."

"He travels a lot. But he does come home occasionally, and one time when he was here for a few months, he and I—oh, I was stupid enough to think there was going to be something permanent between us. I, the Independent Oppenheimer, was ready to make a commitment. When Quillon said he had to speak to me about something serious, I was sure it was going to be a proposal, and I was ready to tie the knot. Instead, he told me that he felt we were both getting in too deep, and it would never work out, and he had to leave in two weeks for Africa."

Katherine stopped. "I'm sorry."

Mimi stood, swinging her satchel, looking down at her sandaled feet. "Yeah. Well." She started walking again slowly. "He was probably right. It wouldn't have worked out on a long-term basis. We're good friends on the rare occasions he's home. But I was used to doing the ditching and here I was, ditched. So for the first time in my life, if not quite the last, I turned briefly to my own tradition. I went to a rabbi and by some rare stroke of luck I got a good one, and told him my story, made my confession, as it were, that all my life I'd been afraid of personal commitment, and at last I was ready and Quill wouldn't have me, and I did not find rejection easy. In fact, I hurt like hell. He pulled on his beard— yes, even though he was Reform he had a proper Orthodox beard, black and curly and beautiful, and it came close to making me horny. Shut up, Mimi, I'm being vulgar because it's easier than admitting it hurt. I was feeling disgusted with myself, and the rabbi gave me back a sense of value. How I loved him for that. He really cared that I was hurting. I went to talk with him several times. I was very disappointed to discover that he was happily married, had several children, and was a devoted husband." As Katherine laughed, Mimi joined in. "Maybe I should have become a practicing Jew then, but I didn't."

"Why not?"

"That old lack of commitment, maybe? And I well understood that my motives were mixed every time I went to the rabbi, and I had a hunch that he was as attracted to me as I to him, and I didn't want that on my conscience. And ultimately I felt that all religious institutions are equally empty. But probably the biggest reason was that after Quill ditched me I was back at not being able to commit myself to—anything, it seems."

"Your work," Katherine reminded her.

"Yes. That. Thank God, or I'd have given up on myself entirely. I've lived a selfish life. I'm not a good Jew, Grandmother Renier's Episcopalianism didn't take, and by and large, I don't blame myself for rejecting what Christians and Jews have done to their establishments." They had crossed crowded Eighth Street and were heading for the Square. "This used to be one of the pleasantest parks in the city for a stroll. Now it's just another Needle Park."

Katherine indicated an old woman with a bulging plastic bag digging through one of the trash baskets. "Does she really have everything she owns in that bag?"

"Likely. And one sees so many bag women lately. It's not a nice world."

"I know." The words were barely more than a sigh. "Despite everything, we're—oh, Mimi, we're incredibly lucky."

"We've worked hard," Mimi said, "and still do." They walked past a bench where two old, unshaven men sat, raising bottles concealed in brown paper bags. "It's become as crummy around here as any place in the city. Let's take this seat. It's the best place to wait for the bus."

The sun was not overhot; the breeze was gentle. Katherine felt relaxed. "By the way," she said, "your friend, Mother Cat—of wherever it is—"

"Siena. But she's well aware that even the Sisters call her Mother Cat behind her back—and sometimes to her face."

"Yes—asked me to come up to her convent and talk to the Sisters about—music, I guess."

"Music and you. Music and discipline. Music and vocation. I've gone several times to talk about being a physician. They're a bright bunch of women and I think you'll enjoy them."

"What would have made them want to be nuns?"

"What made you want to be a pianist?"

"I'm not sure there was much *want* about it. I was surrounded by music all my life and it was my gift."

"I have a hunch that Mother Cat would say the religious life is *their* gift." Mimi stopped as one of the big buses turned to make the journey uptown. She helped Katherine up the high step. "Overlong legs are an asset in boarding buses. One advantage of getting on here is that we have a choice of seats. Let's sit on the right so we won't have the sun pouring in on us." When they were seated, she continued, "Catherine of Siena, the original, was an extraordinarily powerful woman for her time."

"Which was?"

"Fourteenth century. She was virtually the Pope for a while. But she never learned to write, so she dictated all her works. Like most great people, a paradox. I don't understand *why* she never learned to write, since she did so many other things that women of her day didn't do. Probably because she never had time. She had a vision which sent her tootling off to Avignon to end the schism in the Church when they had two Popes. And, whether she dictated or not, according to Mother Cat she was a sound theologian."

"What was her theology?"

"Haven't the foggiest. But if it was good enough for Mother Cat I suspect it's something even I wouldn't quarrel with. And what do I mean by that?" she asked out the window of the bus. The air-conditioning was broken down, and the passengers had wrestled the windows wide to catch the breeze. "Not afraid to ask questions, I suppose. Open to change, but skeptical enough to check out carefully whether or not the change is creative—i.e., the way I've done with new theories and practices in surgery. The less use of the knife, the better. I don't operate unless there's no alternative. As a result, I have no yachts or Park Avenue condominiums, but I do afford an extremely pleasant duplex on Tenth Street, and I don't begrudge you one penny of the rent."

"I, too, have to earn my living," Katherine murmured modestly.

"You're no fool," Mimi said, "thank heaven. I'm not surprised

Mother Cat called you. She can smell quality miles away. Even where one would least expect it—as with Fatima Gomez."

"Will she get the training?"

"Unless Yolande loses interest, yes."

"Why would she lose interest?"

"With Yolande, who knows? Has she told you anything about her early background?"

"She indicated that it wasn't easy."

"She'll probably tell you all, sooner or later, and it won't be the true version. Most of us distort our childhoods one way or another, rearrange the past to make it more bearable. Yolande is more blatant in that as in most things. But I suppose she has cause. She was born in Buenaventura, Colombia, a town ill-named. I got off there once, after a vacation with Quillon on a freighter—it was business for him, relaxation for me. Before we docked we were warned to take off our watches, our rings, so they wouldn't be stolen from us as we walked down the gangplank. The area was steamy and filthy and god-awful poor. We drove from there across the Andes to Cali—Christ, it was beautiful—but as we left Buenaventura we saw tumbling-down huts with children of all shades playing in the filth. The natives are very black, but evidently many of the women are available to the sailors. Quill said the poverty is so desperate they have to get money any way they can—and the kids are a mixture of every nationality."

"How ghastly," Katherine said. "No wonder she needs to make up stories."

"She had a squalid beginning, all right. She was discovered—if that is the correct word—by an American sailor with an ear for music and a flair for being an entrepreneur. He brought her to New York and sold her—for that's what it was—to some small-time Sol Hurok when she was an early adolescent."

"Her life sounds a horror."

"I daresay it was. But don't make the mistake of being sorry for her. Many people have horrible lives, and most of them don't have the good fortune to become pop stars, or end up marrying bishops. I do sound absolute, don't I? It's my training. In surgery I sometimes have to make absolute judgments, and once a choice is made I can't go back on it." She peered out the window to look at the street signs. "Perhaps I've done better with my choices surgically than . . . And you surely had choices to make. No choices, no life."

"Yes. I had choices." Katherine lapsed into silence. The late-afternoon summer heat bore in on them, mingled with body odors, gas fumes, the smell of burned rubber, dust, debris.

When she had called Wolfi, almost knocked out, as it were, by Justin's suggestion that she bear him a child, all she could think of was getting on the train to Munich. Blindly, thoughtlessly, she had fled Justin and Paris and gone to Wolfgang, to the Great Grey One who would know what she should do. It was, perhaps, the last totally childish act of her life.

--◆{ 5 }◆--

"Penny," Mimi said.

"Choices," Katherine said. "All the strange choices we have to make during a lifetime. Without music I'd have gone into despair. But despair is—is death."

"We don't always choose our choices." Mimi looked down at her strong hands, already slightly soiled from the bus trip. "What about Emily Davidson? I'll be most interested to have you hear her play—even just accompanying for the rest of the family tonight. I just want to make sure the piano is the right choice for her. She's young enough—had your Justin ever composed before his hands were broken?"

"Not seriously. And he wasn't as young as Emily. Wolfi—Cardinal von Stromberg—encouraged him."

Mimi smiled. "It amuses me that you, too, got tangled with the Church."

"Not really. Only with Wolfi. And he died." She closed her eyes. She would not think about him. Not now, with Mimi, with her perspicacity, beside her. As the bus lumbered uptown she opened her eyes and said, "Did I tell you? I'm going to be a great-grandmother." She had not told Mimi before, and it was a good way to change the subject.

"How splendid!"

"Kristen called me."

"Kristen is your special grand, isn't she?"

"They're all special to me. But she's the musician."

"And she has your black hair."

"So did Julie. That black hair, first in Julie, now in Kristen, is in startling contrast to the blondness of Eric and his family. Kristen's eyes are dark, like mine. Julie's eyes are pale, strikingly pale under her dark brows."

"Where does she get them?"

She could not reply again, "From her father." Mimi had seen Justin's pictures, and Justin's eyes were as dark as Katherine's. So she simply continued, "The Olaffsens are a close family, and they've taken Julie into their lives, as one of them. Eric—her husband—Eric is big and kind, but I've never felt particularly close to him." She visualized her son-in-law, always smiling benignly, his eyes squinting slightly as though to protect them from the brilliance of sun reflected against water, against snow, despite the paucity of the sunlight in Norway much of the year. Eric was a cipher to Katherine. There was something behind the eternal benevolent smile, but she did not know what it was. It revealed itself, perhaps, in Nils's writing, strange, dense, Scandinavian novels; in Gudrun's fierce determination to be a lawyer, to be involved in politics. She saw Eric more in those two children of his than she did in himself, though surely Gudrun's shrewdness was inherited as much from her mother as from her father.

"What about the other three grands?" Mimi was asking.

"Gudrun is second, after Kristen, a blonde, a Valkyrie, a lawyer, and is probably going to be in Parliament one of these days. Nils is a novelist, beginning to be known in Norway. Juliana, the baby, is simply a darling, domestic, placid, very much the favorite of the Farmor." And that was all she needed to say about Juliana.

The Farmor had been the first to notice that Juliana lagged behind the others in development, had not been horrified by it, as Julie and Eric had been. Instead, she had been protective, nurturing, bringing out the child's lovingness, her contentedness with herself and her life.

Katherine was closer to Kristen, just as the Farmor was closer to Juliana. These invisible threads binding this person to that person, and not to the other, were nobody's choice. They simply existed.

What had happened to the thread between Katherine and Julie?

Mimi nudged Katherine. "Christ, it's hot. We get out at the

next stop." She had a gate key, given her by the dean, so they could enter the Close at 110th Street, at the West Gate. Mimi slammed it shut behind them. "Although anybody can climb over who wants to. Even I could, in a pinch, though it would hardly look dignified."

"I'm very glad you have a key," Katherine said. "My legs are considerably shorter than yours."

One of the peacocks screamed at them, and then displayed its magnificent tail as they crossed the Close. A large group of people, many of them festooned with cameras, were trooping toward the exit.

"Oy veh," Mimi said. "The tour buses are lined up outside. We get more than usual on summer weekends, and sometimes it can be a nuisance. It's hard for the Davidson kids to realize that they live in a place that's one of the sights of the city—it's just home to them."

They climbed the iron steps to the No. 5 door, which Mimi pushed open, putting one finger to her lips. The service was in progress. Mimi shut the door silently behind them, and they slipped into seats.

The Wooden Madonna

 I

Bishop Chan was in the lectern, reading from the Bible, and when he concluded, Felix rose from the shadows of the choir stalls and stood at the head of the steps where there was a standing mike. He wore a soft grey cassock, and he looked small and frail, but when he spoke his voice was strong, and he had a quiet authority which Katherine liked.

She was too busy looking at him, thinking that he did indeed look like a bishop, to hear his first words. She picked up as he was saying, "Job is one of the dark books of the Bible, and although it is shot through with light, it has never been one of my favorite books. I turn more often to Jonah, which says much of the same things—that God's love for his Creation is boundless, and that all he wants from us is that we love him in return.

"But today's reading from Job has one of the greatest cries of affirmation in the entire Bible. Out of the depths of his pain, loss, anger, Job cries out, *I know that my Redeemer lives!* and he adds the equally extraordinary words, that he himself will see him, face to face. Not now, not in the midst of this mortal journey, because we couldn't bear it now. Moses asked to see God, and God put him in the cleft of a rock and protected him with his hand, and Moses saw God's hindquarters as he passed by.

"God's hindquarters. That's all we get, in this earthly part of our journey. But it's the glimpses that keep us going.

"The New Testament reading, too, is a promise, a promise that what God creates, he will not abandon, that ultimately we will be as we were meant to be."

For a moment Katherine had a glimpse of Juliana, successful at cross-breeding chickens, and yet unable to complete fifth-grade work.

". . . and then we, too, will see God face to face, as Adam and Eve did when God walked and talked with them in the cool of the evening—before the choices made then and throughout the centuries brought us to the world of pain and confusion in which . . ."

Choices again. Katherine looked at Felix, but she was no longer listening, even though she was feeling grateful that she liked what he was saying, that his delivery was authoritative and vibrant. When he preached, the years seemed to drop from him. Odd: she had never heard Wolfi preach. Wolfi, she thought, would have liked Felix, despite the fact that the two men were totally unlike.

Had anyone ever gone running to Felix as she had gone running to Wolfi?

She had left Justin and Paris, fled blindly to the station and phoned Munich, leaving a message for the cardinal that she was on her way. She took a taxi and went directly to him, not thinking, simply running.

He was waiting for her in the great library. He embraced her tenderly, then held her at arm's length, looking down at her with his deep-set eyes. 'Are you willing to do this for him?'

'Do you think I should?'

He shook his head, smiling gently. 'This is not in the realm of shoulds and oughts, my child. It is in the realm of love.'

'You think I should, then.'

Again he shook his head. 'Katherine, you did not hear me.'

She moved closer to him, and rested her cheek against his chest, receiving from the cardinal the kind of comfort which circumstances had kept her from receiving from her own father. 'I would do anything to make him happy.'

'Even this?'

'He's—oh, Wolfi, you know how proud he is. He said there've been rumors—someone else from Auschwitz—if I have a child, that will stop it all. Why should it be public knowledge? It would make everything all smutty.'

'Do you want a child, Katherine?'

'I never even thought about it. At least not for a long time, since it wasn't possible.'

'But before?'

'Oh, I thought about it. I suppose everybody does—romantic pictures of a baby in an old-fashioned cradle.'

'And now? Have you thought about it?'

'No. Justin's asking me—it was all so unexpected—I just—'

'I want you to go to your hotel.'

'I don't have a hotel. I came to you straight from the train.'

'Very well. I'll have my secretary make a reservation for you.' He crossed the room to one of the long library tables. 'You've stayed at the Vier Jahreszeiten?' She nodded, and he gave quick instructions on the phone. 'The chauffeur will drive you. I want you to stop off in the cathedral—I know you and Justin are not churchgoers—but I want you to go there and hold your love for Justin, for what he has asked you to do, up to God. Then I want you to go to your hotel and have dinner and go early to bed. Come to me tomorrow.'

She did what she was told.

She knelt before a side altar with a statue of the Virgin and Child, simply knelt there, looking at the serene acceptance in the face carved in wood.

She slept little. Again and again she saw in her mind's eye the wooden Madonna cradling the baby in her arms, saw the half-smile on the young woman's face as she looked down at the Child.

In the morning she took the tram and went back to the cathedral to look at the statue again. The love in the wooden face was still there, simultaneously tender and stern.

At three she went to the cardinal.

'I will do it for him,' she said, and told him about the statue and the effect it had had on her.

'She, too, was asked to bear a child in a strange way. She, too, said yes.'

'But, Wolfi—it's one thing to say I will have a child for Justin, and gladly, but—oh, this sounds so stupid—how do I find—how do I go about—h-how—' She broke off, stammering.

'Neither did I sleep last night. I would like to be the father of your child.'

No. No!

'If Justin could sit down and reason objectively, I think that he would choose me.'

'But—you're—you're—'

One arm still about her, he led her to a deep leather sofa, sat down beside her. 'A priest? A celibate? Yes.'

'Then—'

'Katherine, I am still a man. There was no celibacy in the priesthood in the first centuries, it is not intrinsic in the vocation. I love you. I have loved you since I first heard you play.'

Then Willie was right, the world was right— 'Then what they say . . .'

'They? They? Who are they? No, Katherine, I am not what they say. I have known that there was slander. I am sorry that you had to hear it. That you believed it.'

'But I didn't! Not till—oh, Wolfi— Your vows—'

'I take my vows seriously. But the Church has always been realistic about a man's human needs. I do not, despite the gossip, make a practice of unchastity. If I did, how could I possibly offer myself to you now? Don't you see that it would be something I could do for Justin and you, before God—'

Shocked, she heard her own voice, 'Wolfi, have you ever before—' and bit off her words.

He replied gravely, 'I have told you that I do not make a habit of giving in to my weaknesses. This would not be a moment of weakness.'

She looked down at her feet and noted that the toes of her shoes were scuffed.

'Katherine, do not probe into what is better left untouched. I am by nature a passionate man, and yet I have, with God's grace, managed to hold my passions to a minimum. This I do not consider a passion.'

Why was she horrified? Was she a child about promises? Her promises to Justin? The cardinal's promises to God?

'Is this truly such a shock to you?'

'Yes.'

He sighed, reached his hand toward her cheek, drew it back. He sat beside her silently, grey, grave, and she did not know who he was. There was a discreet knock on the door and his secretary came in, silent, inconspicuous, spoke a few words softly, and left.

The cardinal said, 'Go, then. Go back to the cathedral and to the Holy Mother and see what she has to say. I will call you at— seven o'clock.' He kissed her on the forehead, gravely.

She went back to the statue. But now: was it a difference in light? The young woman's face had lost its look of serene acceptance and was stern and sad.

There were no answers anywhere.

--◦◦{ 2 }◦◦--

She shook her head and moved carefully from the past to the present, away from the cathedral in Munich, to the larger one in New York.

She turned her attention to Felix, heard him saying, "The psalmist sings that he has never seen the good man forsaken, nor his children begging for bread. But good men and their children go hungry every day. And we come to the ancient question: If God is good, why do the wicked flourish, and the innocent suffer? They do; the wicked flourish, and children die of malnutrition or drugs; there is continuing war and disease and untimely death, and we cry out, Why!?

"And God answers by coming to live with us, to limit himself willingly in the flesh of a human child—how can that be? The power that created the stars in their courses contained in an infant? an infant come to live with us, grow for us, die for us, and on the third day rise again from the dead for us.

"And what did this incredible sacrifice accomplish? Nothing. On the surface, nothing at all. More than half the world is starving. The planet is torn apart by wars, half of them in the name of religion. We have surely done more harm throughout Christendom in the name of Christ than we have done good. Rape and murder and crimes of violence increase. We are still grieving over the tragic death of Bishop Juxon. So what is it all about? How can it possibly matter?

"I don't know how it matters; I only know that it does, that when we suffer, God suffers, and he will never abandon the smallest fragment of his creation. He suffered with us during his sojourn as Jesus of Nazareth. And from the moment of Creation on, he suffers when any part of his creation suffers. Daily I add to his suffering and only occasionally to his gladness. But he will not give up on me, not now, not after my mortal death. He will not give up on any of us, until we have become what he meant us to be.

"I know this. I do not know how it will be done, but I know that it will be. I know that my Redeemer lives, and that I shall see him face to face." He stood for a moment, regarding the congregation with a gentle and loving gaze. Then he said, "Amen," and returned to his seat.

The dean rose in his hooded stall, and read some prayers, to which the congregation replied, "Amen." Then he seated himself, leaning back in expectancy. A long, low organ note moved slowly, subtly, distance adding to the mystery of sound.

It was one of Justin's orchestral pieces, a strange cry of loneliness and anguish which transcribed well to the organ. Then Llew shifted to Thomas Forrester's music, to the merriment, the clashing terror, and the final gentle triumph of the *Second Kermesse Suite*. The young organist had undoubtedly chosen it to please Katherine, but it stirred up memories of such intense pain that for a moment she thought she was going to faint.

"Are you all right?" Mimi whispered.

"Just a little hot," she managed. The suite was over, now; Llew was playing some of Justin's ballet music. She was all right. Her breathing slowed, steadied, and she was able to listen to the rest of the concert with pleasure.

Yolande wore, this afternoon, a white chiton with gold embroidery at the hem, in which she looked stunning. Mimi murmured, "Allie buys most of Yolande's clothes, and I must say he has exquisite taste," and then moved across the room to Suzy, leaving Katherine to her hostess.

"Allie sends his apologies and hopes to be home before you leave," the bishop's wife said, gesturing Katherine to a seat. "One of his priests, up in the diocese, is in the midst of a crisis, and Allie's gone to see if he can help."

"I'm sorry," Katherine murmured.

"His wife is having an affair with the senior warden and the parish is scandalized. Allie's hoping to put things back together, or at least in some kind of proportion. He's brilliant that way. I can't tell you how many marriages he's saved—he learned in the fire, after all." She glanced at Katherine. "Are you thirsty? There's iced tea as well as alcohol."

Fatima, carrying a plate of small cakes, looked up at the bishop's wife with the same gaze of adoration that Katherine had seen before, then started around the room with her plate.

Yolande brought Katherine a glass of iced tea, which she was glad to have, as she was still feeling a little shaky. She turned to thank Llew for the concert, but Yolande informed her that he had left the Cathedral immediately to go downtown to Katherine's neighborhood to have dinner with the organist from the Church of the Ascension since a mutual organist friend was in town just for the evening.

Very well. She would write him a note when she got home. He had played superbly, and his transcriptions were excellent.

Yolande pulled up a hassock and sat at Katherine's feet. "Are you all right?" Yolande asked. "I feel—I sense—that something has upset you."

Katherine answered, "I'm all right now," and changed the topic. "I do love your Hunter."

Yolande turned her dark eyes toward the bright and peaceful painting. "If I'm upset, and I look at that mountainside for a few minutes, it will calm me, get me back into perspective—sometimes even more than going to the chapel. Felix tells me you have a superb Philippa Hunter, a sort of Madonna and Child, though he says it's really you and your baby."

"A Madonna is far from anything I could ever be." Katherine

sipped the cold tea. "Though I suppose any picture of a mother and infant can be interpreted that way. Llew's concert was beautiful, wasn't it?"

Yolande swallowed the wine in the bottom of her glass. "Llew is a superb musician, and his music is bringing him back into life. Oh, Katherine—may I call you that?"

"Of course."

"There were so many years when my singing and the electric reaction between me and the audience were all that kept me going. I didn't even know that two people could love each other with respect until I met Allie. I had been taught by my manager—by all the men I met—to equate sex with love. I thought that my chemistry, which has always drawn men to me, was love. But it wasn't. It was just the futile attempt of a prisoner to pretend, you know, that the bars weren't on the windows and the doors weren't locked. You married young, didn't you?"

"Yes."

"How did you meet each other?"

"Justin was my piano teacher when I was in boarding school in Switzerland. I think I loved him the first time I met him."

"And he loved you?"

Katherine smiled. "I was only a child. But I was a child with talent, and that was important to him—my talent, not my self."

"And your childhood crush—it was that, wasn't it?"

Yolande Undercroft could be as perspicacious as Mimi. "In the beginning."

Yolande half closed her eyes. Her voice was a monotonous murmur. "I see you. I see you. Small for your age. Like Allie. A hideous school uniform. Long black braids. Big eyes in a peaked face. And talent. Yes, you had talent. That school was regressive for you, wasn't it?"

Katherine looked at Yolande in amazement. Was this the 'gift' she had mentioned? But she answered, "Yes. After my mother died, my father and stepmother were very busy—in the midst of their own careers—and Father was convinced that I ought to have a conventional education. Though that hideous boarding school was their last attempt."

Yolande's eyes were still hooded. "And then you started to study

with your Justin, and then—something happened—what?—wait
—he left. He began to make a name for himself, and he went to
Paris."

That Justin had gone to Paris was all that Yolande could have
known. Katherine felt uncomfortable, almost afraid.

"You went to study with him again—later—in Paris—you'd
had an unhappy romance—am I right?"

"Yes. But who hasn't? After mine blew up I went back to France,
to resume study with Justin."

"And you weren't a child any longer and you fell in love."

"Yes."

"How sweet. And how simple. I wish it could have been that
way for me. And you had two children?"

"Yes."

"I wish I could have . . ." The bishop's wife reached to the
coffee table and a silver filigreed box set with precious stones,
opened it, and took out a cigarette. "You don't mind if I smoke?"

"I do mind." Katherine tried to sound politely regretful. "I'm
sorry, but cigarette smoke stings my eyes."

Casually, the bishop's wife put the cigarette back in the case. "I
started smoking early, cigarettes for my asthma. I still find it soothing. I doubt if my cigarettes would bother you. They come from
Peru. They're very special, you know, pure tobacco used only by
priestesses of the highest caste. I was trained high in the Andes in
all the duties of such a priestess. Of course, our religion, like the
Western, has deteriorated, and one of our duties, when we
reached the age of ten or eleven, was to be available for the priests.
Sexually," she underlined. "They had perverse tastes, and there
was nothing we children could do but, you know, submit." She
rose. "Please. Will you come with me for a moment?"

There was such pleading, such pain in her eyes that Katherine
said, "Yes, of course," and followed her to the little chapel, leaving a buzz of general conversation behind them.

Yolande genuflected toward the altar, then looked at Katherine,
closed her eyes, and turned toward the prie-dieu. "Of course, some
of the girls came to like it—what the priests wanted. But brutality
of any kind has always been repugnant to me. I learned early that
if I screamed it was worse, it lasted longer. So I would bite my
lips, my tongue, till my mouth was full of blood, but I made not

a sound." She turned her back to Katherine and briefly pulled the chiton up over her head. Across the tanned skin were ridged white welts, scars long-healed, but still livid.

Katherine cried out in horror. Her own prison beating had left scars which were barely noticeable, which Mimi had found only with the touch of her sensitive fingers . . .

"Oh, it's all right, Katherine, don't feel sorry for me. It was all long ago. The thing is, you know, it's made all physical violence a horror to me. If Allie and I had been able to have children I could never have raised my hand to them. I could never, *never* hurt anyone." She was trying to tell Katherine something beyond the words.

But what? Katherine, unlike Manya, or Yolande, had no gifts of prevision.

Yolande's voice quivered with intensity. "When there is violence in our neighborhood, I can *feel* it, physically. I *felt* the bullet rip into Merv. We live in a very wicked world, and I could not survive without my faith in Jesus. How different Jesus is from the gods we were taught to worship in Peru, gods who drank our blood and throve on human sacrifice. Once a year, after she had been used by all the priests, one of us was sacrificed. It would have been my turn next, if I hadn't managed to slip away when they were all drunk on the sacred wine. It was a hideous life, you know, but it taught me to be tough."

How often had Yolande felt the lash? No wonder she had to rearrange the past. What had once been invention for publicity was now necessary protection, rather than pretense.

Slowly she turned to face Katherine. "It also taught me to detest perverts. Thank God Allie is totally normal." Then abruptly, "Your first child was a boy, Michel?"

"Justin Michel Vigneras, after my husband. We called him Michou." She added quickly, "Then we had a daughter, Julie—after my mother. She lives in Norway, and I have four splendid grandchildren."

Yolande spoke softly. "I know your son died when he was quite young." Then, in a harsh voice: "But you had him. You had two children. I was never able to have a child. When you have been abused by as many men as I have, it does something to your—Jesus, what am I saying? I had abortions, and then my

tubes were tied. I was making big money on TV and a baby would
have held me back. So I was told. They had conditioned my reflexes to believe them, so I let myself be talked into it. As far as I
am concerned, I was forced. It made me an easier—you know—
lay. Until Allie, I thought all men were beasts. Your Justin, I take
it, was not a beast."

"No. He was, like most artists, a complicated person."

"He loved his children?"

"He adored them."

"He was a good father?"

"A marvelous father."

"I don't even know who my father was. And your father was a
composer, like your husband? How do they, you know, compare?"

"I've never made comparisons."

"Haven't you?" Yolande looked at her skeptically. "Whose
music do you think will last longer, will still be around in a hundred years?"

"That's something no one can tell, till considerably more time
has passed." It was warmer in the chapel than in the living room,
and Katherine felt tired. She sat in one of the rush-bottomed chairs.

Yolande, too, sat, just across the aisle. "Why do you say that?"

"All artists inevitably reflect their own culture. If anyone had
asked a contemporary of Bach's for the composer most likely to
be admired in a hundred years or so, he would likely have been
told Telemann."

"Your father, though," Yolande pursued, "he really belongs to
—well, not quite the nineteenth century, but surely he belongs to
another generation—and his music is still quite popular."

"Actually, it's coming back. For a good many years after his
death he was hardly played at all. Now there's quite a Thomas
Forrester revival, which naturally delights me."

"I asked Allie to get me some of his records," Yolande said. "I
don't know much about classical music, but I liked his—so merry,
so lighthearted—does it reflect his personality?"

Katherine smiled. "Anything but. He was a brooder. But then,
I think he was only part of himself when he was with people, and
complete only in his music. My stepmother, Manya Sergeievna,
could make him laugh, but I don't think anyone else could. Odd,
isn't it—Manya Sergeievna was a brilliant star in the theatre in her

day—but when an actress dies, her art dies with her. Not many young people today have even heard of her."

Yolande looked apologetic. "I haven't. I'm sorry. But then, in a few more years no one will remember Yolande Xabo. A singer's career is even shorter than an actress's, while *you* can go on and on, since your instrument is outside you, not part of your own body. How I hate the body giving out before my understanding of music does. How I hate it!" She stood up and walked to the altar, gazing at the crucifix. "If I were the jealous type I might well be very jealous of you, still able to give concerts."

Katherine looked at Yolande's slender back, and bowed head, and the small chapel suddenly felt as though a cold chill had come over it.

But then Yolande turned, and her face was alive with interest. "And your husband's music?"

"My husband was one of the most delightful, amusing people in the world. I tend to have inherited my father's broodiness, but Justin could laugh me out of my darkest moods. But his music— his music was born out of war and pain. He has much to say to our torn-apart planet."

"You've been with music and musicians all your life, haven't you?"

"Yes. I've been very fortunate. It's my world."

"One world—" Yolande sighed. "I've known so many—that's why I try to help young artists. Fatima Gomez has an amazing voice. I was born with beauty as well as talent, but Fatima—well, her voice may overcome all the rest of the obstacles. It's amazingly like mine at that age." She genuflected once more to the altar. "I suppose we ought to get back to the others, but I did want a little time alone with you, and this seemed the only way to get it. I love this chapel. It gives me great comfort. The last couple of years have been—you know—hell."

--⊰ 4 ⊱--

The young bishop was waiting for them. He greeted Katherine, apologizing for his delay.

"It's good to see you," she said. "I gather you had some kind of crisis to solve."

Still holding her hand, he replied, "I'm not sure all crises have solutions. Maybe resolutions, if one is given the right things to say at the right moment."

Yolande put her arm about her husband. "That is your gift, Allie. You are very blessed. Is everything going to be all right? I told Katherine what it—you know—was about. I hope you don't mind."

"Not at all." The bishop let Katherine's hand go. "All I could do, for today at any rate, was to stop my poor young priest from acting too impetuously. His wife's a fool, but a nice fool, and I think she's learned her lesson. That pompous senior warden I'm not sure of. When people start using Jesus to justify wrongdoing, there's not much they're able to hear. Well, enough of diocesan problems. How was the concert?"

"Excellent," Yolande said, casting a long side glance at Katherine.

"Do sit down, Madame," the bishop said. "This chair is a good one for you, I believe."

"Thank you." Katherine felt tired from the tension in the chapel with Yolande. She looked at Bishop Undercroft and tried to visualize him as Felix had seen him in San Francisco, but could see only the young Lukas. Lukas had not looked like a Greek god; with his height and strength he was more like a Viking. Or, irony of ironies, a young wolf. *Lukos* is the Greek word for wolf. But she had not known that until long after both Wolfi and Lukas were dead.

"I have a little treat for you," Yolande broke across her thoughts. "Fatima is going to sing for us. I've kept telling you what a, you know, lovely voice she has, and I think it's time you heard it. She'll be less self-conscious with her mother not there. Mrs. Gomez doesn't think much of music."

Fatima was standing at the head of the steps to the living room, looking clumsy and embarrassed. The formidable Mrs. Gomez, Katherine thought, would indeed likely have intimidated her daughter even further. Yolande went to the record player and put on an orchestral recording of some folk songs. Fatima stood stolidly through the first song, frozen in her lumpish fright, looking as though she were never going to open her mouth, but at the second song she began to sing. And suddenly she was no longer ugly or stupid-looking. Her voice was clear and pure, and she sang with her eyes closed, her arms dropped loosely to her sides, lost in the music. The simple melodies showed off her range well; it was even wider than Yolande's, and the quality of the voice was infinitely richer. Katherine was grateful that Yolande had trained the child with these simple songs.

When the record ended, Fatima opened her eyes. The applause was enthusiastic.

As the child started to scurry off, Yolande said, "Wait, Fatima, you must take a bow now. You did very well, and I'm proud of you."

Blushing painfully, the girl bowed in clumsy imitation of Yolande, then scuttled off.

Yolande looked at Katherine, "What do you think?"

"She's extraordinary."

"A good investment on my part, *n'est-ce pas*?"

"I should say that Fatima has a superb teacher."

Yolande blushed with pleasure, and the group began talking about Fatima and her surprising voice, and again Katherine withdrew, leaning back and resting.

After a while she realized that the dean was no longer there, and then Suzy rose, thanking the Undercrofts and saying that it was time to leave. Katherine pushed out of her chair, murmuring her thanks, and Yolande said, "It was more than a pleasure to be with you. It was a privilege. Thank you for letting me talk to you. I can't tell you how much that means to me. I don't have many women friends. I need someone who understands music, as you do." She stood at the door to Ogilvie House, elegant in her white and gold, waving them off.

The air outside was oppressive. One of the peacocks strutted by, dragging his long tail in the dust. Topaze emerged from behind some bushes.

"What are you doing here?" Suzy asked rather sharply.

"Waiting to take Fatty home. Ma doesn't want her on the subway alone."

Suzy's manner softened. "Do you want to come in and wait?"

Topaze shook his head. "Too hot. Just wanted to say good night to the music lady."

"Good night, Topaze," Katherine said, and he bowed, deeply, then moved away from them onto the grass.

"Poor kid," Suzy said. "He quite often walks Emily home from school in a funny, protective, old-fashioned way. And I'm grateful to him for that." She opened the glass doors to Cathedral House and a blast of hot air rushed out at them. "The office air-conditioners are off for the weekend. Sorry. It's fairly comfortable once we get up to the apartment."

"After climbing Mount Everest," Mimi said. "You go on up, Suzy. We old folks will take it more slowly."

"You go on, too," Katherine urged. "You're used to dashing up and down stairs at Tenth Street. Felix and I will climb at a pace suited to our exalted age."

At the first landing, Felix stopped to mop his brow. "How did you like my homily?"

"It made me believe that you were truly a bishop."

He laughed ruefully. "Is it so difficult?"

"Not difficult at all. And I liked what you said. It reminded me of Wolfi."

"Thank you." Felix bowed slightly. "Thank you, my dear. You couldn't say anything that would please me more. I'm glad you had a chance to see me functioning, at least a little."

They started up again, and at the second landing Felix paused once more. Despite Katherine's arthritic knees, the stairs were not as hard on her as they were on Felix. Rather curiously she asked, "How on earth did Mrs. Gomez come to cook for the Undercrofts?"

Felix said carefully, "She is a magnificent cook."

He was prevaricating. "How did they find her?"

Again carefully, Felix said, "The cook Yolande had returned to South America, and she needed someone."

"So how did she find Mrs. Gomez?"

"People who can afford servants know where to ask around, and I think Yolande's old cook knew Mrs. Gomez, who is, I must say, a far better cook. However, according to Emily, Mrs. Gomez got fired from her last job because she hit one of the children in the family."

"How would Emily know that?"

"I suspect Tory told her. Little pitchers have big ears. We'd better start climbing again, or they'll be sending out a rescue party for us."

And indeed, Jos and John were coming down the stairs, offering help.

"We're slow," Felix said, "but like the proverbial tortoise we get there, and without any help from you young hares."

He had been holding out on her, Katherine thought, though she was not sure why she was so certain about this. But there was more to Mrs. Gomez coming to work for the Undercrofts than that they needed a cook.

Dean Davidson had changed to blue jeans and a striped T-shirt; he had cooked the dinner, some kind of Spanish stew with beans and sausages and vegetables, rather highly spiced. Katherine was glad she had a hearty digestion. She sat at his right during the meal and relaxed into the general noise of family dinner-table conversation. Emily and Tory argued until Suzy threatened to send them from the table. Jos prodded his mother into telling him, in detail, about some complicated emergency heart surgery she had performed that morning. Felix and the dean, ignoring the rest of the conversation, began discussing who would be elected the new suffragan bishop.

"It will be hard to find someone with Merv's irenic qualities," the dean said, "and a peacemaker is what we need in this diocese."

"Mother Cat is generally popular," Felix said.

"True, but I doubt very much she'd accept being put up for election. St. Andrew's is very dear to her heart."

"Sister Mary Anna is an excellent headmistress and takes care of most of the administrative work."

"Also true. But Mother Cat wants nothing to do with ecclesiastical politics."

"They'll ask her to run, anyhow," Felix said.

The dean smiled at Katherine. "One thing that kept me from the Church for a long time was all this politicking, but I suspect you don't escape it anywhere."

She nodded. "But I was lucky. My husband, and then my manager, kept me out of it."

"We've discussed it enough for tonight. The subject's going to be around until autumn when we have Diocesan Convention. This is not going to be an easy election. In one of C. P. Snow's novels there's the very political election of a new master of a college, and one of the dons says, 'I want a man who knows something about himself. And is appalled. And has to forgive himself to get along.'"

--⊷❧ 5 ❧⊶--

"Now." The dean clapped his hands for attention. "Let's get organized so that we can make music." With a wave of his arm he swept everybody from the table, shouting out instructions. Jos and John did the dishes, while the little girls prepared coffee, and then they all assembled in the airy living room. Katherine was placed in one of the comfortable chairs by the fireplace, where she waited expectantly.

John was as good as she had hoped he would be. She heard Dave murmur to his wife, "John approaches the violin the way I approach the chalice and paten."

Felix's playing was better than Katherine had anticipated. His technique was rusty, but he handled the bow well, and his tone was clear. Dave played the English horn as though pouring through it all the pain and loneliness of his life, of the lives of everyone around him, everyone surrounding the Cathedral. After a certain amount of badgering by Felix, he played the overture to the third act of *Tristan*.

"That does something to me," Mimi said. "I'd like to put my head down and howl."

"Let's have something cheerful." Dave took sheaves of music from a mahogany rack. "Something we can all play. Warm up your recorders, Suzy, Tory, Jos. Here, let's tackle this Vivaldi, and then we can try some Diabelli."

The three recorder players were adequate, though certainly no more than that. Dave had switched from the horn to the flute and murmured that his lips were out of shape, but he played well.

Emily, accompanying, was tense, scowling at the music. She played with precision, and she listened, Katherine noted, to the other instruments. But whether or not she had the same kind of talent that John did was impossible to tell from her accompanying.

Then, without warning, Emily banged her fists down on the keys with a loud discord, shouted, "It's intolerable! I'm playing horribly!" and stormed out of the room. In the distance came the sound of sobbing and banging.

"Leave her," Dave said to Suzy.

"How can she be so awful?" Tory demanded indignantly.

Felix started to rise.

"No, Bishop," Dave said. "Don't go in to her."

"But she's in pain—"

"Not really—" Mimi started.

Felix cut in, "I didn't mean physically."

"Please, Bishop," Dave restrained him.

"I do apologize," Suzy murmured.

"Let's get on with the music," John said.

Jos looked at his recorder. "Em's temper's never been the best, but lately it's been getting out of hand. Why do you let her get away with it?"

"I don't think we're letting her get away with it," Suzy demurred.

"My dears." Felix held up his hand for silence. "Don't you see what Emily is doing?"

"No," Tory said.

"What, Bishop, please?" John asked. "She's always had a quick temper, but since her accident—"

"Since her accident she's been spoiled rotten," Tory said.

"Hey, hold it, Tory," John warned. "You used to be the spoiled baby and you resent—"

Again Felix held up his hand. "Children. Quiet. Your parents have not spoiled Emily, nor have you. But she's angry. Wouldn't you be?"

Tory scowled. "Sure, but I wouldn't take it out on everybody."

"You would if your talent—that which is death to hide—had been taken away in one instant."

Tory looked sullen. "Since I don't have any particular talent, I wouldn't know."

"Tory," Suzy remonstrated.

John repeated, "Hold it." He looked directly at Katherine. "Uncle Bishop is right, Madame Vigneras, Em was terrified this evening. She knows she can't ever dance again, but she doesn't know whether or not she can play the piano. Can she?"

Katherine returned his gaze. "I don't know, John. I couldn't tell enough from her accompanying. One thing I do know, she has the artist's drive. And I've seen one talent destroyed and the drive turned in another direction. When she has her program worked up I will listen to it, but I will not insult her by making a decision on the basis of this evening."

"Thank you," Dave said. "Some people tend to be sentimental where Emily is concerned, and she sees through it immediately. I'm not happy about her explosions, but I think she has a certain amount of cause."

"And you leave her alone," Mimi agreed. "That's the best way of handling a tantrum. Pay it no attention."

"Well—" Suzy sighed and turned to Katherine. "You've certainly seen us naked and unadorned."

"I have children and grandchildren," Katherine said. "And I agree with Felix and Mimi—and John—about Emily."

"Right," Dave said. "Shall we get back to some music?"

"How can we," Jos asked, "without Em?"

"Shall I try to get her to come out?" Suzy suggested.

"No." Mimi spoke quickly.

Again Suzy sighed. "As a mother I leave a great deal to be desired. I'm away from my children—at the hospital too much—"

"We like you the way you are," John said. "Part-time you is better than most full-time mothers I know."

"Thanks, John, that's balm to my heart. But if we're to go on playing, shouldn't I—"

"No." Katherine eased herself out of the chair with the help of her stick. "I'll accompany."

She was not accustomed to accompanying, and she found it a challenge to listen to the others, to try to guide them. Tory had a tendency to accelerate, so Katherine emphasized the beat and the melody until the child had checked herself.

"Oh, wow," Tory said when the suite was over, everyone

finishing more or less at the same time. "That was terrific. I could feel myself speeding up and then Madame Vigneras pulled me back. And I never understood that sort of hiccupy—"

"Syncopated," John supplied.

"Yes, that part."

Dave set more music on the piano, in the stands. "Just one more. That is, if you can bear it, Madame."

"One more. I'm enjoying it, but it's getting late." Katherine looked at the music. "Good. I'm moderately familiar with this. My eyes are no longer what they used to be for sight-reading."

"A lot better than mine," Felix said. "We haven't played that for ages and I fumbled all over the place."

She smiled at him. "You're not half bad, Felix. Ready?"

He pushed his half-moon spectacles into place. "It's hot. They always slide when it's hot. Yes, let's go on."

While they were playing, Emily came back and sat on the sofa beside Mimi, not speaking. Mimi patted her gently, and continued listening to the music.

When they had finished, Emily rose and went to Katherine. "I'm sorry. It was extremely discourteous of me to fly off the handle like that."

Katherine regarded her, nodding acknowledgment. This apology was not coming easily.

"I have an absolutely vile temper," Emily continued. "I'm sorry it got out of control, everyone, truly I am."

"We missed you," Felix said. "You cover up for my mistakes better than Katherine does."

"You didn't make mistakes—" Tory started.

Felix said, "Where we really missed you, Emily, was in the ballet music, because you play that with more authority than anyone else. Which makes me think—don't you have a ballet dancer as one of your tenants, Katherine?"

Katherine had almost forgotten about Dorcas and her problems. For a moment it seemed to her to be heartlessly tactless of Felix to bring her up, but then she realized that to refuse to talk about ballet with Emily was as stupid as refusing to talk about someone who has died. "Yes. Dorcas Gibson. But she isn't dancing now, she's pregnant."

"Very pregnant?" Tory asked with interest.

"Very visibly pregnant, at any rate. Do you know her, Emily? Was she in your company?"

"Yes, but we kids didn't see much of the real company—except those who teach in the school. During the *Nutcracker*, I got to know her a bit a couple of years ago when I was dancing Klara, the little girl, and she was the Sugar Plum Fairy. I wasn't supposed to dance Klara—it was a girl a year older, but I'd been told I'd have a chance the next year. But she got a stress fracture in her foot the day before the opening, and I slid into the role. A good thing, because I couldn't have done it the next year." Her voice was factual, with no residue of self-pity. "Dorcas is nice. She talked with us kids, and told us stories about when she'd been in the school, and she helped me with a couple of steps where I was getting out of rhythm. I like her. I hope she has a nice baby."

"Is her husband a dancer?" Tory asked.

"He's a banker or lawyer or something gross like that," Emily said.

"What's he like?"

"He's a turd," Emily stated categorically.

"Emily!" Suzy protested.

"Don't you mean a nerd?" Jos suggested.

"Turd."

The air was becoming charged again. Felix said, "Did you know that once upon a time, thousands of years ago, I played the violin in a nightclub in the Village? I was awful, but it was all that kept me from starvation for a full season. Now, children, it's past my bedtime." He wrapped his violin in a white silk scarf before tucking it in its case.

Mimi rose. "Bedtime for us, too." She glanced at Katherine. "I have to be at work early tomorrow morning."

"As do we all," Suzy said. "Dave has been known to throw people out who haven't left at what he considers a suitable hour."

Emily let out a guffaw. "One time he left the room and came back in his pajamas, carrying his toothbrush."

"Don't tell Madame Vigneras all my secrets." The dean turned to Katherine and Mimi. "I'll drive you home."

"No, Dave. You or the boys walk us to Broadway and see us into a cab."

The dean walked with them and stayed till he'd closed the door of their taxi.

—◦⊰ 6 ⊱◦—

As they neared Tenth Street, Mimi suggested, "How about a back rub?"

"I'd love it. But, as you said, you have to be up early."

"I'm wound up. It'll help me unwind. Take your bath and I'll be down."

Katherine, too, was wound up. Emily had touched her more with her outburst than with her calm courage. The child was going to attack life like an eagle; but a one-taloned eagle is woefully vulnerable.

—And no one can help her, she thought, —as no one could help me. We're on our own. No wonder I yell for a God I do not understand in times of stress. Every time I've tried to depend on a human being it's been disastrous.

She took her bath and lay down on her bed, waiting for Mimi.

The cardinal, her idol. She had gone running to Wolfi. He would tell her what to do, would make it, somehow, all right.

But he couldn't. She had been a blind fool. He had no answers for her. The carved wood statue of the Virgin had no answers.

She had left the lights and shadows of Wolfi's cathedral and told the chauffeur she wanted to walk. She moved blindly through the streets. Munich had become a familiar city, but she recognized nothing. She groped in her handbag for her dark glasses, as though they would disguise her pain, and walked directly into Lukas.

Not yet Lukas. Into Kommandant von Hilpert.

He caught her and held her. 'Madame Vigneras!' In prison he had called her Katherine.

'Kommandant von—'

'*Nein.* Herr Hilpert. Lukas. Please, Lukas. You are trembling, you are cold, you need coffee.' Without hesitation he took her arm, led her along the street, around a corner, into a small cafe. He seated her and ordered coffee, '*Mit Schlag ober*, and pastries.' He looked across the table at her. 'I thought never to see you again.'

'I'm sorry . . .' She was still half in shock, and seeing Lukas von Hilpert was almost as shocking as the cardinal's proposal.

'What is it?'

'Nothing,' she said quickly. 'I was just—very depressed.'

He rested his hands on the table. She noticed that he wore a wedding band. 'Were you? So was I. It has been a dull day. Until now. But why are you in Munich? I saw no notice of a concert.'

'I came to see Cardinal von Stromberg.' So unused was she to evasions that she blurted out the truth.

'And have you seen the eminent cardinal?'

'He wasn't there.' Nor was he, the great *éminence grise* she had been running to see, the marble statue who had never existed except in her own imagination, the earthly father who would make all things well.

'My wife is one of his many admirers,' Lukas said, and dismissed him. 'I have been to your concerts. How you have matured in your playing!'

'Thank you.'

'I wanted, but I did not presume, to come backstage.'

She nodded. She would not have been pleased to see him. She did not understand why she was pleased to see him now.

'Your husband's music is played frequently.'

'Yes, he is becoming a fine composer.'

'He is all right?'

'Moderately. He was tortured at Auschwitz.'

He made an anguished face. 'I did not know. There was much that I did not know when I talked to you in that funny school building outside Paris.'

'There was much I didn't know, either. I can't condone what the Germans did, but—oh, God, what the Americans did—' She looked out the window at the rubbled street. 'This was retaliation above and beyond—'

She had not tasted her torte and he gently pushed her plate to her. 'Bombs are never a solution. That is true. But we Germans, with our poisonous religion, caused all this devastation.'

'Religion?'

'Oh, yes, believe me, religion. You went to see a cardinal? Do not ever look for help in religion. It is all a lie, a diseased deceit.' For a moment the tension of lines drawn between nose and mouth reminded her of Justin, despite Justin's fine-boned darkness and von Hilpert's muscular fairness. 'I embraced the Nazi religion with all my soul. I believed that we were building a better, purer world, and that I was part of this army of holy people. You find this amusing?'

'Not amusing at all.'

He leaned across the table toward her. 'Katherine—unlike the majority of my fellow countrymen I cannot pretend, now that the war is over, that nothing really happened, nor that I, myself, am unchanged, and we can pick up and go on as before. I cannot pretend, to myself, or to you, that I had no personal responsibility whatsoever for all that happened, even the things I did not know about.' A slight smile eased the severity of his face. 'Eat,' he urged. 'I knew that we were working on the atom bomb, and I knew what was involved. We would have used it just as ruthlessly and stupidly as you did. When you are a religious fanatic, the cause of your religion is all that matters, not human life.'

Again she looked out the window, shuddering at the devastation of a block of buildings shattered and gutted by bombs and fire. 'This—all this outside—is nothing in comparison to Hiro—' She broke off, swallowing painfully, and took a sip of her coffee.

He cleaned up some last chocolaty crumbs. 'I am grateful that we did not get the atom bomb first. But it is a burden on the conscience of all humankind.' He laughed, an unamused, angry snort. 'I talk like this and eat cake.'

She took, then, a bit of her pastry.

'Religion is a virus, virulent, deathly. It is a lesson I had to learn the hard way, and at the expense of many other people.'

'What are you doing now?' She closed her eyes briefly against the surrounding destruction.

'I manage a number of theatres, not only here, in Munich, but in other cities. I am the manager, in fact, of the hall in which you have played, but I thought it best not to make myself known to you.'

'So it was you who sent me the roses in the lovely crystal bowl!'

'You liked them?'

'I was overwhelmed. A bowl like that is not what one expects from the usual manager.'

'You kept it?'

'Wasn't I supposed to?'

'But of course.'

'I love it. I take it with me whenever I travel. Thank you.'

A crisply uniformed waitress—all uniforms in Germany tended to be crisp, she thought—offered them more coffee from a large silver pot. Behind her came a waiter, also crisp, with a bowl of whipped cream and more pastries. Katherine accepted the coffee and cream, 'but nothing more to eat, please.'

'You have been to the Heiliggeistkirche?' von Hilpert asked.

'No.' The coffee was fragrant and tasted almost as good as it smelled. 'I've never had time when I've been here.'

'Well, then.' He smiled, as though deliberately moving out of darkness. 'We must go, so that you can see the ten original Maruska dancers which Erasmus Grasser carved in wood for the town hall— I think you do not have other plans? We will not talk of horrors but of art; of creation, not destruction.'

They spent the rest of the afternoon together, until the museum closed, and then he asked, 'Where are you staying?'

'The Vier Jahreszeiten.'

'When are you returning to Paris?'

'My husband doesn't expect me till after the weekend.'

'Then you will have dinner with me?'

If she had dinner with him she would not have to see the cardinal. 'But don't you—'

'My dear, any plans I might have had—and I assure you that in fact I had none—would be unimportant in comparison with this opportunity to spend an evening with you. I have wanted, when you have played in Germany, to get in touch with you, to do more than send you flowers as any anonymous manager may do, but I have considerably less assurance than I did. How would Madame Vigneras respond to a message from her erstwhile jailer, her enemy? But I am not your enemy now.' Again his face contorted into an unhappy grimace. 'My children are confused because West Germany is such a good friend of the United States, and why, when, as they say, we were at war with the United States? And why is the United States quarreling with Russia, when they were allies during the war? Friend, foe, it is all on paper; people, human beings, are shoved around for the sake of power and greed. Power. I believed in it once.'

'When you were commander of the prison.'

He slapped the fist of one hand into the palm of the other. 'I used up all my believing then. Now—I believe only that this day is good because chance sent you blundering into my path, and you are being kind to me. That is enough to believe. I believe what your music says when you are playing. Isn't that enough?'

'Yes, it is enough.'

'And—' He smiled at her. 'You went to see a cardinal and he was not there?'

'Yes.'

'You are religious? I have offended you?'

'No. I am not religious.'

'Then why would you need to see a cardinal?'

'He is a friend—a lover of music—'

'Sorry, I can see that you do not wish to talk about it. Above all things, I do not want to hurt you, and if you care about the Church—'

She stretched her fingers. 'I play the piano. Wolfi—the cardinal—came to one of my concerts, and we became friends, through music.'

'You are still a child, and I am hurting you, and I do not wish to hurt this beautiful child.'

'I am not a child.'

'You have a child's vulnerability. Come. I'll take you back to your hotel, and I'll come for you at seven.'

---⊷{ 7 }⊶---

She bathed, changed, then picked up the phone. The cardinal had said he would call her at seven. If she did not call him first, he would call her, and not finding her might well call Justin. She did not want a search party out for a missing pianist.

His secretary was put on the phone. 'Yes, Madame Vigneras. The cardinal said I was to get hold of him if you called. Please wait.'

It was so long before the cardinal came on the line that she was on the verge of hanging up. Then she heard his warm tones.

'Katherine, I'm sorry to have kept you waiting for so long. May I come?'

'No—'

'To talk—'

She shook her head at the phone. 'No, Wolfi. I don't know what Justin was thinking of, or you. I can't just go to bed with someone in order to get pregnant, and then say goodbye and thank you very much. I can't—I can't make love without being involved with the—the—'

'But, Katherine, we are involved. We've been making spiritual love for a long time.'

'You've been making it with Justin, too, then.'

'But of course. That is why this would be so right, for you to bear a child for Justin by me.'

She shook her head at the blind instrument again. 'No. Wolfi, you are a priest, a cardinal—'

He spoke patiently. 'I know. I would not enter into this lightly, or at all, believe me, if it did not seem so—so arranged in heaven.'

'No.' And then, slowly, 'I would be involved with you in a different way. Our friendship has been more important to me than I can say. But this—it would be a completely different kind of involvement. I couldn't just make love with you and get pregnant and go back to Justin and then never—never—'

'Of course not. That was not what I had in mind.'

Her throat felt constricted. 'How could Justin suggest this? How could he think I could just go to bed with someone with nothing but pregnancy on my mind?'

'*Kinderlein.*' The cardinal was again the priestly father. 'I doubt if Justin was able to think it through that clearly. He is simply crying out of his own pain. Do you realize how devastating this is for him?'

She replied stiffly, 'Yes, I think I do.'

'You are a woman. There is no equivalent in a woman's body. This intractable integrity is pride on your part.'

Where, before, had her integrity been something to be accused of? In her pain she could not remember. She did not have any feeling of pride, only of being battered.

The cardinal continued, 'You can perhaps guess at what he is feeling, but you cannot understand. You cannot understand his desperate need to have you give him a child of your body, to call his own.'

She could not talk any more. She murmured, 'I'm sorry, Wolfi, I'm sorry,' and hung up.

But she did give Justin the child he wanted. Not the cardinal's child—Lukas's.

—⋅⋯⊰{ 8 }⊱⋯⋅—

After dinner Lukas looked at her, saying, 'We need each other. I think, for tonight at least, you need me as badly as I need you. I do not ask why. I do not need to know. But you need me.'

They walked in the direction of her hotel, his arm protectively around her. 'Shall we stop at a drugstore?' Lukas suggested.

She did not need to ask him to explain. 'I am prepared.' Prepared for what? To become pregnant. She did not like deception, Justin's, the cardinal's, her own. But she was tangled in it. She said, 'Lukas, you talk about your children. What about your wife?'

'My wife.' His voice was flat. 'Perhaps my wife, staying with my wife, is a small reparation for—oh, for the French school where you were prisoner. It is my wife's house we live in. I love her parents—how ironic that is—I love my children. But my wife is a self-centered hypochondriac, incapable of loving anything except her own imagined illnesses. I am always grateful that my work takes me to many cities. I stay away as much as possible. When I am at home I am with my children. My wife does not sleep in the same room with me, much less the same bed. You need not feel that you are taking anything from her.'

'I'm sorry. After you promised not to ask me anything.'

'I ask you nothing.'

He was tender, gentle.

Justin's lovemaking had been frantic, almost violent, as if in some kind of anguished premonition. She had been excited as their love exploded with brilliant fireworks, almost frightened. She had responded to the urgency without realizing that such a pitch of passion could not be sustained.

Lukas brought her slowly up to the heights.

In the morning, he said, 'My parents-in-law have a small castle in the mountains. We will go there for the weekend.'

'But your parents-in-law—how can—'

'They love me. They understand. I stay with my wife for their sake as much as for the children. I do not absolve myself of all blame for my wife's condition; they do.'

More than one night with Lukas was needed . . . 'Yes.'

He kissed her gently, murmuring, 'Katherine, I do not pretend to know what sent you fleeing to Munich, and I do not want to know. All I want is to rejoice in this beauty. When I was your jailer I was too bound up in ideologies, and zeal for conversion, to be human. And I had had, after all, an adolescent crush on your mother. I want to reassure you that your mother in no way comes between us. It is you I want, you.'

She pressed her cheek against the springing gold hair on his chest, so different from Justin's softer black. 'I know.' There was no question.

He stroked her slowly and rhythmically. 'I know, too, that when this weekend is over, we will not see each other again. Not this way.'

How did he know? What did he know?

His hand stilled as he stated, 'You are in love with your husband.'

'Yes. I always will be.'

"All right. No questions. For whatever reason I am being given this gift, I accept it with incredible joy. And yet—' His hand began to move again. 'Somehow, even when it would have seemed the most impossible, when you rejected me in prison, and you were right to do so, I always knew that one day this would happen.'

—·⊰{ 9 }⊱·—

They drove for half a day, and then took a miniature train.

'There are no cars in the village where the *Schloss* is.'

'What is it called?' she asked.

'Let it be nameless. A fairy-tale village, with a castle of dreams. I must warn you—it is very small—it hardly bears the name of *Schloss*—but it is old and beautiful and I love it.'

They were greeted with deference by an elderly couple who

came out from the small cottage that served as gatehouse. Was this where Lukas came with his—

As though reading her, he said, 'I come here often with the children, for skiing in winter, hiking in summer. And we are always here for Christmas. We have a great tree, and it is like the first act of the *Nutcracker*.'

He brought her a heavy shawl. 'It is colder here than in Munich. If you need anything else, my mother-in-law's clothes will fit you.' They walked through the winter-bare woods, the trees just starting to soften against a pearly sky. They slept in a vast four-poster bed. He asked her if she was taking precautions, and again she replied, 'I am prepared.'

The elderly couple fed them, mostly with vegetables from the root cellar, or from the pantry filled with canning jars, and with their own wine from the damp, cool cellars. They drew her bath, laid out her clothes, clucked over her with loving approval, and she was grateful.

The prison on the outskirts of Paris had been the darkness of nightmare. This was the golden light of fairy tale. While it was happening, it was forever; there was no time.

And then it was over.

Lukas put her on the train and then walked swiftly away.

She did not cry on the train, not until she got back to Paris, to her husband, and then she hid her tears, did her utmost not to let him see that she was in deep depression. She had been right when she had cried out to the cardinal that she could not sleep with someone in order to get pregnant and then forget it. During that intense weekend at the *Schloss* she had, in fact, fallen in love with Lukas, and the knowledge that it was over, that she would probably never see him again, seemed intolerable. When she worked at the piano she saw the music room in the *Schloss* where she had played for Lukas on a square rosewood piano with a light, sweet tone. Resolutely (like a heroine in a Victorian novel, she thought bitterly) she would push the images away. She and Justin went on a brief tour through Scandinavia, and that helped. When they returned she went to the doctor, who confirmed that she was pregnant. When she told Justin he exclaimed, 'So that's why you've been so moody!' He was radiant at the news. How could he be? But he was. 'We must call Wolfi,' he said.

She asked, calmly, 'Does he know that we—that we are doing—this?'

'Of course,' Justin said. 'I tell Wolfi everything.'

And what would the Wolf have told Justin? 'You call him.'

'He will want to talk to you, too.'

'No. I can't. Not about this. This is—private—between you and me.'

'But Wolfi will be the godfather.'

'You talk to him. I can't.'

He put it down to the kind of aberration to be expected of a pregnant woman. When he dialed the operator she left the room, left the house, and walked for an hour.

Gradually Lukas receded from the forefront of her mind. She did everything in her power to feel that the life within her belonged only to herself, to (but how?) Justin.

--◦◃{ 10 }▹◦--

"Katherine!"

Abruptly she returned to the present, to New York, to Tenth Street.

"Where on earth were you?"

Mimi was standing by the bed, holding alcohol and lotion. "I had a phone call from a colleague in Detroit which kept me so long I was sure you'd given up on me."

"No, I'd never do that, Mimi."

"You were certainly off in space somewhere. I had to call you three times before I could get you away from wherever you were."

"Not so much space as time. I told you I'd come home to come to terms with my memories."

Mimi turned off the lights by the bed, leaving only the reading lamp by the chaise longue to hold back the shadows. Katherine relaxed under the strong, competent hands. She was no longer remembering, or thinking; she was content to let the tensions flow from her body, to enjoy the comforting movement of the sure fingers. Sleepily she asked, "Do you know the garden-apartment tenants?"

Mimi's hands slowed, then continued, "By sight. They've only

been here a year. I doubt if I've spoken more than a few words
with them. Why do you ask?"

Still sleepily, Katherine murmured, "I was wondering why
Emily Davidson called him—Terry Gibson—a turd."

"Emily, like me, tends to make snap judgments. I would guess
that, like me, she's usually right, but not always. Gibson strikes
me as a total Establishment type, striding along with his briefcase,
concerned about making money and his male macho image and not
much else. Not Emily's type."

"I'd like to have seen her dance the *Nutcracker*."

"I did," Mimi said. "She was stunning. She knocked your breath
away and then melted your heart. Now be quiet. You're waking
up and I want you to go to sleep."

Katherine relaxed, letting all her muscles loosen, and sliding into
a dream of Emily dancing, and being pursued by the giant rodents
from the ballet. When the phone rang, her limbs jerked in shock.

"The world breaks in again." Mimi reached for the phone and
handed it to Katherine, who rolled over to take the receiver.

"Hello."

"So the famous Madame Vigneras is up to her old tricks again!"
a voice said. "We know what you are doing right now, you and
the great Dr. Oppenheimer. You may think that you are better
than other people, but we know that you are worse, and what you
are up to, and you cannot hide from us—"

Katherine slammed down the phone.

"*Ma mie!* What was it?"

Katherine's voice was cold with rage. "One of those filthy calls
accusing—"

"Accusing who of what?"

"You and me of—" She glanced toward the window.

Mimi replaced the phone on the night table. "It's entirely my
fault. People assume I'm lesbian, and anybody who's my friend
must be one, too. It's nasty, but not to be taken seriously."

Katherine was trembling. "The other time they brought in Felix,
too—they accused me of being his mistress."

Mimi laughed, a robust laugh of mirth. "Dear Felix. Well, in the
morning we'll call the phone company and get your number
changed."

"I like my number," Katherine said stubbornly.

"Too bad. If you don't want these calls to continue, you'll have to have a different number and a private listing. I've had to do it, too. I can't be bothered with people using the telephone as a receptacle for their vomit."

Katherine lay down. She felt as though the anonymous caller had physically assaulted her. She had expected anonymity in her retirement, no more horrors of dead rats, perverse callers. "Vomit. That's what it's like. We had one caller in Paris who breathed into the phone, but never said anything."

"I think I'd prefer the outrageous suggestions to breathing," Mimi said. "You never know what a breather is going to do. Those who get their sexual kicks verbally seldom do anything violent." Her voice was brisk, matter-of-fact. "You are all tense, just as I had you beautifully relaxed." Her hands began to knead, bringing calm back to tight muscles.

"Why," Katherine demanded, "are people determined to think of one in terms of sexual activity?" Realizing that she was repeating her words to Dorcas, she said, "I do not like to be limited. I am all of myself. But first and foremost I am Katherine, pianist."

"Hush," Mimi said. "If you can delineate people according to their rutting habits, you don't have to make allowances for normal human complexity. I love you, Katherine. I don't want to make love with you, but I love you, and that is natural. I love to touch you, and that, too, is natural, and I don't give a hot hoot in hell if it is misinterpreted. As to what is normal and what is abnormal, probably all sex which is not purely for the purpose of procreation is abnormal, so let's not worry about being normal. And stop looking out your window. Nobody is looking in. That idiot phone call didn't come from across the way. It's connected, somehow or other, with the Cathedral."

"The Cathedral? Why on earth—"

"Last winter I had a few similar calls. I got a friend from the hospital to stay with me for a week, and when one of the calls came in I hotfooted it downstairs to Quill's. Fortunately, this was one of the times when he was home, and I got hold of the operator while upstairs my friend kept the caller on the phone, and the number could therefore be traced. It was from the front reception desk at Cathedral House. At midnight."

"And who was it?" Katherine's voice was shocked.

"No way of telling. It could be somebody who'd got hold of a key and had a duplicate made. It could be somebody who works at the Cathedral, from one of the canons down to one of the maintenance men. It could be anybody. I saw no reason to go to Dave about it—I'd satisfied my own curiosity. He has enough problems. I had my number changed. And that was that."

"Oh, Mimi." Katherine closed her eyes. "I thought retirement was going to simplify my life. No more crises, no more personality clashes, no more of life's complexities. I thought I could sit with my piano and my books and sort out my memories and die with everything tidily arranged."

"Katherine, I know you're naïve, but not that naïve, please."

"I did not expect this kind of thing."

"Nobody expects it. But there are a lot of sick people in the world, and more yearly. The statistics are not pretty. As to being straight, I doubt if anyone worth knowing is entirely straight. We all have our kinks and quirks. My own private life wouldn't pass any vigilante group's regulations for moral virtue. Katherine, you are never going to quiet down if we keep on talking. Be quiet. I love you, and I value our friendship, but I love you in the most straight way possible. You know that. So pay that idiot phone call no mind. Tomorrow, first thing, I'll get your number changed."

--⊶{ I I }⊷--

When Mimi had left, Katherine felt quiet enough so that the poison of the phone call no longer burned. She curled up comfortably, turning her mind to happiness, dreaming first consciously, then slipping into the shallows. She was standing by the piano in the house in Paris, Justin beside her, his hand spread out over her belly, an expression of bemused joy in his face. She had felt quickening that day.

'*Minou*,' he said softly, 'wanting this child is not just to appease my gargantuan pride. I want your baby. Not just any baby, *your* baby, which is as close to having *our* baby as we can come. And it will be *our* baby, and we will be a family.'

She could feel the tiny movement against Justin's hand. That there was life within her suddenly became real.

He continued, 'We are one, you and I, and I do not underestimate that. But it will be good for us to be a family. Good for our
marriage. I do not like my pride, but it is a fact. I cannot seem to
get rid of it. But this is far more than that; it makes that negligible.
Do you understand?'

She was not yet far enough away from the physical presence of
Lukas. Justin, she thought sadly, had come further than she. 'I'm
beginning to.' And then, leaning against him, 'I understand that I
love you. And you love me.'

'And we will love the baby. Our baby,' he said, and held her
close.

---···❦{ 12 }❦···---

In the morning, while she was having coffee, someone from the
phone company rang, giving her a new number, and telling her
that it would be in service by early afternoon. She would give her
new number to a few people—only a few. She would write to
Julie immediately. Mimi. Felix. Probably Dorcas. The Davidsons?
Would she have to explain to the Davidsons? What a stupid, un-
savory business. She looked at her watch. With the change of time
and Kristen's odd, musician's hours, she'd likely be at home.

She was. "Mormor, to what do I owe this pleasure?"

"To an anonymous phone caller. I'm changing my number. Do
you have a pencil handy?"

"Yes, here, let me get my book. Okay."

Katherine gave her the number, and Kristen said, "I had an
anonymous caller once, before I married Martin. He made all kinds
of lewd suggestions. What a bore for you."

"Mine doesn't make suggestions, and I can't tell if it's male or
female. It accuses me of various peculiar sexual activities. It's quite
absurd."

"What are these ridiculous accusations?"

Kristen's voice was amused, and the very amusement took away
from the ugliness of the calls. "For one thing, I'm supposed to be
carrying on an affair with Felix—my retired bishop friend."

"I wouldn't put it past you," Kristen said. "Is he attractive?"

"Not in that way, though I find him endearing."

"Mormor, I'm glad you called. I was thinking about you."

"Were you? Why?"

"Oh, lots of reasons. I suppose the world is beating at your door, as usual, people pouring out their woes? There's something about you that makes people want to bare their hearts to you. Sometimes we used to get jealous, afraid you'd love some wounded sparrow more than us."

"Never. You know that."

"I do now. Mormor, did you feel sick when you were pregnant?"

"When I was pregnant with your mother. For the first three months I felt miserable. It goes away."

"Promise?"

"Promise. Are you going to a good doctor?"

"The best in Oslo. Mormor, I'm getting cold feet. I want this baby, but I'm just beginning to do well professionally. The only thing that gives me hope is that you did it, too, had babies and kept on with your music."

"I hope you'll be a better mother than I was."

"Nonsense. But I'm lucky. Martin's mother is more than willing to take care of the baby while I'm working."

"Good."

"She frightens me a little," Kristen said. "All that domestic energy. I'm more comfortable with you, Mormor, and not just because we are related by blood. I'm your kind of person. I'm making some new recordings, by the way, all of Mozart's stuff. I should have them ready for you for Christmas. Mormor, I have to ask you something."

"What's that?"

Kristen sounded unwontedly hesitant. "I know that retirement doesn't mean you aren't busy—but—will you come, when the baby is born? I need a buffer between me and Martin's mother."

"What about your own mother?"

"I love Mor. You know that. But she's terribly busy with the business. And she's not a musician."

Katherine paused. Then, "I want to come. Even if only for a few days. But not if it will hurt Julie. We don't have to make a decision right now. I will come if it seems the right thing to do."

"At least you didn't give me a flat no."

"I could never do that. Now. Have you got my new number?"

"Yes. Thanks, Mormor. I love you."

"And I love you."

Why was it so easy with Kristen and so precarious with Julie? Why was she so zealous about not hurting Julie's feelings when Julie could hurt and not even seem to be aware of what she had done?

---&{ 13 }&---

Katherine and Justin, Julie and Eric, shared their wedding anniversary, more by chance than design. Norway is at its loveliest in early June, and when, on rare occasions, usually a major anniversary, Katherine and Justin were able to be in Aalesund, it was a great joy. There was a time when Katherine, on tour through Europe, got a call from Justin. Julie had suggested that they come to Aalesund for their mutual anniversaries. Katherine would be in Germany and she could fly to Bergen and meet Justin there, and they would then fly the little grasshopper to Aalesund. Justin had had pneumonia in the early spring and was still very frail; it was an effort for him; but they had wanted to be with their children and they had supposed that they were wanted.

The thought of three nights in Julie and Eric's guest room, looking through the pine trees across the fjord to the still snow-capped mountains, was a refreshing one, coming as it did in the midst of a rigorous tour. It would be a delight to have the grands come scramble into bed with them in the morning, to do some brisk walking, to relax. When Katherine and Justin met in Bergen, stopping for tea in their favorite small hotel, they were filled with anticipation.

'And that we have been married all these years is a miracle,' Justin said, stirring sugar into his tea. 'That you should still love me—'

'That we should love each other,' Katherine said. 'Yes, it's a miracle, and I'm grateful. And it will be lovely to share it with the children.'

But when they arrived in Aalesund, Eric's brother, Leif, met the plane, looking embarrassed, shifting from one foot to the other. He was taking them to the hotel, he said, because the Farfar and

Farmor had come from Trondheim to share in the festivities and were staying at the house.

Katherine would never forget the look on Justin's face, the paleness as though the rebuff had been a blow, for it slowly changed to a flush. She felt anger and pain for herself, but outrage for her husband.

'Let's go back to Paris,' he whispered in French.

'No. We have to see it through.'

What had it all been about? It was a major anniversary for Katherine and Justin, not Julie and Eric. Wouldn't it have been more natural for Eric's parents to have been put in the hotel?

When they saw Julie she was all spontaneous effusion, kissing them, welcoming them, assuming that of course they understood. What were they to understand? Eric, beaming as usual, explained that his parents were not used to hotels and would be less shy if they stayed in their usual place in the guest room. And they were used to the children and all their noisiness, and he was sure Katherine and Justin would prefer the peace and quiet of the hotel; they would, wouldn't they?

There was only hurt in the explanation, no comfort. Julie gave a big dinner party the next night in Katherine and Justin's honor, but they still felt as though she and Eric had rejected them.

Eric had been behind it, rather than Julie. But Julie had not seen what Eric was doing, had not understood the pain it caused, and this lack of awareness on her part was added pain.

That's past. Long past. It doesn't even hurt any more. Not terribly.

She heard the postman in the vestibule, and went out to get the mail. Some fan mail. Something that looked like a greeting card. Catalogues which made pleasant browsing when she was too tired to read. A note from Nils saying that his novel had been accepted enthusiastically by his publishers, but that he had to cut three hundred pages from the eleven hundred. He was furious. A long letter in Juliana's round, careful handwriting; it was full of news of the farm; Katherine would save it to read carefully at bedtime. A note from Julie, businesslike, dutiful. Perhaps she should phone Julie, rather than writing, but her daughter was not likely to be in until after five, Norwegian time. She opened the rather bulky greeting-card envelope. In it was a get-well card. How odd. She looked at it curiously. It still felt bulky. She opened it, and there, she realized, after a moment of blankness, was a used condom.

Whoever made the obscene phone calls wasn't satisfied with the sound of his or her own voice. Instead of being horrified, she was furious. This was filthy, and stupid, and abominable. What shocked her was that if the phone calls were somehow or other linked to the Cathedral, so must this unsigned card and its contents be.

She put it all in the fireplace, went into the kitchen for a match, and burned it.

--·◄│ 14 │►·--

The next morning she woke feeling heavy and headachy. She drank her coffee and played through her early-morning exercises, and the heaviness lifted somewhat. In the kitchen she prepared water-cress and cream-cheese sandwiches. It had been arranged that Llew would drive her up to the Cathedral and the Bösendorfer, and she was fixing him a light lunch. It would surely lighten her mood to work over the program, and she was looking forward to the lunch with Llew, who had assured her that he was going to be in the neighborhood anyhow, and it would be no trouble to pick her up.

Just as all was in readiness and she had turned back to the piano, the doorbell rang, followed by an urgent knock. "Who is it?"

"Dorcas."

Sighing, she opened the door.

Dorcas said flatly, "Well, he's done it again."

Katherine looked at her questioningly.

"Been with Ric. I went to have lunch with June—she called and asked me. I didn't ask her. We had lunch at her apartment. There was a baby in a cradle—so sweet—and another in a high chair, and June was feeding him while we ate. It was all—oh, beautifully do-mestic. And then, while we were eating homemade oxtail soup, and that was beautifully domestic, too—she told me calmly that Ric has always been what she calls AC-DC."

Katherine waited.

"June said Ric was highly sexed, and she wasn't particularly, but she was his number-one person, the one he came home to. He's the father of their children and a good father, she said, and his outside affairs don't hurt their marriage. And then—oh, God, Madame Vigneras, she said she'd asked me to lunch to talk because she didn't want Terry getting too serious about Ric. I think she was a little afraid that if Terry got too serious it might threaten her domestic setup, but she *said* she didn't want Terry hurt, because he's a nice guy. Terry hurt? What about me?" Dorcas's voice, which had been rising as she talked, suddenly broke. "I couldn't live like June. It isn't a compromise I could make."

Katherine sat down beside the distraught young woman, moving her hand gently over the long brown hair.

Dorcas made an effort at self-control. "Maybe I'm too absolute about marriage vows, too old-fashioned. I know this kind of thing isn't supposed to matter any more—but that's how I feel."

"I tend to be rather absolute myself. Do you know that this is true? Is June possibly a troublemaker? Have you talked to Terry?"

"No. Should I?"

"I can't make your decisions for you, Dorcas, but I'd think you'd want to find out the truth."

"And if he admits it? If he wants a setup like June and Ric's?"

Katherine rose, remembering Kristen's words: young people had always come to her, and the grands had not always been pleased—when they knew about it. She was still corresponding with one of Nils's friends, now married and living in Copenhagen. "You will have to find out what you can and what you cannot live with. If you continue to feel, as you say, absolute about your marriage vows, I think you have grounds for annulment."

"Wouldn't that—annulment—make my baby a bastard?"

"I don't think people think in terms of bastards nowadays. You could certainly, in any case, get a divorce."

Dorcas shuddered. "I never thought I'd raise my baby alone. But if I have to, I have to." There was an almost visible steeling of her spine. "Thank you for letting me talk. It does help me to think about it all a little more objectively. Terry makes a good salary. I'm angry enough to want to sue him for the world."

"You haven't talked to him yet," Katherine cautioned.

"I suppose that's only fair. But he's already given me a bundle of lies. He promised to go with me to a marriage counselor and he broke the appointment. So, I'll go back to dancing as soon as I can. I'm a good dancer, there'll be a place for me in the company. But

I'll never be a real prima donna. I've had to come to terms with a lot of things while I've been pregnant, and that's one of them. I'll get solos, I'll do moderately well, but I don't have the—the passion for it you have to have if you're going to be one of the great ones. That wasn't easy to accept. I'd made up a glamorous picture of myself that just wasn't real."

"You're very brave," Katherine said. —What would I have done if I had had to accept that I wasn't quite first-class as a musician? My entire life has been predicated on the fact that I am.

"Not brave. Just realistic. About time I dropped my dreams of being a great dancer and having a beautiful marriage."

"Don't be too hard on yourself. It's good to set your sights high."

Dorcas pushed back her long, Alice-in-Wonderland hair. "The thing is, in New York, people all have to do or be something. Something with a name, like doctor or dancer or director. Mother and wife don't count."

"If feminism means anything, it means that you're free to be a mother or a dancer, or both, whichever you choose."

"Not in New York City. And I can't go back to Cedar Rapids."

"Do you want to?"

"No. My parents are dead. I haven't anyone or anything to go back to. But there was a reality, growing up there, that I seem to have lost, and it was a good reality."

"Your reality is largely within you," Katherine said, "and that's where you are going to have to find it."

--⊰{ 15 }⊱--

The doorbell rang, and Katherine was glad she'd already prepared lunch.

"I almost forgot," she said. "Llew Owen, the organist at the Cathedral, is coming to take me uptown to practice. I'm giving a benefit—"

"Yes, I know." Dorcas rose cumbersomely. "We already have tickets." She looked down, murmuring, "Thank you," as Katherine went to the door.

Katherine introduced the two young people, and Dorcas left immediately.

"Something wrong?" Llew asked.

"Everything. You know, Llew, there are worse things in the termination of a marriage than death. I will always miss Justin, but no one can take our marriage away. We had it. And you had yours. But hers has just been smashed to bits."

"Irreparably?"

"I'd guess so."

"And she's pregnant—"

"Yes. There's no good time for a marriage to fall apart, but this is about the worst time I can think of."

His mind was not on Dorcas. "The other day—when you were practicing in St. Ansgar's—will I ever play like that, with that much wisdom?"

She pushed his words aside with her hand. "It took a great deal of painful experience to give me any wisdom at all, and my music is much wiser than I."

He nodded. "I've learned that. It is healing me, whether I want to be healed or not."

She moved to the kitchen. "Being alive hurts. I have found it best not to rush for the aspirin bottle." She took the plate of sandwiches out of the refrigerator, lifting off the damp tea towel which protected them. "Sit down, Llew, lunch is simple." She set the sandwiches on the table, brought out two bowls of soup.

"You're very kind to have gone to all this trouble for me."

"Nonsense. I haven't had much chance to do any cooking in the past years, and I'm enjoying making mud pies."

"Mud pies, nothing. This soup is fabulous. What is it?"

"A French way of using up lettuce when it starts to bolt. Lettuce and chicken stock, basically. Most of these sandwiches are for you. They're only a bite each."

Llew ate hungrily, giving full attention to the food, accepting two more bowls of soup. Then he looked around appreciatively. "What a beautiful picture!" He indicated the portrait over the mantelpiece. "Is it you?"

"Yes, and my son, Michou. I love it. It's probably my greatest treasure."

"I can see why. Dee and I—our apartment's in Diocesan House, up at the very top. We fixed a room for the baby and I don't—I don't know what to do about it—the crib, the wallpaper Dee put on. Every time I go in I see the bear and the lion in the crib—what should I do?"

She answered crisply. "Why don't you give the baby's things to Dorcas? I don't think she's bought anything yet, and with her marriage breaking up, she's not likely to. Then change the paper. How big a room is it?"

"Not very big. Big enough for a baby. I'm not sure I could get rid of anything there—it seems—"

"It seems like accepting that your wife and baby are dead? They are. Don't hold them back. Don't let them hold you back. Your love isn't going to change with the wallpaper."

He looked at her across the table. "Your son died when he was young, didn't he?"

How long ago was it? And it still hurt. No wonder this young man found it difficult to give away his baby's crib, the toys his wife had bought.

"Llew, I understand grief. You must know that it will never leave you entirely. There will be odd moments when it will wash over you like a wave. But *you* must leave *it*." She picked up the soup bowls. "You've had enough?"

"More than enough. Thanks. Now I won't have to worry about dinner."

"Don't start skipping meals," she warned. "It's all too easy when you live alone. I know." She returned for the sandwich plates. "Just let me rinse these off."

"I'll do it," he offered eagerly. "That was my job, doing the dishes."

She glanced at him, then stepped aside to let him take her place at the sink.

He worked briskly and efficiently. "The car's right outside. I was lucky. A car drove off and I grabbed the place. I don't have air-conditioning—" He suddenly sounded anxious.

"Don't worry. I'm beginning to get acclimated."

"It's never too bad in the Cathedral itself."

He drove well, and although the car was somewhat shabby, the springs were still good. "You and Bishop Bodeway are old friends, aren't you?"

"I knew him, long, long ago. And then we completely lost track of each other until recently. We've both done considerable changing."

"He's very special, Bishop Bodeway. After Dee died he never once said any of the silly things that people say. He didn't even say any of the good things. He cried, and so I cried, too. And he talked about Dee and the baby instead of avoiding it, like most people. I wish I'd been around when he was Diocesan, and I'm more than grateful he's about the Close as much as he is."

Felix was surely a good example of the ability of the human being to change or, if not change, to develop in directions which might not have been suspected. And she had come far from the introverted adolescent who had known Felix so long ago and who had thought that the only way to live with hurt was to put a hard shell around it. That was the danger for Llew, but perhaps his music would keep him from it as, she believed, it had made her shed her protective carapace and move into love.

And once the shell is gone, it is gone. She was as vulnerable now as she had been when she first met Felix.

Parents and Children

I

The afternoon in St. Ansgar's chapel, slightly to her surprise, was
without untoward incident. No one, as far as she knew, for she
was deep in concentration, came in. When she was tired and needed
to stretch, she walked around the ambulatory; once she walked to
the end, down two steps, and saw an elderly woman dropping
change into the large chest for donations. She smiled, thinking that
this was perhaps one of Felix's old women with her widow's mite.

As she passed St. Martin's chapel, which Felix had said was always open for prayer, she paused, sensing a sound. Huddled in one
of the chairs was Topaze, his face in his hands, his shoulders shaking
with sobs. She hesitated, wondering if she should go in to him,
then decided that whatever caused it, his grief was private. He
could hear her at the piano; if he wanted her he could, and probably would, come to her. She returned to the Bösendorfer.

When she played the *Hammerklavier Sonata* she could always
hear Justin's voice, sometimes gentle, sometimes shouting at her in
excitement, crying out that a single note could be, all by itself, a
crescendo. 'You are part of the piano,' he often said. 'Each movement of your head, of your body, is as much a part of what you are
playing as your hands on the keys. You never saw Rachmaninoff
play. He counteracted the most erotically emotional of his work by

sitting at the piano as still as marble, no movement of torso, or head. That balance was part of his playing, part of the music.'

He took her to the ballet. 'Your movements must be one millionth of a millimeter of what you are seeing, but it must be indicated. Every slightest movement of your head, your neck, says something.'

For a while he had her take ballet lessons. 'You are not comfortable with your body, and the things I had hoped to teach you I cannot teach you.' She studied with a friend of Justin's at the Ballet Russe and learned quickly to take delight in the disciplines given her body. The ballet lessons stood her in good stead. She was not slumped.

They made friends with many of the dancers in the company and Justin began to compose music for the ballet. He made a quick success with a ballet to Molière's *Le Malade imaginaire*, but comedy was not his forte, and both he and the company were happier with the music he composed for Sophocles's *Antigone*.

The study of ballet was reflected in Katherine's playing. She acquired a new understanding of cross-rhythms with syncopations and sudden sforzando, but the old problem with her hip caused the actual dance lessons to cease.

'You have learned what you needed to know,' Justin said with no sympathy. 'You are comfortable with your body; you are beginning to understand it. Stop being sorry for yourself. You were born to be a pianist, not a ballet dancer. Now pay attention to this crescendo. You are not listening, you are not understanding. Where are your ears? Don't you hear that the crescendo doesn't lead to a fortissimo but to a pianissimo? Play it, and let me hear.'

He never stopped teaching her, she thought, sitting in the shadows of St. Ansgar's chapel, striving to push her as close to perfection as the human musician can get.

A movement disturbed her and she looked toward the pews to see Emily Davidson, eyes tightly closed, her expression one of intense concentration. When the music did not continue, she opened her eyes. Katherine fluttered her fingers in the child's direction. "How long have you been here, little mouse?"

"Oh, a while. When I used to watch ballet—especially the prima ballerinas—I saw what they were doing, and why, and how. I think I hear what you're playing, but I'm not sure why or how.

When a ballet dancer does something unexpected, I expect it. I understand that it has to be that way. But you do things and I don't expect them. I know they're right, but I don't expect them." She spoke with unselfconscious intensity.

"How do you know they're right?" Katherine asked with curiosity.

"Because they *are* right. Do you know anything about ballet?"

"A little."

"Sometimes you'll see a dancer move up into the air so slowly you wouldn't think anything that slow could be *up;* and then the coming down is even slower. You do that with your music. Especially in—I think it was *Le Tombeau de Couperin.*"

"Close," Katherine said. "It was some of the original music Ravel used in *Le Tombeau.*"

"Oh. But then you'll do something I don't understand at all, and I wonder if I'm just fooling myself when I think I can give up being a dancer, just like that, and be a pianist instead."

It was not just living in New York, as Dorcas had suggested, that made Emily need to be something. The child had not only exotic beauty but extraordinary determination and drive. Katherine said, "Talent in any one of the arts usually indicates understanding and talent in other branches. You've just shown that you have real understanding of music. Why don't you play for me now?"

The color drained from Emily's bronze skin. In the odd lighting of St. Ansgar's, her face took on a greenish hue. She murmured, "Maybe it's better this way, before I have time to work up a panic."

Katherine rose from the piano and Emily took her place. She played with technical competence a fairly simple Handel minuet. Then a Beethoven sonatina. She played well, as she had played when she accompanied the family. She listened to the music. Her wrists and her fingers were well placed. But the quality which John displayed when he merely picked up the violin was missing.

Katherine's heart sank as she stood by the piano. She could not lie to the child. Neither could she destroy her. What could she say?

Emily began a new piece, something Katherine did not recognize. It started out sounding like a piano rendition of one of the songs Yolande had sung, but then, instead of going into fear and sadness, it became lilting, merry, then dropped into wistfulness, and ended suddenly with a major arpeggio which flew all the way up and off the keyboard.

"What was that?" Katherine asked sharply.

Now color flooded Emily's cheeks. "Oh. It's one of Mrs. Undercroft's songs. Tory has a tape of it and plays it till I could scream. I like the beginning, but then it does things that give me the heebie-jeebies, so I changed it around so it says something I like to hear, and then I let it dance off the piano."

"You mean it's your own composition?"

"Well, it starts off with something Mrs. Undercroft—"

"Have you composed anything else?"

"Oh, sure."

"Play me something, then."

Emily hovered her hands over the keyboard as though thinking through her fingers, very differently from when she was about to start something from the classical repertoire, and then played what began as a derivative seventeenth-century minuet and suddenly changed rhythm and dashed into extraordinary leaps up and down the keyboard as she modulated from one key to another and finally dropped back into the prim little minuet.

Emily's playing of her own compositions had a freedom it totally lacked in the pieces she had obviously studied with a piano teacher.

Trying to hold down, for a moment, her enthusiasm and relief at Emily's talent as a composer, Katherine asked, "Does your teacher encourage you to write your own music?"

"Oh, no, he doesn't like it. But I thought maybe you would."

"And your parents?"

"Oh, they like it, all right, but they're both so busy they don't have much time for—"

"First of all," Katherine said in her most authoritative voice, "you will change piano teachers. Whoever you have is all wrong for you. Then you will learn harmony and counterpoint. The more you know of the old disciplines, the freer you will be to go off on your own. I'm not sure about you as a pianist, Emily. Your teacher has taught you some dreadful habits. Thank God you break them when you play your own music. But you *are* a composer. On the other hand, you need exposure to every kind of music possible. When I think of what you did with Yolande's—"

Emily interrupted. "You think I have talent?"

"I *know* you have talent." Katherine looked at her watch. "It's time for Llew or somebody to come and take me home. Are your parents going to be in this evening?"

"I think so. Unless one of them has an emergency."

"I'll call them. As for the piano lessons themselves—would you like to study with me?"

Emily's voice was small. "I'm already sitting down."

Katherine made a conscious effort to keep her tone level. "I'm a hard taskmaster."

"Madame Vigneras, I'm not afraid of work."

"I know you're not. But you have a lot to *un*learn, and that will be very hard work."

"Do you really mean it?"

"Hard work? Yes."

"That *you* will teach me?"

"I'll speak to your parents and if they can arrange transportation for you to come to me, we'll start at once."

"Madame Vigneras—" There were no dramatics in Emily's voice. "This was life-and-death for me."

Katherine spoke softly. "I know, my child."

"I could have been dead, and you've made me alive."

"It's your own talent, Emily. All I can do is help it grow."

"I can't say thank you. It's too—"

"You'll thank me by working." It was too intense. Katherine turned in relief as someone said, "Madame Vigneras," and she saw Mother Cat coming in. Emily gave a small curtsy, and Katherine marveled that she made so little concession to her artificial leg.

The nun smiled at them in greeting. "Madame Vigneras, a special chapter meeting has been called, something to do with Bishop Juxon's death, so Llew can't drive you home—the organist is part of the chapter. But Sister Isobel is waiting outside with the car. Are you planning to come to us on Sunday?"

"Yes, of course."

"One of us—I hope I'll be the one, but I'm not positive—will be down for you around four-thirty. I hope that will be convenient."

"Fine."

"And we'll get you home at a reasonable hour. We need our sleep, too. Will you be all right on your own, now?"

"Of course."

"The steps don't bother you? I should get back to the meeting, but—"

"I'll help her down the steps," Emily said.

The nun nodded. "Thanks, Emily. And then go on home, please."

"Yes, ma'am." Emily bobbed again. Perhaps manners were coming back at last.

—⊷⊰ 2 ⊱⊶—

Katherine was, she had to admit, curious about Sister Isobel, who once upon a time had been Allie Undercroft's wife, and who had gone through the agony of losing a child, and who was now a nun. Katherine did not know much about the religious life; in European cities she had often seen nuns, but fewer each year as more and more of them left their Orders or stopped wearing habits, or wore uniforms which made them indistinguishable from airline hostesses. She liked the habit worn by Mother Cat and the Sisters, simple, loose, light blue for summer; all of it, from wimple to scapular (as Mimi had told her), easily washable and drip-dryable. Sister Isobel, waiting by the car, looked cool and comfortable. Katherine knew that she must not be much younger than Mimi, but there was an open youthfulness about her face which made her seem far younger. And the habit helped. A wimple is a most becoming article of clothing for an older woman. Nuns, she thought, should never have relinquished it.

"Welcome, Madame Vigneras." Sister Isobel held the door open for her. "We are all looking forward to having you come talk to us."

"Thank you. I'm looking forward to it, too," Katherine replied, somewhat stiffly. Why should it be more difficult to speak to a nun than to a bishop? Familiarity with Felix, probably.

"Goodbye, and I love you," Emily said breathlessly, and leaned forward to kiss Katherine softly on the cheek. " 'Bye, Sister."

" 'Bye, Em. Get on home." The nun watched as Emily walked across the Close, waited until she was in the vestibule of Cathedral House, then started the car. She was easy and relaxed and drove well, heading for the park. "You and Emily seem to have become friends."

"She is an amazing child."

Sister Isobel stopped for a light. "That she is. But we have many amazing children in our school. Kids on the Upper West Side of this city tend to have had amazing things happen to them early in their lives, and some grow on them, and some fall apart. How is Emily as a musician?"

"She's a composer," Katherine said. "Did you know that?"

"No, but I'm relieved to hear it. I didn't think she was a pianist." "Why?"

"I've gone past while she's been having her piano lesson."

Katherine leaned back as the nun turned into the park. The trees were beginning to look tired and dusty. To break the silence, she said, "I don't think Emily's teacher is the one for her."

"How right you are." Sister Isobel waved one hand in the direction of the Natural History Museum. "Odd to think this was out in the middle of the country when it was built. Emily's teacher just loves little children." Katherine smiled at the irritation under the nun's words. "People who just adore little children are seldom good with them, and to treat Emily as a child is to court disaster. I wonder if we could change her teacher?"

"Yes. I'm going to teach her."

"Alleluia!" Sister Isobel negotiated around a taxi. "I love Emily, and I love music. I played a little before I entered the Community, and still practice when there's time."

"What's your instrument?"

"Clarinet. Easily transportable. I sometimes play faux-bourdons for festive Vespers. We all love music. Sister Agnes plays the harp. You should have seen her when she arrived to become a postulant. She seemed a mere baby, in blue jeans and sweatshirt, with her enormous harp. And frightened—she looked like a lamb expecting to be slaughtered. You'd never think it now. She teaches math, is highly organized, and only when she touches the strings of her harp do we get a glimpse of the delicacy of spirit which is underneath all the efficiency. It's what makes her such a fine teacher, and so loved by the students."

"What do you teach?"

"A little bit of everything. Some cellular biology to the high-school kids. Handbells to fifth and sixth grade. And the recorder to some of the little ones who are musical but who can't afford violin or piano lessons—such as Topaze Gomez. And I go about quite a lot to conduct retreats. We all have to have our hand in a number of things. We have lots of highly gifted students, and a lot of grievously wounded ones."

"Like the Gomez children?"

Sister Isobel nodded. "They have a weak father, who was a tool of stronger men, and a mother who's a born hater—if there can be such a thing."

"What about Topaze?"

"Basically he's a bright, outgoing child, and he has considerable spiritual gifts. But I'm worried about him."

Would a child with spiritual gifts sell information? Then she remembered the small, hunched figure in St. Martin's chapel. "Why?"

"I'm not sure. I think he's frightened, but I don't know of what. The father's in jail, so he's no longer a threat. He used to beat the kids."

"No wonder they're wounded."

"And his mother puts too many burdens on Topaze, talks too much, fills him with her resentment and hate, and Topaze simply doesn't understand resentment and hate. It's not in him. But he's frightened and he clings to us too much. He's been at early Mass every day this week, holding on to his faith in a kind of frantic desperation. Well—he's not the only child I worry about. As for poor Fatima, unless something can be made of her voice, I don't know what life is going to hold for her."

"Tory Davidson seems very fond of her."

"Tory's friendship with Fatima is an enigma. It's partly propinquity because the Gomez kids are around the Close. And I think Tory feels somewhat like Zola championing Dreyfus. All she knows about Gomez is what Fatima has told her, and the poor child worships her father."

"Even though he beat her?"

"Evidently physical abuse does not preclude a desperate kind of love, especially in a child."

—And poor Fatima, starved for love, is trying to find it in worshipping Yolande, Katherine thought, and decided that to question

Sister Isobel about that would be the acme of tactlessness. "How about Tory himself? Where is she going to go?"

Sister Isobel shook her head. "She's one of our brightest students, but she has no particular direction. And she has a strong jealous streak which does her no good. Perhaps she likes Fatima because there's no competition, and Tory can be Lady Bountiful. I've noticed a marked cooling off lately. Perhaps—" She stopped behind a car which had braked suddenly, and when she spoke again, she said, "A lot of our students receive what little love they get from the Sisters. We have a large number of single parents who drop their children off at school at eight in the morning on their way to work, and pick them up in the evening on their way home."

"I can see that your hearts are full, as well as your hands."

Sister Isobel nodded, nosing the car through the dense traffic they moved into as they left the park. "It's a good life."

Katherine wondered if Sister Isobel, knowing that Katherine lived in the same building as Mimi Oppenheimer, would guess that Mimi might have mentioned the nun's disastrous marriage. If so, the Sister gave no sign of embarrassment, but continued to chat about the school and the students. The traffic eased after the Port Authority Building. "By the way," Katherine said, "I'd appreciate it if you'd drop me off on the corner of Sixth and Twelfth—I need to pick up some groceries if I'm to eat this evening."

"Gladly. I can tell you're an old New Yorker. I, too, have never learned to call Sixth Avenue the Avenue of the Americas."

--✣ 3 ✣--

Katherine said goodbye to Sister Isobel, and walked down the street to the grocery store, where she picked up eggs and the makings of a salad. When she came out of the store with the brown paper bag in her arms, she was somehow not surprised to see Topaze.

"Carry your bag for you, music lady?"

This was surely a better way of earning money than selling information, so she handed it to him. "What brings you down to my neighborhood?"

"I like to ride the subways," Topaze said. "I was lucky and saw

Sister letting you out of the car." He shifted the bag from one arm to the other. "I heard you playing this afternoon, music lady."

—And I saw you crying, Katherine thought.

"I like to hear you play. It makes me feel everything isn't going to fall apart."

"Thank you," Katherine said. "It holds things together for me, too. Is something bothering you, Topaze?"

"My father's in prison."

That was not what he was crying about. "Yes, Topaze, I know. You told me."

"Ma says it's unfair. She says everything's unfair for people like us."

"Unfortunately, life's not very fair, Topaze." They were nearing Tenth Street. "Do you like school?" She tried to lighten the air.

"Yeah. Mrs. Undercroft pays for it. Ma says we need to know the right people, and find out how to use them."

Evidently Mrs. Gomez did indeed talk too much to her son. They turned east on Tenth Street, and Katherine said nothing.

"I like the Sisters," Topaze continued to chatter. "They don't mind what your parents are like. They look at *you*, and that's all they see. When I'm with them I'm Topaze, not the bishop's cook's son, or the son of a jailbird."

They had reached the house. Katherine took the bag of groceries.

"Can't I carry it in and put it in the kitchen for you?" Topaze was begging, but somehow she did not want him to come in.

"I'm sorry but I have a phone call to make, and surely it's time you got back uptown." She got out a quarter, put it back, and pulled out a dollar. "Thank you for carrying my groceries."

He took the dollar and stuffed it into the pocket of his jeans. "You want to know anything, music lady?"

"Topaze, I am pleased to give you something for carrying my groceries. I am not interested in buying information."

"Not selling it to you. Telling you for free."

"Topaze, child, there's nothing I want to know from you. Do you understand?"

He shook his head. "Doesn't want you to give the concert."

Startled, she asked, "Who?"

"They sit, and laugh and laugh."

Again she was surprised enough to ask, "Who?"

But he simply turned and started down the street, calling back, "Take care." The way he spoke, it was not the casual, usual, nearly meaningless phrase.

--◦◆{ 4 }◆◦--

As soon as she got into the apartment and put the bag of groceries in the kitchen, Katherine put Topaze and his disturbing conversation behind her and went to the phone to call the Davidsons. Tory answered, and shouted for her mother.

Suzy came immediately to the phone. "Madame Vigneras, I scarcely got in the door before Emily was all over me. Is it possible that I heard correctly?"

"If what you heard is that I would like to give the child piano lessons, and that she shows considerable talent for composition, yes."

"I'm overwhelmed. I've never before seen Emily speechless."

"She has some bad teaching to unlearn," Katherine warned.

"I'm sorry—we didn't know—" Suzy sounded both confused and apologetic.

"Her teacher may be quite adequate for the average child whose parents have piano lessons on the agenda. Emily needs something different."

"I'm totally unmusical—but I should have realized. And Dave— it's not an advantage to children to have highly motivated professional parents. We were just so grateful that Emily's life was spared—"

"Now," Katherine cut in briskly. "Logistics. I live downtown. Emily lives uptown. How are we going to manage?"

"At your convenience, of course."

"My convenience is highly flexible. I'll need to see her once a week."

There was a moment's pause on the other end of the line. Then, "Jos has only one class on Mondays, between three and five. He could drop her off on his way to N.Y.U. and pick her up when he's through, and she could sit and read when her lesson is over if two hours is too long."

"Two hours is fine."

"Thank you. We don't want her going on public transportation alone, at least not the subway, and the bus trip seems endless."

"Monday afternoon will suit me splendidly."

"And—Madame Vigneras—whatever you charge—"

Katherine replied crisply, "Pay me whatever you were paying the other teacher. I'll see her Monday, at three."

Odd how things twist and change. When she had first met the Davidsons she had thought that it was John who was going to be her favorite, John whose gentleness reminded her of Michou. But it was Emily she was going to take into her life.

Ah, well.

She was hungry, so she headed for the kitchen. She was poaching herself some eggs for supper when the doorbell rang. Sighing, she went to the door, calling, "Who is it?"

"Terry Gibson. Dorcas's husband. May I come in for a moment?"

This was not going to be easy. Katherine opened the door. "Do come in and sit down. Just let me turn out the flame under the frying pan."

"I'm interrupting you—I'm terribly sorry—"

She was not prepared for his beauty. From the discussion at the Davidsons' she had expected Terry Gibson to be wearing a dark business suit, to look more conservative, less like an artist. He was wearing black Levi's, and a fawn shirt open at the throat. His slender neck and barely visible Adam's apple made him seem young and vulnerable. His hair, which was neither long nor short, was fair and clean-looking. Underneath the clear skin the bone structure was delicate and strong.

Dorcas was not beautiful. She had the kind of undistinguished plainness which could sometimes flame into beauty on a stage, but she was not beautiful. Terry, Katherine thought, reverting to the language of her youth, was a knockout.

She turned off the gas. "It's all right. Don't fret."

He sat on the piano bench. "I'm terribly unhappy about Dorcas's decision."

Katherine asked carefully, "What is Dorcas's decision?"

"Oh, God." Terry put his face into his hands. "She's so absolute. And of course she's right. But I don't want to go."

"She wants you to?"

"Yes. And I want—oh, please, Madame Vigneras, I want my wife and baby."

She was touched by his obvious misery. She asked, gently, "Why does she want you to leave?"

"She doesn't understand the—oh, the horrible ambiguity of life. She's so young—ballet dancers tend to be babies when they start out. She's only nineteen. Over ten years younger than I am. The awful thing is—oh, it would have worked out, I know it would have, given time, if she hadn't—well, it was premature. Am I making any sense?"

"I think I see where you're leading," Katherine said. "But perhaps you'd better be a little more specific."

"You've lived such a long full life, you do understand, don't you, about ambiguity and how feelings aren't always things one can control?"

"Yes, I understand that."

He crouched over, his hands between his knees, as if in physical pain. "I never meant her to know. If I'd had time, I could have worked it out. But she came blundering in and of course she was horrified, she absolutely fell apart, and I couldn't make her understand . . ."

"Understand what?"

"Fidelity isn't just who you—who you are physically attracted to, who you, maybe, make love with. There's much more to it than that. Anyhow, men and women have different needs."

At this, she looked at him with astonishment. "Good Lord, I thought that went out with the nineteenth century."

"I'm sorry." He was immediately apologetic. "Some things went out with the nineteenth century, yes, and some things are going out with this. Attitudes toward love are different—" He shook his head, and closed his eyes for a moment, breathing deeply. "I'm trying to rationalize, and that isn't any use with you, is it? I'm not happy about myself, but I am who I am. I love Dorcas. And I love Ric. God, I love him. I never meant to love him. For a long time I didn't know he was—was the way I am. He made the first— Well. I don't know what to do. I don't want Dorcas to break our marriage."

He was, she thought fleetingly, too beautiful. He was used to getting his own way. "Do you and Dorcas," she asked, "look at marriage in the same way?"

"Evidently not." Briefly, his voice was hard. "I didn't tell her, before we were married, because it didn't seem pertinent, that I had been with men as well as women. AC-DC, as Ric's wife so graphically puts it. I thought—well, I suppose I thought she knew. And if she didn't know, it was better not. She's gorgeous when she's onstage, you know, radiant, a firebird. But she doesn't—and she can't cope with—" His words dwindled.

Katherine looked at him, seeing that he wanted the marriage his way, that if Dorcas could not cope, neither could he. She said, "Believe me, Dorcas doesn't want your marriage to end. But she does want a faithful husband."

He sighed, a gusting of air. "If only she hadn't found out—"

"Wait a minute," Katherine said. "That wouldn't have worked. It never does."

"Why not?"

"Dorcas may be young and naïve, but she's not stupid. Isn't she worth working for?"

"She's so unbending, so *absolute*," he repeated. "She doesn't understand the ambig—" He stopped himself. "I don't know what to do."

"Could you possibly try being faithful?"

"Can't someone make a mistake?"

"Of course. We all make mistakes. No one is totally faithful. Not even Dorcas. But your intention, if I understand what's behind your words, is to continue to be unfaithful, and that's not the same thing as making a mistake, picking yourself out of the mud, and trying again."

He rose slowly, moving with a feral grace. "I should have realized you're too old to understand, another generation. I'm terribly sorry, I didn't mean—you've been more than kind, listening to me. But—"

But, she thought, underneath the charm, the sensitivity, was a selfishness which Emily had evidently seen. The sensitivity was for himself and his own needs, not others. Not even his wife's.

She murmured, hardly realizing that she was speaking aloud, "Yes, you are a turd."

"I beg your pardon?"

She flushed. "I don't think it's going to work, Mr. Gibson. You and Dorcas have totally different intentions about your marriage." She, too, rose. "I'm sorry. I haven't been much help."

He moved to the door. "You've been brainwashed. You've heard it all only from Dorcas."

She did not say that she had tried to listen to him. She felt sad for Terry, sad for Dorcas, sad, too, for herself. But the girl was probably well rid of him in the long run, though she would not know that now, still torn with loving him, carrying his child. Katherine felt a heaviness in her chest, a heaviness which contained Dorcas's pain.

She turned her mind from Dorcas and Terry by reading a mystery story. But her attention was not on the book. On the surface, it would seem that Dorcas and Terry ought to be able to work things out, to make a go of their marriage. But something deep within her told her they could not. Terry might be more than ten years older than Dorcas, but in many parts of himself he had not crossed the bridge of thirteen. He had the same intense self-centeredness which is normal in an adolescent but not in someone who has reached thirty. And Dorcas would bear her baby alone.

Katherine had come to America to have her baby, her father and stepmother, who had sent her so blithely to France, now assuming that she could not get adequate medical care in Europe still raw with wounds from war. Justin, agreeing, had come with her, eager to be part of the process of birth. Katherine had had the support which Dorcas would not.

Katherine and Justin were based at the farm, which was Manya's pride and joy. She had a farmer caretaker, twenty milk cows, and a small flock of sheep. In the darkness just before dawn the roosters would crow, each announcing his kingship. Also three dogs, in and out of the house, and several cats, which made Justin sneeze and so were barred from their bedroom. Katherine and Justin were given the comfortable guest wing, although she would have preferred to be in the small, blue-paneled room which had been hers as a child.

'Nonsense,' Manya had stated. 'It's not big enough for a double bed, and where would you put the baby? And you know how sensitive your father is to noise. In the guest wing you'll be off where he can't hear the baby cry. Face facts, Katya. Tom loves you, but he does not love noise. And in the wing you'll have your own bathroom, and a separate room for the nurse.'

'What nurse?'

'Katya, a nurse for the baby. I don't want you getting over-tired.'

'But, Aunt Manya, I'm going to nurse the baby.'

'I'm delighted to hear it,' Manya said, 'especially since nursing is out of fashion at the moment. Even so, you'll be preparing for a concert, and a nurse will be helpful. Remember, I'll be around only on weekends, unless the play closes sooner than I expect.'

The pregnancy itself, unlike the second one, had been easy. She had no morning sickness, felt full of energy, and spent long hours at the piano without fatigue. They stayed in Paris until a month before the baby was due, then sailed for New York. Katherine was large by then, and when Tom and Manya met them, Manya cried out, 'Thank God you're here, Katya. You look as though you're going to drop the baby on the dock.'

They went to the apartment on the East River, and the next day she saw the fashionable obstetrician who had been recommended to Manya. He assured them that there were several weeks to go, and there would be no problem in Katherine's being at the farm, which would be much more comfortable than a small apartment. 'First babies are always slow in coming, and you can phone me if you have any warning signals, pains, a show of blood.' He was brisk, and Katherine sensed that under the professional bonhomie lay a coldness. But she knew he had a fine reputation, and she assumed that it is not always necessary to like one's doctor. She was to see him once a week.

Justin asked, anxiously, 'Is he taking proper care of her?'

'Of course,' Manya assured him. 'Pregnancy is not an illness, and Katya could probably give birth at the farm, with us helping, and no problem.'

'I'm fine,' Katherine assured him. 'And our child even kicks in rhythm when I'm practicing.'

Due date came and went. Manya spent the weeknights in the city, driving to the farm after the performance Saturday night, and Katherine drove down with her on Mondays to see the obstetrician, then took the afternoon train back to the country. She felt heavy, but still full of energy, and she and Justin spent much of each day in the library while she practiced. She was to give a Town Hall concert in what they had assumed would be two months after the baby's birth, but which would now be sooner.

'Too soon, unless you start labor right away,' Justin said when Katherine was two weeks overdue. 'We should see about canceling before it's too late.'

'Nonsense,' Katherine pooh-poohed. 'It's quite likely the baby will decide to come tonight, and if not, tomorrow night.' She had been having a low-grade backache, and mild cramps like menstrual pains, for over a week. When the cramps first started she was sure it was the beginning of labor, but the doctor said no, it was only a false labor which often preceded the delivery of the first child, and to pay it no attention.

'Minou, I don't want to go into the city today.'

'Justin. Darling, you've got to get that recording finished. You were promised that this was the last session and it shouldn't take more than a couple of hours. I'm not in labor. Go. You'll be back in good time for dinner, and I'll suggest to the infant that tonight would be a good time to make an entrance into the world.' She moved as close to him as her swollen belly would allow, and he put his arms around her, bending down to press his lips against her dark hair.

'He is going to be the most beautiful baby in the world,' she whispered.

'He?'

"Certainly. I've ordered a boy. Just wait and see.' She did not care a whit whether the baby was a boy or a girl, only that it be complete, be healthy. But she sensed that a boy would do more for Justin's precarious pride than a girl.

In the afternoon she went for a walk in the woods behind the house and barns, enjoying the scents of autumn, the leaves drifting from the trees, the path half-covered and occasionally slippery as she stepped on fallen apples with their strong, cidery smell. Without warning, her water broke and she felt a small deluge. And then the first real pain came. It surprised her with its strength. She doubled over, unable to stand against it, gasping, tears rushing to her eyes. As quickly as it had come, it was gone. Her heart pounded with excitement. This was the time. This was the baby's time. It had started at last. Somehow, despite the constant life within her, she had not quite believed it.

She turned and started back to the house.

—Justin will be angry and upset, she thought. And then, —I'd better get Father to drive me to the hospital, and he hates being interrupted when he's composing.

The pain came again. Nobody had prepared her for quite how fierce labor pains were. Again she doubled over, suddenly frightened, catching at a small maple to keep from falling. Why were both Manya and Justin in the city, and, she suddenly realized, with both cars? Even if she interrupted her father, how could he get her to the hospital? Why was his studio on the far side of the house? Help. She needed help.

The pain left, and she hurried along, stumbling over twigs and roots. The closest phone was in the barn. She would go there and call the nurse in the doctor's office. They would tell her what to do.

The pains were coming more closely together. The hundred yards to the barn seemed miles. She moved toward it blindly, not sure she would make it. Where was the farmer? Why was there no one around?

She reached the barn door. The cows were already in their stanchions. She held on to the door, smelling hay and cow manure and old wood, a strong, healthy smell. Despite the pain, she nearly laughed at the idea that she might drop her baby in the barn. When she could let go her hold on the door, she moved into the barn and switched on the light, and with the light came a swishing of tails, a moving of heavy bodies in the stalls. She looked down the length of the barn, down the double rows of stalls; it seemed a great number of cows, face to face. The cow in the stall nearest her raised its head inquiringly. The sweet, summery barn smell rose around her. The cows stamped, snuffled, disturbed by the light, and perhaps by her presence, too. The cow by Katherine let out a long golden stream, plash, and then shook her stanchions. The phone was on the far wall; why would anyone put the phone on the far wall? Of course: it was the wall nearest the house. One of the cats swished past her, rubbing affectionately against her legs. She bent down to stroke it, could not stand up again. She counted.

One was supposed to count through pains. Seventy-seven, seventy-eight, seventy-nine. It was over. She started to walk down the straw-strewn floor between the stalls.

When she finally reached the phone, she dialed the operator. 'I'm sorry,' she gasped. 'Please help me. I'm starting labor.' Manya had insisted that she memorize the doctor's number. Wise Manya.

Would a phone operator be as helpful now as then? She was connected with the doctor's office, with the nurse.

'Come to the hospital right away,' the nurse said.

She gasped through pain. 'I'm alone. I'm in the barn, here in the country. My husband's in the city and I can't get hold of anyone—' The pain eased. She was half-laughing, half-crying at the ludicrousness of the situation.

'You'll have to come to the hospital at once,' the nurse said.

'I don't have a car. I'm seventy-five miles from the hospital. I—' Her voice broke off as the contraction came again.

From the distance she heard the nurse. 'I don't know what to tell you.'

'Mrs. Vigneras—' A voice from the far end of the barn. Mike, the young farmer.

She left the phone hanging, dangling, and groped her way toward him. 'The baby—'

He strode through the barn, soothing the cows, lifting her up in his strong arms, carrying her out to his pickup truck, putting her into the front seat. 'Hold on. We'll get your daddy and he'll drive you to the city.'

'He can't. My husband has the car.'

'Then we'll just have to use the truck. Don't worry. I'll get you there in time. And if I don't, I've helped many a cow with her delivery.'

Again Katherine was assailed with laughter. Mike drove to the house, ran across to the studio. 'He's not there, and I don't think we ought to stop to try to find him. Let me get you to the hospital.'

He drove with such skill that Katherine was not nervous at his speed. She was too involved with the contractions, which were now coming close together, to notice how fast he was driving. In between the pains she closed her eyes. Once or twice she dozed.

---- ❧ 5 ❧ ----

In the hospital she did not have the care and concern she had received from the young farmer. Ultimately she was left in a labor room with three other women, one screaming thinly like an animal caught in a snare. She wished that Mike had pulled the truck over to the side of the road and let her have her baby there. He would have been with her, would have known what to do. Here, with three other women, she felt abandoned. They were isolated within their own pain. A nurse gave her a shot which turned the pain into a nightmare. Once, she was aware of voices in the corridor, arguing, Manya trying to get in to her, to tell her that Justin was on the way.

Another shot. The shots did not take away the pain; instead, they blurred her sense of herself, so that she felt lost in an anguish over which she had no control. Then there were the bright lights of the delivery room and someone clamping an ether mask on her face. No one asked her anything, by your leave, or would you like. No one told her anything. She was pitched into darkness.

She came back to consciousness slowly. She still felt wet between the legs, but when she put her hands on her belly it was flattened. She opened her eyes and saw Justin, Aunt Manya. 'Is the baby born?' She asked it, she learned later, half a dozen times, and was assured, each time, Yes, yes, it's a baby boy, a beautiful baby boy.

The experience of Michou's birth was not beautiful. She looked at him when he was brought to her and was grateful that he was complete. But she felt nothing more than a calm, intellectual pleasure. Justin and Manya were furious at the fashionable obstetrician, and the inhumanity, which was far more degrading than impersonality. But they were told that everything had been quite normal. And the baby was fine. It was done.

When Michou was put to her breast (none of the other mothers on the floor were nursing), feeling began to come back into her, an aching tenderness. She touched his delicate ears, his small button of a nose. Justin held him, during the hours when he was allowed to visit, in an awed manner.

'My God, how he adores that child!' Manya cried. 'What a father!'

All Katherine felt was a strange lethargy. She did not even think of Lukas; thinking of Lukas took more energy than she possessed. She wondered vaguely if Justin had thought about who the baby's father might be. She knew that he had called to tell the cardinal of his birth. But she felt nothing, neither about Lukas nor about Wolfi. A grey exhaustion wrapped around her like a noose.

When she was back at the farm she was grateful for the nurse, a kind Frenchwoman delighted to be able to talk in her own language. After a few days, she was concerned about Katherine, her lack of appetite, her lack of energy. 'It is not natural,' Katherine heard the nurse, standing outside the door and speaking in a hushed voice, tell Manya.

But nothing was natural. Justin being the proud father was not natural. The cardinal, calling from Munich and insisting on talking to Katherine, was not natural. He did not even talk about the baby. 'I am being sent to Rome,' he told her.

Cursorily, she congratulated him.

'It is not an advancement,' he said. 'I am what I think you Americans would call being kicked upstairs.'

She did not have the energy to ask why. She did not want to know why.

Then he said, low, so that it sounded indeed as though the ocean lay between them, 'It should have been my baby. I will never understand.'

--◦◦⊰{ 6 }⊱◦◦--

She reached for her bed lamp, then sat up in bed. She was hot and yet she was shivering. She turned her mind carefully from the past. Emily Davidson, who reminded Katherine of herself, Emily, who might or might not be able to play the piano, with some unlearning, but who nevertheless had music coming out of her fingers. Perhaps her ballet training, living with the body's response to music, had been preparation, not waste. Wolfi said once that nothing was ever wasted, nothing. Michou?

Almost without volition, Katherine left her bed and went to

the piano. After Michou's birth it was expected of her that she practice on the piano in the library; that, after all, was what the nurse was for, to free her to go on with life. It took more effort to explain that she was too tired to work than to go to the piano.

'You're not thinking!' Justin shouted at her.

'Sorry.'

'Don't you feel well? Is something wrong?'

'I'm just tired.' She did not want them to worry. She assumed that this was how one felt after having a baby, although the nurse told her she was bleeding too much.

Sitting for the portrait was the easiest of all those tasks she was expected to perform. She could be still, holding Michou, and Philippa Hunter was a quiet young woman, as committed to her work as Katherine and Justin were to theirs. They talked little, but during the quiet hours of the sitting they became friends.

But other tasks quickly wore her down. As Katherine's energy dwindled, the nurse became more concerned. The doctor was phoned once, twice, and after a third call he had, rather reluctantly, made an appointment. She would be in New York for the Town Hall concert and could come and see him the next morning.

Sheer willpower took her to the theatre, propelled her onto the stage. The surge of adrenaline Yolande had talked about poured like fresh blood through her body. She moved, as in a dream, through the program, playing well. During the intermission she did not lie down, saying that if she lay down she would not be able to get back up again. Back on stage. Ravel. Satie. Poulenc. Two encores. And finally the bowing, the smiling, smiling toward the top balcony where the young musicians sat, and suddenly, as the curtain was being lowered, blood, blood pouring down, staining the ivory satin of her dress, staining the floor.

Justin came leaping across the stage, first pushing away the stagehand who had started to lift the curtain again, crying, 'A doctor, quick!'

And she was back in the hospital again.

The highly recommended physician had left in part of the placenta.

Dilation and curettage. Pain. Pain worse than the labor pains. And a sudden high fever. Puerperal fever. Childbed fever.

Penicillin. At least in the frenetic post-war world the eminent obstetrician had penicillin, the new wonder drug. Katherine, unlike Llew's wife, did not die. The fever abated, leaving her weak, exhausted, lethargic. She lay in the hospital bed, listening to Justin telling her that Michou had lifted his head to look around, that he was already grasping a rattle, that his reflexes were amazing for so young an infant, and she tried to feign interest. If Justin cared so much about this child, so should she.

He told her that Manya was buying the Hunter portrait for them, that Philippa Hunter, herself, felt she had made a major breakthrough in her own work, that Katherine need not worry about more sittings, the painting was finished. She listened to Justin and there was nothing to say. It was as though there were a wall of glass between herself and the rest of the world. She could see people, could hear them, but she could not reach out to touch them, and they could not touch her.

Manya came to the hospital daily, bringing flowers, a bottle of Yardley's lavender water, a pretty bed jacket. 'Penicillin is a depressant,' she told Katherine. 'That's why you feel so low.' But she could not quite mask her anxiety. 'Depression is a side effect of the antibiotic. As soon as it's out of your system, your spirits will lift.'

She did not believe Manya. Depression enveloped her like a fog which was never going to dissipate.

Justin brought a silent keyboard to the hospital so that she could work her fingers for a half hour a day. And then one morning she woke up with an aching arm, two fingers swollen, knees inflamed and full of fluid, her hip an agony. She could hardly walk to the bathroom. She could not get into a comfortable enough position to sleep. The two affected fingers hurt as though someone had crashed down on them with a hammer.

More doctors, more medications. She lay on her side, on her good hip, her face to the wall.

They sent her from the hospital to the farm. Perhaps, the doctors said, if she were in familiar surroundings, back with her husband, her baby, she would improve. She and Justin could resume their sex life, the doctors said; that, too, might help, they said.

The nurse was there with Michou, who nuzzled against her breast; the milk was long gone. The nurse gave her a bottle of formula to hold, put Michou in her arms.

Winter had come. The ground was white. Fires were kept blazing in all the fireplaces. But she was always cold, and the inner cold was more penetrating than the outer. She did not like to go into the library with the big piano reminding her of her inability to play even the simplest pieces. She felt a weary sense of loss, as though someone had died.

--··◦❧{ 7 }❧◦··--

And then, one day, Cardinal von Stromberg.

She was in the bedroom, lying on the chaise longue in front of the fire, wrapped in a steamer rug, and he came in. Out of the grave in which she had entombed him. Without knocking, he came in.

He was dressed in a dark traveling suit, but he was still a cardinal. Tall. Strong. The Great Grey Wolf. He stood looking down at her, not speaking, his steel eyes softened with compassion. She looked at him, and the weariness and iciness increased, and she closed her eyes against him.

She felt him move, and opened her eyes to see him kneel by the chaise longue. He reached out his hands and put them on her head, and she felt a tingling warmth move through her body. He began to murmur the prayers for healing, and then, in English, said, 'Use these unworthy hands, Lord, for the healing of your child, Katherine. Use these sinful hands to return her to health and to her work which helps heal your broken world. Use your sad and sorry servant, Lord, in your service. Amen.' Then he rose, looked down on her, and left.

She found out later that Justin had called him, and that he had come on the first possible plane, rented a car at the airport, come to her, and then driven directly back to the airport and the next plane, as silently as a great grey wolf . . . .

There was no immediate miracle. Perhaps it was not even Wolfi (though it was), but slowly the swelling and stiffness subsided. And as her body healed, her energy, her *joie de vivre*, returned.

She spent first an hour at the piano, then two. Her appetite became healthy. She laughed as Justin tossed Michou into the air and caught him, and the baby crowed with pleasure. At bedtime she would give Michou his last bottle and sing to him, while Justin got ready for bed, constantly interrupting himself to come gaze at mother and child. He was painting her portrait, in his way, as much as had Philippa Hunter.

--◦◂❙ 8 ❙▸◦--

She had worked through the pain of the memory of Michou's birth and the weeks that followed, but she was now as awake as though morning had broken. She left the piano, walked slowly back to the bedroom, and turned on the light by the chaise longue. She would read awhile. Something dull. Kant.

She looked out the window and saw a dark shadow in the garden below. Dorcas. She was sitting by the fountain, which plashed gently. Her body drooped wearily. She was caught in her own private hell and Katherine ached for her, though it was likely Dorcas's pain which had triggered the old memories. Now that she had moved through them, she looked at them, and the hurt was gone.

She went back to bed then, and slept.

And dreamed. She did not believe people who said they never dreamed. For some reason they could not or would not remember their dreams. In this dream it was dark. The cardinal was lying on the rocky lip of a cliff, leaning over, holding Dorcas's hands and pulling her, slowly pulling her up from the chasm over which she was suspended, pulling her up to the cliff's edge until he was on his knees; and then, as he raised her up over the edge of the cliff, he rose to his feet, and set her beside him on the solid rock.

His face was beaded with sweat. He was panting from effort. And he looked at his hands, which were bleeding, and as Dorcas gaspingly thanked him for saving her life, he murmured, 'And with these hands,' and looked at them with wonder and with awe.

---·◆{ 9 }◆·---

As the dream ended, the phone rang.

She should be used to it by now. There were many times in her life when the incessant ringing of the phone had made it seem a monster. As long as it was not the anonymous caller . . .

It was Julie. "Well, Maman, I happened to call Kristen and got your new number."

Katherine tried to ignore the rebuff in her daughter's voice. "Yes, darling, I did send you a note, and I'd planned to call you late this afternoon so I'd get you before bedtime, but a couple of crises intervened."

"Crises?" Was there a slight thawing? "Anything wrong?"

"Not with me. I was up at the Cathedral working on the benefit"—she *had* written Julie about that—"and then one of the dean's children came in and I had to hear her play. She was studying ballet, but she lost a leg in an accident, so things are very rough for her, and that took longer than I expected. And then when I got home I got involved with the tenants below me. She's pregnant, and their marriage is breaking up, so it's all rather a mess. And by the time I was able to get away it was too late to call." She was, as always, overexplaining, trying to justify herself in Julie's pale, judgmental eyes. She reminded herself of an invented sonata Justin sometimes used to play at parties—his hands allowed him at least some fooling around on the piano—where the concerto began at least a dozen times, had three very short movements, and then worked up to the ending for as long as the laughter of the audience allowed. But there was no laughter on the other end of the phone. It wasn't much past midnight in New York, so Julie must, as always, be up early.

"You seem to be having your usual effect on people."

"They're just—people in need."

"Kristen said you've been getting anonymous calls."

"Nasty ones. That's why I have a new number. Do you have it in your book?"

"Yes. Do you want me to call the others, or have you already done so?"

Katherine said mildly, "I'd appreciate it if you'd mention it to them." She had been stupid, stupid, to call Kristen and not Julie, thereby making Julie feel stepped over. "I sent them airmail cards, but mail gets less and less reliable." Julie had been a cuddly baby, a warm, loving child. Should artists simply not have children? Do we do terrible things to them by our very existence? Will Kristen hurt her unborn child simply by her being?

What had Katherine done that was so terrible to her daughter? Julie was happily married, or at least seemed to be, now that Eric had settled down. The business was as much hers as his and Leif's, and it was flourishing. Despite the problems with appalling inflation and taxation, they were prospering.

"Are you there, Maman?"

"Yes. I'm here."

"I just wanted to check on you and make sure you're all right. You are getting on in years, after all."

"I'm fine. Thank you. Don't worry about me."

"That's all I wanted to know. I've got to go. Good night, Maman."

"Goodbye, darling. Thanks for calling—" But Julie had already hung up.

Sometimes Julie was warmer, more talkative. Indeed, yes, it had been a mistake to call Kristen first.

Suzy and Dave too were overbusy parents, and their children were likely paying for it. But surely they would not have chosen not to have their children, any more than Katherine would have chosen not to have Julie and Michou.

Was Julie jealous? Had she read too many good reviews in the papers, too many interviews which held up the family as the perfect model of what a family ought to be? From where had the image come? She had never fostered it, nor had Justin.

After Julie's marriage, Katherine had tried to keep in touch with her daughter by occasionally taking her on concert tours with glamorous destinations—Majorca, for instance—paying for baby-sitters so that Julie was able to get away for a much needed rest. But while they had enjoyed the time together, Katherine had never felt at all close to this dearly loved child. Katherine, the mother, had opened herself freely, and Julie, the daughter, had accepted graciously, but had given nothing of herself in return.

She seemed more Norwegian than her Norwegian in-laws; and she was, in fact, half Norwegian/Finnish, so small wonder. And if she had been suffering from Eric's infidelities, it was not surprising that she had kept her sorrow to herself.

Katherine sighed, and turned over onto her back. Does one ever stop being a mother, and vulnerable where one's children are concerned? Her grands held a special and beautiful place in her heart. But Julie and Michou were the children of her body.

No point in blaming herself overmuch, or wallowing in false guilt. She was who she was, and she could not, at this late date, change herself. Could she ever? She doubted it.

So be it.

She returned to bed and tried to sleep.

Julie's conception had been both simpler and more complicated than Michou's. When Justin had said, tentatively, that he would like another child, her reaction had been quiet. He had put his arms around her, tenderly. 'There's no reason you should go through what you did at Michou's birth. I've talked with the doctor. That was all the fault of that idiot obstetrician!'

'I know. I'm not afraid.'

'Minou, if I thought there was any chance of a repetition of any of it, of the arthritis—'

She moved her fingers softly against his face. 'My hands are all right.'

'Michou is nearly three. In the logical way of things—'

'I know,' she said. 'Don't push me, my love. We'll see.'

And he had not pushed.

--→{ 10 }←--

There was no need to go running to anyone. Wolfi was in Rome, but evidently doing well. He was moving, rather than being kicked, upstairs. Justin phoned him frequently. It was tacitly understood that when Wolfi called she would talk with him briefly, but that she would not call him. Justin questioned her about her reluctance, but accepted her explanation that she could not explain, that it was part of the horror of her illness after Michou's birth, and that despite her gratitude to Wolfi, he was still a reminder of pain and fear. 'It's totally irrational,' she had said. 'It's just something I can't help.' And Justin had accepted the irrational far more easily than he would have accepted a reasonable excuse. Artists are irrational. Women are irrational. Women who are artists are doubly irrational. Women are irrational where their children are concerned; therefore, Katherine was trebly irrational. She smiled and did not try to disillusion him.

There was no question in her mind as to who the next child's father would be. This time there was no blind running. She called Oslo.

Erlend Nikulaussen had been after her for some time to spend a night with him, a weekend, laughing at her reference to her marriage vows. When she called him to suggest that they spend some time together he took it matter-of-factly. 'But how splendid! I'm due two weeks' holiday in ten days. Can you come with me?'

'Where?'

'Do I have to tell you? Can it be a surprise?'

Yes, it could be a surprise.

'Can you get away? What will Justin think? How will you manage?'

'I'll manage.'

'And we'll be perfectly secure, where I'm taking you. No one there knows us. There'll be no gossip.'

Fortunately, while Erlend cared little about marriage vows, he did care about gossip. He was not married; or, rather, he had not been married for several years. There was no wife for Katherine to worry about.

She flew to New York, where he met her, and only then did he tell her where they were going, to the northern end of Jamaica, to Norseman's Cove.

'It's a private hotel,' he said, 'owned jointly by about fifty of us, all Norwegian. Some people are buying private property, but that involves caretakers and all kinds of responsibilities, and worrying about whether the unrest at the southern end of the island will come to the north, where we aren't hated. Odd, you know: I don't mind being hated by other musicians who are jealous of me, but I would mind very much being hated by these gentle black people. We'll have one of the cottages, and it will be beautiful.'

It was. They stayed in a small stone cottage up on a cliff overlooking the ocean from their bedroom, the cove and the sinuous lagoon from the living room. There were terraces, balconies, sliding doors, a profusion of green of every shade, of vines and wind-carved and curved trees and more vines, of flowers and birds like flying flowers. It was one of the most sheerly beautiful spots Katherine had ever seen.

And the most physical two weeks she had ever spent. Erlend, half Norwegian, half Finnish, held a surprising sense of play, and their lovemaking was interrupted by wild joys of laughter. They were tumbled over by waves in the cove, and then swam in the soft, clear water of the lagoon, and there in the water he would come to her and make love and make love and make love—

It was something to be made, like music. It was like the moment when the piano has to join the orchestra, and Erlend would draw her into the music—

Sometimes it was like the flute, clear and sweet; and sometimes the piccolo, laughing in merriment; and sometimes the entire orchestra; and then she would be taken into the music, the keyboard joining with the strings, the brasses, the celebration of the timpani.

At the end of the two-week holiday, Erlend startled her by saying, 'Divorce Justin and marry me.'

'Erlend, you're out of your mind.'

'I'm completely in it. Katherine, I've been with many women, I've been married twice, but nothing has ever been like this.'

'I made it clear that this was two weeks for us to be together, two weeks and nothing more.'

Erlend reached for her. 'We make love together the way we make music. You know you play for no other conductor the way you play for me. You can't tell me that love with Justin is better than love with me.'

She drew away. 'Comparisons don't come into it. I'm Justin's wife.'

'Then why did you come with me?'

'You've been trying to get me to go off with you for years. You said it was perfectly natural for a woman to—'

'But I didn't know it would be like this, and neither did you.'

'Erlend, when we've played together, when we've given a concert series, I know that I will never play that way for anyone else. But it's over. We go on. You go to your orchestra and to other soloists, and I go back to my piano—to other conductors. And that's the way it is now. I'm going back to Justin.'

Finally, seeing that arguments were useless, that even more love-making was not going to change her, he let her go.

And so, in beauty and play and loveliness had Julie been conceived.

This time there was no aftermath of depression. She had enjoyed every moment of the two weeks in Jamaica, enjoyed, outrageously enjoyed making love with Erlend, but she had not fallen in love with him. She would go on seeing him, playing with him in Oslo or wherever he was conducting; he was her good, true friend, but that was all. When he died, several years before Justin, died as he would have wished, of a heart attack while conducting the Sibelius violin concerto, there was no need to hide her tears. She wept for her friend, wept in Justin's arms and was comforted.

—◆{ I I }◆—

And Erlend, thank God, never knew why she had gone to Jamaica with him. Once, when the children were small, when Erlend had yet again asked her to marry him, saying, 'Just because you've borne two kids by Justin . . .' something in her had relaxed with relief. If Erlend did not suspect, no one else in the world could possibly have the slightest suspicion.

And it had been far easier, while she was carrying Julie, than it had been with Michou, to think of the life within her as belonging to Justin. Julie's birth had been in a small private clinic outside Paris. Labor was hard, but Justin was with her, rubbing her back, wiping her face with a cool cloth, and had seen Julie bursting forth into the world, screaming lustily. The doctor had placed her immediately between Katherine's breasts, and Justin had looked down at his wife and daughter, laughing and crying simultaneously. She would never forget that moment, the small weight of the infant, still wet from the amniotic fluid, her cries of outrage at the harshness of life suddenly stilled as she lay against the secure warmth of her mother's body and slipped into a contented sleep.

Manya and Tom came on the next plane. To their relief, there were no problems after the birth. The placenta had come out easily, and complete. In a few days she had regained her energy, was home, hovered over by Manya and Tom, and by Nanette, who was enchanted with the new baby, Nanette, who had told Katherine well before Justin that it was time for her to give Michou a sister.

Katherine nursed Julie for a year, taking her along on the few concerts outside Paris she had accepted. Manya and Tom, delighted at her swift return to full vigor, went back to the States. But Manya, as long as she lived, was always there when needed, arriving in less than twenty-four hours, once flying became the normal mode of travel. And so for a few years the children had a loving grandmother, who gave the family with lavishness her warm, openhanded love.

Katherine was still thinking of Manya, half in a dream, when the phone rang again. If it were not for the grands, she would take it off the hook at bedtime. And it was one of the grands: Juliana. Juliana wrote frequently, called seldom. She and her Edvard did not have the money to spare for overseas calls. When Juliana called, it was always because her sense of her grandmother's need was greater than her own natural frugality and timidity, and her timing was always accurate. "Mormor?" The voice had the sweet treble of a child.

"Juliana!"

"Mormor, did I wake you?" The small voice was anxious.

"It doesn't matter, darling. It's always lovely to hear from you. Are you and Edvard all right?"

"Oh, fine, Mormor, everything's fine."

"How did you get my new number?"

"Mor called."

So Juliana had sensed that her mother's call might have been upsetting. "I've been getting some nasty anonymous calls, and in order to stop them I had to have my number changed. I sent you an airmail postcard."

"I'm glad Mor called, then. Mail takes forever, and I like to be able to get in touch with you. Just in case."

As a child, too, Juliana had wanted to know just exactly where everybody was. She had not had a favorite blanket, or a favorite toy, but she could not sleep at night unless she knew the whereabouts of the entire family, which was not always easy, with the older children away at school, Katherine on tour. "I'm glad you called, darling," Katherine said, "but let's not talk long. I don't want to run up your phone bill. I'll call in a few days and then we can chat."

"Oh, good. Thank you, Mormor. I just wanted to make sure I had your number, and the right one, and that you were all right. I love you and I think of you lots."

"I love you, too, darling, and I loved your last letter."

"I'll write again soon. Can you read all right on that thin paper?"

"I can read it with no trouble at all."

When they had said good night, Katherine lay down and slid into sleep, dreaming both of Juliana and of Manya, so totally different, and yet so alike in the lavishness of their love.

The Discipline of Memory

As Katherine continued to regard the past, it became easier to recollect it with tranquillity, and the happy times surfaced more often than the tragic ones. When she was at the piano working on the benefit program, Justin's presence was almost tangible, and she could sense him urging her to give another concert for Felix in the autumn. It was never too late to add to one's repertoire. Ronald Melrose had written a new sonata she would like to try, an intricate blending of current popular music reflecting the culture of these difficult years, balanced by an almost fugal classicism, a fine and innovative piece of work. She would enjoy working on that. And Justin's influence was still with her; it was ingrained in her fingers, her ears, her kinesthetic memory, a kind of total intimacy that would always be with her.

In the morning, on impulse, she called Dorcas. It was the sort of impulsive gesture Manya might have made; and that, too, had left its permanent imprint on her. "Come up and have *café au lait* and a croissant with me."

Within two minutes Dorcas was at the door, dressed in a flowing gown of sprigged dimity. "Thank you. I'm not contemplating suicide, not with the baby, but I'm too close to contemplating it for comfort. Terry's gone. At last. He spent all night packing his stuff into our suitcases and all the boxes he could get from the liquor store, and he's gone."

"Where? Or does it matter?"

"It probably matters more to June than to me. He said he was going to a hotel, but he didn't say which. He didn't even ask me to call him when the baby comes. He just said he'd have the proper documents drawn up and he'd see to it that we're taken care of financially. If it weren't for the baby, I wouldn't touch a penny. But a single parent can't afford to be proud."

"You've done a lot of thinking, haven't you?" Katherine looked at bubbles touching the sides of the saucepan of milk and took it off the flame.

"I've had to. Breaking up a marriage with a baby on the way shouldn't be done without thinking, so I've thought. And you know what I bet?"

"What?" Katherine poured coffee and milk simultaneously into two large Royal Copenhagen cups.

"June isn't going to let Ric go, and I don't think Ric is going to want to leave June and the kids for Terry. So what I bet is that within six months after Terry and I are divorced, he'll be married again."

"Not to you."

"Definitely not to me. When something's killed, it's killed." She looked at Katherine over the rim of the cup. "You must have had lots of things killed during your lifetime—"

"Lots," Katherine agreed.

"And you must have been through a lot of hurt and pain—"

Katherine nodded.

"And yet, when I'm with you, what I feel coming from you is a sense—not just of contentment, but of happiness. I mean, you seem to me to be a happy person."

Katherine put jam generously on her croissant. After a moment she said, "I don't think much about it, being either happy or un-happy. But I think I am far more happy than not. Life has been rich and full, and I'm more than grateful." She smiled slightly, to herself, because her memory flipped to that unhappy anniversary when she and Justin had gone to Aalesund, and it did not hurt. For the first time she looked at it without pain. What she remem-bered now was Kristen's insistence on sleeping at the hotel with

her grandparents, Kristen, the only grand old enough to sense anything wrong.

"Madame Vigneras—"

Katherine licked apricot jam off her fingers. "I'm here. I was
just remembering something which hurt me a great deal, a long
time ago, and I was being grateful that I can look back on it without pain. Is Terry really gone? Or was he playacting?"

"Lawyers playact all the time, I think. As I look back on our
marriage, I can see now that I was making the whole thing up—
Terry, myself, the marriage. It was never real. And that's over.
I'll act when I'm onstage; I'll pirouette and smile, or fall dying
gracefully into the arms of my partner, whoever he is, even Ric,
but I'll keep it for the theatre. Terry wanted a pretend world for
all time. Never real. And I want to be real. In my private life. And
when I dance, too. And I can't be real with Terry. I'm glad he's
gone." There were no tears in the girl's eyes, though her voice was
brittle as crystal.

"What about the apartment?" Katherine asked. "Was that part
of the act, too?"

Now the eyes glistened, but the tears did not overflow. "It was.
But it needn't be. We'd probably have had to move, after the
baby. With only one bedroom, it's just right for two, not three.
You know, Madame Vigneras, our apartment is much more you
than it is Terry, as far as I'm concerned."

Katherine cocked an eyebrow. "Is it?"

"Much more. And, under the circumstances, I'm grateful for
that. So long as he's willing to pay for it—and he makes plenty, it
won't bleed him—I'll keep it, for the baby's sake. Terry's pretty
well stripped the place. There isn't much of him—or us—left in it.
So I can make it a home for myself and the baby."

"When is the baby due?"

"In about a month."

"How much sleep did you get last night?"

Dorcas looked surprised. "None."

"Then I want you to go into my bedroom and lie down. This is
the day Raissa, who cleans for me, comes, and I'm going to send
her downstairs to clean up and make the place habitable. I know
you're not sleepy now, but if you'll lie down and breathe slowly—
do you dance the *Goldberg Variations?*"

"Yes, it's one of my favorites."

"Then dance it in your mind's eye and ear. Move from slow movement to slow movement. Feel it in your body. Don't think of anything else. You'll go to sleep. And I have a lunch date with Felix—Bishop Bodeway. We're going museuming, so you won't be bothering me. And I'll be back by mid-afternoon."

Dorcas nodded mutely, and Katherine settled her in the bedroom. As she returned to the living room, the dean called, with Katherine reaching for the phone on the first ring, not to disturb the girl.

"Madame Vigneras, I just wanted to add my thanks for your kindness to Emily."

"It's not kindness. She has talent and courage and she needs a better teacher than the one she's had."

A slight pause. "I should have realized. Yes, Em does have courage. And she's named for another Emily of great courage, Emily de Cortez."

"The pianist?"

"Yes."

"You know her?"

"She used to live up in this neighborhood when she was a child, Emily Gregory. After she was blinded in an accident, I was her reader for her schoolwork, and I watched her fierce struggle to become independent. When we named Emily after her, I never thought—"

Katherine said, "I didn't know she was blind. She's a fine musician."

"Very few people do know. She wants to be known for her music, not as a blind pianist."

"She's succeeded, then. She's surely the best-known interpreter of South American composers. I thought she had to be South American herself. I take it her husband is Pio de Cortez, the conductor?"

"Yes. When Em was in the hospital I reminded her of Emily de Cortez, and she snapped, 'You can play the piano without eyes, but you can't dance without a leg.' And I said, 'You can play the piano without your left leg.' So I feel responsible for turning her toward music."

"You gave her hope," Katherine said. "One can't live without hope."

"But if I was wrong—"

"And you can't live without risk. You know that. I wouldn't be taking her on if I didn't think there was real talent there. Particularly for composition. I look forward to working with her."

She said goodbye, hung up, and prepared to leave. She had arranged to meet Felix for lunch at the private dining room of the Metropolitan Museum, and then to see a special exhibit of French Impressionist painting.

He was waiting for her just inside the entrance. "Shall we eat first, or look at the paintings?"

"Let's have a glimpse of the paintings, eat, and then go back to the exhibit. I love the Impressionists, but I tend to drown in them if I look at too many for too long."

"How right you are." Felix took her arm and led her through jostling people until they got to the gallery with the special showing. It, too, was crowded, but Felix managed to sidle them in until they were standing in front of a Degas ballet dancer. "This always reminds me of our youth—" Felix pointed at the dancer lacing up her pink toe shoe. The girl in the painting reminded Katherine of Dorcas, and the present. "Young and innocent," Felix said, "though I suppose her innocence was short-lived. Loss of innocence— Have you had any more horrid calls?"

"No. Changing the number seems to have taken care of it."

"Good." They moved on to the next painting, a Rouault head of Christ.

"Surely he wasn't an Impressionist," Felix murmured, but stayed, staring at the powerful face. "Oh, Katya, there are so many times when I'm assailed with doubts. I've based my life on the unreasonableness of this"—he nodded at the painting—"death and resurrection, on the unreasonableness of this love, of all love. Sorry, I'm sounding like one of my sermons." He put his hand up as though to cover his clerical collar, and, realizing that people were listening, moved on until they were standing in front of a van Gogh, a painting of a fiery sky.

She replied quietly, "In a way, so have I based my life on the unreasonableness of love."

"I know, my dear, and I'm grateful. You've shared your wisdom with me and made me less afraid."

"Afraid of dying?"

"Of anything. Of dying not so much as the manner of dying.

Of horrid phone calls. Of bad dreams. In the old Office Book there's a Compline hymn which I still say every night, old-fashioned or no:

> *From all ill dreams defend our eyes,*
> *From nightly fears and fantasies;*
> *Tread underfoot our ghostly foe*
> *That no pollution we may know.*

No pollution. What a prayer in a polluted world! Ill dreams—how I wish we could rid ourselves forever of them."

"Perhaps we learn from them." What kind of dreams had van Gogh had in order to paint that incredible sky?

"Perhaps. But the nightly fears and fantasies? Do you fantasize, Katherine?"

"Not so much any more. I used to. When Justin was alive, if he was ten minutes late coming home, I fantasized everything terrible that could possibly happen to him. And usually the terrible things that in fact do happen are things we never could have suspected." She said abruptly, "What is it about those threatening calls that frightens you so terribly?"

"I'm not sure. What makes you ask?" He moved them on, shuffling with the crowd, until they reached a Renoir family, full of gentleness and warmth.

"Because I think you're more frightened than anonymous phone calls justify. Why?"

"If I knew why, I might not be so frightened. Maybe it's just that I'm too old to let human sickness slide off me any more."

"You said Wolfi's books mean a lot to you, that he speaks your theology for you?"

"Yes. I know he wouldn't react so stupidly."

A crowd of students pushed by them. "Wait. Listen. I'm not sure whether it was in one of his books or whether he was quoting . . . Anyhow, he said Satan could never tempt Jesus because Jesus did not possess anything, no worldly goods, no reputation. There was nothing Satan could threaten to take away, because Jesus had nothing."

"Oh, yes, that's true."

"So what do you have that anybody could take away from you that you're so afraid? Are you afraid of dying?"

"Yes, but they can't threaten me with that. They've never threatened me with my life, but even if they did, I don't think they could frighten me, because my life is God's."

"What, then? Your reputation?"

"No. I'm too passé to have that be a problem. But Allie's—"

"Can't you give Allie credit for taking care of his own reputation?"

A pause. Then, "You're right again."

"If they, whoever they are, know they are succeeding in frightening you, they'll go on. If you aren't frightened, they'll stop."

A longer pause. "You make me ashamed."

He moved down the gallery. She followed. He sat down on a bench vacated by three students, and she sat beside him, looking at a Seurat beach scene. "I don't want to make you ashamed. I overreacted to my anonymous phone caller in the most absurd way. I just don't want you to be frightened when you needn't be."

"I *am* ashamed. What's happened to my faith that I've let myself be blinded by panic? You're absolutely right. I don't have anything they can take away. What few things I've gathered in my apartment are only material things, and I sit lightly to them. Thank you, Katya, my dear, dear Katya. You've brought me to myself again. In my foolish panic I seem to have forgotten everything I believe. I won't forget again."

"You still have no idea who's behind this—this terrorism?"

"None."

"Do you want to know?"

"Not particularly, now that I realize how foolish I've been."

"Let it go, then. I've been foolish, too." She thought briefly of the used condom and decided against saying anything. Manya had once told her that anyone who has suffered extreme pain becomes more rather than less sensitive to it. So, since the hideousness of the motive behind the dead rat, she, too, had become more, rather than less, sensitive to acts of hate. Perhaps this was Felix's problem, too.

"I loathe their dragging you into it," he said.

"I'm dragged into it only if I let myself be. We had anonymous phone calls in Paris, too. I occasionally had them when I was on the road, staying in the best hotels. They're nothing new. Human nature doesn't seem to change." She pushed up from the bench, and he followed while she led him to look at a Lautrec whore. A superb exhibition. "I'm enjoying working on the program for your benefit. I think it's coming along."

"I can't ever thank you enough, and I bless you for it—and mostly for you. Ready for lunch?"

The private dining room was light and spacious and not crowded. "In the winter you have to book weeks ahead for a table," Felix told her.

"Felix"—Katherine spoke abruptly—"when I asked you how Mrs. Gomez happened to cook for the Undercrofts, you didn't tell me the truth, did you?"

Felix picked at his salad unhappily. "I didn't lie to you."

"But you didn't tell me the whole truth."

"Why do you want to know?"

"Because I have the feeling it's important. Why are you holding back?"

He stirred his iced tea. "You live in the same building with Mimi Oppenheimer. She doesn't like either Allie or Yolande."

"Please give me credit for having my own opinions. I don't know either Allie or Yolande well, but I like them."

"You do?"

"Yes, Felix, I do."

He speared a cherry tomato, spattering the cloth. "Things that belong in the past ought to be left in the past."

"That would be ideal." She watched him mop up the stain. "However, the past produces the future. What about the Undercrofts and Mrs. Gomez?"

He spoke softly. "Some people can't forgive the past, even when it's been repented, atoned for, redeemed. You can forgive the past, Katya, I know, because you've forgiven mine. All right. I'll tell you. When Yolande was singing, being worked half to death by her manager, she took drugs. Gomez was her supplier. Katherine, this is privileged information."

"I'm not going to tell anybody. Half the world took pot."

"Not just pot. Heavier stuff. Allie told me, so there's no seal of confessional—" He sounded anxious.

She repeated. "I'm not going to tell anybody."

"Gomez wanted to go straight, after the birth of the kids. But he's a sullen man, and he couldn't keep a job. Mrs. Gomez supported the family for years, but she acquired a bad reputation. Not as a cook, but as someone with a bad nature and an unpredictable temper. It wasn't exactly blackmail when she begged Yolande to take her on. Yolande needed a cook—"

"But Mrs. Gomez wouldn't be above letting the world know that the bishop's wife had been a drug taker, and who knows, might still be one?"

"She isn't—"

"But Mrs. Gomez could have been a threat. Could be a threat."

"It sounds horrid put like that, but I suppose it's true. Mrs. Gomez does have a violent temper, and not everybody can control her. There's one tale that she lost a job with a UN diplomat and his family by chasing the maid around the table with a carving knife during a sensitive diplomatic dinner party."

Katherine laughed. "I can believe it. How does Yolande manage to control her?"

"Yolande is paying for the children's education. That's a sizable stick. Now I've told you everything. Are you satisfied?"

"I wasn't looking for satisfaction. It does make me understand a little better why Yolande doesn't want the Gomez contingent living in her house. But those poor kids are always underfoot, and Topaze tends to follow me around, making cryptic remarks."

Felix leaned across the table toward her. "Don't take Topaze lightly."

"Believe me, I don't take Topaze lightly at all."

After lunch they were both too tired to go back to the crowded gallery, so Felix offered to get her a taxi. While they were standing at the curb, waiting, Felix asked, "Has that journalist from the *Times*—Jarwater, or whatever her name is—been in touch with you?"

"No," Katherine said. "Nobody has."

Felix fluttered his fingers. "I don't understand. Yolande is usually quick to get after all the media. Perhaps she knows the name Vigneras is enough—heaven knows, we're already getting as many calls for tickets as her secretary can handle. Even I didn't realize quite what a drawing card you are. Still, it seems unlike Yolande . . . Oh, good, here's an empty taxi." He kissed her, saw her into the cab, and shut the door.

--··⇥{ 2 }⇤·--

When Katherine returned to Tenth Street, Raissa had finished with the garden apartment and reported that it was habitable, though bare-looking.

When the baby came, it would fill up.

But, Raissa said, there are unfaded places on the wall where pictures were taken down.

Katherine went to her big cupboard, out in the public hall and under the stairs, undid the padlock, and took out some pictures which would do until Dorcas found something of her own. Raissa took Dorcas's having a baby without a husband compassionately but unsentimentally. In her world, these things happened all the time. Her chief concern was that Dorcas had no mother to help out. "Her parents are dead," Katherine said, "and there's only a sister living in California." Raissa shook her head, then picked up the pictures and went back downstairs.

Dorcas emerged just as Katherine was ready to wake her. "I slept all day."

"You needed to."

"I thought I'd never sleep again."

"You'll sleep tonight. Emotion is physically exhausting, and you must rest for your baby's sake. I'm being picked up in about an hour to go uptown for the evening—an early one. I'll be home around nine if you need me." A social day, indeed.

"Thank you." Dorcas held out both hands to Katherine. "You've been terrific, way above and beyond the call. But I won't bother you. Not unless there's some kind of dire emergency, like June's coming after me with a hatchet."

Katherine laughed. "I doubt that she'll find it necessary. Ultimately, it's Terry I'm sorry for."

They both turned, startled, as the doorbell rang.

Katherine went to the door, calling out, "Who is it?" She had a peephole but she found it easier to identify people by voice than by the distorted image.

"Llew. Llew Owen."

She opened the door and he came in, his short-sleeved blue shirt rumpled from the heat. "I came down to return some music to Yorke—my friend at Ascension, and since it's just around the corner, I thought I'd—" He stopped in confusion as he saw Dorcas. Dorcas, in her turn, blushed, and rose, steadying her overbalancing belly with a graceful movement of the arms.

"You've met, I think," Katherine said. "Dorcas Gibson and Llew Owen."

"Well, barely," Dorcas said. "I think I was fleeing, just as Mr. Owen was coming for lunch. And I think I'd better flee now, too."

"Oh, don't, not because of me," Llew said, and his glance slid from Dorcas's face to her body, and then to the floor.

Dorcas said, "I'm very pregnant, and Madame Vigneras has been putting me back together, because I'm a married but husbandless mother."

Katherine sighed inwardly. It seemed to be a trend in this day and age for the young to feel they had to announce defiantly whatever was wrong, instead of, as she had been taught, keeping it decently private. "Sit down, Llew," she said, "and I'll pour us all some tea. I have the kettle simmering."

"Thanks. Just what I need." He sat on the sofa across from Dorcas. "I'm sorry."

"I'm sorry, too. I never thought it would happen. But I'm not sorry to be having the baby."

Katherine put her hand lightly on Dorcas's shoulder. "Llew lost his wife in childbirth, and the baby, too, a little over a year ago."

"Oh. God." Dorcas covered her face with her hands. "I'm sorry." And then her frightened face peered through her fingers. "In childbirth?"

"It doesn't happen often," Llew said. "Statistically. We just happened to be one of the statistics."

Dorcas spoke through her hands. "I'm a statistic, too. My husband just left me."

"Enough statistics, then," Katherine said briskly. "Let me fix the tea." She turned her back on them and went to the kitchen.

Although she could easily have heard whatever was going on, she closed her ears and fixed the tea tray. Let them manage the conversation themselves. She turned her thoughts away from them until the tea was ready, then she pushed the tea cart into the living room, hearing Llew say, "How did you get into ballet? Don't you have to start very young?"

Dorcas replied, "I was what I suppose was a hyperactive child—nobody'd heard of such terms in Cedar Rapids—and my mother couldn't stand me getting into everything all the time, and there was a small ballet school in town, and she put me there, and that's how it all began."

As they saw Katherine coming in with the tea tray both Dorcas and Llew rose to help.

"It's light and moves easily," Katherine said. "It's one of my favorite things I brought with me from Paris. But I'll put it in front of you, Dorcas, and you can pour."

Dorcas picked up the teapot and looked at Llew. "What do you have in it?"

"Milk, please. No sugar."

She poured. "Madame Vigneras?"

"Just as it comes today. I'm out of lemons. Thanks, dear."

"Madame Vigneras, you had two children, didn't you?"

"Yes, and I'm still here to tell the tale."

"Was it—was it all right?"

"I had a bad time with Michou, my first. But he was such a charming child—the bad parts are quickly forgotten. As for Julie, she slipped out like a little fish."

"That easy?" Dorcas asked.

"Oh, my dear, nothing worth anything is easy. Birthing a baby is hard work. When a woman grunts in childbirth, it's a work noise, the same kind of noise sailors made in the old days when they were hauling on the ropes. It's good work, but it is most definitely work. And it is the most excitingly creative thing a human being can do." She smiled slightly as the memory of Julie's tiny wet body lying between her breasts flicked across her mind, and then was replaced by the loneliness and anonymity of Michou's birth. "Who is going with you when you start labor?"

"To the hospital?" Dorcas asked. "Me, myself, and I."

"Nonsense," Katherine replied. "Not in this day and age of

understaffed hospitals where women on the obstetrical floors are expected to have someone with them. Can't your sister come?"

Dorcas closed her lips and shook her head.

"Someone from the company?"

Again the shake of the head.

Llew said, "I think I can understand that. A ballet company must be as intimate as a Cathedral Close, whether we like it or not. They're all probably tied in with the breakup of the marriage, aren't they?"

Dorcas nodded in mute gratitude.

Katherine tried to keep her sigh inaudible. "All right. If worst comes to worst, I will go with you. Your landlord isn't the best person in the world at a time like this, but at least better than nothing."

"You're far more than a landlord!" Dorcas cried. "You're Katherine Vigneras! And I couldn't ask that of you."

"You're not asking. I'm announcing. Now, my children," she started to dismiss them, and stopped as she heard Llew.

"Dorcas, the real reason I came by this afternoon was that . . . well, a while ago Madame Vigneras suggested that you might be able to use the crib and things I have, and it's taken me this long to . . . I don't know if you already have everything—"

"No. I should have done something, but—everything's been so—so unexpected."

"I've got everything." Llew was looking, not at Dorcas, but at the portrait of Katherine and Michou. "It certainly isn't doing me any good, and, as Madame Vigneras said, it's only making me hold on to—" He took a breath. "So if you could use it all, it'd be a favor to me."

"Oh! I would love to—to borrow—"

"Fine, then. Yorke and Lib—he's the organist, just up the street, they have a big old station wagon, so they could help me get the stuff down to you. There are—there are some clothes Dee made—"

Dorcas's eyes brimmed, but she did not refuse the offer. "You're more than kind, and I . . . it would mean a great deal to me. I don't deserve this, or Madame Vigneras, or—"

"Great heavens, child, if it were a question of deserving, none of us would have much. That's splendid, Llew, that you have friends to help. Now, my children," she started again, "if you've finished your tea, I'm going to send you on your way. I'm being called for in a few minutes, and I have to change."

Llew leapt to his feet, picking up the cups and saucers and setting them on the tea cart, which he wheeled out to the kitchen. "I'll wash these," he called back. "It won't take a minute."

⸺⁂ 3 ⁂⸺

Mother Catherine of Siena came herself, tall and slender and, Katherine thought, serene, though no doubt the serenity was hard-won. They shook hands and went quickly to the car, which Mother Cat had left running, double-parked. "I drove around the block three times and couldn't find a space, so gave up. I was certain you wouldn't keep me waiting."

Katherine accepted this as a compliment and got into the car. "Thank you very much indeed for coming all this way for me."

"Our privilege." Mother Cat eased the car into the traffic. "Our usual pattern on our special Sunday evenings is to have Vespers, followed by supper, and then we sit around and enjoy our guest. I hope you won't find Vespers painful; some of the Sisters are getting old and a few of them tend to squeak, and we have one old dear who is deaf and doesn't have the slightest idea how loudly she's singing, because she lets the batteries in her hearing aid run down. I can't speak to her about it too often, it shatters her so."

"I survived a musical evening at the Davidsons'," Katherine said, "so I don't think I'll have too much trouble with Vespers. We used to sing a lot when the children were little, and we sang with great enthusiasm, but our musical talent was not vocal—except Michou's. He had a pure, boy soprano's voice."

"We have an excellent choir at the school," the nun said. "I'd love to have you hear them sometime. Rather to everyone's surprise, Fatima Gomez has a beautiful voice."

"I've heard her," Katherine said. "Mrs. Undercroft had her sing for us the other night. It's an amazing voice for an adolescent."

"It is, indeed. Poor Fatima. Her mother is trying to convince her—and us—that she has a vocation to the religious life. She'd love to get rid of Fatima and we are constantly having to remind her that the child is thirteen years old, and right now what she needs is enough education so that she'll be able to earn her living. Fatima is very good with the pre-schoolers, and I'm letting her help out with the little ones in our play school this summer."

"So you run a summer school, too?"

"There's a great need for it here in the city."

"And you know all their names and all their problems?"

"That's a large part of my job. When the new ones come, in the autumn, it takes me a while. But I learn, slowly."

Katherine glanced at her in admiration. "I can't conceive of it—knowing that much about that many people."

Mother Catherine laughed. "Not all of them have that many problems. Some of them, like the Davidson children, come from warm, supportive families. What *I* can't conceive of is your being able to hold in your memory all the music that you know."

Now Katherine, too, laughed. "Different disciplines. We both need our memories in different ways."

"Yes, and I'd be glad if you'll talk to the Sisters a little about that. The discipline of memory needed in their work, and the discipline of coming to terms with their own memories. For that is what you are doing now, isn't it?" At Katherine's surprise, she said, "I've watched it in the retired Sisters. I'm not far from it myself—all the things I haven't had time to think about because I've been too happy and too busy. And I didn't enter the religious life until I was nearly thirty, and there's a good bit I need to sort out and come to terms with. In my youth I sometimes reminded myself of St. Augustine praying, 'Lord, make me chaste, but not yet.' But he got there."

"And you got there, too."

"In my own way. I've been extraordinarily blessed in spending most of my life doing the work I love best. I think that's why I can speak to you so easily. You, too, have spent your life doing what you were meant to be doing."

"There's a price," Katherine said slowly. "I couldn't do anything except be a pianist—but I wasn't as good a mother as I should have been. I'm not as close to my daughter as I would like to be, and I'm sure it's because of my own lacks as a mother. I was on the road more often than I was at home when Julie was growing up."

"There's always a price," Mother Catherine said, "and it has to be paid. I don't always see problems among children or Sisters until too late, when the damage has been done. Sometimes I see a problem and can't fathom what causes it—again, until too late. Now. We're nearly there. The convent is four brownstone houses. We added the fourth a few years ago, and what a difference it has made, especially in the chapel." Mother Cat stopped on a steep hill above the Drive, pulled on the emergency brake, got out briskly, and walked around to help Katherine. From the convent Sister Isobel emerged to park the car, greeting them both with evident pleasure.

Katherine was taken upstairs in a small elevator, and into the guest section of the chapel, behind the Sisters. The chapel was a long room, the length of the four houses, simple and yet warm, with a few icons and a fine ivory crucifix above the freestanding altar. Most of the stalls were filled with Sisters; some were kneeling, others sitting, hands in lap, quietly. Katherine was the only person in the guest section, and she relaxed, not trying to kneel on her arthritic knees, simply sitting and letting the quiet seep into her. In one corner of the chapel was a wooden Madonna and Child, and it startled her by its resemblance to the Madonna and Child in the cathedral in Munich. This young girl's face was enigmatic; Katherine could read nothing. One hand was holding the Child, the other spread out as though in wonder, and Katherine spread out her own hands, once more marveling.

A small bell was struck several times, and the Sisters crossed themselves and knelt.

Katherine enjoyed Vespers. The age range of the Sisters was great, and there were far more young ones than old. It was not difficult to pick out the Sister who let the batteries of her hearing aid run down; every once in a while her voice, cracked and off-key, would rise above the others, but there was such an ineffable look of joy on her face as she sang that Katherine understood why Mother Cat could not speak to her too often. The younger Sisters had clear, light voices, and appeared to be throwing the verses of the psalms back and forth to each other, in a way that reminded Katherine of a ballet Justin had written music for, in which the dancers played battledore and shuttlecock.

After Vespers she was taken downstairs in the elevator by the deaf Sister, who beamed at her until she felt bathed in sunlight.

Not all the Sisters had that quality of total inner light, and it was, she suspected, the result of a lifetime of devotion.

Supper was simple and delicious. The novices and postulants cleared up, and then returned to the living room and sat on the floor. One of the postulants, in her blue denim dress, leaned her head trustingly against the knee of one of the older nuns.

After Mother Catherine's brief introduction, Katherine spoke about her early training in music, the early acceptance of discipline, of the structure without which there is no freedom.

"And I am," she concluded, "a born worker. I really can't take any credit for it. And I am stubborn, and that's not always a good quality, though it can be helpful at times." She talked to them about Justin, about their marriage, their love, once she had done enough growing up, and how they had worked together. "He was the perfect teacher for me, hard-driving, but he knew, always, just what I needed to learn. And he could make me laugh. I got some bad reviews after a concert in Japan, and my pride was sorely wounded, because I thought I had played well. I still think I did, but we'd chosen the wrong music for that audience. Justin could not reason me out of my hurt feelings, so he made me play scales, which I didn't want to do—except that he always read to me when I played scales. This time he read P. G. Wodehouse and got me laughing so, I almost fell off the piano bench. Justin had a wonderful ear and was a great mimic, and could put on a perfect English accent—or any other, for that matter. He translated *The Jabberwocky* into French and read it with a Marseilles twang, and by the time he was done I was back in proportion."

When she finished, they applauded sweetly, and began asking questions, nothing prying, nothing embarrassing, and at last one of the older Sisters said softly, "Tell us about your miracles, Madame Vigneras, please. You cannot have lived as full and vital a life as you have without some miracles."

She held out her hands and told them about Michou's birth and its aftermath, and, finally, the Great Grey Wolf coming to her.

They did not misunderstand when she referred to him thus. Many had read and admired his books. "He was a very great man, a saint," one of them said. "How fortunate you were to have known him."

"Yes," she replied. "I learned a great deal from him."

Sister Isobel accompanied Mother Catherine on the drive back to Tenth Street, so that the Superior did not have to return to the convent alone.

"I hate to accept that a solitary woman driver is no longer safe after dark. There have been too many incidents of people being attacked while the car is at stop lights, even with the doors locked."

"Of course," Sister Isobel remarked, straight-faced, "I am total and absolute protection."

"We ought to have a dog," Mother Cat said, "a big, black, gentle dog with a loud bark."

"Why not?" Sister Isobel urged. "You know we all want one. I'm never happy when the younger Sisters doing lockup have to walk even the short distance home from school."

"I'll think on it."

"We'd all love it."

"I know. That's the problem."

Mother Cat pulled up in front of Katherine's house.

"I'm most grateful for this evening. I've enjoyed it—far more than I expected. And I'm grateful for the ride home, too."

Mother Catherine left the ignition on. "May Sister Isobel see you in?"

"Oh, don't bother. I'm perfectly all right on my own."

But Sister Isobel got out of the car and put her hand on Katherine's elbow to help her up the steps.

"Thanks, again," Katherine said as she put her key in the lock.

--◦⊰{ 4 }⊱◦--

Sister Isobel stayed in the vestibule, waiting, while Katherine opened the door and reached for the light switch.

In the fragment of time it took for them to see the room, Sister Isobel turned toward the street, calling, "Mother! Come quickly!" She followed Katherine into the living room, her hand restrainingly on the older woman's arm.

The first thing that was apparent was chaos. Chairs were overturned. The piano bench was on its side. All the drawers of the music cabinet had been pulled out and music scattered over the floor. Katherine raised her eyes and looked at the picture over the mantel and gasped in horror as she saw that it had been slashed with a knife, Michou's face cut through and through.

Mother Catherine came swiftly into the room, righting chairs. The three women were silent, shocked. At last Mother Cat said, "It seems that the only real damage is to the portrait. Nothing else has been harmed. None of the music has been torn, only thrown about at random." She moved to the telephone, skirts swishing, and dialed.

"The police," Sister Isobel murmured.

"No—no—" Katherine said.

Mother Catherine spoke into the phone. "Dr. Oppenheimer? Good. I'm glad you're home. Will you come down to Madame Vigneras, right away, please? Vandals have been in the apartment. Good. Thanks." And she hung up. "We will, I suppose, have to call the police."

Again Katherine protested, "No. Not yet."

Mother Cat looked again at the devastated portrait. "The father of one of our students is a curator at the Metropolitan Museum responsible for the restoration of paintings. This can be repaired so that you won't be able to see that anything has happened to it. Sit down, Madame Vigneras."

Blindly, Katherine moved to the grey wing chair and lowered herself into it. "But why? Why?"

They turned as they heard a key in the door to the kitchen, and Mimi let herself in. She was wearing pajamas and a short blue robe. She looked at the scattered music, at the portrait. "Christ, Katherine—"

"Who would hate you so?" Mother Cat asked.

Katherine shook her head numbly.

Briskly, Mimi told the two nuns about the anonymous phone calls.

"It is time to call the police." Mother Catherine of Siena went to the phone. Katherine could hear her crisp, authoritative voice, but the words made little sense. The police, however, were quick in coming. Mimi had scarcely gone to the kitchen, saying, "I'll make tea. It always helps to boil the water in time of childbirth or other crisis," when they heard the siren of the police car, saw the light swinging across the windows, followed by a shrill ring on the doorbell. Mother Cat nevertheless peered through the peep-hole before opening the door.

The two policemen were courteous and efficient. They were annoyed at the Superior for having righted the furniture, but she replied calmly, "You can get fingerprints from the chairs, anyhow, and from the music chest and the portrait. I felt that it was more important to put a little order back into the room for Madame Vigneras than to leave what we can perfectly well describe. The chairs and tables were overturned. They were not scratched or hurt. Even the lamps were not broken. The only damage is to the portrait."

"But why?" Katherine asked. "Why?"

Mimi took over, describing the anonymous phone calls. She did not mention any connection with the Cathedral, for which Katherine was grateful, although she did not understand why.

"How did they get in?" Sister Isobel asked.

The police examined the locks to both doors. There was a possibility that some kind of passkey had been used on the vestibule door.

"But it's a Yale lock."

"Yale locks are no longer adequate," one of the officers said. "They are not difficult to pick by anyone with even the smallest talent or experience. I advise you to add a Medeco lock."

"I will see to it," Katherine said, "first thing in the morning."

"Thus," Mimi added, "carefully locking the stable door after the horse is stolen."

The only baffling thing to the policemen was that nothing had been taken. It was not a simple breaking-and-entering case. Some-one wanted to upset Madame Vigneras. "But this is fairly common," the senior officer said, "random acts of violence for no purpose." He looked around the apartment again. "Your radio hasn't been touched, nor your stereo, but I see that your television is gone." He seemed satisfied at this discovery.

"I don't have a television," Katherine said.

This disappointed him.

The younger officer said, "Very odd. The bedroom radio is still there, too. They appear to have concentrated on the living room. Nothing seems to have been disturbed in the rest of the apartment."

It obviously was not an important enough case to interest them.

They made Katherine promise to keep in touch, and said they would keep the case in an open file. They asked if she was all right.

"I will stay with Madame Vigneras tonight," Mimi announced. When the police had driven off, she marched back into the kitchen. "Now we will have our tea. I suppose it is necessary to call the police as a matter of form, but they're not going to do anything about it. Mother—Sister—will you stay and have a cup of tea with us?"

Mother Catherine glanced at Katherine's ashen face and nodded assent. Then she took the portrait down. "This is what really hurts, isn't it?"

The defacement of Michou. Yes. Her entire body was filled with horror. This was far worse than . . .

"It's a Hunter, isn't it?" Mother Cat asked calmly.

"Yes. Of me, and my son, Michou." She shuddered.

"We should put something else in its place until it's restored."

Katherine spoke through cold lips. "I sent most of my spare pictures to my tenant in the downstairs apartment—"

Mother Cat looked around, then took a picture off the wall by the entrance to the kitchen, a seascape about the same size as the portrait, a painting of blues and greys and soft mauves, and hung it over the mantel. "There. That will do for now."

Mimi wheeled in the tea cart. "I've made a mixture of all the most soothing ingredients. This is lousy, Katherine, but worse things have happened. You weren't hurt. Thank God you weren't here."

"It was someone who *knew* she wouldn't be here?" Mother Catherine of Siena suggested.

Who? Dorcas knew. But this could have nothing to do with Dorcas. Even if Terry had come roaring in, feeling destructive, he would not have simply overturned the furniture and damaged the portrait. Had she told Llew? Felix? She must have, she did not remember. Nothing seemed to add up.

Sister Isobel was busy gathering up music manuscript, setting it in tidy piles on top of the rosewood chest. She had put all the drawers back in. To the casual observer, the apartment would appear to be pleasantly normal.

Mimi put a teacup into Katherine's hand. "Drink. It will help. You have to work through this, and I will be here."

Mother Cat put down her cup and knelt at Katherine's feet. "Madame Vigneras, your son died when he was very young, didn't he?"

"Yes. When he was seven."

"How did he die?"

Katherine raised her teacup with trembling fingers, took a sip of the soothing liquid.

"Would it help if you told us about it?" the nun suggested.

Katherine continued to sip her tea. Her reaction to the deface-ment of the portrait was witness to the fact that she could still be reached and hurt; she had not shed her attachment to possessions. Did her words to Felix in the museum mean nothing, then? Did she believe them? But it was not so much the portrait as Michou . . .

The three other women remained silent.

⋯⊰{ 5 }⊱⋯

Perhaps she could tell them about the actual death itself, but there was much else that she could not tell.

She had been invited to play at a music festival in a small town in Bavaria, a festival which had become famous because of the caliber of the artists who came each August. She and Justin had decided to bring Nanette and the children, to make it a family holiday. They had not done anything together as a family for too long, and there was a *kermesse*, a carnival, at the same time as the music festival, which the children would enjoy. They were put up, comfortably, in a small chalet of their own. The first evening, they took the children to the *kermesse* and Katherine had a vivid image of the joy in Michou's face as he rode a white horse on the merry-go-round, a horse with a flowing wooden mane and flaring nostrils. Nanette would not let little Julie on one of the big horses, but rode with her in a small carriage made of two wooden swans.

She remembered eating ice cream with the children, and then taking them to the chalet and singing them to sleep.

The next night she was playing. She had worked often with the conductor of the chamber orchestra; she was easy with him. There was no precarious moment as the piano joined the orchestra; he would draw her in as gently and securely as Erlend. They would be playing Mozart works with which she was thoroughly familiar. So she persuaded Justin to stay with the children. The *kermesse* was at the side of the lake, and there were small pedal boats which Michou had been begging to ride, and fireworks after dark. Nanette, as always, would see to it that there was no danger.

She walked through the soft August evening to the theatre.

A man was in her dressing room, waiting for her, a tall man with a fair beard, and spectacles with heavy frames.

'Lukas!'

'So you do recognize me.'

'It took me a moment.'

'May I sit down?'

'Of course.' But she was trembling.

'Your husband is at the *kermesse* with the children.' It was a statement.

'How did you know?'

'I made it my business to find out. I need to see you alone.'

'Lukas, what is wrong?'

'I am not here because of something that is wrong. I am here because your son, Michou, is also my son.'

She sat at her dressing table, looking at his face in the mirror.

'There have been many pictures of you and your husband and your children. It is obvious that Michou is not your husband's child. You are both dark.'

'My mother was fair—Justin's sister was fair—'

'And Michou looks exactly like me.' He reached into his pocket and pulled out a snapshot. 'Look.' It was Michou, and it was not Michou, because the clothes were too old-fashioned. 'So,' he said, 'I grew a beard. I wear spectacles I do not really need. Did your husband never suspect?'

Still looking at him in the mirror, she shook her head.

'I will never understand that weekend,' Lukas said, 'why you were willing to spend it with me. It was obvious to me then and has been obvious to me ever since that you are in love with your husband. But for me, that weekend was the only lovely thing to happen in many years. I kept it to myself, as a treasure. And then I saw pictures of the child . . . Katherine, I want to see my son.'

She shook her head.

'I will be discreet. I manage this theatre, too. I will come to your husband and introduce myself. I will tell him that many years have passed since the war, and that I am an admirer of his compositions as well as your playing. All this is true,' he added as she continued to shake her head. 'I will not reveal anything. It will be forever our secret. He will never know that the boy is not his. But Michou is my son and I have a right to see him. Tomorrow is Sunday. You are not playing again until Monday. I will invite you out to dinner at the *kermesse*—the entire family—'

'Justin may not accept.'

'But he may.'

Sighing, she nodded, still not looking at him directly, but in the mirror.

'Perhaps I should have waited until after the performance to speak to you, but I was afraid that your husband would be here by then. If he is, I will speak to him.'

She was grateful that night for the daily discipline of long hours of practicing, for the music which took over, first her fingers, and then, as she moved into it, her mind. She did not, she thought, play brilliantly, but she played well enough so that no one would notice there was something wrong.

At the end of the concert the conductor congratulated her on her magnificent performance. 'I have never heard you play better.'

And Justin was waiting backstage. 'That was superb, my love.'

So.

Then Lukas came.

At first Justin's face hardened, the fine lines from nose to mouth whitening as they did when he felt anything intensely. But he listened to Lukas, and at last he said, 'You are right. We cannot hold hate in our hearts forever. My wife has made me see that.' And he accepted Lukas's invitation for the following evening.

During the day, while Katherine practiced, the children paddled in the shallow waters of the lake, under Nanette's watchful eye. They both had long naps, in order to be allowed to stay up for the evening, and then Nanette dressed them. Michou wore soft green lederhosen with embroidered suspenders; while Julie was arresting in a smocked blue dress which set off her dark hair and strange pale eyes.

Lukas took them to a restaurant at the water's edge. He was charming to both children. He talked to Justin about his work, and it was apparent that Justin, despite himself, liked the other man. Lukas described the *Schloss* and his happy times with his children there. His wife, he explained, seldom came, since she was an invalid and preferred the comforts of the city. He did not hide the fact that it was not a happy marriage. There was nothing in his behavior which could cause Justin or anyone else any suspicion about his motives in arranging the evening. Like the cardinal, he was a lover of music; it was music which brought them together.

After dinner they walked through the grounds, lit by long chains of tiny lights which blew softly in the summer breeze like bright stars caught in the trees. Nanette carried the children's sweaters, and Katherine had swung hers lightly about her shoulders. They all rode the merry-go-round, Nanette relaxing enough to allow Lukas to take Julie up on one of the horses with him, watching and waving each time the merry-go-round swept past. Katherine and Justin, too, were up on horses, Michou between them, laughing at the rocking motion as the horses went up and down on their poles. Julie, in Lukas's arms, was shrieking with delight. Michou, looking from Justin to Katherine, was lit with joy.

After the merry-go-round, Nanette stood on the grass verge, holding the children's hands, while the grownups rode the Ferris wheel. Then Michou pointed to a ride, a circle of swings where the children were tightly strapped in, and as the ride progressed, the swings lifted farther and farther up and out.

'Is it all right?' Lukas asked Justin.

Justin nodded. 'It looks safe enough. There are children smaller than Michou.'

'Me, too!' Julie cried.

But Nanette was adamant. 'No. You are too little.'

Lukas bought the ticket for Michou and saw to it that he was safely strapped into the swing. Then he hefted Julie onto his shoulders.

This was the only part which Katherine could tell Mimi and the nuns, and perhaps Mother Catherine of Siena was right and she needed to say it out loud.

"At first the children were all laughing with pleasure. And then the swings went faster and faster—we suddenly realized that they were going too fast—and the laughter turned to screams of terror, and I could see Michou's face and his fear—"

Lukas had thrust Julie into Nanette's arms and rushed toward the machinery that controlled the swings.

"We could see the young man who worked the swings pulling and pulling on the level, frantically trying to slow them, to stop them, but they went faster, and faster, and then there was a terrible explosion, and the central column, to which the swings were attached, burst into flames. Everything was fire—"

It had been a disaster horrifying enough to be in newspapers all over the world. All the children were killed.

--*❦{ 6 }❦*--

"I remember," Mother Catherine of Siena murmured.

"It was difficult to identify the bodies, they were so burned—" Katherine's voice remained quiet, without a tremor.

"Stop it—" Mimi reached out and took Katherine in her arms, but it was Mimi who was crying, her tears soaking Katherine's dress.

Manya and Tom had flown over immediately. There was a funeral, of which Katherine remembered little, because what she remembered was always the look of terror on Michou's face. And, a few days later, Justin, looking at the paper and saying, 'He's killed himself.'

'Who?' she had asked indifferently.

'Von Hilpert. It says he was killed in a shooting accident at his *Schloss*, but of course that's nonsense. He felt responsible and he killed himself, poor bastard. It was a way out of everything for him, that disastrous marriage—'

His words hardly registered.

Justin went on, 'I never thought I'd feel sorry for a Nazi, but I feel sorry for him. It wasn't his fault. It might have happened the night before; Michou wanted to ride those swings and I said, "Not tonight, maybe tomorrow . . ." '

Manya had stayed with them for a month, delaying the rehearsals of her new play. Tom, with recording commitments in New York, had gone home shortly after the funeral, unable to bear more than his own pain, which he worked out in the *Second Kermesse Suite*, music which started out with gentle merriment, moved into laughter, and then rose slowly to a climax of terror and pain, and finally resolved into a gentle and accepting peace.

Nanette was half ill for weeks, sick with self-blame, not hearing when they told her over and over again that it was she who had kept Julie from going on the swings, that she was in no way to blame, that it was an accident, that there was nothing she could have done to prevent it.

It was Manya who held things together, took care of Julie, sang to her, told her stories, took her to the park, bought her a new hoop, roller skates, despite Nanette's protestations of danger.

'Life is dangerous,' Manya stated. 'You will only hurt the child if you try to protect her from all the little dangers of ordinary living. Let her skin her knees; let her live like a normal child.' And she took Julie and went out, and they came home with a tricycle, with which the little girl was delighted.

Justin, like Nanette, would have kept Julie wrapped in cotton wool, but understood that he could not, so he left her to Manya for those first empty weeks, and saw to it that Katherine practiced for the requisite hours. He did not read to her while she played scales; it was months before he opened a book to read aloud to her. Like Thomas Forrester, he worked through his rage and horror in composition, an opera based on Robinson Jeffers's *Medea*, perhaps his best work, but so full of anguish when Medea's two little sons are slaughtered that it was seldom played, while Forrester's *Second Kermesse Suite* was heard over and over again . . .

Katherine patted Mimi's shoulder. "It's all long past." She looked across Mimi to Mother Catherine of Siena. "You're right. I needed to say it aloud. We had a bad time afterwards. I don't know what we'd have done without my stepmother, who stayed with us, even though it meant postponing a play. And then Wolfi—Cardinal von Stromberg—came from Rome."

This time Justin did not send for him. The day after Manya left, Katherine was at the piano, practicing, dutifully, dully, the music dead under her fingers. And then, without warning, she was picked up off the piano bench and held in Wolfi's arms, held tightly, painfully, until at last she was able to cry, to shed the tears which even Manya had not been able to bring from her dry eyes.

--*{ 7 }*--

Mimi wiped her hands across her face. "I've got you all wet with my tears."

"It's hot," Katherine said quietly. "They'll dry."

Mimi turned to the two nuns. "It's terribly late, and you have to get up. I'll stay with Katherine, sorry help though I am."

Katherine touched Mimi's cheek gently. "I needed your tears."

Mother Catherine stood with her back to the fireplace. "You know I'd almost forgotten, but when I was a novice the convent was broken into. A thief came through the skylight. It was a weekday, so most of the Sisters were in school. I was home with grippe, and when he looked in my cell I screamed, naturally, and he fled as though I had frightened him, and raced downstairs. One of our older Sisters was at the door. She was so forgetful that opening the door was about all she could do. But she was a most loving person, and what she wanted most in the world was to be of help in any way that she could. So when she saw this strange young man running down the stairs, she asked him if she could help him, and he said, 'I'm a thief. Give me your money.' And she tinkled a laugh and said, 'My dear, we are just poor Sisters and we don't have any money.' And she turned the pockets of her habit inside out. 'Here,' she said, 'here's a stamp. Now you can at least write a letter to your mother. Would you like paper and an envelope, too?' And while he watched, openmouthed, she found him a note pad and an envelope with the convent return address on it, and then added, 'Now, there are people with much more money down the street who don't have our vow of poverty. Why don't you try them?' and opened the door for him and ushered him out. She at least had enough memory to tell us what happened, and hoped she had done the right thing and been helpful. I suspect that he was very new at being a thief, and what I've always hoped is that Sister Domina turned him toward a more honest living."

Katherine glanced at the seascape hanging over the mantel behind Mother Cat. "If he wrote that letter, I wonder what his mother made of the envelope? Now you really must go. Thank you, all of you, for being with me. It's been more help to me than I can express. But I'm fine, now. Mimi, you, too. Go on upstairs. I don't need you. I'm all right."

"You may not need me," Mimi said, "but I need you. I'll just stretch out on your sofa. Thank you for being so thoughtful as to buy a sofa long enough for someone like me."

"Justin was tall," Katherine said. "I'm in the habit of buying furniture for tall people. Wolfi was tall, too. I had an even longer sofa in the house in Paris, and he occasionally slept on it."

When the nuns had gone, Mimi said, "I'll draw your bath."

Katherine nodded mutely. She was too tired to bathe, and yet she knew that the warm tub would relax her. "Thanks, dear Mimi. And thanks for being here. And I'm glad you didn't mention to the policemen that it might be someone from the Cathedral."

"Let them do their own homework." Mimi was brusque. "I did not think it would serve any useful purpose for them to go up to the Close and question everybody there. If we're to find out who's behind all this nastiness, we mustn't make anybody suspicious." She headed for the bathroom, and Katherine heard the sound of running water, smelled the fragrance of what must be an enormous quantity of bath salts.

She looked at the place where the portrait had hung and understood that she would not want to have been without any part of her life, even the most terrible.

It had been difficult to relive Michou's death, to tell the tellable parts to Mimi and the nuns. But now it was done. And death could not change the brief years of Michou's life, which had been sheer, unadulterated joy. It was not, she thought, climbing into the tub, a sentimental whitewashing of the truth; the truth was that, once she was well after the trauma of his birth and its aftermath, Michou had been joy for them, and this joy had been the source of a deepening of Katherine's and Justin's love, which death had, ultimately, strengthened. It was either that, a firmer bonding, or breaking apart entirely.

The cardinal had helped them, too, coming as often as possible after Manya had gone back to the States. After Michou's death, Katherine was able to see Wolfi again, to love him, not as she had loved him before, but acceptingly, quietly, not expecting more than it is possible to expect from another human being.

If Justin ever wondered about the paternity of either of his children, he never mentioned it. He *was* the father. He said, once, 'I thought perhaps we should talk about having another child, but it would seem like trying to replace Michou, and we can't do that.'

'And it might hurt Julie,' she had replied. 'She might think that she wasn't enough for us. Besides—we are so busy. We travel so much—' And who would she have turned to, who would have been the father of a third child? No, Michou and Julie were enough.

Throughout the years she would occasionally wake, wet with cold sweat as she saw, in her sleep, Michou's terrified face. As Felix's nightmares would never leave him, so this one would never leave her. It was during the worst of these nightmare times that she had developed the habit of getting up, making bouillon, so that she would be awake enough to go back to sleep without moving directly back into the terror. Such phantasms are something we all have to endure, one way or another, she thought; Justin surely had more than his share from Auschwitz.

Wolfi made a special point of coming to them for Julie's birthday, the first without Michou. The Great Grey Wolf was fully back in favor with his Church. They heard rumors that he might be the next Vatican Secretary of State.

He arrived just before the party, half a dozen little ones to dress in party clothes, play games, take home prizes. After Nanette had taken Julie off to bed they had sat talking, late, and the cardinal decided to spend the night on the sofa. Katherine was up early the next morning, and started to tiptoe past him to the kitchen, when he sat up and called to her. She turned back and sat on the sofa beside him. 'Lukas von Hilpert was Michou's father, wasn't he?'

For a moment she did not answer. She did not move, nor did the expression on her face change; though he had taken her by surprise, she had learned that much control. 'Justin does not know who Michou's father was, and he does not want to know, because he *was* Michou's father. If I tell you yea or nay, then that will make a difference. As long as I am the only one who knows, it is better for Justin.'

He kissed her hand again. 'Yes, *Kinderlein*, you are right. I was wrong to ask.' He sighed. 'You have grown, ah, how you have grown. Why must it be pain that makes us grow? Your music— I wept through most of your last concert. Good tears, purgative tears. You take all that you have learned, and then you give it to your audience. That is why you are so much loved.'

She had brushed this away, embarrassed. 'I do have excellent stage presence. Justin has seen to that.'

'Justin and Katherine. Katherine and Justin. I thank God for you every day. Why did it take Michou's death to bring us back together as we were before?'

'It's not as we were before, Wolfi. I'm not as I was before. And you're not, either.'

'No. We have both moved a long way. I do not think you know how much you have taught me.' This last was murmured in so low a voice she was not sure she had heard.

She told him, then, about a concert she had given in Munich a few weeks before. She had gone back to the cathedral. To the ancient statue of the Virgin and Child. How could a wooden face have so many changes of expression? Now the young woman looked old, and full of grief. She held the baby as she might have held the man when he was taken down from the cross, and the baby's face was ancient; the painted eyes held all the wisdom of the world. Katherine had bowed her head against all that wisdom, and when she looked at the mother again, the carved face was bright with love. Grief, and the acceptance of grief, yes. But love was the strongest expression, and the love seemed to be saying: You can bear this. You can bear it and go on living.

'And I am bearing it, Wolfi. At first I didn't think I could, but I am, because I know that if I didn't bear it, Justin couldn't.'

'You do know that? That you have to bear it with him, for him?'

'Yes. I know that. And thank you, Wolfi, for coming for Julie's birthday, for making it merry. I'm not sure we would have been able to laugh and play without you.'

'Whenever you need me,' he had promised, 'I will come. If it is humanly possible. I will come.'

How much did Julie remember of Michou? Of the amusement park and the explosion? Nanette had whipped Julie around, the child's face protected by the grey skirts, had taken her immediately back to the chalet. Nanette, in anguish for Michou, but holding the little one from horror. There was nothing she could do for Michou, but she would try to keep Julie untouched.

And that, of course, was not possible.

Was Michou's death part of what had wounded Julie? Did the grief for Michou make her feel unloved, unwanted, unneeded? It had not been possible to hide that Michou's death had split their universe apart. Perhaps Julie needed to get back at Katherine for Michou's death.

Too much psychologizing was not a good idea; she swished the warm scented water about her.

---⊷{ 8 }⊷---

Mimi helped her out of the tub. "I'm feeling very stiff tonight." Katherine winced.

"You hurt," Mimi said. "I'll try to massage away the pain. You've been through a lot this evening. No wonder your body had to let out a shout."

Katherine tried to quieten under the massage, but she could not banish visions of the living room, of the seascape where the Hunter portrait should be hanging, the piles of music to be sorted and put back in the cabinet, possible calls from the police. And Emily was coming the next day for her first piano lesson. She couldn't disappoint the child.

"Relax," Mimi ordered. "I'm going to stay with you till you fall asleep."

"Mimi," Katherine protested. "You won't sleep as well here as upstairs in your own bed."

Mimi rode over this. "Tomorrow we will put on the lock the police suggested. On both your doors, the one from the kitchen to the hall, too. I don't think there's going to be any more trouble tonight, but someone did get into your apartment, and therefore you are vulnerable. Of course, I sleep soundly, and I am told that I snore loudly. My snoring itself would probably scare an intruder away. No more talking."

Slowly the tenseness eased from Katherine's body. She had not realized how tightly she was in its grip until Mimi began to massage. It seemed that every smallest muscle was tightly coiled. After a while Mimi turned out the light with one hand, continuing the gentle massage with the other. Katherine did not know when it was that Mimi pulled the sheet up and went into the living room.

--⊰{ 9 }⊱--

A little past nine in the morning Mimi came in with a breakfast tray, *café au lait*, a soft-boiled egg, and a brioche.

Katherine rolled over sleepily. "You're spoiling me."

"I think you could do with a bit of spoiling."

"And I don't have a bed tray—"

"I got it from upstairs. I've been to the locksmith around the corner. He'll be here at ten. As soon as he's done the locks, I'll take off."

"Don't you have to be at the hospital?"

"Not till eleven. I gave them a ring."

"You shouldn't have changed anything for me."

"Don't be an idiot. I'm frankly fascinated and filled with curiosity."

"And you think it's all connected—the phone calls—last night—"

"Elementary, my dear Watson."

"Why did *you* get anonymous phone calls last year?"

"Could be a number of reasons. I'm connected with the Cathedral in several ways—through Iona, and Sister Isobel; through Suzy and Dave. Anybody who dislikes them could well include me, just out of spite. Or it might be anti-Semitism, which is still raising its ugly head. Dave found a swastika spray-painted on one of the altars not long ago."

"And last night—" Carefully, Katherine cut the top off her egg. "Why would anyone want to slash Michou's face?"

"Don't, *ma mie*. I think it was random. The baby's face is in the light in the portrait, and you're in the shadows. Anyone who didn't know might not even realize it was you and Michou. I'm not at all sure that you, Katherine Vigneras, are the target of whoever it is who is devoured by malignant passion. They—he? she? it?—may be trying to get at somebody else through you."

"But who?"

"Possibly the old bish."

"Felix?" She had not told Mimi about Felix's calls.

"I'm no detective. Unlike you, I do not amuse myself with English murder mysteries. I prefer science fiction or the *New*

England Medical Journal. I simply offer it as a very tentative postulation."

"Who would hate Felix that much?"

"There you have me. Some people hate all bishops on general principle." She paused. "Eat your egg while it's hot, and take your mind off sick people. It's gone so far I *am* going to tell Dave about it, all of it, from the call made to me from the front desk at Cathedral House at midnight, to the vandalizing of your apartment last night. Then he can decide what to do about the police. He has a lot of friends on the force, and he'll know who to go to if necessary. I hope it won't be. Dave's an independent cuss, and if he can work it out himself he will. He's dealt with voodoo and neo-Nazis and God knows what-all and I think he'll manage to deal with this."

"Are you going to call him?"

"I'm going to see him this evening. I called him before breakfast to make sure he'd be in. I didn't worry him; it's not the first time I've needed to go uptown and hash things over with him." The phone jangled and Mimi reached for it, saying, "I am *not* going to have you disturbed until you have had a quiet breakfast." She turned to the phone. "Yes? . . . Oh, hello, Felix. Yes, it's Mimi Oppenheimer. I do live just upstairs, you know. . . . No, she can't come to the phone now . . . Oh, Chr—all right, I'll tell her. She'll give you a call later on. Will you be in your office? . . . Yes, she'll call you as soon as possible. Goodbye, Bishop." She replaced the receiver. "It might have been easier for you to talk with him now and get it over with. Requests for tickets for your concert are pouring in, and it's totally outgrown St. Ansgar's chapel. They're going to have to put the piano in the choir, just at the head of the steps, and seat the audience in the nave."

Katherine finished her *café au lait,* and Mimi poured her some more from two small white china pitchers. "The acoustics will be completely different."

"I assume that's occurred to them."

Katherine put down her cup with annoyance. "It means, among other things, that my practicing in St. Ansgar's chapel has been useless. I'll have to go back up to the Cathedral and work the whole program out with what are going to be totally different acoustical problems."

"You could be arbitrary," Mimi suggested, "and announce that the concert will be in St. Ansgar's or else."

"No." Katherine pondered her coffee cup. "I can't do that. I said I'd do the benefit to raise money, and the more people, the more money. And, after all, what else do I have to do? I keep forgetting that I'm not tucking this benefit into the midst of my usual schedule."

"All right. I just don't want them to think they can use you."

Katherine was silent for a moment. Then, "If you're going to speak to Dave, I suppose I'll have to speak to Felix about last night."

Mimi picked up the breakfast tray and started toward the kitchen. "I think it would be a good idea. You're going to have to call him back, anyhow."

"Somehow—I don't want to tell him over the phone."

Mimi paused in the doorway. "I understand. That's why I'm going up to talk to Dave."

Should the dean know that Felix had been getting frightening calls? That was something for Felix to decide. She would not tell Mimi.

--•⊰{ 10 }⊱•--

At a few minutes before three, Jos and Emily arrived. He waited only till his sister was inside, then said, "I've got to dash to class," and took off.

Emily stood, hands clasped, very still.

She had never been in the apartment before. She would not notice anything different. The picture over the mantelpiece would look to her as though it had always been there. "Don't be afraid, child." Katherine drew her into the room. "I don't bite. And nothing is going to happen this first lesson. We're going to have to feel things out. Sit down at the piano." Emily obeyed, and Katherine went to the music chest, which she had put back in order after Mimi had left. "How's your sight-reading?"

"Fair." Emily's voice and body were tense.

"Relax. You couldn't dance with a muscle-taut body, could you? Neither can you play the piano. We'll start with some duets, just for fun. Here's one of Schubert's I used to enjoy. I'll play treble." And she sat beside Emily.

"It's much too difficult for me."

"I doubt if it is. Don't worry about the pedal. We'll play at a moderate tempo, and if you get lost, just wait until you've found your place and then come in again."

Emily scowled, then nodded.

"We'll count three measures, then begin."

The child was amazingly quick to follow Katherine's lead. The duet was doing exactly what Katherine had hoped it would, making Emily concentrate on the music so that she forgot to be self-conscious. Only once did she fumble and break the rhythm, and then she took her hands off the keys, stared fiercely at the music, counting under her breath, and was back again after only a few measures.

When they had finished the last notes triumphantly together, Emily laughed in delight. "That was like partnering in ballet!"

"Have you played duets before?"

"Only accompanying Daddy or playing with the whole family. But that—oh, Madame Vigneras, I love it."

"We'll play some more together at your next lesson. But now I want to start you on some things to practice at home. Here's a book of Mozart sonatinas, and we're going to go through them, one by one. I think you'll enjoy them. But first I want you to run a few scales for me. Start with C major, then A minor."

For nearly an hour they worked on scales, Katherine gently correcting Emily's wrist position, her fingering. Finally she said, "Enough. That was good work. Scales are dull, until you get the knack of them, then they can be fun. And if you get to the point where you can run through all the scales without having to think, I'll read to you while you do it, the way Justin—my husband— used to do for me. Now let's start this first sonatina. It's sheer delight."

The two hours were almost up when there was a knock on the door, rather than a ring, and a voice calling, "It's Dorcas." When Katherine opened the door she said, "Oh, I'm sorry. I'm interrupting—"

"It's all right. Come in. Emily and I were just finishing a lesson."

Dorcas looked, not at Emily, but at the seascape. "Where's the portrait?"

There were bound to be explanations, and Katherine didn't want to make them. But there was no use prevaricating. "Someone broke into my apartment last night and knocked things around. The only thing that was hurt was the portrait, and Mother Catherine of Siena, who brought me home, took it to be repaired." She kept her voice quiet.

Both Dorcas and Emily looked at her in horror. Dorcas cried, "But I was downstairs all evening and I never heard anything. I thought I heard a siren, but we hear so many I didn't pay any attention."

"It was the police," Katherine said, "but they didn't have any clues. Nothing was taken. You may have noticed that I have new locks. Now, my dears, it's over with, I'm properly protected, and I really would like to put it out of my mind. Emily, Dr. Oppenheimer is going to talk to your father tonight, so please don't say anything till then."

Dorcas looked at Emily, who had risen and was standing at the piano. "Don't I know you?"

Emily made her bob of a curtsy. "I'm Emily Davidson, Mrs. Gibson. I was one of the kids in the ballet school."

Dorcas moved toward her, smiling, then stopped. "You're the one who—"

"I lost my left leg in an accident," Emily stated flatly.

"But we all thought—" Dorcas put her hand up and put it to her mouth.

"That it wasn't an accident?" Emily asked. "Nobody will ever know, so there's no point in brooding about it." Her voice was so brittle that the words came out like shards of glass.

"I'm so sorry," Dorcas said. "I've put my foot in it—" and stopped again.

"You live downstairs, don't you?" Emily asked. "You and Mr. Gibson?"

"Just me," Dorcas said, "and soon, the baby."

Emily winced. "Now I've put *my* foot in it."

Dorcas shook her head as though to clear it. "Llew Owen called, Madame Vigneras. He's coming down tonight with the crib and the things for the baby. And he said just to say when you want to go up to the Cathedral, and he'll come for you, and he's going to be around to see that the Bösendorfer's moved properly and he's sorry for the change—" She stopped as the doorbell rang.

"That'll be Jos," Emily said.

"Let him in, please, child, but double-check first."

Although she was not much shorter than Katherine, Emily was not quite tall enough for the peephole, and tiptoeing was evidently difficult for her. So she called, "Who is it?" and, on her brother's reply, opened the door.

"Good lesson?" he asked.

"For me, it was gorgerific."

Katherine introduced Dorcas and Jos. "It was a fine lesson," she corroborated. "I'll expect you to have that first sonatina memorized by next week. Half an hour a day minimum practicing. Then I'd like you to spend some time doing whatever you want, making up your own pieces, playing whatever you like, having fun. But practicing first. Scales."

"I promise."

"And watch those elbows."

"I promise," Emily repeated.

When she and Jos had gone, Dorcas said, "I'm so sorry I interrupted. I didn't know—"

"Of course you didn't. Emily will be coming on Monday afternoons between three and five. Dorcas, this is the first time I've heard that Emily's accident may not have been an accident."

Dorcas looked uncomfortable. "It was company gossip, and that can't be trusted. We're always looking for drama, especially when things are a bit dull. I wonder what they're saying about me?"

Katherine sat in her grey wing chair and ignored this. "Her parents have never indicated . . . Nor Dr. Oppenheimer."

Dorcas dropped onto the sofa. "Oh, Madame Vigneras, I never should have mentioned it. I was just surprised at seeing Emily. She's so beautiful, and we were all so horrified—everybody thought she had a brilliant career ahead of her—so we just wanted to blame someone." Her eyes strayed to the mantelpiece. "Madame Vigneras, I feel so dreadful about the apartment, and the portrait, and that I didn't hear anything."

"It's a well-built house, and whoever it was must have been trying to be quiet. It's just one of these stupidities that are becoming more and more a part of the contemporary scene. Did you come up about anything in particular?"

"Just about Llew. And—I saw my obstetrician today and he says everything's fine, but it looks to him as if the baby may come in about a week. It's dropped into position, or whatever they call it. I haven't been nervous about it, and today, suddenly, I am."

"Of course you're nervous. But I meant it when I said I'd come to the hospital with you—which hospital, by the way?"

"St. Vincent's."

"Good, that's Dr. Oppenheimer's hospital. I'll speak to her; she may even know your obstetrician."

"He's a dear. He's being terribly kind to me. But—I didn't realize till today how terribly alone I was going to feel, and you've made it all seem possible, and even all right."

"I'm glad," Katherine replied absently. She was thinking more of Emily than of Dorcas. Now that the possibility had been raised that the loss of Emily's leg might not have been an accident, it had a horrible inevitability about it.

11

She called Mimi that evening. She did not want to wait for a chance encounter. But there was no answer. She called twice more, and went to bed. Mimi was, after all, telling the dean her version of all that had happened. Small wonder she was out late.

In the morning, after her coffee and two hours at the piano, Katherine called again, annoyed at herself for not trying earlier, when Mimi was more likely to be in. But the doctor promptly answered.

Katherine asked, "Are you very busy, or could you come down for a few minutes?"

"I'll be seeing patients this afternoon. I've already been to the hospital and just got back, so I'm free till a little after two. I'll be down."

Katherine talked first about Dorcas. Mimi knew the obstetrician and approved. "He's first-rate. Compassionate and competent. You're really going to the hospital with her?"

"There doesn't seem to be anybody else."

"Well, I'll come, too, to keep you company."

"Thanks. I'll really appreciate that. Did you talk to Dave?" Mimi nodded. "What did he say?"

"Dave doesn't say much until he has something to say. He

listened. When I'd finished, he looked a little more tired. He just said that a cathedral attracts neurotics and psychotics, people looking for help and not knowing how to ask for it. Have you spoken to Felix yet?"

"Not yet. I will when I go up to the Cathedral to practice."

"Dave will be mum, meanwhile. As I said, he's not a talker, unless there's a reason to talk. You've got something else on your mind. What is it?"

"Emily."

"That's right. How was her lesson? Isn't she going to be any good?"

"She's going to be more than good, ultimately. Dorcas came in just as we were finishing—they knew each other slightly when Emily was dancing, you remember."

"Yes. Emily called her husband a turd. What else?"

"Evidently it was gossip that Emily's accident was not an accident."

"Are they still going on about that?" Mimi asked in annoyance. "Artists do tend to make things more complex than they need be—sorry, my dear, I don't think you do. Suzy and Dave heard the gossip but there was nothing to substantiate it. I myself can't believe that anyone would deliberately run Emily down. The quicker such gossip is squelched, the better. The thing is to see that Emily gets on with her life, and you're helping with that."

"Wolfi was killed because of an accident—why there aren't more accidents in Rome than there are, I'll never know. He was crossing the street and was hit by a driver who was coming around the corner—an American tourist who swore Wolfi crossed without looking. The bystanders swore that of course the cardinal was careful, and I'm sure he was. Wolfi was too intelligent to get lost in prayer while crossing a Roman road. He lived for several days—he was badly hurt internally, and ultimately the bleeding could not be controlled."

It was not long before Justin's death, but she had been on the road, urged by both Justin and Jean Paul to continue work as usual. She had, in fact, just given a concert in Munich when the cardinal's secretary called her from Rome.

She was not with Justin when he died, but she had been with Wolfi.

His injuries were severe. He had known that he was dying, and had insisted on being brought home from the hospital. His secretary, grey with grief, but with features emotionless, had escorted Katherine to his room and discreetly withdrew. The room could have been a monk's cell: whitewashed walls, a narrow bed, a plain table which served as desk, a straight chair. A washbasin. A small crucifix over the bed.

His hands groped toward hers and she knelt on the bare floor, unaware of the discomfort to her knees. 'It is all right,' he said then. 'Now it is all right. I couldn't go home till you came.'

'I am here.' She held his hands, lightly, not too hard, for fear of hurting him.

'It is all right,' he said again. 'The pain drained away with the blood. Hold my hands tightly so that I can feel you are here.' His hands were cold, cold as the marble floor, cold as the ivory of the figure on the cross. She felt his fingers twitching in hers. 'My love . . . how strange that you . . . feeling no need for all that I profess . . . should have taught me the meaning of promises . . . to my Lord, and . . .' His breath came in shallow gasps.

She felt strength ebbing from her hands into his.

'Under my pillow . . . my rosary . . .'

She freed one hand and reached for the wooden beads, the carving smoothed by use like pebbles rounded by flowing water, and put them in his hand. He was too weak to grasp them, so she put her fingers around his, and the rosary was entwined between both their fingers.

'I have made my confession, received unction. I am ready to go. All that I needed to wait for was to say goodbye to you, my heart's love.'

'Wolfi—' But she would not try to hold him back.

He opened his mouth once more, and a small, pale trickle of blood came out, but no words. The breathing stopped, almost imperceptibly. He was alive, and then, silently, he was dead. She continued to hold the cold fingers, but now he was drawing no life from her. Carefully, she put his hand, holding the rosary, across his chest. She rose, slowly, her knees stiff from kneeling so long, and left the room.

The secretary looked at her questioningly, and she nodded. He looked briefly through the open door at the still figure on the bed, then escorted Katherine to the waiting car. 'Thank you,' he said. 'You were kind to come.' His features began to distort with the effort not to cry. He opened the door and helped her into the dark interior of the car. 'Wait,' he said, 'please wait.' In a few minutes he returned and put something in her hand. The rosary. 'He would have wanted you to have this.' He shut the car door, and as it closed she heard him sob.

--◦◦◦◦⟨ 12 ⟩◦◦◦◦--

Llew came for her early the next afternoon. As she let him in, he looked automatically over the mantelpiece.

Before he could speak, Katherine said, "Yes, the portrait is gone."

"But why? It's my favorite thing that you have."

"Mine, too."

"What's wrong? What happened?"

"My apartment was broken into Sunday night while I was at the convent, and vandalized. The portrait was slashed with a knife. Nothing else was hurt, just thrown around. Mother Cat and Sister Isobel were with me. I'm grateful; I would not have wanted to see such destruction unprepared and alone. Mother Cat has taken the portrait to be repaired. I'd appreciate it if you don't talk about this, Llew. Mimi has told Dave and I will tell Felix. It just seems nastier to make it public."

"Of course. I won't say a word. Do the police think it was local vandals?"

"That's their theory." She hoped he would believe her.

"Do you still want to come up to the Cathedral after this?"

"Of course. It's behind me now. Nothing terrible happened, so it's best to leave the past and get on with the present. I have to check out those acoustics."

Once they were in the car, he was silent till they were moving up Sixth Avenue. Then he said, "It seemed a very final thing to do, to give away all the baby's things."

She was grateful that his mind was far more on his own problems than on hers. "Yes, I know. When my son died, we gave away all his clothes. Death is final, but to hang on to clothes or other possessions is in a way to hold back whoever has died, to make a tomb out of a room and keep love imprisoned there. And so when Justin died, I gave away everything that could be useful."

"Does it bother you that you weren't with your husband when he died?"

"Of course. Part of life is getting used to living with the things which will always hurt you. Far worse than not being with him when he died was that our last hours together were not pleasant, were, in fact, a bitter quarrel."

He thought for a moment. "That would be terrible."

It was. Michou's death had been violent, horrifying. Those last few hours with Justin had been bitter, like dead ashes.

He had not been well enough to travel for a long time. He suffered so many afflictions, most the result of Auschwitz. He, who had never smoked, had a form of emphysema. His liver did not function properly. His heart was apt to race into tachycardia. Mostly he bore his illness with patience and humor. But he was old long before his time.

The night before Katherine was to leave, they had listened to a broadcast which featured Thomas Forrester's work and concluded with the *Second Kermesse Suite*. This music, which had in it the power of consolation for the rest of the world, would always tear them apart. They went to bed, silently, and lay there, holding each other, still silent.

In the morning, while they were having breakfast, Justin spoke. His voice seemed heavier than the lowering skies outside. 'Your father was a better composer than I am.'

Their breakfast table was in front of the windows in their bedroom, which on a pleasant day would be sunny and warm. Now it was chilly, drab. 'That's nonsense,' Katherine had said. 'You can't make comparisons. You're totally different.'

'Comparisons will be made. They always are. Composing was your father's primary need. For me it was secondary. I would never have started composing if I could have gone on playing.'

"But you *have* composed, and you've been . . . you *are* . . . very successful.'

He waved his hand over the breakfast table, nearly upsetting the pitcher of hot milk. 'Success is ephemeral. My music is not going to be remembered, and your father's is.'

'Justin, you cannot make a judgment like that. What is going to last and what is not is nothing any composer can know during his lifetime.'

'Perhaps not somebody who is only a composer. But I am as much critic as composer.'

'Not of your own work.'

'Most certainly of my own work. I am a pleasant person—most of the time. I have an excellent sense of humor. But my music does not. It is too heavy. When I die, it will drop of its own weight.'

'Justin, you are not well, or you wouldn't be talking like this. I don't want to go on this tour. I'll tell Jean Paul to cancel.'

'You *will* go on this tour. Music is the one language that cuts across politics and party lines. And I don't want you here. You will just add to my depression.'

'Justin.' For a moment, all she could do was say his name. She knew that her very presence exacerbated his pain. She knew, too, agonizingly, that beyond a point she could not contradict him. Her father went further in his music than Justin did.

'I wish I could call Wolfi,' she said. 'He could always talk sense into you even when I couldn't.'

'Go!' Justin had finally shouted at her. 'Go, and leave me to work things out in my own way. Wolfi is dead. Nobody can do it for me. Just get out.'

She had left reluctantly, not with any prevision that he was going to die while she was away. It was bitter enough to know that she had not been able to help him. He had still been angry when Jean Paul had come for her in the car, angry at himself, at her.

And she had failed him.

We fail each other, over and over.

She left him, and while she was in Warsaw his heart gave out.

---- 13 ----

She realized that the car was already moving up Amsterdam and that Llew was glancing at her. "Sorry," she said. "I tend to lapse into memories. The important thing to learn is that there is nothing we cannot live with, we artists. I'm not sure I'd have made it without music."

"Yes," he said, and again, a block later, "Yes."

They were silent until they reached the Cathedral. She liked the fact that she could be with the young organist and not feel the need to talk. He helped her out of the car, up the steps. As they went into the nave she said, "I'm really very annoyed at the piano being moved. Can you give me any hints?"

"The nave is long, and you have to account for the time it takes the sound to move from one end of the building to the other. You'll probably want to play at a considerably slower tempo than usual."

"Logical. Yes. I may have to alter my program slightly."

"I'm so sorry," he apologized.

"It's a benefit, and there's no point in a benefit if you don't make as much money as possible."

Slowly they walked down the dim reaches of the nave. "I saw to it that the piano was moved this morning," Llew said. "Not easy. You can't roll it beyond a certain point, because there's no way to avoid steps entirely. I've also called the tuner."

"Thanks. It's ready." She thought she saw a shadow flit around one of the great columns. "You know the Gomez children?"

"How can one avoid them? They're always hanging around."

"Has Topaze ever—"

Llew gave a twisted grin. "Tried to sell me information? Sure."

"Have you ever—"

He looked vaguely embarrassed. "A couple of times, when I thought the kid needed a hot dog from the vendor on the corner. It's all gobbledygook. He can't ever come out with anything straight. Vague allusions—" He stopped abruptly. "I didn't take it seriously, but—"

"What?"

"I gave him a quarter a few days ago to get him out from underfoot, and he said somebody didn't want you to give the benefit. Of course, he made it all up."

"Of course," Katherine said, and hoped her voice did not sound as heavy as it felt. "Thanks for bringing me, Llew. I'm seeing Felix at four-thirty, so I should be ready to go home a little past five."

"Where are you meeting the bishop?"

"In St. Martin's chapel."

A Change of Program

In the front row of chairs facing the steps to the choir and the high altar sat Emily Davidson. "I thought maybe you wouldn't mind if I listen? As a sort of lesson?"

"Listen if you like," Katherine said, "but don't mind if I ignore you."

"I won't mind a bit. Sometimes being ignored is the one thing in the world you want."

The acoustics were immediately and noticeably different from the chapel. Katherine played through the program, slowing down as Llew suggested. The Scarlatti toccata, she thought, did not work; the repetition of the notes which had been clear and separate in the chapel were blurred in the vast spaces of the nave.

After a while she felt a presence, and Emily was standing beside her. "Madame Vigneras?"

"What is it, child?"

"You know that Mozart sonatina you've given me to memorize?"

Katherine held back her irritation. "What about it?"

"Please—I don't mean to be a bother—but if you'll sit where I was sitting, or even a little farther back, I'll play it for you, at the tempo it says it should be played at."

Katherine began to understand what Emily was trying to tell her.

"All right." She pushed up from the piano bench, and went down the steps to the nave, moving back several rows.

Emily played the sonatina through once, and then again, at approximately half the tempo.

Katherine stood, nodding, and then went back to the choir. "I thought I'd slowed down, but I can see now that it wasn't nearly enough. Some of the music I've chosen won't take being retarded so radically. Thanks."

"You're not mad at me—"

"Of course not. I'm grateful."

"It seems disrespectful, but you aren't used to the Cathedral acoustics."

"Emily, you've shown me just what I needed to be shown. Thank you."

"May I stay and listen for a while longer?"

"I'd be grateful if you will. Sit back a bit, and let me know if I start accelerating."

She worked for nearly an hour before she felt Emily's presence again. "That last piece—it's fuzzy."

Katherine rested her hands on the keyboard. "Yes. And it doesn't take being played any more meditatively than I've just played it. I'll have to substitute something else."

"But the Beethoven," Emily said, "it works."

"I'm glad. I would hate to have had to drop that."

"Madame Vigneras—"

"Yes?"

"What Dorcas said yesterday, about my accident maybe not being an accident—don't pay any attention to her. Ballet dancers have an oversized sense of drama. Of course it was an accident." The light blue eyes in the copper-toned face blazed at her.

Katherine said quietly, "When Dorcas brought it up, you didn't seem that positive."

"She took me by surprise. Of course it was an accident. Mom and Dad know it was. So please don't say anything to them, because it would just upset them."

"If they know that it was an accident, why would it upset them?" Why do children insist on protecting their parents? Julie had been protective with Katherine about Eric's infidelities. She, herself, would have gone to any lengths to protect her own mother. Why, when protecting is the last thing that parents want? It is to exclude—

"It was an accident, it was," Emily repeated, and Katherine drew back at the fear in the child's face.

Before she could say anything, Emily raised one hand and turned to the sacristy; the dean was walking toward them.

"Oh, dear—" Emily whispered, and stopped as her father neared them.

"There you are, Emily," he said, not sounding pleased. "When I heard that Madame Vigneras was here, I thought this was where I might find you. First of all, I don't want you bothering Madame," and, before Katherine could intervene, he continued, "and secondly, you did not check in when you got home from school."

"Oh, but I did, Daddy," Emily protested. "You were in conference and Señora Castillo wouldn't even let me check in by telephone, but she promised to tell you I was home, and coming over to the Cathedral, just as soon as you were free."

For a moment he pondered this, then nodded. "Señora Castillo went home with a headache. She gets occasional migraines, so that's probably why she forgot. All right, Em, get along home. I want to speak to Madame Vigneras."

The child's dark, rebellious face for a moment mirrored her father's. Katherine finally intervened. "Emily, I was concentrating so on the music, and so grateful for your help, that I never even mentioned your memorizing the sonatina so quickly. You must have worked very hard."

"I like work. That kind of work."

"Stay with the first sonatina till your next lesson. Don't rush on to the second."

Emily glanced at her. "How did you know that I was going to?"

"I haven't forgotten myself at your age. Keep on with the first sonatina. Memorizing it is only the beginning. Listen to it. Try to hear what it wants you to do with it. Find out where it wants you to accelerate and be merry, and where it wants to whisper something lonely. Look at the Italian, and if you don't agree with it when it says *fortissimo*, find out why. Spend the rest of this week discovering this one piece of music."

Emily's mouth was slightly open as she listened. "It's like ballet, then. My old piano teacher never talked about music like this. Now I understand why I shouldn't gallop ahead. Thank you."

"Go home and work," Katherine said.

"I will. This minute. Thanks, Madame Vigneras, 'bye. 'Bye, Daddy."

--···{ 2 }···--

Katherine came down the marble steps of the choir to where the dean was standing. "Your child has been enormously helpful to me this afternoon. I didn't realize quite how staggering the difference in acoustics is going to be."

He nodded, half listening, not apologizing for the change. "You know Mimi came to see me?"

"Yes."

"There is never an easy time to be dean of a great cathedral. There are always problems most of the world, even the church-going world, could never dream of. There was crisis after crisis during the sixties—"

"And in all decades," she reminded him. "Each one in my life has had its own traumas I could never have guessed at or prepared for."

"Such as this present unpleasantness?" He led her to the first row of chairs. They sat together, silently. The afternoon light slanted down the long nave, touching the columns with soft color, lifting their heaviness to soaring beauty. There was a pervasive odor of limestone, of city grime, a faint residue of incense. Nothing sharp or unpleasant, no turgid smell of pot. The city sounds, too, were muted, so that a passing siren sounded far away.

"A church or a synagogue used to be safe, a place of refuge," the dean said. "When I sang in choir, a cathedral was still a holy place, and untouchable. All the ambulatory chapels were unlocked, with people going in to pray, not to steal. The silver candlesticks and crucifixes were safe. Now even St. Martin's chapel, where we keep the Reserved Sacrament, and which is always open for prayer, has only valueless candlesticks, and a crucifix a thief couldn't sell. Bishop Juxon used to spend several hours a week outside St. Martin's so that people who wanted to pray or weep or just sit someplace small and private, less overwhelming than the nave, would not be disturbed. But, not long ago, and despite a reasonably good lock, someone stole the Reserved Sacrament for anything but a reverent purpose."

"A black mass?"

The dean bowed his head slightly in acknowledgment. "Black masses have been going on since—oh, very early in Christendom, I suppose. They are, it strikes me, an indictment of the Church, a witness to our lack of love. Throughout the centuries we've imposed, arbitrarily, Christian standards on people who had long-standing ways of worship, forcing whatever was our version of Christianity down their throats, instead of simply letting our light so shine that people would want to know what lovely light of love illumined us."

Wolfi, she thought, no matter what his human weaknesses, had been lit from within. The dean, too, had that light, but now it was flickering, faint, dimmed by his confusion at whatever powers of hate were touching his beloved Cathedral.

"Suzy and I discuss our work with each other," he continued. "I undoubtedly know more about the physical aspects of the human heart than most clergymen, and she—somehow I don't want her to know how far things have gone, how unsafe things are. And you've walked right into this hornet's nest, because of Mimi, because of Felix. If you'd returned to New York and just started going to church on Sunday, you'd be aware of none of this."

Trying to lighten things, she said, "If I'd returned to New York and not seen Mimi or Felix, I wouldn't have gone to church, and I'd have been a great deal lonelier than I am."

"Yet here you are, who should be safely outside the dark side of things, plunged right into the midst of shadows which hold hate, and for which I cannot find the source. Mimi should have come to me when she traced that call to Cathedral House. I am more sorry than I can say about it all—the phone calls, and most especially about the vandalizing of your apartment and the portrait. Are you all right?"

"Yes," she said. "I am angry. At first I was frightened, but now I am angry."

"Do you have any place you could go for a while? Don't you have a house in Connecticut?"

"It's rented. Anyhow—no, Dave, I am not running away. That is evidently what they—whoever they are—want me to do, and I will not give them the satisfaction of driving me out of my home. Also, I have just started to give Emily piano lessons, and that is no small investment for me to have made in your child."

"We are eternally grateful to you. But that should not keep you in New York if—"

"Is Emily in some way connected with this?"

His voice was rough. "Why should she be?"

"I have no idea." She did not press him, but changed the subject. "About the vandalizing of my apartment—Mimi told you that she does not think this nastiness is directed at me?"

"Yes, but—Felix? I could understand it better if it were at me. During my lifetime I've inevitably made a few enemies."

"So has Felix."

"But not now. He's been retired for so long, and he's such a gentle person, everyone loves him."

At random, Katherine said, "He still hears confessions. Perhaps he knows too much."

The dean turned sharply, but spoke in a controlled voice. "Our training as priests is rigorous. We are taught to listen, to hear, and then, after the penitent has left, to forget."

"Are you able to do that?" Katherine asked.

"It becomes easier with experience. And it is a self-defense mechanism, a safety precaution. Allie tells of a time when he was first priested, and a bishop came to his church for a confirmation. While they were waiting for him in the sacristy, the rector was talking about how important the bishop was to him, and how he had made his confession to him many years ago, right after he— the bishop—was ordained. It had been, in fact, the first confession the bishop had ever heard. Well, the bishop finally arrived and they got on with the service, and during the sermon the bishop talked about the value of confession, and just happened to mention that the first confession he had ever heard was that of a murderer."

Katherine made a murmur of shock.

"Allie said that this made an indelible impression on him. It was a terrible slip of the tongue on the bishop's part, though Allie said the poor man had no idea what he'd done. But it made Allie realize that nothing heard in confession must ever be mentioned, that it must, in fact, be forgotten." He sighed, deeply. "Are you through practicing, Madame Vigneras? Is somebody driving you home?"

Katherine looked at her watch. "Llew is picking me up a little after five. Felix is meeting me here at four-thirty."

"Yes, I suppose you have to tell him." He checked his watch. "It's almost time for him to come. You'll be all right if I leave you alone for a few minutes?"

"Of course." But suddenly the shadows seemed to stretch out into the nave, to deepen in the bays, to huddle at the bases of columns. Absurd. If she let her imagination play tricks on her, she would be delighting whoever it was who was full of hate.

The dean looked at her shrewdly. "The Cathedral Close has always been a happy place, or at least the joy has far outweighed the pain. We cannot let what is perhaps the sickness of one disturbed mind throw things out of proportion."

He was, she thought, affirming this to himself as much as to her. Resolutely, she held out her hand to him. "Goodbye. I'll practice these last few minutes till Felix comes." She did not watch him leave, but climbed the shallow steps to the choir and sat down at the piano, which seemed to be placed in the open, vulnerably. Anybody could be hidden in the darkness of the choir stalls.

So? Who would it be except one of the Gomez children, who might be ubiquitous but were surely not evil.

--◈{ 3 }◈--

Felix led her into St. Martin's chapel. At the end of her story, he did not speak. They were sitting in the front row, as far from the wrought-iron gates as possible. To their left was a not quite life-sized statue of Joan of Arc. She looked at St. Joan's face, but the carved features held no message for her.

Felix sat silently, his gaze on the hanging lamp, which swayed slightly from the turning of the earth, the heartthrob of the city. There was a faint odor of burning wax. She was shocked at the pallor of his face and the pain in his eyes.

"I never should have called you when you came back to New York. I never should have tried to get in touch."

For a flickering second she agreed with him. "This isn't the first time sick people have tried to get at me. No one is immune, at any time, in any place. The wonder of it is that when it's all added up, the love comes out far more strongly than the hate."

"But you shouldn't be involved in this—"

"Felix, dear, Mimi Oppenheimer is my tenant. It was she who invited me up to the Cathedral to hear Llew Owen play, not you."

He looked relieved, but only momentarily. "Oh, God, Katya, I hate to think that anybody is so determined to hurt me that they'll take it out on you. Is somebody trying to drive me away?"

"It looks like it, doesn't it?" Her voice was flat, without resonance.

"But who? Why?" His voice was hesitant. "Children sometimes make anonymous phone calls, frighten people, just for fun. And the increase of crime by kids, gangs of ten-year-olds stealing, mugging, even murdering—Merv's death will never let us forget that. The world has lost its innocence."

"Has it ever had any?"

"It's not been as bad as this since the last days of the Roman Empire. During the Dark Ages, when almost all vestiges of civilization vanished, people were brutal, basic, but they had a kind of primitive health. I probably wouldn't have survived in such a world, and yet—I think it was probably better than the world we live in today." He was talking against the dark.

"It's futile to make comparisons."

"I know. But we've forgotten how to play. Even children don't know how to play any more. They have to have educational toys, or electronic ones, instead of just banging pots and pans. When the world began to emerge from the Dark Ages, everybody played singing games, like ring-around-a-rosy—"

"Felix." Her voice was sharper than she intended. "Don't romanticize."

He reached over and patted her cheek. "It's a way of avoiding the subject."

"Do you have any idea who the anonymous calls come from?"

"No." Felix batted at a fly. "I've been out of church politics for longer than anyone can remember."

"Felix: I don't know much about your church, or mine, for that matter. But don't you still hear confessions?"

He looked baffled, then startled, then repelled. "No. No."

"I know you're supposed to forget what you hear—"

"I do."

"Can you forget all of it? If, for instance, Emily's accident was not an accident, would you be capable of forgetting that?"

His face went grey as old ash.

"Would you?"

"Confession is private. I do not talk about it. You do not ask me."

"I'm not asking. Even if you can forget, are there possibly people who fear you because of all that you must know?"

"They know—everybody knows—that what is said in confession is privileged."

"All right." He looked so distraught that she knew she could not dwell on it. "You still have no idea who's been trying to frighten you?"

He shook his head. "I've prayed and prayed, but there's no break in the fog. All I know is that for the past two years someone has been trying to frighten me, and in my senility I allowed them to succeed. I don't want you involved in it. If someone wants to persecute me, that's one thing. I've done enough wrong in my life to deserve anything I get. But you—"

"Don't worry about me, Felix. I was a fool to think that retirement would allow me to drop out. I don't think I want to drop out."

Again he patted her cheek gently. The touch was soft as a moth's wing. "How grateful I am to you for giving me back my peace. Now I can bear whatever is happening without falling apart. You've given me back the courage I thought I'd lost. I did have courage, real courage—it held me up the time I was shot."

"Shot!" she exclaimed.

"Didn't you read about it? It was in all the papers, everywhere, not just in New York."

"I'm terribly sorry—when I've been on tour I've gone weeks without looking at a paper. When was it? What happened?"

"It was years ago, when I was Diocesan. It was a Sunday when I was preaching, and some lunatic from a fringe sect took a pot-shot at me. He grazed my shoulder, but that's all, and the guards were on their toes and got the gun and the man. The thing is, I wasn't frightened, even when I didn't know whether or not he'd hurt me mortally. God was with me and I never faltered. I'm really rather . . . rather hurt that you didn't know about it."

"I'm sorry, Felix."

"Maybe it's best. What could you have done? Maybe you've come back into my life at the moment when my need is greatest. You've turned me around, and I can reach out for God's hand, knowing that it is there."

"Felix, dear. Only you can turn yourself around."

Behind them came a sound. "Oh, Llew—" Felix rose and moved toward the beautiful grilled gates, so tottery that Katherine was afraid he might fall. Then the gates were pulled open, and Llew Owen put out his arm to steady the old man.

"Bishop, are you all right?"

"Why, I'm fine, Llew, completely fine. I'm sorry we kept you waiting."

"It doesn't matter. I have the car outside, and we'll drop you off."

"I'm all right." Felix straightened. "The walk will do me good."

Llew said, "It's no trouble to take you," and Felix did not protest.

—◦◦❧ 4 ❧◦◦—

After the almost unbearable tension of that afternoon in the Cathedral, life unexpectedly slipped into a quiet routine. No more anonymous phone calls. No more terror. Once a week someone drove her uptown to the Bösendorfer, and her practicing sessions were without incident. Usually she saw one of the Gomez children, but Fatima skittered away like an overblown shadow, and Topaze offered her no more information. Usually Emily came and sat quietly to listen.

Katherine and Mimi had several meals together, most often in the apartment, occasionally at a local restaurant. One time, when they were eating out, Mimi mentioned that she had received a call from one of Iona's colleagues. "Her birthday's the second Friday in August, so I'm working my schedule out so I can take the shuttle up to Boston. I'll be back early Sunday evening. It's not for a while. I just wanted you to know it's in the offing."

"A birthday celebration—that sounds pleasant." But Katherine's mind was not on Iona, or even Mimi. Emily had been with her that day for a piano lesson, and it was Emily who kept Katherine from being lulled into feeling that everything was all right now, that nothing more was going to happen.

Emily was so transparent to Katherine that there was no way she could hide that she was afraid.

The piano lessons themselves were sheer joy. Emily was getting over her bad habits pianistically. She might possibly turn out to be a performer. But it was her talent in composition which excited Katherine. She had written a fugue for recorders and English horn which not only was charming but had a depth, under the haunting melody, which was far beyond the child's age. The piece was almost ready for performance, not just at the Davidsons' on a Sunday evening, but publicly, with some small, experimental group. Perhaps early in the next season would be a good time. Meanwhile, Katherine had Emily concentrating on music for the piano. If—when—she gave Felix his benefit in the autumn, she might well premiere some of Emily's music.

When Emily was at the piano, her concentration was so complete that there was no room in her for anything else. But when she first arrived for a lesson, or when Jos was a little late in picking her up, Katherine sensed fear, desperate fear. When she tried gently to question the child, Emily froze, and under the unnatural stillness, Katherine felt a barely repressed hysteria and stopped probing. When Emily was ready to talk, she would talk.

Mimi's strong voice broke across her thoughts. "You all right?"

"Oh—fine. I'm just grateful that there haven't been any more nasty phone calls, or Vandals, Goths, and Visigoths breaking into the apartment. It seems they plunder in every century."

Mimi laughed. "So right. I hope the shuttle to Boston isn't hijacked. It's going to be Iona's sixtieth, and we didn't think it should go unobserved, so a small group of us are taking her out to dinner."

Katherine toyed with the remains of her meal. "That should be fun."

Mimi looked across the table at her. "Will you be okay? I hate to leave you alone after . . ."

"Mimi, please stop clucking over me like a mother hen. I've lived alone for a long time. I'm used to it. I enjoy it."

Mimi flushed. "Sorry. I do tend to come on strong."

"And I tend to be overindependent," Katherine said quickly. "I'm grateful that you're around to take care of me, and that you understand and forgive if I bristle."

—Bless Mimi, she thought as they smiled across the table at each other. —How fortunate I am to have found such a friend.

"How are the lessons with Emily going?" the doctor asked.

"Better than I could have hoped. I'm more and more convinced that she's a composer, not a performer, but she'll end up playing the piano more than adequately. But her own music . . . She's working now on a tarantella which I may well put into my own repertoire. It reflects the noises of the city, the constant frenetic movement, in a way that's rather reminiscent of Gershwin. And I discovered that Emily hardly knows his work."

"I'm more delighted than I can express," Mimi said. "As you know, Emily has a special place in my heart."

"Mine, too," Katherine said.

How amazing to acquire a new child at her age! She found herself thinking about Emily frequently, and with concern. At the close of her lesson the next week, Emily put her arms around Katherine, to be held, rather than to hold. She seemed about to speak, and Katherine thought that the child now trusted her enough to tell her whatever was causing her fear. But the doorbell rang, announcing that Jos was ready to take Emily home. When the time was ripe, Emily would talk. Nevertheless, Katherine felt a pang of anxiety at Josiah's interruption of something she felt to be of utmost importance.

Without Manya to confide in, Katherine would have been far less able to move through the pains of growing up than she had been. There had been one summer on the Riviera when she was in her mid-teens, and had slipped into an uncalculated and naïve one-night affair, and had finally confided to Manya her fear that the sorry episode might result in pregnancy. Manya, neither condemning nor condoning, had been there for her during the period of waiting until they knew that there was no pregnancy. It was over this incident that Manya had read to Katherine from the Bible: '*Et non seulement cela, mais nous nous glorifions même dans nos afflictions, sachant que l'affliction produit la patience, et la patience l'épreuve, et l'épreuve, l'ésperance.* That's from Paul's letter to the Romans, and while I tend to quarrel with Paul's attitude toward women, he knew what he was talking about here.' And she repeated softly, translating, 'For we glory in tribulation, knowing that from tribulation comes patience, and from patience comes experience, and from experience comes hope.'

These words might be good ones for Emily to hear.

The beginning of August was hot, fiercely hot. Katherine wilted under the brazen sun, the damp humidity. She thought longingly of the house in Connecticut, of Norway, of Paris, anywhere that the temperature didn't hover around a soggy ninety.

In this intense heat, New York was a city of fear. It was difficult not to pick up the contagion. She took shorter walks and cooler baths. On her walks, if she saw a group of teenagers, she turned and went in another direction. She did not like being afraid, but to walk deliberately into what was likely danger was foolish. She carried a ten-dollar bill in her pocket, and a card with her address and Mimi's number. The paper carried stories daily of people being beaten up, killed, because they had no money when money was demanded.

She came in from her walk, sodden, carrying a grocery bag full of materials for a cold fruit salad, and took a tepid bath. But as she bathed, New York did one of its rapid changes, and a cool breeze came in through the windows. By the time she had put the salad together and Mimi had come downstairs, she felt better.

Mimi remarked on it. "You're perked up, like flowers in fresh water."

"It's the lovely cool breeze. I kept reminding myself that New York's heat waves don't last, but while I felt like melting butter I kept forgetting it."

"Don't be too sanguine," Mimi warned. "There's another low-pressure system on the way."

They were finishing their salads when there was a ring and a knock on the door, and Katherine opened to Dorcas, who said, breathlessly, "I'm having contractions."

Immediately Mimi was all doctor. She asked Dorcas some brief questions, and said, "Good. This is probably the real thing. Do you have an enema bag?"

"I think so. Downstairs. If Terry didn't take it."

"Somehow I don't see him making off with an enema bag. We'll give you an enema now, so you won't have to have it done at the hospital. Go on down and get ready for me. I'm going to give your obstetrician a quick ring and tell him we'll meet him at St. Vincent's in about an hour."

"Thank you." Dorcas moved to the door. "Thank you for being here for me." She turned imploringly to Katherine. "Play the piano, please. Something loud, so I can hear."

Katherine waited till Mimi was through on the phone and had gone downstairs. Then she moved into some Rachmaninoff preludes. Nice and loud. Some Liszt. She wasn't overly fond of Liszt, but he was splashy. And loud.

In less than half an hour, Dorcas returned with Mimi. "She's a fine, healthy young woman," the doctor said. "Things are moving along, and I think it's time to go to the hospital. It's fun for an orthopod to play obstetrician for a few minutes, but I think Dorcas needs her own doctor now. I'll trot down to Sixth for a taxi. We'll honk when we get to the door." She set down a small overnight case. "She's well prepared."

"Llew told me to be ready. And he said he'd pray for me. That's nice of him."

"He *is* nice," Mimi said, and she was off, briskly competent.

Dorcas turned to Katherine. "She's wonderful."

"Yes. She's very special."

"Madame Vigneras . . . I'm afraid . . ." Tears trembled behind Dorcas's words. "I want Terry to be with me. I mean, not the Terry who sleeps around, AC-DC, but the Terry I thought—" She choked on a sob.

Katherine took the girl's cold hands. "Terry isn't with you. But Dr. Oppenheimer and I are. You are not alone."

Dorcas gasped, and her grip on Katherine's hands tightened. "Dr. Oppenheimer says—says—that these are—only dilation pains —not pushing pains—but oh, God, I hurt—"

"Count," Katherine ordered. "Breathe slowly and count. One, two, three . . ."

Up to seventy.

"It's gone." The girl looked at her watch. "Every ten minutes now."

Outside, the taxi honked. Katherine picked up the little blue case, which seemed to her oddly pathetic. "Let's go to the hospital before the next pain comes." Even in this urgency she remembered to double-lock the doors.

In the hospital Dorcas was whisked away and Katherine and Mimi were sent to the waiting room on the obstetrical floor. Mimi said, "First babies can be very slow in coming. Why don't you go home? I'll call you as soon as anything happens."

"I promised her I'd stay till the baby comes."

At that, Mimi shrugged. "And you won't break your promise. I know. I wish everybody honored promises as you do."

"I don't make them casually."

They were sitting on a big sofa covered with brown imitation leather. Above them was a bad reproduction of a Cimabue mother and child. Katherine glanced at it, then away; it spoke to her of nothing but unresolved pain. On the wall across from the sofa was a framed embroidery of a bleeding heart.

Mimi pointed. "What would Cardinal von Stromberg have made of that?"

"Wolfi was able to accept paradox and contradiction. And he— he saw several concentration camps just after they'd been evacuated. He said that the only Christ he could comprehend then was a weeping Christ with a bleeding heart."

"Well—" It was half an apology. "I still wouldn't want to wake up to that every morning."

They were the only people in the waiting room. Venetian blinds covered the windows which looked out onto the street. The head nurse told Mimi that there had been a flurry of activity earlier, half a dozen babies arriving so closely together that everybody seemed to be running in several directions at once, but that now it was unusually quiet. Katherine leaned back and dozed, but woke because the breeze coming in the window was chilly.

"Let me go see if I can find a blanket," Mimi suggested.

Katherine shook her head. "Just shut the window."

Mimi rose and did so, and the chilly draft stopped. "Katherine, you being you, you probably haven't forgotten that this is the weekend I was supposed to be going to Boston."

"Yes. Tomorrow."

"I'm not going."

Fully awake now, Katherine looked at her in surprise. "Why on earth not?"

"I'm not going to leave you completely alone in the house for the weekend with Dorcas away. This cold front is being pushed out by a low, heavy one, and severe thunderstorms are forecast for tomorrow afternoon and evening. The power will go off, there'll be vandals roaming the streets—"

Katherine cut off Mimi's recital of doom. "Don't be absurd. The weather reports are seldom right. And how much help do you think Dorcas would be? She was downstairs totally unaware when someone picked my good Yale lock. And $\overline{y}$ou were upstairs. Neither of you had the faintest idea that anything was happening."

"Okay, okay," Mimi agreed. "But even though things have been calm enough on the surface lately, I still can't bear the thought of your being entirely alone. Now stop bristling, it's only my own foolishness."

"Foolishness is right. You are not going to miss Iona's sixtieth birthday on my account."

"I am not her only friend. It will be well celebrated without me."

"Mimi." Katherine sat up as straight as the sagging springs of the sofa would allow. "Iona is your good friend. This party has been planned for a long time. I am not going to have her disappointed." She stopped as a nurse came to tell them that Dorcas had been taken from the labor room to the delivery room. The baby's head had crowned.

"And that turd Terry doesn't even want to know when his baby comes," Katherine murmured.

"It's coming quickly for a first one." Mimi checked her watch. "No unexpected problems. Yet."

"Why do doctors always expect problems?"

"Because we see them far too often."

—And maybe those who don't see them should get spectacles. Witness Michou's birth.

"Are you warm enough?"

"Fine." She felt irritated, and barely stopped herself from saying, "Don't hover," as she had on occasion had to say to Nanette and Jean Paul. To forestall further conversation, Katherine leaned back, closed her eyes, and slid into a shallow sleep, waking only as she heard Mimi speaking. She pulled herself out of the dank embrace of the sofa. The imitation leather was clammy. She got to her feet and saw a doctor, in his greens, coming toward them, smiling.

"It's a little girl," he announced. "Mother and child both fine, no complications. Afterbirth tidy and complete. I'm sending her back to her room and she wants to see you. The other bed's empty, so I see no reason not to bend the rules a bit. It's a hell of a way for a girl to have her first child. It's a good thing she has you, Doctor, and Mrs.—"

"Vigneras."

"Her landlady? Is that right?"

Katherine's eyes twinkled. "That's right." It was pleasant to be anonymous.

Dorcas was waiting for them, the baby in the crook of her arm, an ordinary, red-faced, ancient-looking, withered, normal baby. Joyfully normal. "Isn't she beautiful?" Dorcas asked.

--⊶❦{ 6 }❦⊷--

They were home before three o'clock. Tenth Street was quiet, most of the windows dark. Lit by the streetlamps, trees threw shadows against the stone. Katherine said firmly, "Now, Mimi, go upstairs to your own apartment, and go to bed. You have to be at the hospital tomorrow morning, don't you?"

"Yup, and I'll check on Dorcas."

"Good. And I'll go see her during the afternoon visiting hours. Now I'm going to take a good hot bath, go to bed, and sleep as long as I can." Slightly to her surprise, Mimi did not argue, but went on upstairs.

It was a long time before sleep would come. Her body had gone beyond fatigue to a hollow wakefulness. Her memory would not leave her alone. She relived not so much the births of her own children as their conceptions, smiling as she thought of Norseman's Cove and the orchestral lovemaking with Erlend. At last she slid into sleep. And a gentle dream of Lukas. Lukas. Once love has been awakened, the flame never entirely dies, and she knew and accepted that it is quite possible to love more than one person simultaneously, one love ultimately adding to—rather than taking away from—the other.

After Lukas's death, so shortly after Michou's, she had not dreamed about him, nor had she been able to think about him for a long time, so closely was he tied in with terrible anguish.

It seemed no more than a logical continuation of the anguish when one day at breakfast, with the morning sun pouring in on them, Justin looked at her over the newspaper. 'Von Hilpert's wife is dead, too. There was some question of an overdose of sleeping pills, but the doctor has diagnosed a heart attack as the cause of death.'

She had listened, almost without hearing.

The phone cut across Justin's unemotional voice, breaking through her memories. She looked at her watch. Nine o'clock. She had slept longer than she realized.

It was Dean Davidson. "Madame Vigneras, my wife's at the hospital, or she'd be giving you this invitation herself, but Mimi forbade us to call you before nine. We do hope that you'll come spend the weekend with us. We have a pleasant guest room and bath and can promise you privacy and as much time at the Bösendorfer as you'd like."

She was too close to sleep to be polite. "Mimi is interfering and I won't have it. Thank you, but I know she's put you up to this, and I am quite capable of spending a weekend alone in my own house."

"Madame Vigneras, I can't ignore all that has been going on.

Someone has harassed you, to put the most innocent possible interpretation on it. Mimi very much wants to go to Boston for the weekend, but she won't go and leave you alone."

"This is emotional blackmail. I have not yet had my coffee. I'll call you back in an hour," Katherine said firmly, and hung up. She felt sleepy, but when she lay down and curled up under the light blanket her eyes opened immediately. Sunlight splashed a puddle of gold on the rug. She swung her legs out of bed.

She was finishing her first cup of coffee when the phone rang again. Dorcas. "Madame Vigneras, thank you for coming with me last night."

"It was a pleasure."

"I can't quite realize it—I'm a mother!"

"There's no doubt about it."

"You were right, it really wasn't bad. Once I'd dilated and started the pushing pains it was almost fun. And my doctor was so kind and gentle." She giggled. "Madame Vigneras, he doesn't have the slightest idea who you are."

"Why should he? The music world is a small one. Does he know who *you* are?"

"He knows I'm a dancer because of my muscles, but I'm not anybody. And he said he'd never even been to a ballet. Madame Vigneras, may I name the baby after you? Will you be the godmother?"

She had not expected this, and she was not sure it was a responsibility she was prepared to take.

"Madame Vigneras?"

How could she refuse the child? "I'd be honored. And I'll be over to see you during visiting hours."

"Oh, will you? That's marvelous. I'm already thinking of her as Kitty, because she's as cuddly as a kitten, so I don't know what I'd have done if you'd said no."

Well. Responsibility or not, Katherine was pleased. Very pleased.

Kitty. She had avoided Kitty and Kathy, although Pete had sometimes called her Kitten—why had she suddenly remembered that? And Manya had called her Katya. Kitty was a pleasant name for that funny, raw little creature who was her unexpected godchild.

She poured herself a fresh cup of coffee and went to the piano, remembering to take the phone with her, although she had forgotten to return the dean's call. Her body jerked involuntarily as the phone shrilled. She shouldn't have brought it over to the piano with her. She should have taken it off the hook.

"Madame Vigneras, it's Emily."

She kept her voice light. "Why, hello, my child, how's the practicing going?"

"Fine. I think. It's much more . . . more flowing than it was. Madame, Daddy said I could call you, since you didn't call back."

She glanced at the clock. After eleven. The time had slid by quickly.

"Please, Madame Vigneras, please come for the weekend. Dr. Oppenheimer really wants to go to Boston."

This was not Emily's fault. Katherine tried to control her temper. "There is no reason whatsoever why she shouldn't go to Boston."

Emily's voice quivered with restrained passion. "I offered to come spend the weekend with you, but Daddy didn't think Dr. Oppenheimer would think that was good enough."

Katherine could not keep the sharpness from her voice. "I have every intention of spending the weekend in my apartment. Alone."

Tears quivered behind Emily's words. "Please, Madame, please come. For—for Uncle Bishop and the Bösendorfer. You'd have lots of time to practice. And—and somebody—might know you're alone in your apartment and might come again and—"

"This is melodramatic," Katherine said, "but I can see I am going to be badgered beyond the point of endurance." She looked around her pleasant room. A car drove up the street and a shaft of light moved across the seascape where the portrait should have hung, cutting it diagonally as the knife had slashed the painting. "I am coming against my will, they might as well understand that. Dorcas has had her baby, by the way."

"Dr. Oppenheimer told us."

"And I am going to visit her at two o'clock this afternoon. I should be home by three. Can someone come for me?" If they were this importunate, they could chauffeur her.

"Of course. Llew or Jos or Daddy. Just bring a nightie and a toothbrush. You won't need anything else."

—I'd rather go to a hotel, Katherine thought rebelliously as she packed her overnight bag. —I hate staying in private homes. I thought I was through with travel and strange beds.

Was she feeling like a petulant child because she had allowed them to override her protestations about staying home alone? Or was she afraid? Afraid of all that she knew, which did not as yet add up to anything comprehensible. The house would indeed be very empty. She did not know any of her neighbors along the street well enough to call them in an emergency. And if she went up to the Cathedral she would, as both Emily and the dean had suggested, have extra and needed time at the Bösendorfer.

The phone rang twice again, to her intense displeasure.

The first caller was Mother Cat to say that the portrait of Katherine and Michou was at last ready, beautifully restored, and that she would bring it down that afternoon if convenient.

When Katherine protested that it was entirely out of her way, the nun said, "I took it down from the mantelpiece, and I'd like to hang it back up. And then I can take you back uptown with me and drop you at the Davidsons'."

Katherine replied with asperity, "It seems I have no private life."

Mother Cat made a murmur of apology and continued, "I had cause to talk to the dean this morning and mentioned the portrait, and that I planned to bring it down, so he quite naturally asked me if I'd mind driving you uptown. Is around three o'clock convenient?"

"Fine, and I'm sorry if I sounded short. My young downstairs tenant had her baby last night, and Mimi and I went to St. Vincent's with her, so it was rather an interrupted night. I'm going to see her when visiting hours start at two, but I should be back by three. I'm not going to stay long."

"If you're not back, I'll wait for you," Mother Cat assured her calmly.

The second call was from Llew, suggesting that he go to the hospital with Katherine to visit Dorcas.

"You know she's had her baby?" Katherine asked in surprise.

"Emily told me."

Of course.

"And then I could bring you uptown," he added.

"I'd love to have you come to the hospital with me, Llew," she said, "but Mother Catherine of Siena is coming down with the portrait—it's been fixed. And she's going to drive me. Maybe you could visit Dorcas tomorrow, when I won't be able to."

He was hesitant. "That does make sense, but . . . but if you don't mind, it would mean a great deal to me if I could go with you. Then I can drop in and see Yorke and Lib."

"All right. Let's walk over. I'll be ready by a quarter to two."

She finished packing. A gentle breeze was blowing through the apartment. The air felt light. There was no smell of an approaching storm.

She did not feel like cooking, or even going to the trouble of making a sandwich. There was some vichyssoise in the refrigerator and she had a bowl of that, then returned to the piano. Thank heavens she still had a large enough repertoire so when the benefit had to be moved from the chapel to the choir she had more than enough selections to choose from to replace the pieces which did not work in the greater space. Otherwise, she would even more annoyed than she was. And she was annoyed.

Annoyance. She had long since learned that annoyance was often a cover-up for fear. When Justin's heart had first raced out of control, a good ten years before his death, her terror until the doctor came was held at bay by anger, not at Justin, but at the threat of a heart attack. She raised him to a sitting position, where he could breathe slightly more easily than lying down, and murmured soothing endearments. 'It will be all right, my darling, try to breathe more slowly, the doctor is coming, it will be all right, my love,' while her own heart pounded in outrage.

Why was she feeling such fierce annoyance now?

Her fingers continued diligently to play, but her mind was not on music. She might just as well be playing chopsticks, and what, indeed was she playing? Brahms's Second Piano Concerto, music totally unsuited for the benefit.

She ran scales until Llew rang the bell.

"You're sure Dorcas won't mind my coming with you?" he asked.

"I think she'll be delighted. She's ecstatic about the baby, but she's in a very lonely position, and she's going to need all the support she can get."

They walked in silence, which Llew broke. "This isn't going to be easy for me."

"What?" Katherine broke out of her own thoughts.

"Going to see Dorcas and the—the baby. But I think it's something I need to do, like giving away the crib, and turning the baby's room back into my practice room. I've avoided seeing babies ever since—I couldn't quite—"

"It's all right, Llew. I think I understand, and I think you are right. You can't spend the rest of your life looking away when someone goes by with a baby carriage. And this way, you'll be doing something for somebody else, and that should make it easier."

"It does. Thanks for understanding." He took her elbow as they crossed the street.

"Dorcas was very grateful that you said you'd pray for her."

"It was the least I could do. You prayed for her, too."

"I don't know much about prayer. I just went with her."

"That's prayer," Llew said, "the best kind. Everything went all right?"

"Fine. No problems."

"And she's really happy about this baby?"

"Yes. You'd think Kitty was the first child ever to be born."

"Kitty?"

"Yes. After me. Isn't that lovely?"

"I think it's super." He was quiet for the rest of the walk to the hospital complex. They were given admission cards at the security desk, with visiting rules written in English on one side, Spanish on the other. Llew said rather crossly, "This used to be a largely Italian neighborhood, and nobody bothered to have things in Italian as well as English. But we didn't have security desks then, either."

The crossness, she realized, was due to his tenseness. It was going to be difficult for him to see the baby.

Dorcas was sitting up in bed, and held out her arms to them. Katherine kissed her, and Llew, rather awkwardly, pressed her hand.

"Would you like to see Kitty?"

"Of course."

"She's in the crib closest to the window, so you can get a good view. She was a bit early, just off being a preemie. But she's adorable. The nursery is right down the hall."

Llew walked silently beside Katherine. The blinds were up at the nursery windows, and they had a good view of the half-dozen tiny cribs. The arrangement had evidently been changed, because the first baby was a little black button. But the next was likely Kitty, for she was indeed tiny, red and wrinkled and bald, as Katherine had seen her the night before. They stood, watching for several minutes. Finally Llew said, "Okay," and they returned to Dorcas's room.

"I'm apt to have a roommate by this evening," she said. "My doctor says he has someone else just about ready. Isn't Kitty gorgeous?"

"She looks exactly like a baby," Katherine said firmly, "a right and proper baby."

There was a knock on the door and Mimi came in, wearing her khaki suit and carrying a small case. She greeted Dorcas and Llew, then turned to Katherine. "Thank you for giving in to me."

"I gave in to the entire population of the Cathedral Close."

Mimi laughed. "I'll pick you up on Sunday on my way in from La Guardia."

"All right, thanks. Have a good weekend, and give my best birthday wishes to Iona."

When she had left, Dorcas said, "I'm glad you're going to the Davidsons' too. That's an awful lot of empty house, after everything that's happened. When we get home, Kitty and I will be there to protect you."

"Dorcas, are you going to have anybody to help out with things when you get home?"

"No, but I have nothing else to do. I can manage."

"You'll be more tired than you realize. I'm going to see if Raissa can give you half a day."

Dorcas pondered for a moment, then smiled. "There's no reason why Terry can't pay for it."

"None whatsoever. Now, my child, I'm on my way up to the Cathedral. I'll call you tomorrow and Sunday, but I won't be able to come by till Monday."

Now the smile was real. "Just knowing that you came with me

last night, that you're here today, that you care, that's enough to keep me from being lonely."

Llew said, "You met Yorke and Lib when we brought you the crib. They'll drop by to see you. It's just around the corner for them."

"Oh, I don't want anybody to go to any trouble."

"It wouldn't be any trouble, and they liked you."

"I liked them a lot. But I don't want—"

"I'm on my way to see them," Llew said. "I'm sure they'll want to come. Take care."

"I will. And thanks."

"It's done." Llew sighed as they walked back to Tenth Street. "And I didn't break into a thousand pieces. Not visibly, at any rate."

"You did very well indeed."

"Dorcas didn't notice anything?"

"I doubt it. She's normally a sensitive person, I think, but right now she's preoccupied with her own problems, and concentrating on the birth of her baby to—as it were—keep the wolves at bay."

"I know those wolves only too well," Llew said. "Cathedrals, it seems, tend to be surrounded by them."

"Not only cathedrals. And, actually, wolves are given a bad name which isn't at all fair."

"I know. It's just part of the—of the mythic vocabulary. Anybody can be dangerous when hungry."

The clarity was gone from the air, replaced by heaviness and a whiff of sulfur.

"I'm glad you're going to be with the Davidsons tonight," Llew said.

Katherine looked at the rapidly clouding sky, and did not reply.

He left her at the apartment. It was five minutes before three, and she wandered about, rather aimlessly checking things, until Mother Catherine of Siena rang the bell promptly on the hour.

"My guardian angel was with me this time and I'm parked just across the street." The nun carried an unwieldy parcel wrapped in brown paper. "I'm glad to see the new locks."

"Yes. Mimi took care of that immediately."

Mother Cat put her parcel down on the coffee table in front of the long sofa and began untying the string.

"I have scissors," Katherine suggested.

"Not necessary. I'm almost done, and I have a habit of saving string." She untied the last knot and rolled the string into a small ball, then began removing the heavy layers of brown paper. "There. Isn't that a beautiful job of restoration?"

To Katherine's untrained eye the painting looked as it always had, a strange and striking study in lights and shadows, the baby Michou's face illuminated. Mother Cat took the seascape from above the mantelpiece and hung it back in its place on the wall near the kitchen. Katherine was silent until the nun had stepped back from the fireplace and begun to fold the wrapping paper.

"I can't tell you how grateful I am," Katherine said at last. "Not having the portrait there has had a strange psychological effect on me. How much do I owe you?"

Mother Cat put the brown paper and the heavy string into a capacious black carryall. "Not a thing. Mr. Robinton refused to take a penny. He said it's the best Hunter he's seen and it was a privilege to work on it. They plan a Philippa Hunter exhibit at the museum in a couple of years, and he hopes you'll lend them the portrait then."

"I'm glad it's not for a couple of years." Katherine looked at the luminous face of the baby, her own face almost hidden by the soft, dark hair. "I don't think I could part with it right now. Would we have time to stay for a cup of tea?" A sudden clap of thunder cut off her last words, and the room was immediately and noticeably darker.

"Did you say tea? I think I'd better stay till the storm is over."

—So Mimi was right, and not just doom-mongering. Katherine sighed as the room was lit by a brilliant flash of lightning followed almost immediately by an ear-splitting crash of thunder, and then a great rush of rain.

"If I may use your phone," Mother Cat said, "I'd better reassure them at the convent that I'm under cover." Katherine indicated the phone and the nun picked up the receiver, holding it to her ear and listening intently. "No dial tone. I'm afraid the storm has knocked it out."

"Let me try the phone in the bedroom," Katherine suggested.

It, too, was dead. There was the prickling smell of ozone in the air. The rain was coming in the windows, so she closed them.

Normally, electrical storms exhilarated her. This did not. Mimi's forebodings must have affected her.

Mother Catherine had closed the windows in the living room. The tea kettle was hissing. Katherine made tea, put cookies on a plate. Mother Cat wheeled the tea cart into the living room. "I hope the power stays on." She turned on the lamp by the piano, and the light was reassuring in the storm-darkened room. After the next flash the bulb flickered, but did not go out, and there were several seconds before the thunder clapped. "It's moving north." The nun leaned back comfortably and sipped at her tea. "Ah, this is good. How are Emily Davidson's piano lessons going?"

"Beautifully."

"Sister Isobel says she has talent for composition."

"Real talent. She's delightfully free when she plays her own work. And beginning to loosen up with other composers. Emily says her old teacher did not like her compositions. Could he be jealous?"

The nun thought for a moment. "It's possible. He's supposed to be an excellent teacher, but he's never made it as a soloist himself. Sad to think he might feel lessened by Emily's gift, rather than excited by it. I can't tell you how grateful I am that she has you. Not everyone has to have a sense of vocation to be complete, but Emily's one of the people who can't survive without it. John, too, but John has gone serenely on with his violin, with no brutal interruption."

Katherine kept glancing back at the portrait, deeply relieved to see it in its place over the mantelpiece. She refilled their cups. A thin splash of lightning filled the room, and the thunder was slow in following.

"All the Davidson children except Tory have recognized their particular talents, and know where they are going. Tory doesn't realize that her siblings are unusual, and she's the more average child in not yet having discovered her focus, and so she's jealous. Very jealous."

Katherine asked, "Is the fact that I'm giving piano lessons to Emily going to add fuel to Tory's fire?"

"Very likely. But her jealousy must not be pandered to, and Emily needs you right now." She opened the windows and a wave of heavy air came in. "Storm's over. For now. There's evidently a chain of them coming in from the Great Lakes. I'll try the phone once more . . . Still dead. This makes me grateful that you're not going to be alone here with a dead phone."

"The way it's been screeching at me today has been worse than the peacocks. I'm delighted it can't keep on at me."

"True. On the other hand, it can be a most unpleasant feeling not to be able to call out. We'll report it when we get uptown. Ready?"

Katherine nodded, indicating her case, then glanced again at the portrait. "Thank you, more than words can ever convey, for having the portrait repaired. I wouldn't have known such a thing was possible."

"A good thing Rose Robinton's in our school, or I might not have known, either. Thank you for the tea." Mother Cat gathered up the tea things and wheeled them into the kitchen.

Katherine followed, standing in the doorway and allowing the younger woman to do the brief washing up. "I was an only child. Michou died at seven, with Julie not four, so I have no experience . . . Are Emily's and Tory's squabbles normal?"

The nun laughed. "Heavens, yes. They'll outgrow them and become friends, I hope. It's Tory's jealousy of Emily that disturbs me, not their sibling spats."

"Jealousy is an ugly thing." Manya's warning seemed to echo in Katherine's ear. But Tory was Suzy and Dave's problem, not hers. Emily she understood in her bones. She loved Emily as she loved the grands. And to love is to be vulnerable.

Music in the Cathedral

It had not rained uptown. "Summer storms can be very local." Mother Cat sniffed. "But it smells like thunder. We'll get it up here sooner or later."

As the nun helped Katherine out of the car, they saw Yolande Undercroft hurrying toward them.

"Madame Vigneras! I've been hoping to catch you. Allie told me you're coming for the weekend. So much better for you than being all alone."

Katherine stifled a sharp reply, said only, "Yes."

"I know you're staying with the Davidsons, but would you come have a drink with Allie and me before dinner?"

Katherine looked briefly at Mother Catherine of Siena, who was standing by the car, her face calm and unreadable. "I'm sorry," Katherine said firmly. "I'm going to spend as much time with the Bösendorfer as possible. I've had to replace several selections because of the change in location."

"Ticket requests are still pouring in. You're very popular," Yolande said. "Are you sure you won't have time for a small glass of wine?"

"I'm sorry," Katherine said again, still firmly. "Once I've finished practicing, I'm going to the Davidsons', and early to bed. This is not a social visit." She sounded far more disagreeable than she intended. And she had hurt the bishop's wife. Katherine sighed inwardly. There was too much intentional hurting in the world for her to add to it unintentionally. "What I would really appreciate is a cup of tea, right now."

"Of course!" Yolande's relieved pleasure was as open as a child's. "Mother Catherine, will you join us?"

—But she doesn't want her.

"No, thanks, Mrs. Undercroft. I'm due back at the convent."

"Oh, well, then. I'll walk dear Katherine back to the Cathedral and see to it that she's all right."

Katherine refrained from saying, "I can take care of myself," and followed Yolande to Ogilvie House.

"Something told me," Yolande said, "to tell the children not to come over for tea this afternoon. I always obey these impulses, and now I know why I had this one."

Mrs. Gomez brought them tea and thinly sliced pound cake. There was a small silver bell on the tea tray, and the cook said, "Ring if you want anything," and left them. Her voice was dour.

But Yolande did not seem to notice. "You're really looking forward to spending the entire afternoon at that piano?"

"Most of the afternoon's already gone. And I still have a lot of work to do."

Yolande handed her tea in a translucent china cup. "What I envy most about you is that you love your work. You've always loved your work, haven't you?"

Katherine took a slice of lemon and squeezed it with her spoon. "Not always. I don't think anyone does, twenty-four hours a day, fifty-two weeks a year. There were times when I was working up a program and Justin was standing by me, making me repeat a phrase over and over, when I was so tired and discouraged that all I wanted to do was put my head down on the piano keys and sob."

"So your Justin *did* abuse you?"

"No, no," Katherine protested. "He just wouldn't let me stop working until he had got out of me the best he possibly could."

Yolande crushed a piece of pound cake to small crumbs. "Jesus, you're lucky. I envy you, envy you. The only time I loved singing was when I was a child in Buenaven—in Peru, before I was, you know, discovered and taken—taken high up in the Andes to the temple and my life was no longer my own. But when I was little,

I could do whatever I wanted, and could sing as I wandered through the fields. That was my *real* singing. I heard the songs I made up, and I loved them, and what my voice could do with them. This is the kind of singing I am trying to teach Fatima."

"I'm so glad," Katherine said.

"Perhaps she's lucky in being unattractive. I attracted men like bees to honey, and once I was discovered, once I was brought to New York and made to sing, not for myself, but for the brutes who exploited me, the audiences who, you know, adored me— then I hated the music. It wasn't mine, any more. And I didn't belong to myself any more, either. I belonged to my managers, as I had—belonged to the priests." She slipped off her white jacket. Under it she wore a lacy shirt through which her scars were visible; or perhaps they were visible only if one knew they were there. She said, "It's hot today. I usually keep my scars covered. I don't suppose anything like beatings ever happened to you in your privileged world."

Katherine felt acutely the bitterness behind the words. She spoke in a low voice. "I was beaten by the Nazis, when I was in prison early in the war. But it was nothing like what you must have gone through. I'm sorry. I wish I could do something to help."

Yolande's voice was even lower than Katherine's. "You can let me hate you."

Katherine looked up, astonished. Yolande was saying in a normal voice, "You *are* helping me, by letting me talk to you, share myself with you." Had she really said those first few words? Or was Katherine picking up something felt but unsaid?

Yolande hated her. Whether the words had been said aloud or not, they were true. Was this the jealousy Manya had tried to warn Katherine about, speaking as she was dying, when she had, perhaps, already crossed the border between the known and the unknown?

—Yes, Katherine thought sadly, —I have loved my music, even when I was angry with Justin for pushing me too hard, I have loved it. Even when I was half dead with grief, music has sustained me. No wonder she hates me.

She felt cold, as though a dark cloud had come across the humid afternoon. She said, "Your singing evidently gave hope to many thousands of people."

"Hundreds of thousands," Yolande corrected. "I pulled them in like those, you know, evangelical TV preachers. Sure, I gave hope to them all. Not to myself."

"But now—" Katherine looked around the beautiful room. "You're married, you love Allie—"

Yolande shuddered. "If he ever stopped loving me, I'd die. And he would, if he knew . . . Why should my life have been nothing but burdens, each one heavier than the last? I feel like, you know, Sisyphus, pushing that stone forever up the hill, only each time the stone gets bigger and heavier. I'm not sure how long I can go on." She reached for her jacket, slipped into it. "You were surprised to have me know about Sisyphus, weren't you?" Then, "If you've finished your tea I'd better walk you over to the Cathedral. I don't want to go on wasting your time."

"It's not being wasted." Katherine tried to reassure the younger woman. "I just wish I could do something to help."

"So do I," Yolande said. "Jesus, so do I."

--◦◦❦{ 2 }❦◦◦--

Yolande insisted on walking Katherine back to the Cathedral, and saw to it that she was seated at the piano.

Katherine started to play in order to turn her mind from the bishop's wife. She did not want to think about their conversation. Not yet. She felt soiled from the jealousy which had washed over her.

Music cleansed her. When the last notes of the *Hammerklavier Sonata* had faded into the distance, she became aware that she had an audience. The first rows of chairs were full of a motley assortment of people, all applauding politely, some enthusiastically. Many of them had cameras slung over their shoulders, and she realized that it was a busload of tourists. Their guide was urging them on, gathering them around him, talking in a dully rhythmic voice; he had said everything thousands of times before.

She turned away from their gawking, back to the music, concentrating on one of the Poulenc pieces she had chosen as a replacement for the Scarlatti toccata. When she had played through it half a dozen times, she looked up and saw Bishop Chan sitting in the front row. He applauded soundlessly, then rose, his knees as creaky as hers, and came toward her but did not climb the steps to the choir.

"Madame Vigneras, I want to thank you for what you've done for Llew."

"I've done nothing. He would have come out of it by himself."

"Perhaps. I'm not sure. He was close to giving in to despair. He needed a push, not from one of us, but from someone outside, someone he trusted." Bishop Chan lowered himself carefully onto the steps, pulling down his dark cassock. "It is good to see Llew moving back into full life again. And Bishop Bodeway, too, is being nourished by your friendship."

"He's nourishing me, as well."

Bishop Chan nodded. "He has been like a father to us all, a grandfather to the younger ones. Children all love him. And he helps Allie whenever Yolande is suffering from an attack of her demons. I think it was Rainer Maria Rilke who said that he feared that if his demons left him, his angels would leave him, too. Is this true of all artists?"

"Possibly," Katherine murmured, thinking of tea with the bishop's wife. Was this an attack of her demons? Or her 'dark angel,' as Allie had put it?

"Sometimes Allie is afraid that Yolande's demons are going to overpower her angels. I am not being just a gossipy old Chinaman, Madame. Yolande is more sinned against than sinning. She can't help her background or the things her career, so very different from your own, did to her. She's worried about something, now. Deeply worried. And it's been getting worse for—oh, maybe two years." He shook his head, and tried to rise from the low, marble step. She felt that she ought to help him, but understood that he needed to struggle on his own for as long as possible. Using his arms, he pushed himself up, scrabbling like a crab. When he was on his feet he looked down at her, his face as inscrutable as Oriental faces are supposed to be, and, she was sure, intentionally so. "I met Yolande as I was walking over here from my office, and she said that you had had tea with her and she was afraid that she might have upset you."

Katherine met his gaze. "I agree with you that she is troubled."

Bishop Chan smiled, his face crinkling into a fine network of wrinkles. "You see, I want you to work miracles with Yolande, as you have with Llew, as you have with Felix. Felix has regained his serenity, and I know that you are responsible for that."

"No." She was angry now, though she tried to keep her face as unreadable as that of the old Chinese bishop. "I work no miracles. Llew, in the natural order of time, was moving away from his grief. Felix is—Felix."

"And he has told me something of what you have done for him. But I mustn't put too much on you, and that is what you think I am doing?" He smiled again. "As for me, here I am, half dead in body, but struggling on. So I must assume that God still has work for me to do. Would you be kind enough to play just one more piece before I go? Something"—and his crinkles moved outward and upward—"something comforting. Strengthening."

She thought for a moment, then moved into a fugue, not Bach, but the master who had so influenced him, Pachelbel. When she was through, holding her fingers on the keys so that the last notes continued to sound, murmuring slowly down the nave, she saw that Bishop Chan had been joined by the four Davidson young ones. Katherine smiled at them all. "I hadn't planned to include that piece in the program, but I think I will."

Emily clapped her hands. "It worked with the space, Madame, it worked beautifully, like little waves lapping at the shore, one following the other, not blurring."

"Em's right," John said. "I don't know that fugue, but I'm going to. Have you recorded it, Madame?"

"Yes. It's one of my pets. It's on a recording of 'music-before-Bach' which I did—let's see—not more than a couple of years ago, so it still ought to be available."

Bishop Chan bowed over Katherine's hand. "Madame. Thank you."

She looked directly into his kind, weary eyes and wondered how much he, too, had added up, and to what conclusions he had come. "Goodbye."

He moved slowly down the nave. "I do like him," Emily said. "Llew loves him, now that he's back into loving again."

Jos spoke through her words, not listening. "What John and I thought we'd do, Madame, is make a fireman's chair with our hands and carry you upstairs."

"No. Thank you, Jos, but no. If I do not exercise my arthritic knees, they'll just get worse. The four of you gallop upstairs at your usual pace, and let me follow along at mine."

When they were outside she looked up at the lowering sky. A warm wind was blowing from the south, and the air felt wet enough to squeeze. At this moment Katherine would not like to be completely alone on Tenth Street with the phone dead.

John insisted on going up the Deanery stairs behind her, putting no psychic pressure on her to move more quickly than was comfortable.

"Em had an awful time with the stairs after the accident. It was almost easier for her at first, when she heaved herself up with her crutches and one leg, than when she got the artificial leg and Mom took the crutches away from her. Now she goes up and down like the rest of us—a little slower, because she can't take the stairs two at a time. I'm very glad she doesn't play the violin. I might be jealous of her if I thought she was getting better than me—I. But she's learned more at the piano lessons with you than in all the rest of her piano lessons put together."

Katherine paused on the red-carpeted stairs to catch her breath. "I gather Emily and her previous teacher had a considerable personality clash."

"Yah, and Mom and Dad don't like us to complain about our teachers. I'm glad she's got you now."

"Thanks." She continued the climb. She liked the Davidsons because, although they tended to treat her like Venetian glass, it was out of consideration; they also allowed her to be a normal human being. They respected her for her accomplishments, but they were used to being with accomplished people. They did not put her on a pedestal.

3

When she reached the Davidson apartment, Emily was waiting. "Mom says I can show you your room. Llew brought up your bag long ago."

She followed Emily through the apartment, through the library into a small hall off which there were three doors. "You'll be private here," Emily said. "We kids are all upstairs, and Mom and Dad are at the other end of this floor." She opened a door. "This is your bathroom. I hope you're not mad for showers. This is the biggest bathroom in the house, but it only has a tub. There's a shower in—"

Katherine stopped her. "I infinitely prefer a tub." She looked at the deep, old-fashioned bathtub, up on claws, and wondered how she was going to get out.

Emily opened a second door. "Your room. The other is a sort of sitting room where the practice piano is—it's not as good as the one in the living room, but we can bang away and not disturb anyone." She led Katherine into the guest room, indeed a pleasant room, nearly square, with a fireplace in which were laid some birch logs. There was an old-fashioned mahogany sleigh bed, with a small love seat at the foot. The wide, uncurtained windows had shutters, open now, and the two largest windows looked directly at the Cathedral, with a good view of the roof, with St. Gabriel, horn raised.

Emily said, "Mrs. Undercroft used to call Gabriel the Christmas angel. But of course he isn't; he's standing there ready to blow the last trump. I don't find him frightening. Tory used to be scared of him, but I've always felt he was taking care of the Close, keeping bad things out. Of course I know he doesn't—at least the statue doesn't—and bad things get in. But I'm still glad he's there. And I'm glad *you're* here," Emily said softly.

Katherine was not glad at all. But she said only, "Since I'm here, we'll work in an extra lesson tomorrow. What's your schedule?"

"Saturday's free. Weekdays I work with the little kids in the play school, and I do some French and Latin tutoring. I'm not that great at French and Latin, but I'm okay, and the tutoring helps me, too. We'd better get on to the living room. I know Mom and Dad want to offer you a glass of wine before dinner."

Tory appeared in the doorway. "Oh, there you are, Madame Vigneras. There's a phone call for you, and then Mom and Dad are waiting."

Mimi checking in, probably, to make sure she was really at the Davidsons' and not on Tenth Street.

"It's hello and goodbye for me," Tory said. "At least for a few hours." She wore a flowered print skirt and a white peasant blouse.

"Off to a party?" Katherine suggested as she followed her.

"Not mine. The Undercrofts are having frightfully important

people for dinner, and they've asked me to help out as well as Fatty. I need the ten dollars." She looked obliquely at Emily.

Emily looked back. "You don't seem very pleased."

"Maybe I'm getting too grownup for it all. But I need the money." They had reached the small library. Tory pointed to the phone. "When you're through, Mom and Dad say just to come along to the living room."

"Hello," Katherine said, slightly sharply.

But it was not Mimi's voice. Instead, a pleasant, lilting voice replied, "Madame Vigneras, at last I've tracked you down. This is Grace Farwater, from the *Times*."

"Oh. Yes. Hello."

"I just found out this morning, by accident, that you're giving a benefit. Someone called the paper about tickets. I would really love to do a small story on you if at all possible."

So Yolande had not made arrangements with the *Times* after all.

Grace Farwater continued. "I gather you're staying with the Davidsons for the weekend. Would sometime tomorrow be possible?"

"I don't think so," Katherine said slowly. "I'd really rather talk to you at home."

"Tenth Street?"

"Yes. How about early Monday afternoon? I give a piano lesson at three."

"Early afternoon would be fine. Would between one-thirty and two be all right?"

"Yes. Fine."

"I do look forward to it, and you're very gracious to be willing to see me at such short notice. You are an inspiration to a great many of us, Madame Vigneras. I'll promise to keep the interview short and not take up much of your time."

"Thank you. Monday, then."

She put down the phone, looked at it for a moment, as though for an answer, then went to join the Davidsons in the living room.

"It's going to pour," Suzy was saying. "I hope the Undercrofts have sense enough to lend Tory an umbrella."

The air had the yellow light which often precedes a storm. "Speaking of rain," Katherine said on impulse, "my daughter lives in Norway, where the sun seldom shines, and I'd like to give her a ring. I'll bill it to my number."

"We could plug the phone into your room," Suzy said, "but it'll probably be easier for you just to go back to the library."

"Yes. Thanks. We don't talk long. I just like her to know where I am."

When she heard the phone ringing in Aalesund, as clearly as though she were calling Mimi upstairs at home, she hoped she would find Julie at home.

Eric answered. "Good to hear your voice, Maman. Julie said she planned to call you. She's right here. You just caught us."

"Maman, is everything all right? I had you on my mind today and, as Eric said, I'd planned to call you."

"Bless you, darling, that's why I called, just in case. I'm not home. I'm up at the Cathedral at the Deanery, for the weekend— so that I can have some extra time at this piano before the concert."

"You're a marvel, Maman, able to sleep in strange beds. I have insomnia if I'm not at home."

"Years of practice," Katherine said. "I'd have died of insomnia long ago if I hadn't learned to adjust. Everything all right in Aalesund?"

"Fine. We flourish."

"Good. I'll be back in my house Sunday evening."

"Thanks for calling, Maman."

She hung up and went back to the living room, glad she had obeyed her impulse to call.

--- 4 ---

The evening passed pleasantly. With Tory absent, there was no squabbling. The dean and Suzy were both entertaining, telling Katherine about the early days of their courtship, and the vicissitudes of a seminarian trying to arrange dates with a medical student when their hours were in complete conflict.

After dinner Jos went to his room to study, and John put a record on the player. Katherine sat in a comfortable chair, eyes closed, listening, hardly hearing the rumbles of thunder, until all at once there was a violent clap, and simultaneously a flash of lightning which seared through her closed lids. She opened her eyes and the lights went out. The needle on the record slowed to a stop, the sound winding down with a groan.

"We'll give it a few minutes," the dean's voice came calmly out of the darkness. "If the lights don't come back on quickly, I'll get candles."

"Oh, Madame!" Emily sounded tense. "I'm glad you're here."

"Actually," Katherine said, "so am I. Thunderstorms are fun when you're with pleasant company, but I no longer enjoy them when I am alone."

"I wonder if it's citywide?" Suzy's voice came from the direction of the windows. "I don't see any lights." Her silhouette was outlined in the next flash of lightning, and the phone rang at the same time that the thunder clapped.

"At least the phone's still on." The dean moved, in the next flash, to the instrument. "Hello . . . well, that's very kind of you, Yolande, but I doubt if the power's going to be off for long . . . Of course, but . . ." He slammed down the receiver. "The phone's dead now, too. That, as you may have gathered, was Yolande, suggesting that Tory spend the night if the power doesn't come back on."

Suzy closed the window. "How about upstairs? This rain is blowing in from all directions, it seems."

Katherine heard the dean calling, "Jos! Check the windows, please."

And Jos calling down, "Right, Dad."

The dean moved through the darkened apartment, occasionally bumping into something, and Katherine could hear windows being closed. The rain lashed into the building, but the lightning and thunder were no longer on top of each other; the storm was quickly passing over.

The dean returned, carrying a candle. The moving light sent flickering shadows over the walls, but it was a relief after the heavy darkness. "I didn't shut your windows, Madame Vigneras; the rain is from the southwest. I have candles for us all, and we'll have to make do. Fortunately, the water supply isn't affected." He gave Katherine an old-fashioned pewter candle-holder, lit the candle, then went round the room, giving light to everyone.

Jos came in, carrying a flashlight. "But I'll take a candle, too, Dad. I don't want the batteries to run down."

Katherine rose, holding her candle. "Under the circumstances, I think I might as well go to bed. Is it really possible for me to take a hot bath?"

"We do have some of the comforts of home left," Suzy assured her, and then, under her breath, "I really wish Tory were here instead of at the Undercrofts'."

"What about the rest of their guests?" Emily asked. "Are they going to have to keep all those bigwigs for the night? Tory and Fatty are probably making up beds. Daddy, can I have an extra candle to put in Madame Vigneras's bathroom?"

"Of course, Em. Get one from the kitchen."

The light of the single candle wavered in the large bathroom, but was adequate. Katherine took a hot bath, trying to relax and not worry about getting out, which she managed to do by turning over in the water and getting up on her hands and knees and pushing up from there. She was smugly pleased at her accomplishment. At first glance, the tub had looked formidable.

She brought the bathroom candle into the bedroom, but even two candles did not give sufficient light for comfortable reading. She moved to one of the windows and looked out. The rain had stopped, though it was still shaking from the trees. The Close looked dark and full of even darker shadows. She saw something move, and looked down. It was hard to tell with the lack of light, but she thought it was Topaze. Poor child, waiting for his mother and sister. Why didn't he wait in Ogilvie House?

She jumped slightly as the clock tower boomed out the first of ten strokes. She moved back toward her bed, listening. Yes, she heard a faint tapping at the door.

Certain who it would be, she took one of the candles and went to the door. Yes. Emily, holding her candle, her hand trembling slightly.

"Please—can I come in for a minute?"

Katherine moved back to her bed and the child followed and put her candle on the night table. Katherine got into bed and indicated that the child should sit beside her.

"I'm scared," Emily said.

It was more than the dark. Katherine said, "I'm not likely to be as much help as your parents."

"I think it's moral support I want," Emily said.

"What are you afraid of?"

"It's so dark."

"You're at home. I'm with you. There's nothing to be afraid of."

The shrill shrieking of several police cars speeding along the avenue assailed their ears. Emily's voice was low. "There's always something to be afraid of."

Nightly fears and fantasies? "Something real?"

"Very real," the child said. A thin wash of lightning flooded the room, then left it seeming darker than ever. There was a pause of nearly ten seconds before the thunder grumbled its way across the sky.

"You've been afraid of something ever since I first met you, haven't you?"

"Yes."

Katherine sensed a shudder moving across the child's body. "I think you'd better tell me about it." Did she want to know? Not necessarily. But she had come to love this child. She had to ask.

"I want to tell you, but I can't."

"Why not?"

"She said something terrible would happen to me if I said anything, and it did."

"Who said?"

Now she could feel Emily's trembling. "I can't tell you. If I told anybody, it would be you, but I can't."

There were times when Manya had had to prod the young Katherine. "I think you must."

Now Emily's arms reached for her, clutched her. Katherine held the child, smoothed the soft, fair hair. Emily whimpered, "I can't. I can't."

Katherine soothed her. "Hush. What are you afraid of? Who has threatened you?"

"I don't dare . . . She said something terrible would happen if I said anything, and it did."

"Who did you speak to?"

Emily clutched at her. "You promise me that nothing will happen, that I won't get hurt again?"

"I can't make that kind of promise. But my instinct tells me that you are less likely to be hurt if you stop holding on to this secret and let me share it."

Emily pressed her cheek against Katherine's shoulder. "You know that Tory goes over to the Undercrofts' a lot in the afternoons?"

"Yes."

"I used to, too, before . . . We'd go there and Mrs. Undercroft would have Mrs. Gomez bring us tea, and little sandwiches and cakes. Sometimes other kids, from Tory's class mostly, came, too. I don't think Mom and Dad liked it much, but they weren't home when we got back from school, and we both got good grades. And Mrs. Undercroft made us feel special."

Katherine pushed the pillows up behind her, so that she could lean more comfortably against the headboard.

The child continued. Now that she had started, her words were splashing out like a small stream released. "She said that we—Tory and I—had spiritual gifts, special spiritual gifts. She said she can sometimes see into the future, and that she can tell what people are thinking. And she said she couldn't have children, and she was sad about this. So we were the children of her heart." The child's last words were cut off by the screaming of an ambulance, the shrilling of more police cars. "I wish the lights would come on," Emily whispered. "If they don't come on soon, there'll be lots of violence. Listen to all those police cars."

Katherine said quietly, "Go on, please, Emily."

"At first we just had tea, and things, and then we used to go into the little chapel in Ogilvie House, Tory and me, and Fatty, and some of the other kids from school when Mrs. Undercroft said we could ask them. And Mrs. Gomez and the maids came. Mrs. Undercroft talked a lot about Jesus, and how he saves us . . ."

"Isn't that what Christians are supposed to believe?"

"I guess. But the way she talked, it seemed that God was so angry with us for being born sinful that he couldn't ever forgive us unless Jesus came and got himself crucified to sort of placate the Father. I think that's ghoulish. That isn't the God I believe in. Anyhow, she took us into chapel more and more often, and she had Tory light the candles, and Fatty and the other kids put flowers on the altar, and before we left, I was the one to snuff the candles."

"Was Fatima made to feel special, too?"

"Well, sort of, but it wasn't quite the same. Tory and I were *more* special, and that was easy to believe, because—well, you know Fatty."

Yes, it was easy to see how Yolande had beguiled the children. Being made to feel special is as potent an addiction as any drug. "What about Topaze? Was he part of all this?"

"He's a boy. Mrs. Undercroft said it was just for us females."

"And then what happened?" Emily did not respond; Katherine asked, "What happened to disenchant you?"

"That's the word," Emily breathed. "It was sort of as if she'd enchanted us. She told us about how she'd been trained as a priestess in the Andes in Peru, and she was still a priestess, but now it was for Jesus, not the old gods, and we were her vestal virgins, Tory and Fatty and I. Then"—Emily's voice dropped so low that Katherine had to lean close to hear her—"one day she wanted us to kiss her. On the mouth. At first. And I didn't want to. I just didn't, I didn't want to."

Katherine said gently, "I wouldn't have wanted to, either." After a silence which was alive with pain she asked, "Then what happened?"

Emily's voice was thin. "She said of course she'd never ask me to do anything against my will, and I thought it was okay, but then she went on to say that I was one of them, whether I wanted to be or not, and that I would have to keep all their secrets. And I thought I ought to tell Mom and Dad. I didn't say it, but I thought it, and she knew I was thinking it, because she said that if I ever said anything to anybody, I'd be sorry. And I said I'd never tell anybody anything, and she made me swear on the Bible I wouldn't, and she said if I did, I'd be sorry, because if you swear on the Bible, something terrible will happen to you if you break your word."

"And?" Katherine urged. The child had to get it all out, if the infected wound was ever to heal.

"I wanted to tell Mom and Dad. I'm older than Tory, and I was worried—but I couldn't tell, not after she'd made me promise. I mean, I *promised*."

"But you broke your promise?"

"Well—yes. And no. I mean, I didn't think I'd said anything, but—"

"What did you say, and to whom?"

"The next day was my piano-lesson day . . . Oh, I wish the lights would come back on, it's so dark."

"What happened the next day?"

"My piano teacher was late. I was waiting for him, and Mother Cat—Mother Catherine of Siena came by, and asked me how I was. And I said I wasn't sure, because you don't lie to Mother

Catherine of Siena. I would have liked to talk to Sister Isobel, because she was my homeroom teacher, but I knew I couldn't talk to anybody."

"And?" Katherine prodded.

"Mother Cat asked me if anything was wrong, and I asked her what she thought of God's being so angry at all of us he couldn't forgive us unless Jesus died. And she said no, no, that wasn't right, but then one of the Sisters came hurrying in with some kind of emergency, and my piano teacher arrived. I had my lesson. And I played him one of the pieces I made up, and he told me to stop wasting my time, and his. So when I walked home I was angry and upset and not paying attention. I didn't even see the car, till—"

"Emily! You think the car hit you because you spoke to Mother Catherine of Siena?"

"She said if I said anything after I'd sworn on the Bible, something terrible would happen."

"No, Emily. No! That has nothing to do with it."

"When I was in the hospital she came to me, when nobody else was there, and said it would be worse for me next time. She leaned over me and her face got bigger and bigger and more and more terrible and—" Emily's voice broke and her breath came in short gasps.

Katherine rocked the child, trying to control her own shuddering, and murmured soothingly, meaninglessly, for Emily was beyond words of comfort.

Emily's arms were tight around Katherine's neck, holding her as Julie had held Katherine after one of the terrible nightmares which afflicted the child after Michou's death.

All that Emily was telling Katherine was nightmare. Distorted nightmare. Fevered phantasm. It was not that the child was lying, Katherine knew that she was not. She believed everything she had said. But it did not add up.

Emily suddenly went rigid in Katherine's arms. "Hush."

Katherine listened. She heard a thin sound, like a kitten's wail.

Emily's body was tense. "What is it?"

Katherine said, "You had better get your father."

Emily took one of the candles and limped out of the room. The remaining candlelight seemed to accentuate rather than alleviate the darkness, the darkness of Emily's nightmare. Katherine heard a door open and slam. Silence. Eventually there was a knock on her door.

"Madame Vigneras, it's Suzy."

"What's the problem?"

"It was Topaze. On the steps leading up to our apartment, howling like a lost beast. He'd managed to get this far in the dark, and was terrified. He'd started to go to Ogilvie House and blundered into one of the peacocks and fell over it, and the bird pecked him. It was probably as frightened as Topaze."

Katherine looked at Suzy, standing calmly in the doorway, her face illumined by her flickering candle. "I think if a frightened and angry peacock attacked me in the dark, I'd be terrified, too."

"They are anything but cuddly beasts," Suzy agreed. "Topaze escaped into the vestibule of Cathedral House. He has a key to the inner door, which he is not supposed to have. But Dave says that when he was a boy he managed to acquire keys to all the doors and gates. Anyhow, Topaze is asking for the 'music lady.'"

"So he, too, knows I'm here?"

"There aren't many secrets on a Cathedral Close—one of many reasons I'm glad I have a life of my own. Since we're all thoroughly disturbed—I'm sorry Emily bothered you—Dave is making hot chocolate for the kids, and I'm making tea or consommé. Sorry I don't have any of Mimi's tisanes. Will you join us?"

The picture of Topaze attacked by the peacock, afraid in the dark, was vivid, ludicrous, pathetic. "Yes, I'll join you." She reached for her robe, and Suzy waited until Katherine had on her slippers. She took her candle and followed the dean's wife into the living room. Several candles were lit, and their flames wavered in the breeze from the now open windows. Katherine sat in one of the fireplace chairs, and started looking about in the blowing light for Topaze.

Sudden as lightning the power came on, the electric light dimming the candles, the music rising into life on the record player. The dean carefully took the needle off the disc. "We'd better wait a few minutes before snuffing the candles."

Suzy reached for the phone on the table beside the sofa. "Still dead."

Topaze scrambled to his knees. "Music lady! I was scared."

"I think we were all at least a little scared, Topaze," Katherine said. "But you're all right now."

The dean set a tray of mugs on the coffee table. "Cocoa is ready. When you're through, Topaze, I'm going to take you over to Ogilvie House and bring Tory home."

"Please—can't I stay?"

"Your mother will be worried about you."

He nodded in mute acquiescence, trying to suppress tears. He lifted the mug and held it against his lips, then took a sip. "Music lady—" His voice was back in control. "You all right?" There was deep concern in the question.

"I'm fine, Topaze."

"Glad you're here," he said. "Needed here."

Katherine thought she heard Emily murmur, "Oh, yes, please, yes," but the words were lost in the general conversation which followed the return of the light.

When Topaze had finished his hot cocoa and said good night, Katherine rose. "Once again I think I will try to go to bed."

Emily, too, stood up. "I'll see you to your room."

"Emily." Suzy was stern. "You are not to bother Madame Vigneras. Say good night to her at the door, and go on up to bed."

"Yes, Mom."

They walked silently to the guest end of the apartment. Had she sent Julie to bed, Katherine wondered, when the child needed her? Shouldn't Suzy have recognized that Emily was in no fit state to be alone? Do we always see it better with someone else's children than our own?

"Would you like to come in for a little while?" she asked as Emily paused in the doorway.

"Oh, I would, but Mom—"

"You're not bothering me, Emily. I'm inviting you." She folded her robe once more at the foot of the bed and looked at Emily. "Would you like to spend the rest of the night with me? What's left of it?"

"You mean here, with you, in your bed?"

"Yes."

"You really wouldn't mind?"

It was not a question of minding. It was what had to be done. Emily stood by the bed, looking thin and old-fashioned in her long, seersucker nightgown. "I'll have to take my leg off."

"Of course," Katherine replied calmly.

"I'd just as soon you didn't look."

Katherine turned away until Emily was in bed beside her. The child nuzzled up to her and fell quickly into sleep, worn out.

Katherine's own sleep was shallow. It was a long time since she had shared a bed. She slid in and out of dreams. Concert halls where she had played dissolved into cathedrals. Yolande appeared in the middle of a concert and knocked Katherine's hands off the keyboard and began to sing. Lukas appeared, saying, 'No, no, this will not do. No wife of mine must behave in this manner.' And Yolande dissolved and Lukas announced that the concert would continue and that he would take Katherine safely home. Dreams overlapped, vanished, returned, always including Lukas, and Yolande, who in the dream was Lukas's wife. Where was Justin? Wolfi?

She woke up and lay on her back, not wanting to disturb the sleeping child. The usual pinkish light from the city shone through the windows. Once more the spotlight illumined the Angel Gabriel. The statue had indeed not kept evil away from the Cathedral Close.

She looked at her travel clock. Two-thirty. What the Scots call the wee sma' hours, during which it is impossible to think reasonably.

She was exhausted when the sunlight woke her.

Emily was beside her, still deep in sleep. On the chair to the dressing table lay the prosthetic leg with its harness of metal and leather. Katherine turned to look at the clock; the hands were just pointing to nine, and as she looked, the hour boomed from the clock tower. Emily stirred, but did not waken.

A gentle knock came at the door, and a pleasant-looking dark-haired woman appeared carrying a breakfast tray, followed by Tory. "Dr. Davidson said not to let you sleep too long. I am Dolores, a friend of Raissa. She would want me to take good care of you."

Emily moaned, and pressed closer to Katherine. The old woman smoothed the fair hair, and the child opened her eyes.

"Breakfast," Dolores said. "Sit up, and I will arrange the pillows. You can help, Tory. Breakfast for two—brown eggs I brought from Brooklyn, and my own bread, toasted and buttered." She handed the tray to Tory and pulled Emily up in the bed, patting the pillows until they supported both Emily and Katherine.

When the tray was settled over Katherine's legs, she left. "On Saturdays I do the ironing. Tory, you can bring the tray when they're done."

Tory perched on the foot of the bed. "Dolores thinks she can boss us around. But Mom says we couldn't manage without her."

"How does she happen to know Raissa?" Katherine opened her egg, which was cooked exactly to her liking, soft, but not runny.

"She's a friend of Dr. Oppenheimer's maid—didn't Dr. Oppenheimer find Raissa for you?"

"Yes, I see."

"And speaking of finding, how come we didn't find you in your own bed, Emily? How come you're with Madame Vigneras?"

Katherine detected a strong tinge of jealousy. "We had rather a disturbed night, if you remember. Didn't you nearly sleep over at the Undercrofts'?"

"I would have, if Daddy hadn't come for me. Anyhow, Mom said Emily wasn't to bother—"

Katherine broke in, "Emily was here at my invitation. We got to talking, and when she fell asleep I didn't have the heart to disturb her."

"She must have meant to spend the night." Tory's glance went to the dressing-table chair. "She took off her leg."

Emily, who had sleepily been breaking bits of toast into her egg, was suddenly wide awake. "Mind your own beeswax. Where's Daddy?"

"In the office with Señora Castillo, catching up on mail while things are Saturday-quiet."

"Mom's at the hospital?"

"She said she'd be home early. No office hours this afternoon. Dolores has a pot roast in the crock pot. It smells good already. My job this morning is to mop the bathroom floors. Em, you're to polish the silver."

"I polished it last Saturday."

"So? That's what Dolores says you're to do."

The conversation sounded casual enough on the surface, but there was enough electrical tension between the two girls, Katherine thought, to light the city. Tory, she realized, was intensely unhappy. —No, she thought again. —Dave and Suzy will have to take care of Tory. Emily is all I can take on.

"I have to go to the bathroom," Emily said.

As Katherine moved the breakfast tray, Tory reached for the artificial leg and tossed it on the bed.

All the color left Emily's face and her pupils enlarged. "*Don't.* Don't ever do that." Her voice was low. She pulled herself out of bed and hopped to the bathroom.

Tory's eyes filled with tears. "I can't do anything right. I was just trying to help."

There seemed nothing to say. If Katherine mentioned that Emily was sensitive on the subject of the leg, it would not make Tory feel any better. "Did the Undercrofts have overnight guests?"

"Just Mrs. Gomez and the kids. They invited the bigwigs—it was an enormously tall African bishop and his wife—but when the lights came back on, a car came for them from their embassy. They thought the power failure was all because of them. Isn't that weird? They thought someone pulled a power switch just to hurt them."

Katherine smiled. "Not so weird. They've probably been hurt so often they're oversensitive."

"But to cause a blackout *on purpose?*"

"They may not have felt that it was on purpose. People are often hurt inadvertently by being in the wrong place at the wrong time. And we all hurt people without meaning to, as you just saw."

Tory's eyes widened. "I never thought of it that way. Shall I take the breakfast tray? Are you finished?"

"Yes, thanks. I'll just keep the coffee."

"Sure." Tory took the tray and left.

Katherine sat leaning against the pillows, sipping coffee. The morning was cool and radiant, the storm spent, the air washed clean. But the storm which Emily had let break at last was still not over.

The child hopped in, picked up her leg, and hopped back to the bathroom. In a moment she walked in. "I shouldn't have snapped at Tory."

"No."

"We didn't get enough sleep. I'm always snappy when I don't get enough sleep. Madame. What I told you last night—do you believe me?"

Katherine held out her arms to the child and Emily moved to her. "Emily." Gently, she kissed the top of the fair head. "I believe that you were telling me what you believe to be true."

"But you don't believe it's true!" Again the child's voice was a frightened wail.

"Hush," Katherine said. "Mrs. Undercroft did not deliberately cause your accident. I am positive."

A faint note of hope came into the child's words. "You promise?"

Katherine shook her head, though Emily's face was pressed into her shoulder so that she could not see. "I cannot promise, Emily, until I have found out the answer to a few questions." Perhaps Yolande had somehow or other, unwittingly, caused the accident which had resulted in the loss of Emily's leg. That could be the burden to which she had referred with such anguish. That, surely, would account for her 'demons' of the past two years. But Katherine had to know for certain that her hunch was correct before she could give the child the reassurance that would still the storm of released fear. She said, "Has Mrs. Undercroft talked to you and the other children about her horror of physical abuse?"

"Yes," Emily admitted. "Once Tory pinched Fatty and Mrs. Undercroft wouldn't let her come to tea for a week."

"So you can see that it isn't likely she would ever deliberately cause physical harm to anyone. In any case, how would she have known of your conversation with Mother Catherine of Siena?"

"What about her gifts of knowing? Please, Madame, please, I don't want to be hurt again."

"I don't want you to be hurt, Emily, and I don't think you will be. Have you never told anyone about this?"

Emily's eyes flared with terror. "No—no—"

"Not even Bishop Bodeway?" Katherine asked implacably.

"But—but—he can't tell, because I told him in confession."

So. Felix could never have forgotten what Emily had told him, no matter what his training. "And?"

"He said what you said. That she wouldn't."

"And he was quite right. She wouldn't." But she had not succeeded in reassuring the child. "Go get dressed, my dear, and then go to the practice piano. Run through a few scales, and then start composing something of your own. Six-eight time, F major. I won't be long."

"You're sure?" Emily asked anxiously.

"I'm just going to wash and dress."

From the bathroom Katherine heard Emily practicing. Scales. Then she began tentatively picking out a melody, first in the right

hand, then in the left. The child was composing a gigue. Katherine
listened for a moment, then finished dressing.

Emily and John made sandwiches for lunch. Jos had Saturday
classes, and Tory was off with Fatima. John was happy to eat early
because he had spent the morning mopping floors at the music
school.

After they had eaten, Katherine and Emily got into the sleigh
bed. Emily took off her leg, then pressed against Katherine, saying,
"If you could promise me everything would be all right, I could go
to sleep."

"Emily, darling child, I don't make promises unless I'm positive
I can keep them. And you're asking for a promise nobody can
make. There are no guarantees that there will be no accidents or
no evil or no pain. I can promise one thing only, and that is, your
music will always see you through anything that happens, and that
is no small promise."

"But, Madame, I told you everything she said not to tell, and
I'm afraid."

Katherine's arms tightened around the child. "I hope that before the day is over, I will be able to wake you up from the nightmare in which you've been living. It *is* nightmare, darling. The
reality of the loss of your leg, of having to stop dancing, of turning
to composing, this you will be able to live with, not bitterly, but
with fortitude and verve. What you have not been able to live
with, what is frightening you now, is not reality, but nightmare."

Emily moaned almost inaudibly.

Katherine continued, "What Mrs. Undercroft wanted of you
girls was ugly, and I'm not surprised that she was ashamed of it,
nor that she *did* threaten you. You can see that she would be afraid
to have it known. But it is pathetic as well as ugly."

Emily made a noise which was neither denial nor affirmation.

"Mrs. Undercroft was demanding shows of love with the same
single-mindedness as a small child, hungrily seeking the kind of
love she did not have when she should have had it. You have always
known that your parents love you, no matter how busy they are."

Katherine waited until Emily made a muffled murmur of agreement. "Mrs. Undercroft had none of that taken-for-granted love. You see, if you're not touched and cuddled when you're an infant, the need for it grows, monstrously. And what can be a normal need in a two-year-old is definitely abnormal in an adult."

At last Emily rolled over and leaned on one elbow so that she could look at Katherine. "Was she really a child priestess in Peru?"

"What do you think?"

Emily shook her head.

"And that's pathetic, isn't it? Whatever her childhood was, it wasn't glamorous. It was unhappy and abused."

"The scars—she showed us the scars—"

"They are real. But the scars on her mind are as real as the scars on her back."

"If she didn't get them in Peru—"

"It could have been anywhere. She lived in a brutal world."

"She did say, oh, Madame, she did, that if I told anyone I'd be sorry."

"You didn't tell anyone except Felix."

"But that was in confession . . ."

"And no one else knew, Emily, dear child. What happened was an accident, a horrible accident. But perhaps it is what has awakened in you the real gift which God has given you, your gift for making music."

"But do I really have the gift?"

"That is something I *can* promise you. Yes. You have the gift. Now close your eyes. We both need some sleep."

With the affirmation of a firm promise, Emily slumped almost immediately into sleep and nestled against Katherine, breathing softly. It was less easy for Katherine. She disciplined herself to breathe slowly, deeply. Scales. F, modulate to C. C, modulate to G. G, modulate to D.

The minor scales. During B♭ minor she slid into sleep.

She woke up, as she had planned to do, a little before three. Emily was still asleep. It was a shame to wake the child, but this was no time for her to move into consciousness and find Katherine gone. She shook her gently. Emily moved closer, flinging one arm across Katherine.

"Emily. Wake up. I have to go to the Bösendorfer. Wake up."

Slowly the long bronze eyelashes fluttered and Emily looked at Katherine. "Is it morning?"

"Three o'clock in the afternoon. Time to wake up."

"I am *wide* awake." Emily jumped out of bed and fell. From the floor she looked disconcertedly at Katherine. "I forgot my leg. Sometimes I still do. Not often, but sometimes." She pulled herself up, got the leg from the dressing-table chair, and hopped to the bathroom.

Katherine had taken off her dress and put her robe on for the nap. Now she dressed again. As she and Emily started down the stairs, she remarked, "I could wish that what goes down doesn't also have to go back up."

"You'd get used to the stairs if you lived with us," Emily assured her. "They really aren't all that bad."

When they reached the choir of the Cathedral, Katherine was absurdly grateful to see Topaze sitting in the front row, as though waiting for a concert to begin.

"Topaze," she said without greeting, "please stay with Emily till I return. I have a small errand to run. Emily, for your delectation, you may play the Bösendorfer till I get back."

Without waiting for a reply, she walked away from them, not looking behind her. As she neared the bronze doors she heard the first notes of the six-eight melody, F major, full of *joie de vivre*. Even in the midst of irrational fear, Emily could listen to the music within her, and let it flow through her fingers.

Katherine descended the steps, carefully, walked around a tour bus, and saw someone, one of the canons, she thought, getting out of a taxi. He recognized her, bade her good afternoon, helped her into the taxi, and she directed the driver to the convent.

She rang the convent bell. Waited. Rang again. Waited. She heard the bell ring inside. She was in the right place. A brightly polished brass plaque bore not only the street number but the name of the Community. She rang again. No one came. Surely someone had to be there. She pressed her finger against the bell and held it.

Finally the door was opened by one of the younger Sisters, who smiled as she recognized Katherine, beckoned her in, and led her into a pleasant, small sitting room. "Mother will be right with you."

The room was simple, but comfortably furnished. There was a medieval triptych over the mantel. She turned as she heard a swish of skirts, and the Superior came in, shutting the door behind her.

"Madame Vigneras." She held out her hands. "We're having a Quiet Day, and we let the bell ring when we're in chapel, but you are certainly persistent, so I sent one of the novices to see who wanted us that badly."

"Persistent I am," Katherine agreed. "I'm sorry to interrupt your Quiet Day, and I won't keep you long. I wouldn't have come without reason."

"I know that," the nun replied, and waited.

"Do you by any chance remember that Emily spoke to you before her piano lesson on the day of her accident, and seemed worried about something?"

"I do," Mother Catherine replied. "She did indeed seem worried. She asked me some vaguely religious questions which were all out of proportion to her anxiety, and I felt strongly that she wanted to tell or ask me something important. And then we got interrupted, and I was deeply concerned. But that evening we heard that she had been struck by a car on the way home."

"While she was in the hospital, did Mrs. Undercroft come to see her often?" She had to know.

The nun looked surprised. "I doubt if at all. Visitors were forbidden. At first, Emily was in deep shock, and then she ran a high fever. Oh." She stopped. Katherine waited. The nun said, "Emily's fever was so high that she was delirious and thrashing around, and they were afraid of convulsions if she couldn't be calmed. Sister Isobel was her homeroom teacher that year, and Emily was very fond of her, so they sent for her, hoping that she might have a quietening effect."

"Did she?"

"Anything but. Emily screamed in terror when she saw her, and kept saying, 'I didn't tell, I didn't tell!' And she called Sister Isobel Mrs. Undercroft."

"You're sure?"

"That's what Sister Isobel told me. It was a most distressing reaction. Sister *was* Mrs. Undercroft for a few years, and though most of the children at school are unaware of this, it's quite possible the Davidson children may have picked it up."

"Did Emily think Sister Isobel was the present Mrs. Undercroft?"

"That never occurred to us. We put the whole thing down to the delirium of deep shock."

"Thank you," Katherine said. "I'll explain everything when I get it all sorted out."

"You don't need to."

Katherine knew that she did not. Mother Catherine of Siena would never refer to this conversation. "I think I'll quite likely want to explain. But thanks. I must go. I left Emily and Topaze waiting for me at the Bösendorfer."

"How are you going to get back?"

"I was lucky enough to get a taxi right outside the Cathedral on my way here. If I don't find one, I'll walk."

The nun gazed at her speculatively. "You don't want to leave Emily and Topaze alone too long. I'll drive you. The car's just outside."

Katherine did not protest. "Thank you. I would appreciate that."

When they reached the Cathedral, Mother Cat asked, "Would you like me to come in?"

"Please don't bother. Get back to your Quiet Day. It would be pleasant to hope all the problems were ended with the storm and I could have a quiet afternoon at the piano."

But that, she thought, was unlikely. There were still some unanswered questions.

When she was finally seated at the Bösendorfer, with Emily and Topaze listening from the choir stalls, she ran a few scales, limbering her fingers before working on the program. Getting the feel of the nave had meant a complete aural and technical reorientation.

When she had played the program through in its entirety, she felt that it was at last beginning to cohere—notes of music, light, space, all in counterpoint. She rested her hands on the keyboard, and looked up to see Yolande Undercroft walking toward her.

From the choir stalls Emily and Topaze rose, and she turned to see them slipping out of the choir into the ambulatory.

"Superb, superb." Yolande beat her hands together in applause. "How privileged we are to have you!"

Katherine remained seated at the piano, her fingers still touching the keys as though for confidence. She did not know why Yolande had come to the Cathedral, or even if it was on purpose to see Katherine. But there was no more time for waiting for the unanswered questions to work themselves out. She said, "Yolande. I want to speak to you about your gift of prescience—of knowing."

"Oh, that. Well, yes, of course." Yolande appeared to dismiss it. "I came to tell you that I've finally been able to get hold of the elusive Grace Farwater, of the *Times*, and I've arranged—"

"She's already spoken to me," Katherine interrupted. "Prescience can work two ways, you see. I think we are all born with considerable powers which we lose as we move into a world that has settled more and more for technocracy. Perhaps we artists are lucky, because we never lose these gifts entirely. You might be interested to hear that there are some things I know about you."

"About me? But I am an open book to you. I have revealed myself to you as to few people."

"I am grateful for your confidence," Katherine said dryly. "Now let's get a few minor facts straight. You didn't call Grace Farwater at all. She found out I was having a concert and called me."

"No, no, I did—"

"It doesn't really matter, Yolande. Your jealousy is more pitiable than anything else."

Yolande drew back. "I don't want your pity."

"I know, and I'm sorry about that, but like your jealousy it is a fact and not very important. What I really need to talk to you about is Emily."

Katherine had kept her voice level; there was no hidden threat in it, but Yolande caught her breath. Then her face closed in. "Emily. Oh, we are all so grateful that you are teaching Emily, giving her a real chance. I, personally, am grateful."

"Yes," Katherine said. "I believe you are."

Yolande looked around as though for something she could not find. "Let's go into one of the chapels where, you know, we won't be disturbed. I have keys."

Yes. Like Topaze, Yolande would need to have what Felix called the keys to the kingdom.

"We'll go into St. Saviour's," Yolande urged, "behind the high altar. It's the Orthodox chapel and has some beautiful icons. I think you'll enjoy seeing them."

Katherine followed her. Yolande took her keys from her handbag and opened the grilled gates. St. Saviour's was a spacious chapel. Light came from four standing alabaster lamps. There was a rug on the floor, a few straight chairs along the sides. A large candle lamp swung over the altar, swaying slightly. Yolande turned to Katherine. "We were all so horrified at Emily's terrible, terrible accident. She had so much talent as a dancer, and it was all taken away in one horrible moment. But now you are helping her to find her life again, and we are all so grateful."

Katherine let her finish. She sat in one of the side chairs and indicated that Yolande was to sit beside her. She waited till the bishop's wife did so. Katherine kept her voice quiet, conversational. "When Emily was in the hospital after her accident, did you go to see her?"

Yolande started, put her hand to her heart. "Why do you ask?"

"I would like to know."

Yolande looked away from Katherine, at the Orthodox cross on the altar. "Of course I went to see her. I felt—oh, I can't tell you how terrible I felt. I've had no children of my own, so . . . I went with Allie; we could go after visiting hours, which was more convenient for Allie." Now Yolande turned to look at Katherine. "Jesus, it was shocking. The poor child was delirious. She looked at me and she screamed and screamed. So Allie took me by the arm and led me away. I never had a chance to say anything, to help. In all that I have been through, it was the most ghastly . . ."

The words had the ring of truth, but the equation had to be completed. "Was the accident in fact an accident?" Katherine was astounded to hear her own words—unaccusing, unemotional.

"Oh God, yes, oh Jesus, yes."

It was all falling into place. "You wanted to frighten Emily, so that she wouldn't tell about the . . . the little services you were holding in your chapel."

Yolande leapt to her feet as though a steel spring had been released. "No!" The sound rose shrilly up into the shadows.

Katherine remained seated, but she forced herself to continue. "You threatened Emily."

"No!" Yolande's voice soared, up, up, to the vaulted roof. "Everybody makes up things about me because I'm not good enough to be the bishop's wife. She wanted to get me in trouble—"

Katherine continued steadily. "You threatened Emily. You told her that something terrible would happen to her if she ever said anything to anybody about your . . . your odd chapel services."

"She swore she'd never say anything. There wasn't anything to tell! She swore she'd never—"

"She didn't tell. I had to drag it out of her last night during the blackout. But you frightened her enough so that she believes you caused the accident that cost her the loss of her leg. She believes you did this to punish her."

"She couldn't believe that! She couldn't!"

"Emily believes you did. I don't, but Emily does. She is terrified of you. You had better tell me what really happened."

Yolande dropped back into the hard chapel chair. "She knows I would never physically— She knows I would never hurt— She knows I could never, after all that was done to me— Physical cruelty is abominable to me— Jesus, you must know . . ."

"Tell me what the truth of the matter is. Then perhaps we can keep anything else from happening."

Yolande dropped her hands from her eyes. Her face was streaming with tears. "Only to frighten—that's all—so she'd—you know —so she'd keep quiet."

"You were ashamed?"

"Nobody would have understood. Everybody misinterprets . . ."

"So who was it you asked to frighten her? Was it Mrs. Gomez?"

"No, no. Him. The fool, the—"

Katherine did not understand much Spanish, but enough to guess at the stream of invective Yolande was hurling at Gomez. The veneer of civilization vanished. Then, slowly, vestiges returned.

"He swore the accelerator stuck, that the car went out of control. I was glad when he went to jail. He's ruined every—"

"But you believe it was an accident, the accelerator did stick?"

"Oh, Jesus, yes. He's a fool, but he's not a murderer, and he had no reason, he hardly knew the child. And then, a few months later, you know, he went to jail for drugs."

"And you thought you were safe?"

Yolande shook her head back and forth, back and forth. "No one is safe, ever."

"You used to take drugs."

"Years ago. I swear. Years ago. I haven't—"

"I believe you. But he was your supplier."

Yolande's eyes were dark, tragic smudges. "How do you know all this?"

"You have almost told me yourself. And when enough things are added up, then certain conclusions become inevitable. You pay Fatima Gomez to keep you informed—" She held up her hand to stop Yolande from breaking in. "So you know Gomez made his confession to Bishop Bodeway after the accident. And so for two years you've been trying to frighten Felix, making threatening anonymous phone calls."

Yolande tried to pull herself up. "Nonsense. Only children—"

"Perhaps a child. But also the child's mother. It was Mrs. Gomez who broke into my apartment and vandalized it, again at your instigation." Katherine stood up. "Now we are coming to the truth. Aren't we?"

Yolande moved her fingers restlessly, like someone ill, like someone dying, plucking at the sheets. "Jesus, she loved it. She is far worse than her husband. She loved every bit of it. She lusts in it."

"And she'll do what you ask her to do, because you are educating her children."

A harsh laugh turned into a sob. "Jesus, money is a weapon. But she's a sadist. I had to stop her from hitting Fatty, at least in my house. She wants revenge on the whole world. It was her idea to go after Oppenheimer, to be a red herring, she said. She hates Jews, that's really why. She hates everybody. She does more than I ask. I never wanted that portrait touched. She hates you, too, as much as—" She broke off.

Katherine looked at Yolande steadily, pityingly. "I know you hate me, Yolande. I know you hate Felix. Hate is eating you, like a cancer."

Yolande lifted a ravaged face. "That shameless faggot. Seducing Allie when he was a mere child."

"That is not true, and you know it."

"They love each other."

"As friends."

"That can be more threatening than sex. I feel, you know, excluded."

"So you are punishing Felix? Are you so jealous of an old man who has long ago paid for the sins of his youth?"

"We never stop paying! We pay for things we never did. I pay for my parentage, whatever it was, I pay for the beasts who used me . . ."

They sat in silence. Katherine felt that she had nothing more to say. All that was left was to try to teach Emily, to develop the child's latent talent. Perhaps a phoenix might rise from these ashes.

Yolande reached toward her with groping hands. "What are you going to do to me? I'm in your power. What are you going to do?"

Katherine drew away. "Does your husband know about any of this?"

"Jesus—" Yolande slid to her knees. "It would kill him. He'd never forgive me. Our lives are in your hands."

"Don't be melodramatic," Katherine said. "When you went to the hospital to see Emily, you didn't speak to her, threaten her?"

"God, no, how could I! What do you think I am? She was delirious, out of her mind, screaming. Allie took me away, it upset me so, he could tell you—"

Katherine did not need Allie to convince her that Yolande was telling the truth. Nevertheless, the visit to Emily in the hospital, which was not evil in intent, had implanted itself in the child's fever-distorted mind, adding to the nightmare, becoming in itself nightmare.

Again the younger woman clutched frantically. "I prayed, oh, sweet Jesus, I prayed, that there would be a miracle, you know, that it wouldn't have happened, that Emily would only have been frightened the way I wanted, not hurt. I prayed . . . I stayed in the chapel all night and I prayed . . . Nothing can make the horror go away. Nothing can make it be all right." Now the real tears came.

Katherine did nothing to check the storm, but let it spend itself.

"I dream about it." Yolande spoke through tears which were coming more quietly. "I dream, I see it happen, and I wake up, sobbing . . . I will never forgive myself, never."

—I can't forgive you either, Katherine thought wearily. —I don't have the power. But you need to be forgiven. For Allie's sake, if not your own. "Yolande"—her voice was soft but it carried strength and the younger woman raised her eyes. "Nothing is ultimately unforgivable in God's sight, when you have repented."

"But he can't make it all right! It's done!"

"*You* can't make it all right. Neither can I. But God can, in ways we may not be able to guess." So much she had learned from Wolfi.

"Allie—I don't think he could forgive me. What are you going to say to Allie? If it should be made public—if Grace Farwater—oh, Jesus, what are you going to say to Allie?"

"Nothing. Nor to Grace Farwater. Nor to anybody."

Yolande looked whitely at Katherine. "You won't tell Allie?"

"What good purpose would that serve? Emily's accident is a burden of horror you will have to carry the rest of your life. Why should Allie be made to bear it, too?"

"But—"

"Would you like me to tell Allie, so that he can help you carry the guilt?" Silence. "If you truly love him . . ."

"I do."

"Enough to spare him this? Enough to carry it alone?"

Yolande bowed her head. "Yes." She stared silently at the cross on the altar, making no motion to wipe away her tears.

"Who is your confessor?" Katherine asked.

Yolande shook her head.

"The high priestess hears confessions and is above making them? I don't know much about your church or confession, but I know enough to know that you won't be able to survive what has happened unless you make yours. And now. You will have to find someone, right away. Do you understand?"

Yolande twisted her fingers together. "Could anyone ever give me absolution?"

"That will have to be between you and whomever you go to. Perhaps the most difficult part will be for you to accept forgiveness."

"From God?"

"From yourself, which I suspect will be a great deal more painful. But you are not to put this off. You will find a confessor."

Yolande stretched out her arms toward the cross. "I will." Then, "But what—" She looked at Katherine beseechingly. "What about the children?"

"You will have to let Tory and Fatima go."

Yolande nodded. "Oh, yes, I know that. They don't know anything. Not really. I made Fatima think it was only a game—that's easily ended. And Tory, you know, knows nothing. But Emily—what about Emily?"

Katherine replied steadily. "I will tell Emily the truth. That her accident was an accident. That you neither caused nor willed it. That you came to her in the hospital to comfort, not to threaten."

There was a long silence. At last Yolande said, "What about Felix?"

"What *about* Felix?"

Both women turned as Felix put a key in the gate and came toward them.

"Perhaps," Katherine suggested, "you owe Felix an apology?"

The old man went directly to Yolande. "My dear, isn't it time all this pain and punishment ended?"

"You know?"

"Once I stopped being a frightened and foolish old man, I realized that you had to be behind those calls. What I don't understand is why."

Katherine said, "You don't have to understand why, Felix. That is going to be between Yolande and her confessor."

Felix nodded thoughtfully, looking from one to the other.

Again Yolande tried to catch air. "I'm sorry—I'm sorry—"

Felix sat beside her, taking the grasping hands and holding them. "Does Allie know?"

"No. Oh, Jesus, no."

"But he knows something has been wrong, very wrong, that your dark angel has been in the ascendant."

"He'd never . . . Oh, Jesus, he'd never forgive me."

"Allie loves you, Yolande. And he has a forgiving heart."

"Do . . . do I?" It was a painful supplication.

"You can learn," he said. "We do learn from our mistakes, and for that I daily thank God. I don't know why you felt that you had to frighten me, but I know that I have been a silly old man. I was an even more silly and stupid youth, but why should I be so afraid that someone would find out about me, about my past, that I should have allowed myself to take such nonsense seriously? I am what I am, and this I give to my Lord, as I am. It is all I have to give, and it is, I believe, enough." He looked gently at the crumpled woman. "I ask you to do the same. We are, perhaps, our own crosses, but we will be given the strength to bear them."

—◦◦⊰{ 6 }⊱◦◦—

The late-afternoon sunlight streamed across the nave of the Cathedral, reached colored shafts to the choir, where Katherine sat at the Bösendorfer with Emily. With a closed, guarded face, the child listened. When Katherine had finished, Emily leaned against her, reaching for her hands. Katherine rocked her lightly, following her words with the assurance of touch.

"It really was a nightmare?" Emily whispered.

"Yes. And it is time to wake up."

A long slow shudder shook the child's slender frame. "She still frightens me."

"You'll get over that in time." —She frightens herself. And she, too, will have to get over that. "Now, my child, let us make music."

Emily looked around. "Here?"

"Here. What about that Schubert duet we played at your first lesson?"

"Oh—I love it. Yes, please."

Katherine reached into her music bag, found the Schubert, and placed it on the rack. "I'll count two measures and then we'll begin." Music, more than anything else, would bring Emily out of the nightmare.

The child's fingers moved on the keys without faltering. The simplicity of the piece cut across all the fear and jealousy and anguish which had surrounded them. The gentle melody was an affirmation. Was prayer.

When they were through, Katherine said, "Now, my darling girl, I want you to go home. There is nothing to be afraid of."

"Will you be coming?"

"Yes." She would have to spend one more night at the Davidsons' in order to safeguard all that which needed to be protected. "I'm going to work, now. But I'll see you in—oh, in an hour and a half."

"All right." Emily rose obediently, then flung her arms around Katherine with a hug and a kiss. "Oh, Madame, thank you, thank you. I'm beginning to realize that I'm awake, that you've taken away the nightmare."

Katherine gave her a light, loving spank. "Then go practice scales."

When the child had gone, she turned to music. She played through the pieces she had chosen, until she came to the Beethoven. Then she sensed movement, and looked up to see Bishop Chan and Yolande walking along the nave, the bishop's arm around the woman in a protective gesture.

Katherine returned to the sonata.

---*{ 7 }*---

She spent the next afternoon at the piano until the music and the great space became one. A tired ache moved from shoulder blade to shoulder blade, and she turned to see Bishop Undercroft standing beside her. So it was not over yet.

"May we talk?" He looked pale and sad.

"Yes."

A group of tourists was coming in. "They're late," he said. "It's nearly time to close the doors. Will you come with me?" He led her down some side steps and into the ambulatory, away from the crowd. He opened the gates to the second chapel. "This is St. Ambrose, the Italian chapel. Isn't it a little gem? We have a lot of tiny weddings here, and most of them hold." His voice was carefully controlled. He pulled the grilled gates closed. When they were seated in the uncomfortable oaken stalls, he said, "I have learned about it all."

All? "All what?" she asked carefully.

"The phone calls. Trying to terrify poor old Felix. And you. Mrs. Gomez slashing your Hunter portrait. I am sick at heart."

"How did you find out?" —And how much? What did Yolande tell you?

"I went into the house and Fatima was having hysterics. And Mrs. Gomez admitted it. She is full of hate, nothing but hate. And because her husband once supplied my wife with drugs, Yolande is afraid of her and did not dare tell me. Why could she not have told me? Was she afraid Mrs. Gomez would hurt her physically?"

"Probably. When one has suffered intense physical pain, as she has, then pain becomes less rather than more endurable."

"It does not excuse her complicity. When Fatima started blurting everything out, Yolande admitted that she knew, that she had not been able to stop it. How could she have let it go on, without turning to me—"

Poor Allie. How little he knew. And that little was bad enough.

"I thought I had taught her to trust me. I have spent our marriage trying to teach her trust. But my faith hasn't been strong enough. I've failed her."

"Allie—hush—"

"Why should forgiveness be so difficult? Forgiveness of ourselves. Ultimately I forgave myself about Ona's death. I thought, after that, no forgiveness would be difficult. But this—I was so outraged, so distraught, that I went to the phone and called the convent and asked for Isobel. And was told that she was not available. But Yolande heard me ask. And to Yolande that was betrayal, and so I have failed her again."

"Hush, Allie, hush," Katherine repeated.

"When Yolande first came to me—despite all the success, all the adulation—she was a broken child. She brought me her lack of faith and asked me to teach her faith. And I thought I had. But that she could not trust me, that she could let Felix be hurt, and you, without coming to me . . . I have failed her."

"We all fail each other," she said, "especially those we love most dearly. And is it so strange?" As an echo, she heard Wolfi's words under her own. "Wasn't Jesus singularly unsuccessful with a great many people?"

He was silent for a moment. "Yes. Of course. Thank you. We live in a world sold on success, even in the Church."

"But love is what it's about, isn't it? Not success?"

He nodded. "Yolande was right. She said that I should come talk to you, that you had been very kind to her, that you knew all about it, and that you had forgiven her."

—Does keeping silence constitute forgiveness? Katherine wondered. —It would not be only Yolande, or only Allie I would hurt if I told him the truth. We must all look at ourselves, and the ill that we have done, and if we are to survive, we must have great compassion on ourselves. "How amazing," she tried to lighten the tension, "that Mrs. Gomez cooks like an angel. One would think that so much anger would cause her soufflés to fall, and I gather they never do."

But he was not ready yet for lightness. "I cannot bear to think that Felix was frightened, after all he has done for me. I gather this has been going on for a long time, someone I love terrorized, and I knew nothing about it. How could I have been so insensitive? I have been like the wasp, guzzling jam, unaware of my own brokenness . . ." He bent over, his eyes dry and tearless.

In St. Ambrose chapel the stalls were separated by high carved barriers of oak and she could not reach over to touch him. If he was this devastated by the least of all that Yolande had done, she hoped that Bishop Chan had reinforced her own advice to the bishop's wife to bear her burden alone. She thought that probably he had, and that he would help her to bear it.

The stall was a little too high for her, hard and uncomfortable. She thought of all the good advice she had given Dorcas about marriage, advice which had turned out to be useless. What did she have to say to this man, torn apart by only a small fragment of the knowledge that Yolande was going to have to carry with her for the rest of her life?

"When she was using drugs she was in touch with at least the fringes of the criminal world—that's how she knew Gomez."

"Hush," Katherine said. "She hasn't used drugs for years, now. You've done that much for her."

"I thought I could do more. In my pride I thought—" Suddenly the tears came.

She felt exhausted, but she could not ignore this naked grief. She reached across the oaken barrier and put her hand over his. "That's all right, let it out, don't be afraid to cry, Lukas, it's all right."

He was suddenly still as marble, the tears arrested. "What did you call me?"

She had not heard.

"You called me Lukas. That was my father's name."

She had known for a long time, since that first meeting on the Close, really. But she had not wanted to know. No one could look that much like Lukas von Hilpert and not be his son.

Still with her hand over his, she said. "Yes. Lukas von Hilpert. I knew him a long time ago. You are very much like him."

"Why didn't you say anything?"

"Because at first I thought it had to be coincidence. You had another name, an English accent with no trace of German—"

"I was only a child when my parents died. It was said that my father was killed in a shooting accident, and my mother of a weak heart. But my mother took sleeping pills, too many sleeping pills. Perhaps by accident. But she called me in—I was the baby and her favorite—and told me that my father had killed himself because of some woman."

Katherine's voice was steady. "Unhappy women often want to make their sons hate their fathers, in order to keep on possessing them, even beyond the grave. You have just seen what an unhappy, jealous woman can be driven to do." —Let him keep on thinking it was Mrs. Gomez, and not his wife. "Your father was one of the most honorable men I have ever known. My husband respected him, too."

He moved from the uncomfortable stall and knelt at her feet, but it was very different from the way his wife had groveled; it was simply to avoid the carved oaken barrier, to get closer to her, closer to the truth. And this truth she could give him. "You truly knew my father?"

"Yes. I knew him well."

"And you say he was an honorable man?"

"He was incapable of doing anything dishonorable."

She was grateful for Felix's reminder of what she so firmly believed. A sick world, greedy for sensation rather than salvation, does not need to have every appetite sated.

"Thank you." The tears started again. "I cannot thank you enough. You have—oh, my God!" It was a cry of joy. "You have given me back my father!" She stroked the fair hair gently. "I know you would not lie to me."

"No." Nor had she.

"When I was sent to England to my mother's relatives, I lost touch with my family. All I remember—except my mother's bedroom smelling of menthol and medicine and her last words to me—is Christmas in the country, at the *Schloss*, and a great tree, like the one in the *Nutcracker*, and I was on my father's shoulders, and even so I could not touch the angel at the top—" Silent tears trickled down his face, and he buried his head in her lap, and she stroked his hair, wiped his tears, as though he had been Michou.

---◦≺{ 8 }≻◦---

When Mimi came for her, the dean insisted on driving them home, asked no questions except, "Is Emily all right?"

All right. Two small words which could mean many things. "Yes. Emily is all right."

The first large concert after Michou's death was in Rome. Had Wolfi somehow managed to arrange it? Katherine and Justin had flown there, arriving only a few hours before they were due at the concert hall. Her fingers ached, taking into themselves the pain in her heart.

'I can't play,' she said flatly.

'You must,' Justin said. 'For me. For Michou.' He said it, but he did not come near her. He rubbed his broken hands together and his own pain was all he could hold.

The cardinal sent his car to their hotel. Katherine got in, still saying to Justin, 'I can't. I don't know what to do. I can't.'

Justin got in beside her, saying nothing.

Wolfi was waiting in the dressing room. He had put a bowl of vivid anemones on the dressing table. Katherine looked at the brilliant color of the flowers, then at the two men. Wolfi put one hand gently on her shoulder.

There was no need of a miracle. Still saying *I can't*, but silently now, not out loud, she knew that she could. That she would.

And the miracle came then, in her playing, in the music which was an affirmation, so that as she rested her hands on the keyboard at the end of the concert, before the applause began, she was able to say, 'All right.'

---◦≺{ 9 }≻◦---

The very size of the Cathedral would always be a surprise. Felix, wearing a light, white cassock, led Katherine across the choir to the Bösendorfer, and she was met with a great thunder of applause from the audience filling the nave, the choir stalls, applause rolling the length of the Cathedral like great ocean waves.

Felix stood beside her, slenderly dignified, until the applause diminished, dwindled, ceased. He introduced her with a tender pride, and stepped back into the choir to take his seat.

She stood by the piano bowing to the audience, first to the gathering in the nave, then to the choir stalls, where the Cathedral family sat—Bishop, Dean, and Chapter; many of the secretarial staff, the maintenance men, the Stone Yard workers, and their families and close friends. There was a feeling of unity here that touched her deeply. She looked slowly around as she seated herself at the piano, taking her time, in quiet preparation for the music.

On her left sat the Undercrofts, Fatima between them. Yolande, in a black dress, looked pale, with less makeup than usual. But there was a marked change: the anguish was gone.

Bishop Chan came in one of the side entrances, saw an empty seat, and slipped into it, looking gently, lovingly at Yolande, then sitting back and leaning his head against the dark wood of the choir stall.

On the opposite side sat the Davidson family and Mimi Oppenheimer. And, Katherine noted with some surprise, Iona Grady. Behind them were the Sisters, the whole Community, with Topaze sitting between Mother Catherine of Siena and Sister Isobel. Llew and Dorcas, Katherine knew, were somewhere in the nave.

She looked toward the Davidsons and caught Emily's eye. The child gave one of her solemn smiles, and blew a kiss.

Katherine returned the smile, and glanced once more at all these people she had known for only a few months. Between them all they held a great many secrets. Between them all they had worked out as much peace as the human being is likely to have.

She turned her mind away from them and focused it on music. The rustlings in the stalls and throughout the crowded nave stopped, and there was anticipatory silence.

For Katherine, as she held her hands over the keyboard, there was nothing but the piano, and she and the sensitive instrument were no more than living extensions of each other.

When the music had fully entered into her, she began to play.